THE GATES
OF HELL

THE
GATES
OF
HELL

MICHAEL LIVINGSTON

A TOM DOHERTY ASSOCIATES BOOK **TOR** NEW YORK

THE GATES OF HELL

A Tor Book
Published by Tom Doherty Associates
175 Fifth Avenue
New York, NY 10010

www.tor-forge.com

Tor® is a registered trademark of Macmillan Publishing Group, LLC.

The Library of Congress Cataloging-in-Publication Data is available upon request.

ISBN 978-0-7653-8033-3 (hardcover)
ISBN 978-1-4668-7332-2 (e-book)

Our books may be purchased in bulk for promotional, educational, or business use. Please contact your local bookseller or the Macmillan Corporate and Premium Sales Department at 1-800-221-7945, extension 5442, or by e-mail at MacmillanSpecialMarkets@macmillan.com.

First Edition: November 2016

Printed in the United States of America

0 9 8 7 6 5 4 3 2 1

For Samuel and Elanor,
who are every reason

ACKNOWLEDGMENTS

Writing a book is never a solitary endeavor. So first and foremost I must acknowledge my family for giving me the time and the energy to finish this novel. Thank you, Sherry, for watching the kids a bit more (not to mention driving through Book One!), and thank you, Mom and Dad, for coming out to help when I'd reached the end of my rope. Kids, I owe you so much for understanding that Daddy had to work.

Friends gave the encouragement and the feedback I needed to cross the finish line. Catherine Bollinger continues to be the finest alpha-and-omega reader I could ask for, and Kelly DeVries is owed much for helping talk me through my moments of writer despair—with bonus Roman troop movements along the way! Kayla Moore made the last push possible, and David Allen kept the wolves at bay when I needed it most. My writer friends Mary Robinette Kowal, Ilana Myer, and Harriet McDougal were lights in times of darkness. Amy Romanczuk is the best unpaid cheerleader imaginable. Thank you all.

At a fundamental level, of course, this novel simply doesn't happen without the strong support of Claire Eddy, my editor, as well as my publicist, Diana Griffin, and all the other fine folks at Tor. Well done, gang.

Last, to all the kind readers and reviewers who loved Book One, your encouragement was simply beyond anything I could have imagined. This one, I think, is even better.

Contents

PREFACE

The Shards of Heaven series, of which this is the second volume, is a historical fantasy. As such, its story is intended to fit within the bounds of known history wherever possible: What occurs within these pages is inspired by real events, happening in real places to real people. Vellica was real, as was Carthage. And so, too, were the writings of Thrasyllus, the sickness of Augustus, the tales of Olyndicus, and even the remarkable boldness of the outlaw king himself.

The reader wishing a basic understanding of the facts of history as they pertain to the characters herein should consult the glossary at the end of this book.

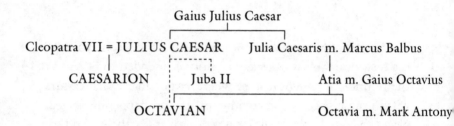

Families of Julius Caesar

Gaius Julius Caesar

Cleopatra VII = JULIUS CAESAR   Julia Caesaris m. Marcus Balbus

CAESARION   Juba II   Atia m. Gaius Octavius

OCTAVIAN   Octavia m. Mark Antony

and Cleopatra VII

Julius Caesar = CLEOPATRA VII m. Mark Antony

CAESARION   Ptolemy Philadelphus

Juba II m. Cleopatra Selene   Alexander Helios

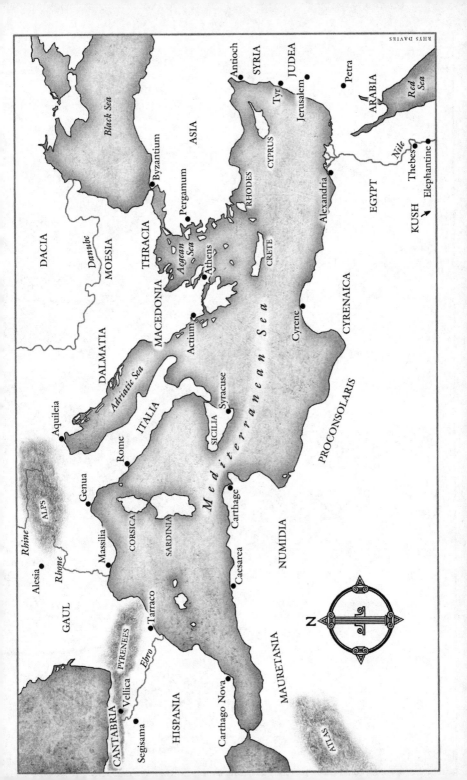

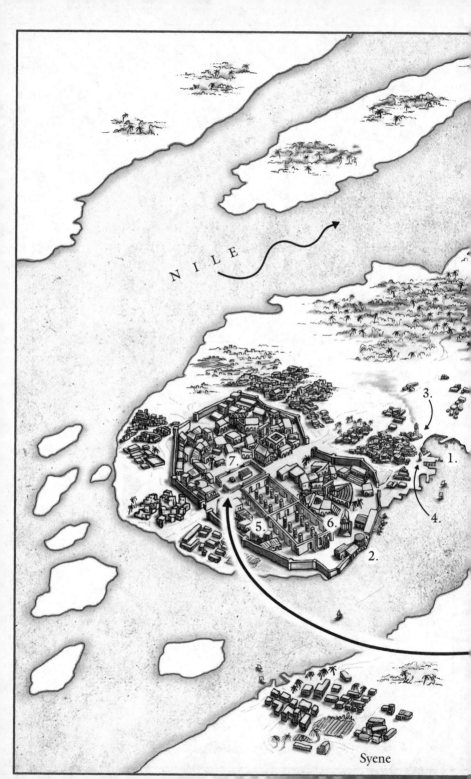

N I L E

1.

3.

4.

2.

5.

6.

7.

Syene

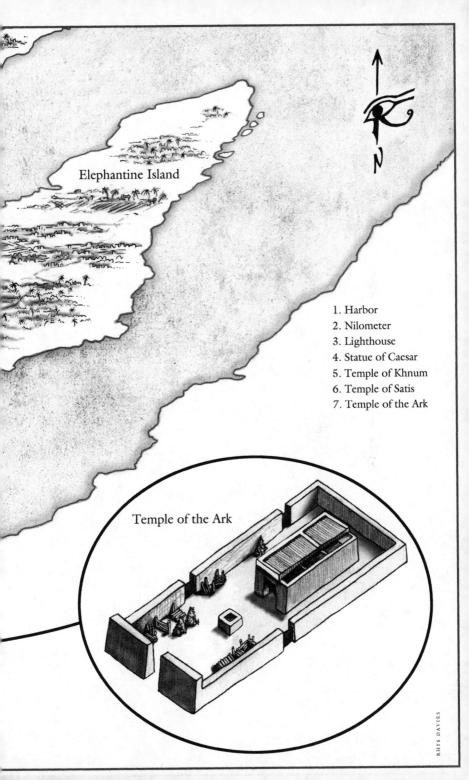

Elephantine Island

1. Harbor
2. Nilometer
3. Lighthouse
4. Statue of Caesar
5. Temple of Khnum
6. Temple of Satis
7. Temple of the Ark

Temple of the Ark

N

RHYS DAVIES

Do the gods build this fire in our hearts,
Euryalus? Or is a god built of each man's desire?

—Virgil, *Aeneid*, Book 9

PROLOGUE

The Dark of the Moon

On the January night that the Republic finally came to an end, thirteen-year-old Cleopatra Selene fell asleep waiting for the emperor's son.

.   .   .

Not for the first time she dreamed she was ten again, sitting on the cold stone bench of a Roman prison cell, her head against Alexander Helios' shoulder as she pretended to sleep. The yellow light of an Italian dawn was just beginning to stream in through a barred window high on the outside wall, taunting them with unreachable warmth.

Helios shifted his shoulder beneath the weight of her head. "Wake up, Selene," her twin whispered.

Selene didn't move her head. "I am awake."

"Did you sleep?"

She let the air out of her lungs, then yawned it back in again and regretted the instinct: the air was thick with the sickly humid reek of mold and mildew and human despair. She coughed and gagged.

"Me neither," he said.

Through the window came the voices of the gathered crowds: jubilant cries of celebration at the festivities of the Roman Triumph, mixed with angry shouts for the death of the traitorous Egyptian royalty whom Octavian had brought back from Alexandria: the children of Antony and Cleopatra.

Selene felt their hatred run like cold fingers up her spine. Before she could shiver she lifted her head from her brother's shoulder and stood, rubbing at her numb arms. The roiling mass of emotion outside had been building for more than two days, but today it would come to a final climax. Today was the end.

"Do you really think Caesarion is dead?" Helios asked.

Selene instinctively started to reassure him, to say that no, of course he was still alive, but she knew he would recognize the lie. "Maybe. Probably." It was the truth, painful though it was to admit. Juba, the Numidian prince she had promised to marry in order to save the life of her old friend Lucius Vorenus, had told her that Caesarion was dead, that he'd been killed in Juba's struggle to find the Ark of the Covenant and use it against their common enemy, Octavian. She believed the Numidian, of course—he had no reason to lie—but even so she could hardly imagine that their older half-brother—tall, handsome, strong Caesarion, so much the image of his father, Julius—could be dead. It just didn't seem possible.

Helios, so slight, so sickly compared to Caesarion, coughed loudly, painfully, and Selene felt a pang of sorrow rise in her gut that she had to fight to keep at bay.

"Caesarion's not here, anyway," she said when he had control of himself again. "Octavian would march him, too, if he was alive. He wants to make a display of us all."

She didn't mention their younger brother, Philadelphus, but she didn't have to. The child, even sicker than Helios when they last saw him, was never far from their thoughts. Was he dead, too?

"Maybe Caesarion's alive, though," Helios said. "Octavian could be lying about it because he's scared. He's using us to keep Caesarion from doing what he wants to do. Maybe that's another reason why Octavian hasn't . . . killed us yet. Like how he wanted to use us against Mother."

Mother. Her brother's voice cracked at the word, and then Selene's dream spun wildly, sweeping her out of the cell, rushing her back through even more distant memories, back to the moment she stood before the vivid and all-too-real image of her mother's agony-contorted face, staring at the world through dry, sightless eyes. The corpses of two loyal maidservants were slumped on the floor beside the throne, themselves twisted by the bite of the asp that Selene had managed to smuggle into the guarded chamber to fulfill her mother's desire for death. The reed-woven basket of ripe-to-bursting fruits was overturned in front of them, and there was an apple in Cleopatra's venom-clawed hand, squeezed to broken mash. The scepter of Egyptian authority was broken into two pieces at her feet, nothing more than the wooden stick that it was beneath the luminescent jewels and the fine gold casing.

Octavian was there, too. He'd made the children come to the chamber before anything was touched, before anything was moved, so that they could see with their own eyes what he'd taken from them, as if Cleopatra's suicide was his victory, not hers.

Even the asp was there for the children to see, coiled in a corner where it had been trapped. Selene, for a moment, had wanted to run to the black thing, to grip its head and plunge its glistening mouth into the soft flesh of her own neck, to let it drink its fill of blood even as she drank of its terrible venom, but the desire for revenge had steeled her against such a surrender. As they watched, Octavian took from among his guard a spear. Then, with slow steps that echoed in that stony place, he walked to the corner and drove the sharpened point into the writhing, hissing creature.

. . .

Cleopatra Selene—daughter of Antony and Cleopatra, once heir to the great Ptolemaic empire of Egypt, now adopted daughter to the very man who'd brought her family to such ruin—awoke from her nightmares, gasping and reaching for the dead: her mother, her father, her brothers.

She found, instead, another young man, a year older than herself, who recoiled from her clutching fingers. As he shrank back, the flickering lamp-shadows around the bed swallowed his gentle features, but it took only a glance for Selene to recognize Tiberius, the boy she'd fallen asleep waiting for this night, the stepson to the man who, she reminded herself, was no longer to be called Octavian. Among everything else that had happened this day, the man who had all but officially ended the Republic—who'd already been accorded the title of Emperor Caesar, son of God—had been declared by the Senate "Augustus": the Illustrious One.

Augustus Caesar. Much though the thought of her adopted father made her ill, Selene had to admit that the name had a certain ring to it. Not unlike the name of Augustus' adoptive father—Caesarion's blood father, she couldn't help noting to herself—Julius Caesar. The Romans had made Julius into a god. Would they do the same for Augustus?

"I didn't mean to startle you," Tiberius said, stirring Selene back out of her dark thoughts. "You looked like you were having another bad dream."

Another. Selene concentrated on breathing deep, allowing her heartbeat to slow. In the two and a half years since her world had ended, hardly a night had passed without a dream of the horrors. Walking with the basket to see Mother. Staring into those unblinking eyes. Trembling in that Roman prison. The smiths coming to their cell with their gritty, blackened hands to fasten the golden fetters to their wrists and ankles, to their necks—collars and chains of their mother's Egyptian gold melted down and made into the very signs of the subjugation of her children, her kingdom.

Selene rubbed at her wrists as if she could feel the weight of the metal on her skin even now. "It's fine," she said. "Just a dream. I must've fallen asleep waiting."

Tiberius smiled in the shadows. "That's all right. I was just glad you were, um, dressed."

Though she was, as always, uncertain if there was some romantic interest behind his comment, Selene took it as mocking play and she rolled her eyes. After all, they both knew they were promised for others. Tiberius was arranged to be married to Agrippa's eight-year-old daughter, Vipsania. And rumors were already swirling that Selene would be married to Juba the Numidian sooner rather than later. "I'm dressed enough," she said, slipping out of bed and lacing up her best sandals. Then she stood and shrugged her shoulders as if to unencumber herself of the memory of her dead mother and the promises for revenge that she kept hidden even from Tiberius. "No one saw you, did they?"

Tiberius gave her a look of mock anger. "No. Of course not," he said, trying to sound exasperated. "So why'd you want to sneak out tonight, anyway? I think the whole city is drunk or passed out." He yawned. "I could use more sleep myself."

The festivities to celebrate Augustus Caesar and his acclamation by the Senate had, indeed, overtaken Rome. This night more than any other, the city would be quiet and still, and the usual fun of their nocturnal walks would be taken away. Selene looked over to the curtains that were pulled shut across the balcony. The rich cloth rocked to the moving air outside as if pushed by the touch of unseen hands. "You'll see," she said.

Tiberius was wearing a good traveling outfit that would

keep him warm but still enable him to move easily: a necessity
for climbing down from her balcony, among other things. She
had already donned something similar, but she went over to her
chest and quickly rifled through it to produce the shoulder
bag she'd managed to make from the soft and gentle cloth of
one of her old Egyptian dresses. Royal linen.

"What's that for?" Tiberius asked.

"A Shard," Selene whispered, feeling the small but heavy
stone statue inside the bag and thinking how maybe after tonight she'd have no more nightmares. Maybe after tonight
she'd dream of Caesar in golden chains, Caesar in sackcloth,
Caesar begging her for mercy. It would take time to master
the Shard, but she was certain she could be patient. Once she'd
learned that killing Octavian wouldn't be enough to sate her
thirst for vengeance, after all—once she'd learned, as Juba had
before her, that true vengeance meant destroying Rome
itself—she'd lived among his family in his house, never once
making an attempt on his life. Yes, she could be patient. Even
with the Shard, she could bide her time. Find it, take it, master it. Then strike.

"What did you say?" Tiberius asked.

Selene turned back to look at her friend, smiling at possibilities he could never understand, possibilities he would surely
think treasonous, even if he had his own reasons to hate
Octavian. First things first, though: she had to get it. And if
she was going to slip inside the Temple of the Vestal Virgins,
the keepers of Rome's eternal fire and its most sacred relics, she
was going to need his help. "I told you," she said, lifting the
bag with its hidden statue to her shoulder. "You'll see."

·   ·   ·

From Augustus' house on the crest of Palatine Hill they moved
through the quiet, darkened streets, shadow to shadow, ever

downward toward the ancient Forum. Tiberius was quiet, as he so often was, and Selene was glad for it. Her mind was on the Shard.

She still found it difficult to believe that one of the Shards of Heaven had been here, in Rome, all this time. How often had she walked past the House of the Vestals, past the ever-burning fire of their temple, not realizing that a piece of her vengeance was so close for the taking? Staggered at the thought of it, she'd had to ask Vergilius to repeat himself at a dinner with old Varro two months earlier, when he'd made an off-hand comment that he was planning to mention the Palladium in the poem he was writing in honor of the man who'd restored the glory of Rome, the man soon to be Augustus. Yes, Vergilius had assured her. *That* Palladium. The statue of the goddess Pallas Athena that had such mysterious power that its presence alone had kept the Greeks at bay during their decades-long siege of Troy. Stolen from the city by Ulysses, the Palladium, the poet said, had eventually been brought to Rome by Aeneas—the Trojan exile and legendary founder of Rome who was the hero of Vergilius' poem in progress—and the artifact now rested under the protection of the Vestals.

Conversation at the dinner had gone on as if the foreign-born girl had never interrupted, but to Selene it was as if the gods of old—gods she had become certain did not exist—had inexplicably handed her the key to her vengeance. Sitting in the Great Library of Alexandria so many years earlier—before the fall of their city, when her brothers were still alive, when she still thought herself, in the tradition of the pha-raohs, a goddess on the earth—she'd listened to Caesarion, their tutor Didymus, and a now-dead Jew discuss the Shards of Heaven.

The Shards of Heaven. It was hard for her to imagine a time

when she had never heard of the fragments of divine power that had been cast out across Creation when the angels—there'd been a time she'd not heard of them, either—tried to open a gate to the highest heaven by giving up the greatest gift of God, the gift He'd given of himself: their souls. Caesarion had died in the struggle over the Jewish Ark of the Covenant, one of the most powerful of the Shards. Her husband-to-be, Juba, had held two more: the Aegis of Zeus and the Trident of Poseidon—the latter now kept under the personal control of Augustus. And here, now, was the fourth and final Shard she'd learned about on that distant morning in the Great Library. The Palladium.

Her mother had defined herself by men: first by Julius Caesar, then, after his death, by Selene's father, Mark Antony. Looking back, Selene could see how Cleopatra had never really had control of her own destiny.

"Not me," Selene whispered to herself as she turned off the paved path, skirting through a shoulder-breadth alley between stone buildings. With the Shard, she'd have power her dead mother could never have imagined. With the Shard, she could be her husband's equal. And if he joined his power to hers—if they gathered the Shards once more—their shared power would reshape the world. Destroy their Roman enemies. Achieve vengeance for them both. Juba had been meant to rule Numidia before Rome seized it, after all, before he, too, had been left an orphan in the house of his family's conquerors.

The alley emptied out into the sacred grove that spread across the base of the Palatine Hill, its darkness thick and deep, impervious to the slight sliver of moon in the sky. Selene forged onward until she felt the stands of growth closing in all around her. When she stopped, Tiberius stumbled into her back.

"What are you stopping for?" he asked, voice quiet in the hushed wood. He moved around through the grassy, winter-dried underbrush between the trees to stand beside her. "And why are we going this way? Thought you wanted to go down to the Forum."

Selene looked around and saw nothing but silent trees in front of her and the black expanses marking walls behind. The air was chilled, but not unbearably so, and it smelled of earth and dried leaves. It was as good a place as any to tell him what he had to know. "Not to the Forum in particular, no," Selene said, crouching down to the ground and keeping her voice at a conspiratorial hush.

Tiberius crouched down, too: close, but not too close. "So? Where?"

"The Vestals."

Even in the shadows of the wood she saw his eyes widen, and he seemed to lean back from her slightly. "Vestals?"

"That's right," she said, trying to keep her tone even, as if she wasn't talking about potential treason. "I want to get into the Temple of the Vestals."

Tiberius blinked. She imagined him trying to decide if she was joking. "Why?"

For weeks she'd rehearsed this exchange in her mind, know-ing she couldn't get what she wanted without his help but knowing, too, that there was no way he would help her. So now, when the moment came, the words flowed easily enough. "You remember the Triumph, don't you? Octavian's Triumph after Alexandria?" Of course he did. She remembered *him*, after all. She remembered how he rode in his stepfather's char-iot, waving happily at the adulating crowds, looking down at the suffering, burlap-clad children of Cleopatra as if they were slaves, not high-born royalty once worshipped as gods. Though they'd never spoken of that day, Selene had always felt his fear that she might remember him from it. She'd felt his guilt and held fast to it, preserving the favor that it would provide even if she didn't know what that favor might be. When Vergilius revealed the Palladium's presence in Rome, she'd known the time for using Tiberius' decent humanity against him had come. "You do remember, don't you?"

Her adopted brother seemed to sigh back into even deeper shadows, his shoulders rising or his face falling, she couldn't tell which. "Yes."

"Octavian—Augustus—took something from me that day."

"Your kingdom," Tiberius whispered, the words hardly audible.

"Yes. My home. My pride. My hope. My family." She let that last phrase sink in for a moment, knowing how Augustus had taken Tiberius' own father from him when he'd forced Livia to divorce because he lusted after her. "But that's not it, Tiberius. He took something else away, too." Selene shifted her crouch, bringing her shoulder bag around so that she could grip the statue inside. She held it up, though she didn't expose it.

"What's that?"

"A statue," Selene said, focusing her eyes on it to help steady her nerves through the lie. "They sell them down in the market and I bought one. It's of Horus."

"Horus?"

"An Egyptian god, son of Isis and Osiris. My older brother, Caesarion, was thought to be the living Horus."

"I . . . I don't understand," Tiberius said. His voice sounded deeply hurt. The guilt all coming back, Selene imagined.

"This statue is a replica of one that Augustus gave to the Vestals. It's a statue he took from my home. It belonged to Caesarion, and I want it back. More than anything in the world."

"You want to steal it?"

Selene imagined him picturing the high cliff of the Tarpeian

Rock at the other end of the Forum, the promontory from which traitors to Rome were thrown, headfirst, onto the stones below, where they were torn apart by the crowds whether the fall killed them or not. "He stole it," she said, her voice both stern and hurt. "It's rightfully mine." She let a few tears fall, hoping that they would catch the scant moonlight on her cheeks. "It's all that's left."

Tiberius was silent for a long time. A slight breeze rustled the trees around them, making the tiniest of singing sounds in the branches. Selene took a hand from the still-covered statue to wipe her cheeks. Whatever he said next, she hoped it wasn't that he wanted to see it.

"So you want me to help you get into the . . . *gods* . . . the Vestal Temple so you can take back the statue and . . . what? Replace it with that one?"

"I . . . I guess so. No one would ever know," Selene said, letting her words start to spill out as she fell into the role of the thoughtless girl. It always made men feel more comfortable, more in control. "Roman sculptors have told me that they need only see a thing once to reproduce it perfectly. The Horus statue has often been on display. And it was real simple. I remember it exactly, and no one would be able to tell the difference between the real thing and this fake one. No one but me."

Tiberius let out his breath. "This could kill us both," he said. "It's sacrilege."

"I'm not going to put out the sacred fire," Selene said. "And I'm not asking you to sleep with one of the Virgins. And no one will know, anyway."

"But if someone—"

"No one will find out. Even if they did, I'd tell them you didn't know what I was doing."

"I don't know, Selene."

The pleading tone in his voice was all Selene needed to hear to know that she'd won, that he'd do it, and she had to fight back a sigh of relief. She'd been prepared, after all, to offer him much more than guilt in return for his compliance, the sort of thing her mother, she was sure, would have tried first. But then, Selene wasn't her mother. She was better than that. "It'll be easy," she said, using her gentlest voice. "I've got a plan."

. . .

From the far corner of the House of the Vestals, near the abomination of an arch that Augustus had built to celebrate his triumph over her parents, Selene looked eastward down the Forum, past the round, column-encircled Vestal Temple with the telltale plume of gray smoke rising slowly from its crown, to where Tiberius was approaching through plazas filled more with litter than with people. Where mingling crowds and noise would typically reign, she saw only a handful of citizens shuffling along the paths or talking in small groups. From their shuffling steps or their overloud talk, it appeared that most of them were drunk on the free libations of the night, just as she'd hoped. And not one of them was taking any notice of Tiberius, who was moving slowly but steadily—building up his nerves, she thought—now passing between the stretching length of the House of the Vestals and the Regia, where the high priest of Rome was supposed to live. The latter was empty now, Selene knew, because Lepidus has been exiled by Octavian years earlier—allowed to keep the title, but not the power. A rare act of mercy. Selene wondered if he, too, desired the emperor dead.

She could see only the back of the temple, but she could hear the movement of only a single Virgin within, muttering arcane prayers and fussing with the sacred fire that marked their goddess's protection over the city. Selene allowed herself a smile, confident that the five other Virgins, like the rest of the city, were fast asleep after the long day of rousing celebrations. And unless she was wrong, the Virgin left the task of tending the fire this night would be the youngest of them, the one Tiberius would know.

"Urbinia?" Tiberius called, his voice just loud enough to be heard in the temple. Not so loud, she hoped, that it would wake any Virgins sleeping in their nearby house. "Is that you?"

There was new movement inside, and Selene rushed quickly from her hiding place to stand in one of the little alcoves between the temple's rear columns. Though the stone walls were thick, she could hear the individual footsteps inside. "Tiberius?" It was a young girl's voice: both hopeful and uncertain. Urbinia.

Selene didn't take the time to smile now, though she felt the lightness in her heart of fortune's grace. She moved as quickly as she dared around the southern side of the temple, in the shadows between it and the long House of the Vestals.

"You're honored to tend the fire this night," Tiberius said from the front of the temple. Coming around the side, Selene could see him again, standing five or six paces from the foot of the steps. He looked strikingly natural and confident. He was a better liar than she'd ever given him credit for.

"Everyone else was, um, celebrating," Urbinia said.

Sneaking closer column by column, Selene could see that the young girl—was she nine now?—was standing in the temple doorway. The backlight of the fire inside danced on the drapes of her linen mantle. There were red and white ribbons beneath her gossamer headdress.

"Well, come down here so I can see you," Tiberius said.

Urbinia took a single step down, smiling—it was no secret she'd held childish feelings for her older cousin before she was chosen to become a servant of Vesta—and then she froze and

started to look back toward the fire. Selene slipped behind a
column foundation only a few paces away and concentrated
on slowing her own heartbeat, keeping her breathing smooth
and even. "I don't think I'm supposed to," the girl said. "The
fire—"

"Looks strong enough for a minute or two, Urbinia."

After a few seconds, Selene heard the little girl give a
brief giggle before she began skipping down the steps. Selene
took one last breath and then hurried out of the shadows and
up the stone staircase like a cat, padding on the balls of her
feet. The light of the fire ahead was blinding after so long a
time in the darkness, but she kept her watering eyes to the
ground, watching each step fall, until she was inside the doorway and could duck out of sight.

"What?" she heard Urbinia ask. "Is something—?"

"Oh, nothing," Tiberius said hurriedly. "I was . . . I was
just thinking what a wonder it is that you get to tend to that
fire. My favorite cousin, a Vestal Virgin. But here, let me look
at you, all grown up."

Selene let out a breath she didn't know she'd been holding, then concentrated on letting her eyes adjust to the inside
of the temple. The sacred fire of Vesta dominated its single
chamber, blazing in a large brass bowl set atop the blunted,
fat pillar of a carved stone base at the rear center of the room.
The polished marble floor around it reflected back both the
light of the fire and the darkness of the thin, climbing column
of smoke that forever rose toward the hole at the apex of the
domed roof. Around the thick stone walls were inscriptions
of dates and names, reliefs of gods and men, and a waist-high
circle of marble-wrought cabinetry of extraordinarily beautiful red and black tones, flecked with a gold that matched tiny
plaques over its low doors. Inside, she knew, were the most
important documents in the Republic. It was here that Julius

Caesar had supposedly placed the will that adopted Octavian as his son and heir, cutting out Caesarion, his natural child with Cleopatra. It was here that her father, Mark Antony, had eventually placed his own will, granting everything he had to his children by Cleopatra and expressing his traitorous wish to be buried with her in Alexandria rather than in Rome. The war that had taken away Selene's family and her home had begun when Octavian had forced the Virgins to hand the will over, an act of terrible sacrilege that was somehow forgiven in the face of the greater betrayal that it exposed. For a moment Selene felt the urge to open all the doors, to turn over the sacred fire and burn it all to cinders and ash, but it would be a small victory. Not the true vengeance she sought.

Atop the cabinets were some of the greatest treasures of Rome: golden eagles, skulls, consecrated stones, and—she saw it on the other side of the room as her eyes adjusted at last—the Palladium, standing beside the statue of Horus that had been so precious to her family.

Glancing outside and seeing that Urbinia's attentions were still thoroughly engaged by Tiberius, Selene padded over to stand before the statues, lifting from her shoulder bag the replica she'd purchased two weeks earlier. The object in her hands was not, as she'd told Tiberius, a replica of the delicately crafted statue of Horus beside her. It was, instead, a roughly cone-shaped lump of rock the deep red-brown color of clay, but with the foggy transparency of quartz. In and around it were laced lines of a darker black that gave it the vague external appearance, she thought, of wet wood. No taller than her forearm, the rock was misshapen by rounded protrusions that—seen through the eyes of imagination—could make the stone seem as if it were the statue of a strong woman, the details of her limbs and the drape of her gown somehow melted away. Where the statue's eyes and mouth should have been the black veins were bolder, creating the appearance of a face. Holding it up next to the real Palladium, Selene could see that it was, indeed, a nearly perfect match. The Roman sculptors were right to boast.

Saying an instinctive prayer to a goddess she didn't believe in, Selene snatched up the Palladium and put it into her bag, placing the replica in its place. She felt a wash of extra heat in the moment it was done, even beyond the roiling warmth of the fire behind her. Nerves, she thought. Must hurry.

As Selene turned to head back toward the doorway, she heard Tiberius' voice, too loudly asking a question. And Urbinia, very close beyond the doorway, replying to him. "I'll just check on it."

Selene spun away, looking but knowing that there was no way out of the temple but the way she'd come in, and that there was no place to hide. Hoping that Urbinia would just glance at the fire, Selene dove behind the round stone base of the sacred flame just as the Virgin appeared in the doorway.

"But, Urbinia!" Tiberius called.

"You can't be on the steps," the girl said, sounding strangely authoritative for her age.

"Oh, I know . . . I—"

"Just wait. It's time for more wood."

Crouching behind the short stone pillar opposite the door, feeling the heat of the fire above her radiating into her skin and singeing the hairs on her flesh, Selene didn't have to turn to know that the small stash of wood was against the wall behind her. All was lost.

"Can't it wait?"

"It'll be only a second."

Feeling tears rising in her eyes, wanting to scream at the injustice of it all, Selene closed her eyes and pulled the Palladium from her bag and embraced it, holding her last hope to her chest. It felt warm there. Comforting.

She heard the footsteps of the girl moving through the doorway. Coming closer.

No! she screamed in her mind, squeezing the Palladium into her body as if she could hide it there, deep down inside her. No, no, no—

Power suddenly shot into her hands, a fire coiling up her arms like a fast-moving snake and lancing into the core of her chest. Selene gasped, falling backward into the small wood-pile, her eyes snapping open. Beyond the smoke of the sacred fire she saw the foggy shape of Urbinia, paralyzed at the realization that someone was inside the temple. Between them Selene expected to see her arms engulfed in flame, a trail tracing out from the Vestal fire to her body like a flickering, hungry tongue. Instead, she saw the Palladium, its ghostly face turned toward her, eyes and mouth somehow an even darker black. And within its depths, visible now as an almost pulsing heart, was a blacker-than-black stone within the stone.

The Shard, she thought with sudden realization. Yes.

The tide of the fire coursing into her body pulled back for a moment, and time seemed to slow around her. Selene closed her eyes and let the tendrils of night pull down inside her like buckets diving for the bottom of a well. She felt the coils of power gather up within herself, deep down in a core of her being that she'd never known. Then, when she could take no more, when she thought that if they grabbed anything more there'd be nothing of her left, she released them back out with a sickening, exhilarating, frightening belly surge of energy.

The air in the Temple of the Vestals unfroze, rushing forward in a roiling storm of smoke and burning embers drawn up from the sacred fire. The force of it threw Selene backward into the woodpile again, and she could hear nothing but a wail of wind like the roar of a vengeful god. Then, a heartbeat later, the throaty storm was moving away and she could hear, in its place, Urbinia's screams.

Selene was dazed from striking the back of her head on the woodpile, her thoughts scattered, churning from fire to flight, from Urbinia's screams to the Shard of Heaven whose power she'd somehow tapped.

Move, she reminded herself, as if she stood outside her body. People will come. Get up. Get away. Go.

The Temple of the Vestals was filled with a fog of dust and ash and smoke, vexed to spinning in slow puffs of cloud flashingly lit by the agitated but still-burning fire. Selene rolled over with a cough and saw through tear-filled eyes the statue that she must have let go when the wind burst out from . . . her? She had done it, hadn't she?

Pulling the now lifeless rock to herself she slipped it into her shoulder bag as quickly as she could, then stood, crouching, feeling a pain in the back of her head and an exhaustion down to the very marrow of her bones.

No, she thought as she started to move. An exhaustion down to the core of her soul.

The air was clearing before her as she stumbled out of the temple and saw the wave of wind still rushing eastward through the Forum, a moving wall of dirt and debris. How long, she wondered, before it lost its energy?

Closer, at the foot of the stone steps, she saw Tiberius kneeling beside a crumpled Urbinia. The girl's screams of horror had turned to the half-wails of pain from the ashes in her eyes. Tiberius looked up at Selene, his own eyes trembling with shock and fear and something that looked like grief. There were shouts from around the Forum. Sounds of people moving. His mouth moved in a silent whisper: *Go.*

Selene thought about going down to him, about trying to see if there was anything she could do to help Urbinia, to assure him that everything was okay, that he'd not betrayed Rome, that there was no Vesta, that there were no gods to be angry . . . but then the shouts were getting closer and she merely nodded her head and ran as fast as her tired legs could take her, back for the wood and the darkness and her dreams of vengeance.

PART I

THE REACH OF ROME

1

First Light

Perched on the leading edge of the barge, his back to the rising sun, Lucius Vorenus watched as the hulking mass of Alexandria rose above the still waters ahead. The last time he'd seen the great city, parts of it were in flames. From the deck of the ship upon which they'd fled that day—a stolen Roman military trireme, far different from this flat-bottomed Egyptian cargo vessel—Vorenus had watched through his tears as gray snakes of smoke grew in size and number, slithering lazily into the bright blue sky above the tiled roofs and great white blocks of Alexandria's buildings, which were fading to the horizon. He remembered how there had been no sound of it, and upon the water he had only been able to smell the sea. Seen from afar those tendrils of destruction could almost have seemed beautiful. But Vorenus knew better. He was a veteran of enough campaigns, a participant in enough slaughter, to know the kind of death and destruction that the conquering Romans had brought that day. He knew what fed the hungry fires.

Yet the city he returned to this morning—that very city—showed no scars of its conquest. The only fire he could see was the one that was shining brightly in the sky, hanging above the rooftops like a beckoning star of morning or a signal upon a towering summit: the beacon of the Great Lighthouse that burned day and night above Alexandria's harbor on the other side of the city. There were no riotous fires of tumult and death. The buildings, which were growing more dense along the canal, seemed to be untouched by war and conflict. The five years that had passed had been more than enough for the Romans to rebuild whatever they had destroyed.

Except for the lives, of course.

Those scars took far longer to heal.

Monuments might outlast the memories of the dead, but among the living there were few things so real as the recollection of loss. Despite all his experience, Vorenus didn't think he really understood that until he'd watched the rising columns of smoke that morning.

The morning Titus Pullo had died.

"Excuse me, sir," said a voice behind him.

Vorenus turned, saw Petosiris, the barge captain he'd hired to take himself and Khenti along the long canal between Schedia on the Nile to Alexandria. Rarely did Vorenus find himself in the company of men who made him feel tall—he was of average height and build for a Roman, quite unlike his friend Titus Pullo, who'd been a towering giant of a man who filled door frames—but the stocky captain made him feel just that: Petosiris was at least a full hand shorter than him. The Egyptian was stout, though, compact in a way that gave Vorenus no doubt that a life working on the decks and the docks had left him a good man in a fight. And that made him just the sort of company Vorenus liked to keep—especially when he was returning to Alexandria as a wanted man. "Yes, Captain?"

"We will be in the city soon." Petosiris didn't frown. He didn't smile. His demeanor was businesslike, which was another of the things Vorenus liked about him. Combined with his native Egyptian skin—darkened further from a life spent under the high, hot sun—the captain's quiet professionalism meant that he could disappear in a crowd, and disappearing was precisely what Vorenus might need. Romans, after all, did not forget. "You weren't specific about where the two of you would like to be let off the ship," the captain said.

"No, I was not," Vorenus agreed. "You'll be going to the granary docks?" Aside from himself, the Egyptian swordsman Khenti, and a wiry young lad who worked as the captain's deckhand, the only thing the flat-topped barge carried on this route was grain: a load of barley making its way from the rich farmlands of the great river to the great city on the sea.

The barge captain nodded. "The lake harbor docks," he said. "South side of the city."

Vorenus nodded. Alexandria sat on a long strip of land perched between the Mediterranean Sea and the shallow shores of Lake Mareotis. The city was served by multiple docks, but those upon the lake would be the first they would reach. And he knew the area well. He'd lived in Alexandria for fourteen years, a legionnaire of Rome tasked with guarding the lives of the royal family: Cleopatra and Mark Antony and their children: the twins, Cleopatra Selene and Alexander Helios; the younger Ptolemy Philadelphus; and of course Cleopatra's oldest son, named Caesarion after his father, Julius Caesar. The last time he'd been at the lake harbor, in fact, he'd been with Caesarion, inspecting the defenses of the southern walls of the city. "That will do quite nicely, then."

"Very well. Do you still plan to return with us back to Schedia?"

Vorenus had paid for passage to Alexandria, but he'd offered the barge captain half again as much coin if he could get them back to the Nile without incident. "A very comfortable journey," he'd said. A quiet one without questions, he'd wanted to add. Even the deckhand had known better than to make inquiries about the ship's extra passengers. "Yes. I think we will. Just the two of us still."

"As you wish, sir," Petosiris said. "We will leave the dock at sundown." Then, not saying whether or not the decision to travel at night was in keeping with custom or in deference to Vorenus' secrecy, he turned to walk back toward the tiller and the shadows of the barge's single sail.

As Vorenus watched the man make his way along the thin line of deck boards not covered by mounds of barley, he was reminded once more of his dead friend. Pullo, he was certain, would have liked the ship and the sweet smells of the grains very much. The big man had reveled in such things in life. "Good women, good food, and good drink is all a man needs," he'd once told Vorenus. They had been arguing, as they often did, about the need to give honor to the gods: back then Vorenus had been a believer in the faith of Rome, the faith of his father; he didn't know then that there had only ever been one God, and that He was dead. "And good friends," Pullo had added with a smile. "So save your libations to the earth. Pour me another instead."

Vorenus smiled and looked up into the morning sky. He'd never met a more loyal friend than Pullo. For years they'd fought side by side wherever Rome had needed them—from Rome to Egypt, from Gaul to Greece—and Pullo had never failed him. Not once. Not even in the end.

The thought brought his gaze down, and Vorenus watched for a time as the water relentlessly rolled under the prow of the ship. He'd been feeling a growing guilt ever since they'd left Schedia, and the closer they'd come to Alexandria the stronger it had become. Vorenus hadn't been certain what it was before, but he felt sure of what it was now: the shame of survival. His friend had never failed him, but he couldn't help but feel that he'd failed his friend.

He knew there was nothing more that he could have done. The death of Mark Antony, and the subsequent speed of the Roman army's advance into the city that morning, had spun matters out of their hands. Looking back, Vorenus knew that it was those terrible events that had made him cease thinking of himself as a legionnaire of Rome. For years he'd been maintaining a stubborn allegiance to that citizenship, even as politics tore the Republic asunder and forced him to take up arms alongside the forces of Egypt and against those who'd been his countrymen—to take up arms against a conqueror then known only as Octavian, not by the self-exalted name of Augustus Caesar, highest of emperors. But the smoke that day carried with it more than the ashes of the fires in the streets; it carried the ashes of his old life. That morning Vorenus was no longer a Roman. He was no longer even the head of the guard for the Egyptian royal family—even if, sailing away from Alexandria, he'd stood watch over Caesarion, the young man who was heir not only to that kingdom through his mother, Cleopatra, but also through his father, Julius Caesar, heir of Rome, too.

Vorenus still cared for Caesarion. He still watched him like an eagle over its young—which made leaving his side for this trip a discomforting if necessary choice—but as important as Caesarion was to him, the young man hadn't been his priority on that morning or on any of the mornings since.

Instead, it was the Shard.

That far-off morning, as they had spirited it away from Alexandria on that stolen Roman trireme, Vorenus had become a Shard-bearer. He swore to himself—for there was no one in the heavens to hear—that he would protect the Ark of the Covenant, as the Jews called it, at whatever cost. As the ship's oars had drawn them ever farther from the chaos of the city, Vorenus knew that they carried a weapon beyond their understanding, and he could never allow it to fall into the wrong hands. To protect the Ark, to save the Shard, he and Pullo had been forced to go their separate ways. Vorenus had barely survived a Roman attempt to execute him as a traitor, only just managing to steal the Roman trireme that would carry the Shard to safety. And Pullo had died preventing the Numidian prince, Juba, from seizing the Ark before it could be saved. Despite the feelings of guilt that ached in his chest, Vorenus knew in the end that it was his friend, that man of mirth and frivolity, who made the choice between his own life and the safety of the Shard.

Not a morning went by that Vorenus didn't think, as he did now, upon that moment, upon that choice. Not a morning went by that he didn't hate and love Pullo for making the choice he made. And not a morning went by that Vorenus didn't hope, when the time came, that he, too, would be strong enough to do whatever had to be done.

Ahead, the southeast corner of Alexandria's walls was coming into view above the jumble of buildings that had been built outside its protection. The massive, engineered solidity of the fortifications made the other structures at its base look all the more ramshackle, as if they were broken toys haphazardly strewn against it by the winds of the surrounding sands, lake, and sea.

Vorenus took a long deep breath, inhaling the organic scents surrounding the reeds of papyrus growing upon the shallows beside the banks. The air was still natural here, the sights still gentle and calm. But soon enough it would be the sights and sounds and scents of the bustling city that was once his home.

When he looked back in the direction of the Nile, he saw that Khenti was making his way forward, his pace strangely unaffected by the narrowness of the tracks between the piles of grain or the gentle rocking of the vessel on the water. The swordsman had been the head of the Egyptian royal guards under Vorenus, but his loyalty to Caesarion had led him, too, away from the city that had been his home. With Pullo gone, there was no one Vorenus trusted more to have with him on this journey.

The Egyptian set down the light pack he was carrying, their only supplies for this trip. "Everything is ready," he said.

Vorenus nodded, smiled, and then turned back toward the city. For a few minutes they stood and stared, lost in their own thoughts.

"This was all farms when I was younger," Khenti said.

The Egyptian's voice brought Vorenus back once more from his memories, and he looked around to realize they had crossed some kind of threshold: though the walls still lay ahead, they were undeniably in the city now. The buildings were close about them, and the streets between were filled with the busy noise of life. The edges of the canal were no longer the domain of papyrus reeds. Instead, tired washing basins and broken drying frames littered the muddy banks, and colorful sheens of oil and filmy bubbles pooled in the shallows. After so long living away from the city, the air seemed thick with the scents of excrement and filth. "The city grows," Vorenus agreed. "There's always work in the city."

Khenti nodded, but he crinkled his nose. "Smelled better as farms."

The canal made a turn, and abruptly the walls of Alexandria were passing to their right. And looming directly ahead of them, where none was supposed to be, was a chain gate across the canal, manned by Roman soldiers.

Vorenus and Khenti exchanged only the briefest of looks before gathering their things and walking, as quickly as they could manage without seeming suspicious, back toward the rear of the barge.

Petosiris was there, one hand on the tiller, the other upon
the line holding wind in the sail. The little deckhand was near
his feet, where he appeared to be checking a heavy coil of
docking rope, unraveling it from one part of the barge floor
to another. "I see it," said the barge captain.

"You said there were no gates on the canal," Vorenus said.

Khenti had taken a position that nearly triangulated the
barge captain between them and one of the larger mounds of
barley. But if Petosiris noted the threat he made no notice of
it. "I said there were no Roman checks on the canal," he corrected. "Haven't been for months."

"This is a problem," Vorenus said.

"I am aware," the barge captain replied. He wasn't looking
at them, just staring up ahead at the gate. The chain across
the canal had been pulled tight, rising up out of the water,
which fell away from its links in drops that sparkled in the
morning light.

Vorenus looked at Khenti, who had pulled back his traveling robes to expose the hilt of his sword. Then he looked to
the stinking water, wondering if it was too late to jump and
try to make their way through the slums and into the city another way.

"Get down," Petosiris said.

"What?" Vorenus asked, looking back to the man. "Why
are we—"

The barge captain made a sharp pull at the tiller, and the
barge rocked sideways and bumped into a small raft along
the shoreline. In the same moment, Petosiris released the line
holding the wind in the sail and lunged to the deck. "Get
down!"

As the barge rocked back and forth, its wake crashing back
against itself in sloshing froth and its cloth sail suddenly flap-
ping free, Vorenus and Khenti both complied. The deckhand

had stayed busy, and as he pulled the last coil loop from one pile to another, Vorenus saw what he had exposed: a small hatch in the deck. Petosiris, on his hands and knees, pushed his fingers into the cracks along its edges and hefted it free. The reek of stale, damp straw washed out behind it. "Go. Hurry," the barge captain said. "Our little accident here can only buy so much time."

Vorenus nodded and started worming his way down into the hidden hold. It was shallow, hardly more than two feet high, but it extended beneath the biggest stacks of barley above. He rolled aside as best he could so that Khenti could join him.

The floor of the little space was entirely covered with the old straw, which had grown musty in the heat. Vorenus sneezed.

Framed by the little square of sky above them, Petosiris frowned. "It would be in our mutual best interests if you didn't do that while you're down there."

Then the hatch closed over their heads, and heavy coils of rope began to be laid round and round above them. The boat once more began to move, inching its way toward the Romans at the gate and the great city of Alexandria beyond.

Doing his best to remain still in the choking, stifling darkness, Vorenus instinctively thanked the gods that he'd chosen well in hiring Petosiris, and that—in a few hours, if his luck held—the stench of stale straw would be replaced by the scents of the scrolls in the Great Library, and the sight of an old friend.

And he prayed—not really sure who he was praying to— that he wouldn't sneeze.

2

SIGNS OF LIFE

Before the new day cast its rays upon the great city of Alexandria, the astrologer Thrasyllus of Mendes awoke to the exotic scents of passion. Sleeping with a prostitute didn't take away the pain, he decided, but it did push it away. If only for a time, it made him feel better.

Thrasyllus opened his eyes, smiling to know that the night had not been a dream. The black-haired girl was still with him in the bare little room, cradled close beside his body in the cool, pre-dawn air. For long minutes he watched her breathing—marveling at her smooth skin, the sensuous curves of her tanned back and shoulder, her chest just hidden from view—until he realized he must be grinning like a fool.

Democritus, he imagined, the scholarly thought coming to him unbidden, would not be pleased with such astonished fascination. It was too caught up in the senses. Too subjective. The girl's body was just an accumulation of atoms, as was his. The old philosopher had, after all, said that a brave man was the one who could overcome both his enemies and his pleasures: "There are some men who are masters of cities," he'd written, "but slaves to women."

Thrasyllus had edited the work a year earlier, but it was only

now, with the fresh memory of the girl's movements still rippling over his sweat-chilled flesh, that he truly understood
what Democritus had meant, and how easy it would be to en-
slave oneself to such sensuality. It was frightening, but it was
thrilling, too. And Thrasyllus was quite certain—watching
as she rolled over, the strands of her long raven hair spilling
across and around the plump but firm roundness of her now
exposed right breast—that the risks of enslavement were
more than worth it. Democritus had clearly never had the
pleasures of such a creature.

Thrasyllus had already planned a sacrifice at the Poseidium
this morning, to pray that the sea-god would give him a safe
voyage to Rome. Or, better still, that the gods would see fit to
have changed old Didymus' mind about passing the keys to
the Great Library to Apion. Looking at this girl, he thought
he might also make a sacrifice at one of the many shrines to
Eros this morning. Another offering would be little trouble,
after all. And it was fitting to thank the gods for what they
gave, not just to beg them for what they might give.

Not that he had much hope that the gods could do anything to make the old librarian change his mind. Didymus was
a stubborn and resolute man, and he'd left no doubt that his
decision was a certainty: Apion was a Homeric scholar, like
Didymus himself. And loyal, long-suffering Thrasyllus, who
had served in the Library far longer?

Why, he was a mere astrologer.

Even editing the works of Democritus hadn't been able to
shake that fundamental identification, which had stuck with
Thrasyllus from the moment he entered the Great Library as a
boy: Thrasyllus of Mendes was, in the mind of the chief librarian, a simple astrologer.

Thrasyllus felt yesterday's anger rising up again—the same
anger that had made him storm out of the Great Library,

relinquishing his position and declaring that he would seek better employment in Rome—so he took a deep breath and looked back at the beautiful girl beside him. The sight of her calmed him.

And calm brought clarity. Democritus was right about that, at least.

What was clear now, Thrasyllus thought, was that it was true. He *was* an astrologer. Had he not looked at the signs after angrily leaving the Great Library yesterday and seen in them a sign of the favor that this girl—the very one he'd adored for so long—would bestow upon him?

And had she not done so?

That it took money to get her to his room . . . well, that was just to get her attention, was it not? Once they were alone, after all, she'd smiled and cooed. She'd traced a line along his square jawline and told him he was young and handsome. She called him her little stargazer. She hadn't needed to do that, but she had done it anyway. And she'd fallen asleep with her head on his shoulder, her delicate fingers tracing lazy, slowing circles through the hairs on his chest.

She'd even told him her name. Lapis.

Thrasyllus had never heard anything so beautiful as that word spilling from her full red lips. *Lapis.* A perfect name. A perfect match for her azure eyes.

The astrologer sighed and peeled himself from her carefully and quietly, slowly rising from the bed. He'd paid for the whole night, but he suspected that one person's definition of "night" might differ from another's. He'd had such debates among the other scholars at the Library. While he'd always defined the end of night to be the rising of the sun, he imagined that for the girl the night might end when she awoke. And any sense that Lapis might have really wanted to be with him this night would no doubt be ruined if she was in haste to get up, to get away, to wash herself of him. That, Thrasyllus was certain, would very much break the spell.

Still, even as the astrologer slipped on his simple garments, he found his gaze returning to the sleeping, azure-eyed girl, as if his mind still insisted on reminding itself that he really had spent the night with her. He'd certainly admired her for long enough, watching from the window of his little upper-story room as other men—and a few women, too—came to the corner and took her hand, leading her away after making their arrangements. Sometimes he thought that she had looked up to see him, too: watching him watching her. But he never thought he'd actually do it himself. He never thought he'd have the courage.

Looking down at her sleeping there, knowing how much he wanted to wake her, to hope for another bout of passion—yet fearing the possibility that she'd only reject him without another batch of coin—Thrasyllus frowned. He still didn't really have the courage, did he? It took knowing that he'd probably never see her again to get the strength to do it. It took this being his last night in Alexandria.

Calm brought clarity.

He was an astrologer. He was also a coward.

Thrasyllus stared at her a minute longer, memorizing shapes, before he turned back to the bare room and gathered the last of his meager possessions into the old leather satchel that his mother had given him when he'd left Mendes so long ago. He wouldn't be coming back here, he knew. And he wouldn't be going back to that little Egyptian town. He'd settled all his accounts. He was meant for better things. All that was left now was the waiting boat. He'd sail for Rome. He'd find a new life there.

Quietly he counted the promised coins out onto the bare table. Setting two extra down, he checked once more that he had enough left to cover the passage to Rome. Just enough, he decided, and he wouldn't have to spend his lucky coin, the only one remaining of those his father had placed in this same satchel so long ago—more than his poor family made in a year of meager earnings.

All for a chance at a better life.

Thrasyllus glanced once more to the sleeping girl, wondering what they would think of him now.

Then, taking one last breath of the night, he went out to meet the day.

Instead, he met two men. One was a small and wiry man with dark, grease-slicked hair. He was leaning against the wall of the hallway, absently flipping a gold coin in his hand. The other was a much larger, broad-shouldered man, perhaps in his fifties, who was sitting down against the same wall of the hallway. He looked up when the astrologer came out, as if he had been sleeping, and the astrologer could see that he was heavily scarred, the wrinkles of his face crossed over with the jagged tracks of countless old injuries, like a doll that had been torn apart and sewn back together.

Thrasyllus closed the door to his room as quietly as he could manage. "Pardon me," he whispered to the men, pressing himself against the opposite wall to step past them.

Instead of helping to get out of the way, the slick-haired man caught the coin he'd been flipping and then pushed off the wall to block the way. And behind him the older one stood, slowly and seemingly painfully lumbering up to his feet to tower over them both. When the smaller man smiled, he was missing one of his teeth. "Been waiting for you," he said. His voice was rough with gravel, and there was the stench of smoke on his breath.

Thrasyllus stepped back toward his closed door. "For . . . me?"

The man nodded, and his smile broadened. He was missing two teeth now. "Have a good night?"

Thrasyllus felt himself blush. "I . . . it's—"

"She's good, this one," the man rasped. Using the coin in his hand, he pointed toward the door.

The astrologer blinked, almost gagged. "What do you—"

"Money," the man said. His smile disappeared and he took a single step closer. "I'll need to be taking some now. Or this brute here will be taking some of your hide."

Thrasyllus looked between the two men. The slick-haired man's eyes glinted with hunger, like a rat's. The other one, whose shoulders reached from wall to wall, had something like anguish on his face, as if he was repulsed by his own behavior, but Thrasyllus was too frightened to think long upon it. Instead, he swallowed hard. "I . . . I don't have any," he managed to say.

"You better be lying."

"No, I—"

The little man's eyes moved down to the astrologer's satchel with a ravenous look. "Leaving town? Then you've definitely got some. Let's see what's in that bag of yours."

"Nothing," Thrasyllus managed. He instinctively pulled the satchel from the front of his hip to his back. "Just books. Papers. Pen."

"Now I know he's lying," the rat-faced man said over his shoulder to the brute.

The door behind Thrasyllus opened, and the astrologer smelled the girl even before he could turn to see her. "Lapis! Get back in—"

The girl's fingertips raised up to brush across his shoulder. "It's okay, stargazer," she said.

"Lapis now, is it?" the little man said from the hallway. He laughed, a coughing, rasping sound. "Good name for a whore. I like it. Might fetch a higher price with a pretty name like that."

"What is—?"

"It's okay," Lapis said. This time she was looking past Thrasyllus. She pulled the door shut behind her and stepped around the astrologer, smiling. The coins he'd left on the table were in her hand. She clinked them together. Thrasyllus, despite his confusion, noted that she was showing only the coins he'd owed, not the two extra. "He paid up," she said.

"He should have paid more," the rat-faced man said. His laughter had subsided, and his voice now had a harsh edge of threat.

"Come on," the girl said. "He's not enough to bother with. Let's go."

The brute remained still, but the little man's hands had balled into fists. "I want more."

The girl's gentle fingers, the tips of which only a moment ago were upon the astrologer's shoulder, now reached up to run across the man's forearm. "He's not worth it." She smiled at the man, almost seductively.

Thrasyllus stuttered. His heart was frightened and breaking all at once. "I paid what we agreed," he finally managed to say. "Inside."

"I want more."

"I don't understand, I—"

The little man stepped up, his hand shooting forward in the same movement. It impacted the astrologer's shoulder, throwing him back against the door.

The world spun for a moment. Thrasyllus saw Lapis turning back. Saw her reaching out for him.

The wiry little rat of a man caught her perfect arm in his

hand, yanked her back toward him. Her perfect hair twirled in the air in slow motion, like a thousand dancing black threads.

Thrasyllus saw Lapis struggle and start to cry out. Something in him broke.

The astrologer shouted. Abruptly, an inner instinct—one he didn't know he had—overrode his cowardice. Despite his own dizziness he lurched forward to try to protect the girl. "Lapis!"

For a moment he saw her face as she rolled over in the rat-man's grip. Their eyes met. Something like a smile began to form on her perfect lips.

Then something heavy and hard struck Thrasyllus on the back of the head, and he saw no more.

. . .

This time Thrasyllus awoke not to the scents of passion, but to the smells of the street: dust and sand, rock and piss. His mouth was filled with grit and the iron taste of blood, and his head pounded as if a horse had been trampling upon it.

The astrologer groaned and lifted his face off the ground. His ears were ringing for a few seconds, but slowly he began to make out familiar sounds: hooves on paved stones, shopkeepers hawking their wares, children chasing balls, doors opening and closing, men laughing, women talking, and everywhere the din of footsteps in a world full of life.

Thrasyllus managed to open his eyes through the thudding pain of it all.

Light flooded in. Too much light, smashing against the back of his aching skull. He squinted, gritting his teeth, but he didn't close his eyes. He didn't give in to the pain.

It appeared to be mid-morning. And he was sitting in the middle of a square in the city.

He sat upright despite the wail of his head. His back was

touching something solid, and he let himself lean back against it, allowing its feeling of permanence to settle the world into place. The pounding in his head began to grow dull, less urgent.

He knew this place. It wasn't far from his room: just down an alley from the corner where he'd met Lapis.

Lapis!

His eyes widened at the thought of her, and he leaned forward as if he might look around for the girl, but the thudding in his skull became a percussive scream and he once more had to settle himself into place.

He hoped she was okay. She'd been kind to him, after all.

And surely that greasy-haired rat of a man—her pimp, he decided on reflection—wouldn't hurt her much. It wouldn't be good for business.

Business. Thrasyllus smiled despite the pain in his body and in his heart. That's all he was for her in the end. Business. He'd been a fool to think differently.

He turned his head to spit out the thick contents of his mouth. The act brought his tongue against the back of his teeth and so he ran it across them, counting.

His smile returned. Whatever blows he'd received after he'd been knocked out—and from the feel of it there had been several—they hadn't dislodged any teeth. That was a blessing, he supposed. The big brute must not have done much of the hitting. If he had, Thrasyllus was certain he'd be in far worse condition.

He leaned back again, looking up at the white stone buildings with their red-tiled roofs. So much of Alexandria was planned—an exact arrangement of right angles squaring off the grid of wide streets, following the patterns established by Alexander the Great at the city's founding—that the few ar-

eas where the plan broke down seemed chaotic by compari-
son. This part of the Old Quarter was one of them. Here the
buildings appeared to pile up atop one another, an organic
randomness that could seem a labyrinth to outsiders. But to
those who lived here, it was part of the charm. It was teeming with its own kind of life, like a tiny village inside the city,
complete with its own little markets and ways and means.
It was one of the things that had drawn Thrasyllus to take
rooms here: the Old Quarter was as close to home as he would
ever get.

At the thought of home Thrasyllus felt for the satchel at his
side.

Gone. The astrologer's smile faded away. He wasn't surprised to find that it was gone, though he'd hoped. It was all
he had left of his mother.

And with it, his passage to Rome.

And even his lucky coin, all he had left of his father.

Thrasyllus sighed and pulled himself to his feet. Only then,
as he put out his hand upon it to steady himself, did he realize
what he'd been leaning against: the carved sandstone pedestal
on which was mounted the sundial that Eratosthenes had
used to measure the Earth some two centuries earlier. The
smooth white marble of the sundial's flat surface was covered
with thin dust, and some of the brass initials that were inlaid
upon its top were missing, but the metal gnomon at its center, a thin spike almost five feet high, still stood straight and
tall and sharp. For Eratosthenes its shadow, along with a man's
shadow cast down into the depths of a Nilometer on the
island of Elephantine on the Great River, had allowed him to
calculate the circumference of the round globe of the Earth.
For Thrasyllus its shadow now confirmed that he'd been unconscious for much of the morning.

And he had nothing. No room, no money, no position. Just the soiled clothes upon his back and the memory of a night that might be best forgotten.

The astrologer looked back up at the gnomon of Eratosthenes stabbing like a needle into the blue Egyptian sky. It was a monument of enormous importance, yet most people simply passed it by. Even Thrasyllus, who knew the tale of Eratosthenes, hadn't known that the sundial was so near his rooms until another scholar at the Great Library had pointed it out.

The Great Library.

The gnomon was, though the astrologer hardly wanted to admit it, another sign. He'd have to go back to the Great Library. He'd have to beg Didymus to get his old job back. He'd even have to humble himself to that damn Apion.

Thrasyllus took another look at the gnomon, shook his head a little to clear it, and then sighed. He had no choice now, he supposed. The gods wished what the gods wished. He could only try to follow their signs.

As he took his first step, his sandaled foot kicked something on the ground. It made a metallic sound as it rattled across the paving stones, and he looked down to see that it was a single coin, its glint just barely visible in the dust of the day.

Thrasyllus bent down and picked it up. Even before he began turning it over in his fingers he knew it.

His father's coin.

Another sign, the astrologer thought. If he'd not decided to walk in this direction, he never would have found it. Maybe, just maybe, his luck was changing.

His mother's satchel gone, Thrasyllus tucked his father's coin into his fist. And then, with a limp that faded the farther he strode from the gnomon of Eratosthenes, he began the long walk to the Great Library of Alexandria.

3

The Palladium of Troy

Amid an open circle of trees, a whisper of wind rose from the earth. Even with the shadows of the coming dawn still long around it, there was light enough in that clear space to see how the wind gathered into the air in thin fingers made visible by the fine dust that they sucked up from the parched ground. It coiled back against itself, and little flares of its growing strength flicked out from its rising, spinning form, licking out into the world like the forked tongues of serpents. Still it grew. Tighter. Faster.

And then, in a sudden rush, the wind tumbled forward as it was released into the half-light, unrolling its pent-up tide of energy into a chaotic cyclone that danced across the open ground and collided with its target on the other side of the clearing.

The empty canvas bag, buffeted by the churning ghost, strained against the branch it was hung upon. Lingering night birds ceased their chatter and sprang out from the surrounding trees. Then the wind was spent, and the cloth shook itself into stillness.

Sitting on a rock at the opposite side of the clearing, Cleopatra Selene took her hands away from the Shard in her lap. Through she was breathing heavily from the effort to engage the power of the artifact, she smiled. Her ability to control the Palladium was growing by the day.

Her new husband, Juba, was standing behind her, and she could feel his joy even before she heard him clap and reach down to put his dark-skinned arms around her in a hug that squeezed her firmly but gently. He bent his head to her ear and kissed her lightly on the cheek. "Wonderful, my love."

Selene turned her head to give him a quick kiss in return. "It's getting easier," she said as her breathing slowed. "Down and then out, just like you keep saying."

It had been more than a year since she'd stolen the Palladium of Troy from the sacred temple of the Vestal Virgins in Rome. That night Selene had triggered the Shard's power accidentally, terrifying Augustus Caesar's stepson Tiberius and partially blinding his cousin Urbinia. Selene had refused to answer Tiberius' confused questions about what had happened, and she had done her best to avoid him in the many months since, despite the fact that he was obviously infatuated with her—and that his feelings were further aroused by the new, supernatural mystery surrounding her. She'd also refused to touch the Shard again, for fear of what it might unleash through her, even if she still wished that she could harness its strength to somehow avenge the deaths of her parents—suicides to be blamed, without doubt, on Caesar and Rome.

It was only with her marriage to Juba of Numidia, just weeks after she turned fifteen, and only weeks before he was summoned to join Caesar here in Cantabria, that she even spoke to anyone of her theft of the Palladium, and of what it really was. She'd done it on their wedding night, after they'd been blessed by the Roman gods of marriage and fertility and ceremoniously paraded into the room where they were meant to consummate the union that had been decreed for them by Caesar. Juba had known of the Shards of Heaven: he'd discov-

ered the Trident of Poseidon, after all—he'd been forced by
Caesar to use it to destroy Selene's parents' fleet at Actium—
and they both knew how he had acquired the Aegis of Zeus
by taking the armor from the tomb of Alexander the Great in
Alexandria. He had saved Selene's life then, and at every turn
he had seemed a man she could believe in, a man she could
trust. It was a test of that trust to tell him about the Palladium,
and she was not surprised that he expressed no shock at the
existence of another such object of power.

She was surprised, however, that he'd responded to her
crime—for a most grievous crime it was to violate the sanctity
of the Temple of the Vestals as she had—with a smile and warm
laughter. Taking her hand, he'd led her to a locked chest.
Opening it up, he had carefully unpacked traveling clothes, old
maps, and even a set of hardened leather armor. Then, staring
at what seemed to be an empty trunk, he'd let out a long sigh
and told her that he, too, had stolen something quite special.
Then he had reached down, pulled off a false bottom to the
trunk, and showed her the Aegis, which he'd managed to keep
hidden from Caesar's prying eyes.

They'd embraced then, not as politically bound titles, but
as unexpectedly kindred souls. She'd cried purely and honestly
and openly for the first time since she could remember: cried
for her dead parents, Mark Antony and Cleopatra. She cried for
her dead brothers: her twin, Alexander Helios, who had died
in the prison in Rome, and little Ptolemy Philadelphus, who
she later learned had died before he ever made it that far. She
cried for her dead half-brother, Caesarion, who was the best of
men. She cried for her vanquished homeland of Egypt, and for
the horror of living as the adopted daughter of the man who'd
taken it all away from her.

Juba had understood. She'd known that he would, even
from the first moment they'd met in Alexandria, when he

helped to save her from the bloodthirst of Rome. But even as they were engaged to be married, even as they came together in tentative, too-formal hugs and greetings, she'd never opened herself to him. Not like this.

Through all of it—the sorrow, the rage, the guilt—Juba had simply embraced her. And then, standing over the Shard of Heaven of Alexander's breastplate, the very Aegis of Zeus, he had sworn that he would support her quest for vengeance, which so closely mirrored his own. And he swore, too, that he would teach her to control the Palladium of Troy, to no longer need to fear the Shard's power. It was, she'd thought as he held her, the most wondrous thing she could have imagined.

How little she knew. They made love that night, but as the months had passed it was clear that their bond was just beginning. They were genuinely and truly in love. And that was surely the most unbelievable wonder of all.

It was that same love that she saw sparkling in his eyes as he stepped around from behind her and eyed the path of the little torrent of wind that she'd unleashed with the power of the Shard. "You'll be better than I am soon enough," he said. "You control it so effortlessly."

"Still tiring," she said. She frowned a little at the bag on the tree. "It's not enough."

"You're getting stronger, though," he said. "You have to start small. You have to build up to it. To learn the Trident I started with a cup of wine."

Selene saw something dark pass over his face. Memories, she knew. Juba was nearly eight years older than she was, but more than once she'd had to comfort him when he woke up screaming from the nightmares of remembering what he had been made to do with the Shard that Caesar did know about: the Trident of Poseidon, which controlled water. "Of course," she said. Selene made her voice quiet and demure, aimed at bringing his attention out of the past. "I couldn't do this without you."

To her relief, when Juba shook his head she could almost see the ill memories fall away. "No, I think you could. Maybe not as fast, but you'd still do it. Strongest person I've ever known. And the most beautiful."

He'd said it to her many times now, but she didn't like hearing it. Somehow it reminded her too much of her mother and her pursuit of power through lovers. None of that interested Selene. She would hold power between her hands, not between her sheets.

At the thought, she looked down at the Shard, which indeed sat in her lap between her hands. It remained an unimpressive-looking thing: a crystalline rock, vaguely the shape of a woman in robes. In Troy they had associated it with Pallas Athena. It protected them. For years it kept them safe. Only after it was stolen from them did the city fall. If the stories were to be believed, the thief Odysseus had paid for that crime—and his failure to control its power—with a wandering journey of years spent away from his beloved homeland.

She was a thief, too, Selene supposed. Only, she would control the Shard. She would succeed where Odysseus had failed. And rather than spiriting her away from her homeland, the Shard would be the key to bringing her back to it.

"Do you think we can really do it?" she asked.

"What's that?" Juba had turned and was looking at the empty bag again. He seemed to be calculating something.

"Destroy Rome," Selene replied, her voice unintentionally small this time.

Juba turned back around. He knelt before her, just as he had on the night he'd sworn his support for her dream of vengeance. He took her hands in his, the Palladium untouched between them. "You know I do," he said. "You know I wouldn't be here if I didn't. I believe in you, Selene. I believe in us."

Selene examined how their fingers enmeshed, his darker skin alternating with hers in a perfect grip that felt complete. "And the Shards?"

"What do you mean? I believe they're real enough." He seemed about to laugh at the object of power between them, but the seriousness on her face gave him pause.

"No," Selene said. She squeezed his beautiful fingers more tightly. "I mean, you say you believe in us. But is that only—?"

"Only because of the Shards?"

Selene nodded, biting her lip.

"No," Juba said. He squeezed her hands in response. "I told you: I believe in us. The Shards are only a means to an end. They are tools. Nothing more. And like all tools each requires a user, one who understands how to use it. That's what Octavian didn't understand. That's what he still doesn't understand, and it's why he can't use the Trident."

Selene pulled their fingers apart and then moved her grip so that she held his hands in her own. She leaned forward and placed gentle kisses on the backs of each of them. "It's what is inside that matters," she said.

"I suppose that's right."

"You're a good man, Juba."

He smiled at that, and then he pulled his hands free and stood. Selene looked up at him, wondering how she'd once thought this man was her enemy. "I like to think so," he said. "Though Caesar might disagree in the end. Shall we try again?"

Selene looked up at the brightening sky, then nodded. "Just one more. Then we should probably get back to the tent."

Her husband, gentle man that he was, frowned. He didn't

understand. "A patrol isn't due this way for another hour. And this morning's war council won't be for at least another hour beyond that."

Selene grinned.

For a moment or two longer, Juba still frowned. Then recognition swept the confusion from his face and he gasped. "Oh!" He blushed. "Right. Just time for one more, then. Unless, I mean, if you wanted to stop now, we could—"

"No, no," Selene said, still grinning as she waved him away behind her. "You said we had plenty of time."

"As you wish, my lady," he said. She heard him settle down into place behind her, to watch down the same line of sight that she had across the open ground toward the empty bag in the tree.

Selene took a deep, long breath. She flexed out her arms and then relaxed them down into her lap, her fingers touching the surface of the Shard.

Locked in the heart of the smoky quartz of the vaguely woman-shaped stone was the Shard itself: a deeply black pit that seemed to capture and hold the light. Lacing around it were black veins, rising to the surface most prominently where the eyes of the woman's face ought to have been. It was here that Selene's thumbs rested, her pads settling into the slight depressions as her fingers reached around to the back of the Palladium to hold it steady.

At once the sensation of a roiling fire began to shoot up through her hands and into her forearms. When first she'd felt it, back at the Temple of the Vestals, she'd feared it would consume her. From what Juba had now told her, the use of a Shard could do that to many people. Why the two of them were able to withstand the shock, able to begin to control it, Juba did not know.

It was enough for them that they could.

So when the shock erupted into her out of the Shard, Selene did not scream. She did not pull away. Instead, she closed her eyes and let it wash over and through her. She brought it into herself. She let herself become one with the power, let it swirl through her veins just as it swirled through those in the stone.

When she felt she had enough, when it seemed that it would wash her away, she swallowed and focused it, pushing it out of herself the same way that it had come: down through her arms, down through her hands, down through her fingers and into the stone she held there.

And then, opening her eyes, she pushed the power out of the stone like the exhalation of a long-held breath.

Amid the open circle of trees, a whisper of wind once more rose from the earth.

4

Alexander's City

The heat in the barge's hold had been so stifling, and the grain-heavy air so choking, that Lucius Vorenus had been certain he'd either suffocate or sneeze long before Petosiris had gotten them through the Roman customs officials and into the safety of the city.

Not that Alexandria was exactly safe for a man who had been sentenced to die by Caesar himself. Even now, quietly making his way north along the widest and most busiest avenue of the city he'd once called home, Vorenus was certain he'd be a dead man if he was recognized.

In that respect, he supposed, he was far safer under the deck of the canal barge. At least there, holding his breath and trying his best to stay silent as the vessel docked at the water gate, he had known the identity of the threat: the Roman soldiers who had stepped aboard to inspect its cargo and the captain's papers.

Beside him in the narrow, shallow space, Khenti had lain with his eyes shut. If not for the steady rise and fall of the Egyptian's chest, Vorenus might have thought him dead. As it was, the swordsman had been still enough that he might have been sleeping.

Peering up through the cracks in the decking above, Vorenus had seen the familiar hardened-leather soles of the sandals
he knew so well from his many years spent as a legionnaire. And
beyond them he had recognized the accents of Rome, of those
he'd once called countrymen.

Petosiris, Vorenus now knew, was a man even more versed
in smuggling than he had suspected. As the soldiers had
poked long spears into the piles of grain and peppered him
with questions, the barge captain had given only the simplest
of replies, and he had stood with his hand on the ship's tiller,
directly beside the coil of ropes that concealed the hidden
hatch.

When the soldiers were satisfied that all was in order, Vorenus had heard the quiet clink of coins being exchanged, and
then the sandaled feet had stepped off the barge, the little
deckhand jumping into action behind them. Vorenus heard
the links of the chain across the canal rattling through a metal
cleat as the chain was allowed to go slack. It fell into the water
with a splash that rocked the barge beneath Vorenus' back.
Then they had unmoored from the dock, and once more they
had traveled along the great canal, headed west over the sunken
chain toward the lake harbor docks and, beyond them, the
teeming city of Alexandria.

As Vorenus had watched through the cracks, the deckhand
had then methodically re-coiled the rope, moving it off the
hatch and into a new pile to the side. Only when it was done did
Petosiris at last open the hatch and bring fresh air and the
bright light of day into the hold. "You can sneeze now," Petosiris had said with a smile.

Vorenus had indeed done so, and even now, two hours later,
his nose itched.

They'd left the barge at the lake harbor, with reassurances
to Petosiris that they would be making the return trip east

when he left that evening. Then he and Khenti had entered the city from which they had been exiled.

It was Khenti who decided that the straightest route to the Museum would be the best one. From the west end of the lake harbor docks they needed only to make their way north across the breadth of the city by walking along the Sema Avenue.

It was a calculated risk. They would encounter far fewer people by making their way through the many side streets of Alexandria, but with fewer people around they would also stand out more if indeed they did encounter anyone who knew them. Amid the thousands of people pulsing along one of the central arteries of the city, they would be, they hoped, lost in the vast sea of faces.

And so, block by block, they made their way north through the thick crowds.

For all that the Roman seizure of Egypt had changed in his life, Vorenus was shocked at how little Alexandria had changed. It was still a city of white walls and red-tiled roofs, and at least the monumental buildings along the Sema Avenue showed not even the slightest scar. The city's people, too, were just as he remembered them. Alexandria had long been a hub of trade between the riches of east and west, north and south, and its incorporation into the growing vastness of Caesar's Rome had done nothing to slow the masses of people from across the world who lived upon or passed through its streets. Walking among them, Vorenus and Khenti were surrounded by a vibrancy of color and dress. They were surrounded, too, by the polyphony of language swirling into a thrum of humanity, punctuated by the squall of birds, the bray and cry of stock, and the clatter of wheels on stone streets. The city even smelled as Vorenus remembered: that bewildering mix of the people, their beasts, and scents of their foods drifting out from stalls and shops.

Indeed, the only thing that had changed were the occasional squads of Roman soldiers marching upon the streets. The people moved around them like currents of water passing around rocks, and Vorenus and Khenti were happy to do likewise, taking care to be as far from Roman eyes as possible.

No one recognized them, and they made good speed despite the crowds. It was only mid-morning when Khenti pointed ahead of them through the crowds. "Vorenus," he said. "The square."

There were two streets in the city of Alexandria that were known far and wide. One was the Sema Avenue, along which they walked, running roughly south to north from the busy docks of the lake harbor to the sprawling Emporium along the shores of the Great Harbor on the sea, at the mouth of which stood the Great Lighthouse itself. The other was the Canopic Way, running from the Sun Gate in the east to the Moon Gate in the west. The royal palaces were on the peninsula of Lochias in the northeast quadrant of the city, but even the royal family—when there had been a royal family—had known that the real center of Alexandria, the true, beating heart of its proud people, was the confluence of those two broad streets. Rare it was for a traveler to come to Alexandria and not walk one of those paths, following it to the wide, open square where they met.

Upon each corner of that square stood a massive building. To the northeast, in the direction of the royal palaces, was the temple to Isis, the Egyptian goddess-queen. To the southeast, fronted by high pillars, was the Sema, from which the avenue they walked had gotten its name. Burial place of kings and pharaohs, it was there, in a statue-lined chamber beneath a pyramidal roof, that Alexander the Great's body rested in its crystal tomb. It had been almost three hundred years since the Macedonian king had conquered Egypt and been declared the

son of both the Egyptian god Ammon and the Greek god
Zeus, almost three hundred years since he'd stood on the bar-
ren shores of a stormy sea and proclaimed that it was here that
he would build the city that would take his name, the city of
Alexandria, wonder of the world.

That it was built, too, in order to house the Ark of the Covenant, perhaps the most powerful of the Shards of Heaven,
was a secret known to few men. For all that he had seen and
experienced, Vorenus had difficulty believing it himself. But,
truly, there were days he had difficulty believing that the fall
of Alexandria to Rome had meant that he himself had become
one of the keepers of that secret, one of the keepers of the Ark.

To the southwest, across from Alexander's mausoleum, perhaps fittingly, was the Temple of Ammon. And at the fourth
corner, to the northwest, lay the beautiful, green grounds of
the Museum. Their destination this day lay at the center of
that vast complex dedicated to the Muses: the Great Library
itself, built of white marble and stone, whose magnificent
dome was crowned by a golden statue of a man holding a scroll
open to the sky.

As they crossed the Canopic Way and entered the Museum grounds, Vorenus wondered at the fact that the Great
Library had not been put to the torch when Octavian—
Augustus Caesar now, he had to remind himself—had seized
the city. When Julius Caesar had come to Alexandria, the first
time that Vorenus had come to this place in service of Rome,
part of the Great Library had indeed burned. An accident, so
it was said, though there were whispers in the legion that Caesar had been concerned about the power of the growing intellectual elite of the librarians. So he had fully expected the
new Caesar to burn it to the ground.

He hadn't, though, and Vorenus was glad for it. He was
never one for books and letters himself, but it was a beautiful

building, and he had grown to appreciate the knowledge of men like his friend Didymus, who had become the head of the Great Library not long after Caesar's death. Didymus, he was sure, knew more than any other man in the world.

If anyone knew why the Ark seemed to have lost some of its powers since leaving this city, it would be Didymus.

•   •   •

Before the deaths of Antony and Cleopatra, Didymus had been a personal tutor to the royal children—to Caesarion and his stepsiblings—and so the librarian had kept an apartment in the palace. It was there that he had become such good friends with Pullo and Vorenus, the three of them sharing the often bewildering experience of being foreigners within the inner circles of Egyptian power. The two Roman legionnaires and the Greek intellectual had spent many nights laughing under the quiet of an Egyptian sky. Fortunately, the fact that those nights were spent in the palace rather than the Great Library meant that there was unlikely to be anyone there who would recognize Lucius Vorenus.

Khenti, however, had come to the office of Didymus more than once, usually in the company of Caesarion himself. So when they approached the doors of the Great Library, the Egyptian swordsman slipped into the shadows of a stand of trees while Vorenus walked on, approaching the dark mouth of the building alone.

There was a librarian standing just outside the door— Khenti had told Vorenus to expect this—and the young man asked him his business. "I've just arrived by boat from Macedonia," Vorenus said in his best Greek. "I bear a message to be personally delivered to the chief librarian himself."

The man blinked and looked him up and down. Whether he was wondering how he could possibly be from Macedonia or he was simply taken aback by the request to see Didymus,

Vorenus could not tell. "And may I ask your name?" the librarian asked.

Before embarking on this trip, Khenti and Vorenus had agreed that they could not use their real names near Alexandria. It would simply be too dangerous. "Philip," Vorenus replied.

The librarian disappeared into the building, and Vorenus turned back toward the trees to see if he could locate Khenti. It was no surprise that he could not. Besides being the best swordsman he'd ever met, the Egyptian, he was sure, could disappear on an empty street at midday.

It was several minutes before the door of the Library opened once more. The first librarian had returned, accompanied by an older man who was clearly a man in charge: he appeared both flustered and exhausted, as if he'd already had his fill of a hard day, even though it wasn't even noon.

"Can I help you?"

"My name is Philip," Vorenus repeated. "I've come from Macedonia with a message for the chief librarian."

The man sighed. "And I am Apion, his assistant. Give me the message and I'll see that he gets it."

"Apologies, sir," Vorenus said, trying to be deferential even though he was much the elder man. "My instructions are very explicit about giving the message directly to Didymus himself."

Apion sighed again, and he rubbed at his temples while shielding his eyes from the bright sun. "Philip," he repeated. "From Macedonia?"

The tone of the librarian's voice was filled with doubt, but it was also scratchy. Vorenus recognized the signs. He'd seen them often enough when Pullo had been too long at the cups. "That's right," he said, his voice suddenly far louder than it needed to be.

Apion winced. Then, after a moment, his shoulders relaxed in a kind of defeat. Whatever doubts he had, he seemed to think that the old man posed no greater threat than the morning sun. "Very well," he said. "Follow me. And please keep your voice down. So you don't disturb the scholars, you know."

Inside, Vorenus found himself being led through a long entry hall lined with five pillars on each side of a long, narrow reflecting pool. He could see offices between the pillars, and there was a buzz of work coming from within them. As men came and went through the doors he saw into two of them, and he recognized them as scriptoria: lines of scribes hunched over desks, quills in hand, carefully copying old books onto new pages.

"You know, you're lucky, Philip," Apion said over his shoulder, voice hushed. "Didymus didn't go home again last night. Another couple hours and you would have found him asleep."

Vorenus nodded and allowed himself a smile. His friend had often burned the midnight oil. His life was his books. Always had been.

The entry gave way to the main hall at the center of the Great Library: a six-sided room of towering walls broken only by the stairs that crawled up their surfaces and the heavy oak doors that led to the wings of the building beyond them, which were no doubt filled with scrolls and books. Between these walls and the high dome above were a line of massive windows that painted everything in a wash of warm sunlight.

The reflecting pool in the entry hall tumbled down a few steps into a circular pool in the center of this larger room, providing a steady and calming patter behind the sounds of hushed voices and footsteps as scholars and their assistants moved around the busy space. Smoothly curved benches bent around the edge of the main pool, and here and there upon it men sat in thought. Vorenus noticed that one of them, a young man who looked up as they approached, had very clearly had the worse of a recent fight. His face was badly bruised, and blood stained the tattered front of his shirt.

"Apion," he said, his voice slurred by swollen lips and cheeks, "you need to let me see him."

Apion's steps faltered and then stopped. Though he'd seemed genial enough with Vorenus, there was nothing but contempt in his face as he turned on the battered younger man. "I *need* do nothing of the kind, Thrasyllus. You quit, remember? You quit and proved once and for all why he was right to choose me."

"But I—"

"You quit," Apion repeated. A smile like a sneer crossed his face. "Thought you'd make a point, and all you did was prove why he chose me. Fool, you're lucky I even let you in the building."

Each word was like another slap to the man's face, but still he opened his mouth to say something more.

"No," Apion interrupted. "Not one word, Thrasyllus. You sit or you go. Didymus will see you when—and if—he wants to do so. Not one minute before."

Thrasyllus closed his open mouth, and Vorenus could see the mix of hatred and defiance and pained self-loathing in his eyes. Something of it reminded Vorenus of young legionnaires that he'd known who'd been subjected to the harsh correction of the lash. He pitied the young man, and when Apion began walking once more, Vorenus met his gaze. He nodded at him ever so slightly in acknowledgment of his difficulties. Thrasyllus stared back for a moment, then he nodded in return, and something like a smile creased the corner of his mouth.

Apion, seeming even more tired now, led Vorenus up two flights of stairs that angled along the walls, where they entered a short, pillared hall not unlike the entry two floors below. At its end was a single door, and Apion knocked at it quietly.

It had been so long since he'd heard the voice from within that when it spoke Vorenus broke into a grin behind Apion. "Yes?" Didymus asked.

"Someone to see you, Librarian," Apion said to the door. "A Macedonian named Philip. He says he has a message for you."

There was a pause of a few seconds before Didymus answered. "Very well. Send him in."

Apion opened the door, turning back to Vorenus as he did so. The pain of the previous night of drinking was even clearer on his face. "He'll see you now," he said.

Vorenus gave him a nod, but before he entered the room he leaned in close to the scholar and whispered, "You don't need to wait here. I can find my way out."

The look on Apion's face was one of pure gratitude. "Thank you," he replied quietly. "I'll be downstairs in my office if I'm needed."

Apion turned and hurried off toward the stairs in the main hall. Vorenus did not doubt that he was hurrying to relieve himself one way or another.

When he was gone, Vorenus stepped into the office of the chief librarian and closed the door behind him.

It surprised Vorenus not at all to see that Didymus hadn't even looked up. He was hunched over his desk, his face hidden behind the long locks of his gray hair. With his quill in hand, he was focused on reading one of the many scrolls strewn in what once might have been piles upon his desk. "Yes?" the scholar asked without moving his head. "What is this message?"

Vorenus smiled happily, taking another step forward. He'd been in exile so long that it was hard to believe he was seeing such a familiar face once more. "That an old friend misses you," he said.

The quill scratched loudly to a halt, and the scholar's head snapped up, the gray strands swaying in front of his eyes. He blinked as if he could not believe what he was seeing. Then he jumped up, overturning his chair behind him and scattering scraps of papyrus to the floor. "Vorenus!"

The librarian had aged considerably in their time apart. The wrinkles were carved more deeply upon his Greek skin, and his back was more hunched than it once had been, but the warmth with which he embraced his friend was unchanged. It was as if time and the war had never parted them. "By the gods, Vorenus, it's good to see you. It's been far too long."

Vorenus patted his back. "So it has, my old friend."

Didymus abruptly pulled back out of the embrace, holding Vorenus at arm's length. Sudden fear gripped his face. "What has happened? Is everything well? Is Caesarion—?"

"He is fine," Vorenus assured him. "All is well."

Didymus let out a long breath. "Thank the gods. I worried, seeing you again." He let go and stepped back, looking the Roman up and down. "And you certainly look well," he said.

"And you."

"Still a poor liar." Didymus smiled.

"I'll not compliment you on your housekeeping, then."

Didymus laughed a little at that, then bent over to unceremoniously clear a haphazard stack of papers from a stool in front of his desk. As Vorenus sat down, the chief librarian walked around to set his own seat upright. "Well, I'm surprised to see you," Didymus said. There was sadness behind his smile. "I confess I never thought I would do so again."

"Like Pullo always said, I'm a hard man to keep away."

Vorenus meant it in levity, but the mention of their old

friend's name was like the breath of a chill wind in the room. Both men fell silent at the memory.

"You know," Didymus finally said, "I never was able to tell you how Pullo died."

"You said he did it to save you. To protect Caesarion and the Ark. Isn't that enough?" Truth be told, it had always been enough for Vorenus.

The librarian's eyes were turned down toward the desk, but he wasn't looking at it. Vorenus could see that his friend was lost in a memory he'd too long kept to himself. "He was wounded, Vorenus. Juba, the Numidian who was looking for the Ark . . . he surprised us. We tried, but we couldn't stop him."

"Pullo couldn't stop him?" Vorenus tried to imagine something short of an angry bull stopping his big friend. Even that was hard to picture.

Didymus shook his head as he looked up for a moment. "I told you, he surprised us. And it wouldn't have mattered. He was wearing the Aegis of Zeus."

"Aegis?"

"Armor," Didymus said. "The armor of Alexander the Great."

At last Vorenus remembered. That night, that last night in Alexandria, the keepers of the Ark had summoned them all to the old Temple of Serapis. They had spoken of Alexander's armor. What it really was. "Another Shard of Heaven."

Didymus nodded slowly, the long gray strands of his hair rising and falling in front of darkened eyes. "Pullo was so hurt, Vorenus. But he knew. He knew what had to be done. He . . . he gave his life to save us all."

Vorenus bit his lip to control his jaw. "A good man," he managed to say. "A better man than I could ever be."

Didymus brushed aside his hair to look Vorenus in the eyes. "He would have said the same of you."

"He would have been wrong, then."

"As he would have said, once more, of you."

Vorenus couldn't help but smile at that. It was true, after all. He knew it. Pullo would have clapped that big hand of his upon his friend's back and laughed at how Vorenus was both the better man and the greater fool—as if such a paradox made all the sense in the world.

Didymus was smiling, too, but then a shadow once more seemed to fall over his face. "And both better men than I could ever be," he said.

Years before they'd known each other, on the night after Julius Caesar was murdered, Didymus had helped an assassin infiltrate Caesar's villa, where he'd nearly killed Caesarion, the son of Caesar and Cleopatra. Pullo had been the one to save the boy. But Didymus was a different man now. Vorenus knew it. Pullo had known it. Caesarion, too, had long since forgiven him. "It's been so long, my friend. What's done was done."

"It isn't just that," Didymus said. "I brought Juba to the Ark. Selene convinced me that he would help us protect the Ark. He wanted to destroy Octavian."

Vorenus thought on it for a moment. "You did what you thought was best," he finally said. "You didn't know what would happen."

"No. I didn't. And I don't think he did either."

"What do you mean?"

"In the weeks afterward I spent time with Juba. He came here to the Library, seeking out information about the Shards. He knew so much, Vorenus. And he was—is, I suppose—a brilliant young man. A voracious appetite for knowledge, and he remembers seemingly everything he reads. I could have made him a fine scholar."

"High praise indeed."

"So it is," Didymus agreed. "Well, I got to know him. And he isn't the wicked man we feared. He truly wanted the Shards, but not to make himself great."

"He wanted to make Octavian great."

"No. Not at all. That's what I'm saying. To the contrary, my dear Vorenus, he wanted to kill him. I imagine he still does, but the experience of using the Aegis of Zeus affected him deeply. It took control of him. It changed him."

Vorenus leaned forward. "How?"

"How did it control him? I don't know. Neither of us did." The frustration in the scholar's voice was palpable. Didymus was a man who thrived on knowledge. Not knowing some-thing clearly rankled him. "But when he attacked us it wasn't really Juba. Not anymore. He didn't even remember what happened later. It was like he was under a spell. And later he wanted to understand how."

"You said he learned a lot."

"Yes. But you can be sure that I endeavored to see that he never learned too much. Certain books I hid. Certain paths I never let him follow."

"Did he still want the Ark?"

Didymus frowned at the question, thinking. "He did and did not. Were he offered its power, he would have taken it. But he would not seek it out. He may not have remembered every-thing he did when he was under the spell of the Aegis, but he knows that it had much to do with his desire to get the Ark. I do not think he wants to ever kill again. But if he was freely offered the Ark, if he had the chance to use it, just once, to gain his revenge, his thirst for revenge against Caesar remains unquenched."

"So long as he's no threat to us," Vorenus said. He settled back into his chair, relaxing. "He can kill as many Caesars as he wants. He just can't do it with the Ark."

"I do believe you are safe from Juba, my friend," Didymus reassured him. "But he isn't the only threat. You're still a wanted man here, Lucius Vorenus. I'm glad you're here, but it isn't safe."

"I know it only too well. Caesar is not a man to forget."

"Indeed so," Didymus agreed. "He would pay a great deal for your head."

Vorenus shrugged. "Flattering in its way," he said.

"An interesting way to look at it," Didymus said. "You might have a touch of the philosopher in you. But if you knew this, and you are still here, then it is not for friendship that you've come."

Vorenus frowned, trying to appear disappointed. "Can that not be enough?"

"No, my friend. Friends or not, you were never a fool. You need something. Otherwise there'd be no reason to risk a journey so deep into the city." He leaned forward on his elbows. "So. What is it, Lucius Vorenus? What brings you to Alexandria?"

Vorenus took a deep breath. "It's about the Ark of the Covenant, Didymus. It's about the Shards."

5

The Cantabrian War

Selene was already gone when one of Caesar's praetorian guards pushed aside the flap of Juba's tent, bringing in the shock of morning light and the sounds of the vast Roman encampment.

"Sir, Caesar requests the presence of the king of Numidia. I am to escort you."

Juba lifted himself up to his elbows and blinked into the light for a moment before resigning himself to closing his eyes and nodding firmly. "Thank you, praetorian."

The guard stepped away, and in the darkness once again, Juba rose from the bed he shared with the beautiful young daughter of Antony and Cleopatra. He readied himself as quickly but as properly as he could, taking extra care to don the uniform of his station. The wording of the invitation, after all, meant that he was needed not just as the stepbrother of Octavian—Juba refused to think of him by the name Augustus—but in his more formal role as ruler of the land of his birth, the land that his father had ruled before Julius Caesar had destroyed him and made young Juba an orphan before adopting him in a display of that particularly Roman mix of arrogance and grace. Augustus Caesar had restored the title to Juba when he'd given him the hand of Cleopatra Selene, who was herself in title the queen of Egypt after her mother's suicide. It was fitting, Octavian had said, that she be married to a king.

Not that either title held substance: the lands of their birth were entirely under Roman control now. Their grand names were nothing but decrees that befit the plans of the increasingly powerful Caesar. Juba wondered sometimes if he'd been made a king only to show how one more king answered to the emperor of Rome.

Just thinking about it made Juba want to spit.

Instead, he straightened the purple sash that marked him as a member of the royal family and then pulled aside the flap of the tent.

The first thing he noticed, as he blinked out of the darkness, was that part of the wooded hillside to the west was on fire.

The siege of Vellica, the Cantabrian hillfort perched there, had met with little success over the past weeks, so on this morning the Roman assault had begun with pots of oil and flame. Heaved by catapults into the smoke-scattered sky, the bundles rose and fell like a dark, scattered rain, exploding into the enemy fortifications in bursts of red and brilliant orange.

It wouldn't work. Even the Roman legions, lined up in their rows at the foot of the hill of the encampment, ready to press an advantage across the little shallow valley should it appear, seemed to know it. Juba could see that many men hadn't buckled their armaments, and even the standard of the golden eagle, emblem of the might of Rome, was held at the slightest angle, as if the bearer below was talking to another man in the ranks.

Juba knew enough of Rome to know that such an act ought to bring the whip, but Octavian didn't seem to mind such things so long as he got what he wanted in the end. Besides which, it was in the nature of a siege that the besieged and the besiegers alike both suffered in the stalemate.

Not that you would know it for a stalemate based on the number of Romans that had been lost here. For all that he had seen of war in his twenty-three years—the great fleets clashing upon the stormy waves at Actium, the towering engines crashing against the gates of distant Alexandria—Juba had never seen anything quite like the horror that had welcomed the Romans in Hispania.

In the weeks since he'd come to the frontier, Juba had seen enough death to last him a lifetime—and still the barbarians refused to surrender to their inevitable defeat.

"Sir," said the praetorian guard beside the tent. "Caesar is waiting."

"Of course," Juba said. He took a deep breath of air that was—despite the new fires across the valley—fresher than it had been for several days. The winds of the night had pushed away the fetid air of the encampment, which had been as oppressive as the summer sun here.

The praetorian was holding out his arm to indicate the path to the command tent, though Juba had walked it often enough to know the way. As if he had no other care in the world, Juba nodded and started making his way toward the field headquarters of the emperor of Rome, the man he and his wife were determined to kill.

.   .   .

In his tent, Augustus Caesar was sitting with several other commanders at the central table. He smiled when Juba entered. "My brother," he said. "I hope I didn't wake you from any activities this morning?"

The fact that Juba had brought Cleopatra Selene with him when summoned to the frontier had been a source of more than a few lascivious comments through the weeks—the emperor himself had joked that the Numidians must be a most lustful people, given that their king was so insistent on continuing his passions on the campaign. Juba allowed the comments, even encouraged them, because it was easier than the truth of why he'd brought her along. It was true that they were in love—genuinely so, much to Juba's delight after the arranged marriage—but it wasn't sex that kept them together here, secreting off alone to the hidden little hollow they'd found behind the lines. It was vengeance.

And, he thought with a wry smile, a little sex, too.

"The lady Selene sends her regards, Caesar," Juba said. He looked down, feigning some embarrassment.

Octavian laughed and motioned to a seat to his left. There were a few more snickers, but things quieted down quickly.

Sitting down, Juba noticed that Octavian's stepson was watching him from the other end of the table. Juba, almost ten years older and growing up in the same household, had often looked upon Tiberius as a younger brother, and he'd always felt a kind of affinity for him. After all, he suspected that Tiberius, like himself, might have felt little love for Caesar. It was Octavian, after all, who had forced Tiberius' mother, Livia, to divorce his father when he was three years old. But something had changed recently. Tiberius, now that he was fifteen, was old enough to accompany his stepfather on campaign, and some said that Augustus Caesar intended for Tiberius to rule after him. Juba wondered if perhaps the distance he was feeling between them was simply a result of Tiberius growing into a sense of himself as a man. Or was it something else?

Juba nodded at the young man, smiling as amicably as he could. Tiberius stared at him for a moment, a clouded look upon his face, before he nodded in return, the barest hint of a smile on his face. Then he turned away toward one of the other, older commanders and engaged him in conversation.

Juba let out a breath, not even sure why he'd been holding it. Then he took stock of the rest of the men in attendance. It was Carisius who had not yet shown up. He'd been one of the field generals who'd been directing the campaign in Cantabria before the emperor's arrival, and it wasn't like him to be late.

Rather than engage in meaningless talk with the other men, Juba busied himself with examining the large map of Cantabria that had been pulled out upon the table. The Roman positions, along with those of the enemy Cantabri, were wooden blocks of various size and shape upon it.

The campaign, they all knew, had been a difficult one.

Shortly after having himself declared Augustus Caesar, Octavian had ordered up his legions to begin preparations for an advance on distant Britannia, whose shores Julius Caesar had left twenty-seven years earlier. The new Caesar, it was widely known, intended on further legitimizing his position through a show of military force and the integration of new lands into the empire. But fate, it seemed, had different plans. The armies had only reached as far as southern Gaul when word arrived that the Cantabri, a barbarian tribe in northern Hispania, had rebelled against Roman authority. They'd murdered tax collectors, destroyed dozens of Roman villas and farms, and they were even threatening a massive assault on the central Roman town of Segisama. It was an outright rebellion, and it had to be stopped.

Juba hated his stepbrother, but he could not help but admire the efficiency with which he pivoted his massing forces, transferring his legions out of Gaul to the shores of Hispania. From the port of Tarraco they had marched up-river into the higher plains, and as the new year began Caesar had established a new base of operations in Segisama, where he initiated plans for a two-pronged assault that would strike Cantabria in the spring. One army would march northwest toward Arecelium. The other, under his personal command, would march north.

Juba and Selene, newly married, had remained in Rome during those months, reveling in their love and their shared thirst for Caesar's destruction. They had listened to the reports as they came in. They had pored over maps, trying to glean the truth from the glowing accounts of glory that even the messengers knew for lies. And Selene had begun learning to control the Palladium, in the hope that it could be used to destroy Rome upon Caesar's return.

And then one day the messenger came with news of the glorious victory over the Cantabrian forces at Amaya, along with the request that the king of Numidia set out to join Caesar on the frontier.

They knew there could be only one reason. Octavian once more intended to use the Trident of Poseidon to destroy his enemies. And he needed Juba to do it.

It had been six years since Juba had used the Trident in war—since he had killed hundreds by raising a wave to crush Mark Antony's flagship at Actium—but for Juba the memory was still far too close. That he'd not yet been made by Caesar to use the artifact was simply a blessing that he considered too good to be true, as was the determination of Selene to remain by his side even as they rode past the piles of the bloating, bird-pecked Cantabri dead still unburied outside Amaya. More than once on their journey, Selene had woken him from a nightmare—when he wasn't waking her from her own.

That he had not been called upon was curious to him. When he thought about it, he wondered if perhaps it was because there was so little water here. Even during the spring rains that fell as Juba and Selene had made their way up from the coast, it was clear that this was an arid climate: a landscape of rocks and red-brown earth, shrub-trees and tiled-roof houses with white walls to keep off the heat. Now that it was summer, the dryness of the air was enough to leave cracks like red spiderwebs across the backs of his hands.

In a strange way, though, it felt like home. Juba wasn't like most of the men in the army of Augustus Caesar, a fact that was clear at a glance: he might be a Roman citizen, an adopted son of Julius Caesar himself, but his dark skin made him an outsider. He was a Numidian, and in the end he had more in common with the enemies of Rome than he did with those of the Eternal City. This had not gone unnoticed by the men. Juba knew that behind his back he was called the "dark prince," among other, less dignified titles. He was a foreigner, yet in this foreign, desolate landscape much akin to his North African birthplace, he felt at home. That fact made life here in the Roman encampment at the edge of the world more than merely bearable. It made it comfortable.

So long as he didn't have to use the Trident.

The sound of a commotion outside stirred Juba from his thoughts, and he looked up as the flaps parted and Carisius hurried inside. A short but stout man, the general was flustered and concerned. "Caesar," he said, "it's Corocotta. There's been another attack."

Octavian stood. "What? Where?"

"On the southern road." Carisius swallowed hard. "Sir, he's hit the supply line."

．　．　．

There was a terrible stillness in the meadow where the ambush had taken place. The men who'd been driving the supply wagons, and the horses that had been pulling them, were all dead. Even the birds had gone quiet in the trees, as if fearful of what they had seen. The road itself was black and dusty gray, littered with the charred remnants of the inferno that had consumed the supply train. The little air that moved under the mid-morning sun raised ghosts of ashen dust that danced and disappeared like stolen memories. The hot summer air was thick with the sickly sweet smell of burned flesh.

Juba had heard rumors of such attacks on his journey up from the coast. At first they were small, just a few men who'd gone missing on patrol. Then it was a detachment sent out from Amaya to scout the passes, who'd failed to report as expected. Then another. And another.

All of the missing men were found quickly, Juba was told. After all, it wasn't hard to follow the smoke that was left behind.

Cantabri prisoners had told Caesar who to blame. It was a man named Corocotta, who was said to be the leader of a band of Cantabrian warriors trained to move at speed in what was for them familiar wilderness. Rather than fight the Roman legions on their terms, Corocotta and his men were determined to fight through ambush and terror.

And it was brutally, dangerously effective. The name of Corocotta was whispered among the men like a story told to frighten unruly children. He was a horror who burned men alive. He was a phantom who could appear and disappear at will.

More than once Juba had seen men choose the punishment of a flogging over the fear of following orders to scout beyond the lines.

Which was, Juba suspected, exactly what Corocotta had in mind.

Caesar had dismounted from his horse when they'd reached the site, and he was standing, alone, beside the broken, scorched remnants of just one of the many wagons in the supply train. The fire had burned it down to a slumping hulk on the ground. The spokes of its wheels stuck out from the fire-twisted mess like the bones of a dead animal. What was left of the two

Roman drivers lay on the ground nearby, blackened beyond recognition.

Octavian wasn't looking at the corpses. He was staring at the back of the destroyed wagon, at the gutted crates of supplies.

Tiberius had stayed behind in the encampment, but most of the other Roman leadership had come. Caesar's praetorian guards had made a securing ring around the perimeter of the meadow, and within that the high-ranking men were fanned out among the wreckage, taking stock of what had been done. The loss, it was clear, was total. Carisius was not far away from Caesar, and Juba could see that he was in a conversation of heated whispers with another of the generals about how soon they could logistically replace the supplies that had been lost—if indeed they could protect the road well enough to get supplies through at all.

Juba himself had remained on horseback. He had no interest in being any closer to the dead than he already was.

"I want a price on his head," Octavian finally said. So quiet was the ruinous meadow that he did not need to raise his voice to be heard. And the few men who had been talking ceased at once.

Carisius exchanged pointed looks with the man he'd been arguing with, and then he strode toward the emperor. "Caesar?"

Octavian didn't look up. He was still staring at what was left of the supplies in the back of the wagon. "Corocotta," he said. His voice was steady. "One million Sesterces to the man who captures him. Dead or alive."

Carisius actually pulled up short. And Juba imagined that he heard several others swallow hard. "Caesar," Carisius started to say, "one million Sesterces—"

"Should get the job done," Octavian said. At last he looked up and met the general's eye. "Don't you think?"

Carisius started to say something more, then thought better of it. "It is a wealth unimaginable, Caesar."

"Good. I want the word sent out through the camp. But more than that, I want it sent in every direction. Pick twenty Cantabri prisoners. Send them out into the countryside with the same message. One million Sesterces for Corocotta. Dead or alive."

"Yes, Caesar," Carisius said. He gave a slight bow. "Any orders on which prisoners should be released?"

Octavian's gaze had returned to the wagon, and he absently waved his hand in the general's direction as if shooing a fly. Juba had seen the gesture before, years earlier, when his step-brother had admitted that he'd broken into the Temple of the Vestals to steal Mark Antony's will and use it to declare war on Egypt. "The old, the lame, the women," he said to Carisius. "The weak ones, I suppose. Now go. All of you. Send a burial detail in an hour. I want to speak with the king of Numidia alone."

Carisius and several of the others looked over at Juba quiz-zically, but they said nothing. Augustus Caesar was not a man to stand for objections. Instead, after saluting the emperor's back, they remounted the horses and rode back up the road toward their encampment. Only the praetorians remained, silent as statues around the edges of the clearing.

Juba watched the others go, the hooves of their horses kick-ing up the dust of men, materials, and dry earth. Only when the last of them was gone did he dismount.

Octavian still had not moved, so Juba walked to him, try-ing hard not to step upon the charred corpses near his step-brother's feet even as he tried not to look upon them.

"A hard blow," Juba said when he got close. It seemed right to speak in a quiet voice here, and so he did.

Octavian nodded, but he didn't look up from the debris in the back of the wagon. "A smart one. Corocotta is wise to attack our supply lines. We are stretched too thin here."

"Perhaps your bounty on his head will help inspire the men."

"Perhaps so." Octavian shrugged. "But I don't think it will matter."

"Won't matter?"

"They won't catch him. I have been trying for weeks, but he somehow kills everyone he meets. He burns them." Octavian's head raised to scan the meadow, pausing for a moment on the blackened corpses strewn amid the remains. "Like these men here."

It was the first time he'd actually acknowledged the dead men in the meadow, and it pleased Juba that he'd finally done so. He might hate Octavian and so much of what Rome stood for, but he truly believed that most of the men were loyal, strong, good men. Juba could never hate them for doing what they'd done. "Perhaps the released prisoners," he said to his stepbrother. "It only takes one to get close enough to him to kill him. And a million Sesterces—"

"Is nothing when weighed against Roman lives," Octavian said. "And Corocotta not only took the lives of these men, but he also endangered the lives of every man back in camp, my brother. We need this road open. We need the supplies." He turned his face to the sun for a moment, almost as if he was saying a prayer to the gods. "Coins can be replaced, Juba. The men cannot be."

It was a noble reason. It was a true and good reason. And not for the first time Juba felt an unsettling appreciation for the man he and Selene were determined to kill. Whatever else he was, Octavian was a leader. Perhaps he wasn't as fiery as Mark Antony, but he was focused and efficient. These were good qualities in a man who would rule—even if it meant, as Juba knew all too well, that he could be cold and ruthless when needed.

"But this isn't what you want to talk about," Octavian said, their eyes meeting for the first time since they'd come to the meadow. "You surely must be wondering why I sent for you, my brother."

"Not just missing me?" Juba asked hopefully.

Caesar's smile seemed genuine and warm. "You know that it was more than that, Juba. You served me well at Actium. You served Rome well."

Actium. Juba had used the Trident of Poseidon that day. Octavian had made him use the artifact to kill before—he'd used it to topple a trireme at sea, and he'd used it to kill Quintus, the slave who'd raised him—but never on the scale that he did at Actium. There he'd raised a towering wave and used it to crush ships, to drown hundreds of men. Juba fought hard to keep the memories of that day out of his mind. He fought hard to keep at bay the dead faces in the water and—perhaps worst of all—the glorious feeling of unbridled power that had coursed through him as he'd summoned the power of a god.

"I know you do not like to use the Trident," Octavian continued. "I have seen what it took from you. You have not been the same man since that day. And I am sorry for it."

The admission was so unexpected, so honest and true, that Juba could only stare at him. Octavian reached out and gripped his shoulder.

"I never wished to cause you pain, my brother. Truly this is so. I have only ever wished to do what is right for Rome." He let go of Juba's shoulder in order to sweep his arm across the meadow. "These men, all this death . . . I don't want any of this."

"No one should," Juba said.

When Octavian turned back to him, there was a fierce fire in his eyes. "I will have a world at peace, Juba."

"You'll have the world be Rome."

Octavian blinked for a moment in a look like confusion. "Could it be anything else? You've seen the rest of the world. Look at these men here, what this Cantabrian bastard has done to them. Rome is law, my brother. Rome is civilization. Rome is the future. We both know that. And yes, I will have the world be Rome, even if you and I must kill a thousand Corocottas to do it."

Juba felt like shaking him, screaming at him that killing Corocotta would only breed another like him—but then he, too, blinked. "You and I?"

"Yes, Juba. I sent for you for a reason."

"The Trident. You want me to use it to kill this man."

Octavian nodded as if this were the most obvious conclusion in the world. "You will do what is right, my brother. I know that you will. You're a good man, and you always have been. You're a better man than I ever will be. You'll do what's right. You'll help me avenge these men."

Juba felt like a caged animal, looking for a way out. "But the Trident is no use here. There's no sea. And even if I met this Corocotta, a common legionnaire has a better chance of catching him than I do of using the Trident to kill him."

Octavian began to grin. This time when he reached for Juba's shoulder it was to turn him toward the wagon. He pointed to the crate he'd been staring at so closely. "Look closely at this box, my brother. Tell me what you see."

Most of the crate had been burned to crumbled planks of wood mixed with whatever had been inside of it, but one side was still partially intact. There was a black scar across it, a line of fire. "It looks like someone has run a flame across it."

"So it does," Octavian said. "Only—"

Juba squinted at the line. "Only the scorch doesn't extend up," he said. "It's not right. It's too even. The flame of a torch would have licked upward."

Octavian patted him on the back as if he were a prized student. "Exactly so, my brother. Ever the smart one. You've seen in seconds what it took me weeks of visiting such sites to see. What not *one* of these other fools has yet to see."

Juba looked up at him in confusion. "But if not a torch, what?"

"You know what. You of all people know what."

Juba stared for a moment, weighing the impossibilities. But of course Octavian was right, even if he didn't know what the Shards of Heaven were. If there was a Shard to wield water, and a Shard to harness the wind, then there was a Shard to control fire.

And Corocotta had it.

6

The Astrologer's Plan

From the stone bench in the middle of the library he'd once hoped would be his, Thrasyllus watched Apion lead the strange man up the stairs and out of sight. Whoever the man was, the astrologer was sure of this: he was no Macedonian. If that was so, it stood to reason that his name wasn't Philip, either.

Plus, Thrasyllus couldn't shake the feeling that he knew the man somehow. When their eyes had met, something about him had seemed familiar.

Apion, the man who Didymus had chosen over him to assume the position of chief librarian when he retired, had been in the middle of lecturing him on moral responsibility when they were interrupted with news of the coming of this messenger who insisted on seeing Didymus. Thrasyllus was sure that Apion knew the man was lying—whatever else he was, Apion was no fool—but he also clearly saw no harm in bringing him into the presence of the chief librarian.

Thrasyllus turned to look down at the pool behind him. The waters were a constant ripple from where they tumbled down the steps from the reflecting pool in the entryway. With his finger, he pushed into the cool surface and made a slow circle that cast little ripples of its own. They were quickly rolled over and disappeared.

That was a difference between them, Thrasyllus thought to himself. Apion trusted, where he suspected.

Looking up, he saw Apion hurrying back down the stairs, alone now. His face was pale, and it appeared he might be sick. Clearly, after Didymus had announced his decision—and after Thrasyllus had made a show of storming out—Apion had celebrated his appointment through the night. He was paying for it now.

Even sick as he was, though, the other scholar managed to stare daggers as he scurried by on his way to relieve himself in the back rooms.

Thrasyllus wanted to sneer back, but he couldn't manage it. That kind of anger required pride, and he felt like the last of it had been beaten out of him today. Sitting here bruised and penniless, prepared to beg for a position—any position—at the Great Library, he knew he had nothing left.

So instead he turned his gaze back toward his finger swirling in the water and watched the current erase the signs of his passing, wave by tiny wave.

Spurred by a sudden anger, he pulled his finger out of the water and shook it dry.

No, he told himself. He would not just roll over for Apion. When the scholar came back he would settle for nothing less than the third in line at the Library. And he would demand several coins in advance, to hire new rooms and make a fresh start. He would not leave the Great Library with nothing.

As if spurred by a sudden shout, Thrasyllus abruptly smiled—painful though it was to do so. He reached into his pocket and pulled free his father's coin. Then he held it up to the light, examining its worn edges, its rough surfaces. Not nothing, he thought. He still had this. It was battered by what it had been through, and it was still smeared with dust, but with work it would gleam once again. And it was still worth something.

Just like him.

Beyond the coin in his hand he could see the top of the stairs, where Didymus kept his office. He remembered how years earlier, when the city had fallen to Octavian, he'd stood up there himself. He was a much younger man then, but already he'd spent most of his lifetime here in this place. So many of the librarians had fled when the Romans advanced, for they were certain that the legionnaires would finish the work of Caesar and put the Great Library to the torch. Didymus had told them all to go, but a few of the librarians had stayed with him, barricading the doors as best they could, and vowing to stay with their books to the final end. Apion had left, but Thrasyllus had been among those who stayed. He had nowhere else to go.

He remembered running from room to room, window to window, shouting back the news of what he could see of the Roman forces who were forming up on the Museum grounds. He remembered how he looked out one of those windows, just when they thought all hope was lost, and had seen a dark-skinned man and a little girl approaching the doors alone. Didymus had been sitting down here by the pool—near to this very spot, in fact—when Thrasyllus had shouted it down to him. He never understood the look of shock and unreadable awareness on the chief librarian's face when he heard that Juba of Numidia and the lady Cleopatra Selene were coming.

Back in the present moment, Thrasyllus blinked.

Lady Selene.

That was where he'd seen this Philip from Macedonia before: with the royal family. It wasn't often that he'd gone to the palaces on Lochias, but on occasion Didymus had sent for a book to further his teachings to the royal children. And Thrasyllus was certain he'd seen the man there.

He couldn't possibly be who he said he was.

Thrasyllus pulled the coin into his fist. Then, looking around him to ensure that Apion wasn't watching, he stood and hurried up the stairs.

Didymus worked day and night, but he wasn't truly indefatigable. Eventually exhaustion would overtake him and he would fall asleep, facedown amid the papers on his desk. As his assistant for so many years, Thrasyllus knew which boards in the hall would creak. So as soon as he left the stairs he knew exactly where to step so that his movements made no more sound than the steady hum of noise from the rest of the building. It took him little time at all to make it to the librarian's office, and to silently place his ear to the door.

"I do not think he wants to ever kill again," Didymus was saying. "But if he was freely offered the Ark, if he had the chance to use it, just once, to gain his revenge, his thirst for revenge against Caesar remains unquenched."

Revenge against Caesar? The astrologer's mind raced as he closed his eyes to focus in on their words. Who were they talking about? And what ark?

"So long as he's no threat to us," said the man who called himself Philip. Thrasyllus heard the sound of a chair settling under a man's weight. "He can kill as many Caesars as he wants. He just can't do it with the Ark."

This wasn't just any ark. This was *the* Ark. Thrasyllus racked his mind, certain that he'd heard of such a thing before.

"I do believe you are safe from Juba, my friend," Didymus continued. "But he isn't the only threat. You're still a wanted man here, Lucius Vorenus. I'm glad you're here, but it isn't safe."

In a flash, the astrologer's contemplations about what the

Ark might be disappeared, replaced with the clear memory of exactly who Philip of Macedonia really was: Lucius Vorenus, the former head of the palace guards, who'd been condemned to death by the conquering Caesar when the city fell, but who'd somehow survived his intended execution. His name had been on the lips of the city for weeks while an enraged Octavian sent his soldiers chasing every whisper of a rumor of the man's whereabouts.

"I know it only too well. Caesar is not a man to forget," Vorenus replied.

No, he is not, Thrasyllus thought to himself. And then, as if reading his mind, Didymus said, "Indeed so. He would pay a great deal for your head."

Leaning against the door, Thrasyllus couldn't help but smile at his good fortune. Here, here in the Great Library itself, was a man that Caesar would pay riches for. Here was an opportunity for Thrasyllus to prove his worth. An opportunity far greater than any he'd had before. He'd read the sign of the gnomon of Eratosthenes rightly, by the gods. After all he'd been through, he was meant to come back here and see this man. He was meant to be the one to find Lucius Vorenus and turn him over to Caesar in return for a reward that was beyond anything he could ever receive as a mere librarian.

All he needed to do was to find the nearest Roman soldiers. There would be some not far away, he was certain. There was always a company near the main square.

Thrasyllus pulled his ear away, looking to the ground to measure his retreat to the stairs, but then he froze, thinking.

What if he learned more? Surely more information would mean more appreciation, would it not? And the two men were still talking. And what if Didymus was equally a traitor to Rome? Would Caesar take him, too?

The thought frightened the astrologer, but then he remembered the way the older man had looked at him with such disappointment when he told him that he'd chosen Apion instead.

Besides, he reassured himself, Caesar would surely not kill the old scholar. He'd just remove him from his office and replace him with a new chief librarian. Not someone with questionable loyalty, like Apion, but someone who had proved his worth.

Thrasyllus, smiling, could think of only one suitable candidate. So he leaned his ear once more to the wood.

"You need something," Didymus was saying. "Otherwise there'd be no reason to risk a journey so deep into the city. So. What is it, Lucius Vorenus? What brings you to Alexandria?"

"It's about the Ark of the Covenant, Didymus. It's about the Shards."

The Ark of the Covenant? Yes, that was it. Didymus had once had him spend several months trying to determine a date when the Israelites fled Egypt—the Exodus, the Jews called it—and he'd had to read Greek translations of parts of their sacred book to do so. It spoke of a great Israelite leader named Moses, of the powers given to him by their god. And it spoke of how that god had given him a special object, a sacred vessel of extraordinary power: the Ark of the Covenant. Didymus had never said why he was interested in dating the event, but it was clear enough now that it was because of the Ark. It had been found.

"It is safe?" Didymus asked.

"For now. It's on the Nile."

There was the sound of moving cloth from inside the room. "No, do not tell me where, Vorenus. I do not need to know."

"But where it is, Didymus, might be the problem."

"How so?"

"Because it is not as powerful as it was here in Alexandria. So he says."

"He's tried to use it again?"

"He does not wish to do so. He does not think that a man should wield such power, he says."

"Always was a good man," Didymus said. "The best of what a man could be. He is well?"

"So he is." Vorenus laughed. "And he's in love, if you can believe that."

Didymus laughed, too. "I can, indeed. That beautiful Jewish girl, is it? Hannah. Yes, even someone so inexperienced as I am could see the look in his eyes when he looked at her. And she at him. Strange how love can be."

"So it is, I suppose," Vorenus said. "I've only loved once. And that was lost a long time ago."

"I know it only too well, my friend," Didymus said. "We cannot choose the ways of the heart."

There was a pause, and Thrasyllus imagined the two men smiling sadly at one another as they shared a memory he did not understand. Instead, he was reeling with thoughts. Lucius Vorenus was living somewhere on the Nile, and he had the Ark of the Covenant. The reward Thrasyllus would get from Caesar was going up by the minute.

"So he wants to know what more I've learned about it?" Didymus finally asked. "He wants to know why it isn't as powerful now?"

"He instructed me to ask exactly that," Lucius Vorenus said. "He doesn't want it for the power, you understand. But if he needs to use it to keep it safe, he wants to know how."

"I understand. And you're right about what you said earlier, my friend."

"What's that?"

"Well, it does indeed have to do with where it is."

. . .

Standing outside the Great Library, Thrasyllus made his decision. It was, he suspected, one of the most important he would make in his life.

There was a small squad of legionnaires marching across the grounds of the Museum. In seconds he could run to them, tell them that Lucius Vorenus, at this very moment, sat with Didymus in the Great Library. There would surely be a struggle, but they would take him. Didymus would be removed. Apion would be discredited. And whatever reward there was, it would be his.

Perhaps the Great Library would be his, too, if his luck held.

But he didn't run to them. Instead, he walked in the opposite direction, back toward the empty room that had once been his quarters here in the city, back toward the gnomon of Eratosthenes that had, on this very morning, been the sign that sent him back to the Library.

He wouldn't hand Vorenus over to Rome. Not yet, anyway. He and Didymus could talk on about their old memories and lost friends, unsuspecting that they'd been discovered. They'd been doing so for at least ten minutes when Thrasyllus had finally decided that he'd learned all he could and slipped away before he might be caught.

And how much he had learned! Didymus hadn't wanted to be told where the Ark was, but Vorenus, that old fool, had told him anyway: Elephantine Island, on the Nile.

Elephantine! Leaving the Museum grounds and crossing the Sema Avenue, headed east toward the Old Quarter, Thrasyllus felt like laughing. After they'd beaten him this morning, the pimp and his brute had dumped him in the square, at the base of the sundial that Eratosthenes had used to measure the circumference of the Earth. Thrasyllus had seen in it a sign that he should return to the Great Library. Returning to the

Great Library, he'd discovered Vorenus. And now, having discovered Vorenus, he knew that the greatest artifact of the Jews was on Elephantine—the very island that had the well that Eratosthenes had used to complete his calculations.

The plans of the gods were unexpected at times, but he was confident that they had one. To know it, you just had to read the signs. He'd told that truth to Didymus more times than he could remember over the years, but the old scholar would hear nothing of it. Didymus didn't believe in signs. Thrasyllus wasn't sure if he believed in the gods. Even in announcing Apion as his second librarian, Didymus had made sure to belittle the astrology over which Thrasyllus often labored.

But the gods had their plans. Thrasyllus had no doubt.

And he had a plan, too.

Lucius Vorenus had told Didymus that he'd come to Alexandria by barge. He would no doubt return the same way. And somewhere on that quiet canal, out of sight of anyone else, Thrasyllus would capture him. Then they'd go to Elephantine, and with the information from Vorenus he would capture the Ark. It was, from what Vorenus had said, guarded by little more than some boy and the Jewish girl he loved.

When he had the Ark, he would turn Vorenus over to the Romans. He'd take his reward. And then he'd bring the Ark—*his* Ark—back to Alexandria and learn to use it. Because that was the other thing he'd learned today: Didymus told Vorenus how he'd discovered that the Ark, and the other objects like it—Didymus mentioned that Juba of Numidia had one—were more powerful in certain places. They could draw more power, he said, from sacred spaces. The heart of Alexandria had been one. Another, he said, was Carthage. So Thrasyllus would bring it to Alexandria. He would study it. He would learn to wield its power. And then he'd have something far greater to give to the most powerful man in the world.

What wealth would Caesar give him for that?

His practiced steps brought him into the Old Quarter now. Rounding a corner, he saw ahead the little square with the sundial at its heart. The metal gnomon in its center struck upward toward the sky, toward the gods whose power might soon be within his reach.

Thrasyllus had his sign. And he had his plan.

He just needed to find Lapis, her pimp, and his brute.

7

TIBERIUS

CANTABRIA, 26 BCE

Selene and Juba had made love as dawn was breaking over Hispania. Then, with her husband snoring in peaceful serenity, Selene had gone to what passed for baths in this wretched encampment. It was hardly the comfort that she had known in Rome, living within Caesar's household, and it was nothing at all like the finery of the baths she'd enjoyed in Alexandria, but bathing was like holding on to a memory. It helped her remember who she was.

The praetorian who'd been assigned by Caesar to see to her safety among the men—a duty that the man clearly disdained, viewing it as akin to watching over a child in the middle of a war he'd much rather be fighting—had told her upon exiting the bath that her husband had left the encampment with the other Roman leaders and was not expected back for an hour or more. She'd thanked him, receiving a rough grunt of acknowledgment, and then decided to take an indirect route back to her tent.

Roman encampments, she had learned, were always roughly rectangular in shape: first a ditch was dug, the removed earth being piled just inside of it so that any attacker would have to first climb down and up out of the ditch, then up the mound of earth that had been in the ditch. Atop this inner earthen rampart, the legionnaires then would build a wooden palisade wall, further increasing its defenses. Four towered gates, one in the middle of each side of the great rectangle, were constructed to give the force inside the maximum amount of maneuverability, but the main gate was always faced to the main road or main danger: here it was the road coming up from Segisama, though the Cantabrian hillfort of Vellica was only across the valley.

Everything inside the encampment had its designated place. Roads running between the gates intersected at the staff headquarters, and around this the tents of the many officers and their legions—and all the other additional staff of what amounted to a temporary and astoundingly mobile town—were placed in well-ordered and precisely regulated rows within further quadrants. Even the latrines had their place, set beyond a wide, open space between the walls and the tents, cut down against the base of the mounded earth and carefully constructed so that the human waste ran away from the encampment.

For all that order, for all that precision, a Roman camp was also a place of both sweltering heat and dirt that—no matter that they'd not seen rain for weeks this summer—was perpetual mud. It was also, to her continued despair, a place of harsh smells: smoke from the cooking fires, the reek of oil on leather and bronze, and urine from men and horses.

Shortly after they'd first arrived, Juba had assured her, with loving laughter, that one never really could grow used to it all—at least he never could—but that in time she would grow better at hiding her disgust. Walking between tents, her head held high and face impassive but for the slightest smile of authority, Selene was certain that she'd mastered the art of masking things well. It seemed she'd been doing it her whole life.

Her mother had taught her so much before she took the asp and died. How to pretend. How to manipulate. How to seduce.

And how to love.

Selene was sure her mother wouldn't approve of the status of the man who had become her husband—Cleopatra was a woman who had seduced two of the most powerful men in the world—but she had no doubt that her mother would approve of the way that she loved Juba. The Romans accused her mother of so much in attaining the affections of first Julius Caesar and then Mark Antony—spells, love potions, and far worse—but Selene knew the truth of it. She'd seen it in her mother's eyes when she looked at Selene's father, and the way she spoke of Julius Caesar it seemed there was no doubt that she'd looked at him the same way before his assassination. It was love. Simple and real. She'd loved them, and they'd loved her back.

It was a lesson Selene had learned well. She had Juba's love.

She'd also, in the end, learned a great deal from her mother about vengeance. She would have that, too.

The Roman soldiers she passed would often stop what they were doing, stare for a moment, and then bow slightly, murmuring in her wake. They were unaccustomed to having a young woman in camp, but she felt no fear among them. It wasn't just the praetorian who, she knew, trailed along somewhere behind her. It was the fact that most of the men just seemed glad for something beautiful to look upon—even if for only a moment.

Selene also felt safe because the camp, despite all its filth, remained a remarkably well-ordered place. Growing up she'd heard jokes about the Roman need for order, but from inside the ranks of the Roman army she could see so clearly that the strict discipline of the men, extending from their actions upon the field to the precise layout of their tents, was perhaps their greatest strength. And she found that comforting.

By the time she reached the tent that she shared with her husband, at least an hour had passed since Juba had departed. And whatever else she expected upon pulling aside the flap that served for a door, she didn't expect to see Tiberius standing in the dim light.

"Tiberius," she gasped, frightened.

He was standing in the middle of the tent. He had his back to her, his head lowered. It almost looked like he was staring at the bed. "It's Lord Tiberius now," he said. "I'm fifteen, you know. I'm a man. And Caesar sees fit to judge me among the leadership."

Selene swallowed hard. "Of course. I'm pleased to know that Caesar thinks so highly of you. It is well deserved."

When he turned around to face her, she saw for a moment the old darkness in his eyes. Tiberius had long been plagued by a kind of melancholy, something she always tried to cheer him from when they were younger. But then it passed—or the light changed, she couldn't be sure. He looked softer, more like the young boy she'd known, though his body was indeed that of a young man. He was stronger now. And more stubborn. "But we need no formalities, Selene. We grew up in the same household. We are like family, you and I. It is important for us to remain devoted to one another."

"It is," she said. Why was he here? What did he want? "I'm devoted to what's important."

Tiberius gave her a tight-lipped smile. "I've no doubt."

Selene moved away from the door toward the little writing desk Juba had placed in the corner of the room. She tried to move with an unconcerned grace, though she felt an uncertain fear in his presence. Her heart quaked and her mind spun with questions. "If you're looking for my husband—"

"I'm not," he said, cutting her off. "I'm looking for you."
She felt his stare following her, though she didn't dare turn
to look.

"Oh?" As casually as she could, she let her eyes roll across
the small chest where she kept the Palladium. It hadn't moved.
The lock appeared undisturbed. That, at least, was a relief.
"I can't think that I'm of much importance here."

"You are to me," he said.

Selene felt his stare leave her, and when she chanced a glance
back she could see that he was looking toward the ground,
and that he'd begun a kind of slow pace across the floor. "We
did indeed grow up together," she said, turning her gaze back
to the desk before he could look up again at her.

"It's more than that," he replied. His voice was quiet. "You
know that."

Selene didn't know how to reply, so instead she said
nothing. She stared at the desk, wondering what to say or do,
wondering what Tiberius intended, and longing for Juba to
return. When she turned, she gasped instinctively. The young
man had walked up behind her in his pacing, and they stood
nearly face-to-face.

"There's more," Tiberius said.

Selene berated herself for having been startled, but her heart
simply refused to stop pounding in her chest. The air was hot
and swelteringly thick. Tiberius was standing, she realized, directly between her and the flap of the tent. If he did something, she wondered, should she cry out? And if she did, would
anyone come? Or would the praetorians simply stand guard
as she was overpowered?

"What happened that night?"

She blinked at the unexpected question. "What night?"

"You know which one," he said. "In Rome. The night you
broke into the Temple of the Vestal Virgins."

Selene did her best to seem impassive, thinking of all her mother had taught her about the game of kings. "You were there," she said.

"And I know what I saw. Or what I think I saw."

"So what do you think you saw?"

"A wind," Tiberius said. His gaze moved off of hers as he remembered. "A sharp wind on a windless night."

Selene said nothing. Please, she thought, please let Juba come soon. Her guard had said it would be perhaps an hour, had he not? Surely her husband would come soon. Please.

His gaze returned to hers. Piercing and probing. Angry and lusting. "It wasn't just a little statue of Horus that you stole, was it?"

"I don't have time to talk about this, Tiberius." Selene stepped to the side and began to walk around him, toward the flap of the tent. "I need to—"

His hand shot up and gripped her arm hard, stopping her with unexpected strength. "Was it?"

Selene shrugged her arm. "Let me go, Tiberius. Let me go or I'll—"

"You'll what, Selene?" His grip tightened painfully. "Scream? No one here will care. The praetorians will keep the peace well enough. I've tested that before."

Selene swallowed hard. "My husband," she said plaintively.

"Is away," Tiberius sneered. "And it was wrong to marry you to him. A jewel like you, in the hands of that dark-skinned beast—"

Her free hand came up almost of its own accord. Without a moment of thought, she struck him hard across the face. She gasped at the suddenness of her own anger, even as she pulled her hand back.

His head had turned with the blow, but Tiberius did not react for a moment. Then he let her go and slowly raised his hand to his face, rubbing at his reddened skin. His jaw rocked back and forth, as if ensuring that it was still functional. "I don't think that was wise, Selene. I will be Caesar myself one day."

May that day never come, she thought. To Tiberius she said, "And it was Caesar who chose him for my husband. Do you disapprove of his choices so?"

The young man hadn't expected that reply, and she could see him working over in his mind how best to respond. They both knew that he didn't dare insult the decision of his step-father. "Marriages can be a matter of convenience," he finally said. "I know that more than most. Caesar chose rightly for now. But perhaps, if you still please me, I'll find you a more suitable match one day. And I'll not leave you out ruling some frontier land. I'll have you in Rome, where the daughter of Cleopatra should be."

Selene wanted to throw up, but her face, she hoped, was once more every bit as impassive as her mother taught her it could be. She made the slightest bow of her head, an acknowledgment of his authority but not an acquiescence to his threat. "May I go now, Lord Tiberius?"

His jaw clenched once, twice, and then he stepped out of the way.

Selene nodded once more. As she started to step past him, his hand once more caught her arm, tight enough to make her wince. He leaned in toward her, close enough that she could feel his breath upon her cheek. She refused to look at him. She simply stared at the tent flap, willing her husband to come through.

"You know I'll find out, Selene." The voice of Tiberius was calm, quiet, yet it was full of a kind of threat that she would not have thought such a young man capable of—at least be-fore now. "What you took from the temple that night. How you caused that wind. It was you. And I'll find out how. I promise you."

He let go of her, and Selene walked away, head high and proud and impassive. She pushed open the tent flap, blinking as she stepped into the light. The praetorians had a kind of perimeter around the tent. Their backs were turned away from her, and they stared out into the churning masses of the encampment.

Selene didn't know where to go, but she didn't dare stop moving. Without knowing why, she turned and began walking in the direction of the command tent.

The praetorians let her pass. Whether the man who had been assigned to be her guard still followed her, she did not know. But she assumed that he was there.

Tiberius had frightened her. In short minutes he'd pushed her to the point that she wanted to crumble down into the dust. She was scared, and she was angry that she was scared. Fear made her feel weak. It made her feel like that little girl locked away in a Roman prison, waiting to be paraded in golden chains with her now-dead brother.

Coming around a bend in the well-worn path—trying to hold back both her terror and her self-loathing rage—she saw Juba walking toward her. He wasn't looking up. He was staring at the ground in front of him as he walked, his shoulders hunched with fresh worry. But when he looked up and saw her, whatever brooding thoughts he'd had disappeared into a moment of happiness that was suddenly struck away by a new concern.

Selene tried to smile, tried to erase whatever her husband had seen upon her face, but she knew she couldn't hide the roiling emotions that played there. She wanted to both weep and scream.

Then he was there, reaching out to swallow her into his

loving embrace. She buried herself against his chest for a moment, squeezing him so tightly she could feel the air coming out of his lungs.

"What's wrong?" he asked. "What's happened?"

Selene wanted to say so much. But whatever had happened to Juba while he'd been away, it had brought new weight for him to bear. She didn't want to burden him even more with what had happened to her.

Besides, she thought, her mother would never have allowed herself to feel such weakness, much less show it. She would have steeled herself against the fear and anger. She would have been strong.

"Nothing," she whispered. "I just . . . I need you to hold me. That's all."

8

Signs of Death

The trap was set along the north side of the canal, where generations of footfalls from a nearby farm had cut a deeply sunken track through the grassy tufts of the higher embankment. The worn track led to a small wooden dock on the water, framed by thick reeds. Knee-deep in the water there, hidden in the concealing brush, the three hired bowmen had their recurved bows at the ready.

Thrasyllus was crouched above them on the sunken dirt path, hidden by the deeper shadow of the embankment on either side. Between the scholar and the bowmen, close enough to whisper between them, crouched the rat-faced man and his brute.

All of them were staring out at the water as the sun glowed a fierce red upon the horizon. A sign, Thrasyllus was certain, of the blood to come.

Finding the men who'd left him bruised and battered that morning had not been difficult. He'd only needed to find the beautiful, black-haired girl who called herself Lapis—wherever she would be, her pimp and his brute would not be far away.

He'd known just where to look for her, of course. For months he had lurked in the shadows, watching the busy street corner where she stood every evening. For months he'd watched as she took the hands of other men and even some women, watched as she was led away from the corner to private rooms and the delights of the flesh. He'd gone to the same corner last night, when he thought this day would see him leaving Alexandria for good.

Some things changed, he'd thought with a smile.

But, thanks be to the gods, some things never did: Lapis was there, just as she ever was, waiting for the next man, as if the events of the night and the morning had never happened.

She had recognized him, at least. That was some comfort. She'd even appeared concerned, calling him "little stargazer" and begging him to leave before Seker—that was the rat-faced man's name, he'd now learned—showed up.

But of course Seker was just the man Thrasyllus had come to see.

When the pimp arrived, Thrasyllus had been surprised to see that he was alone. Perhaps, he'd thought, the morning had proved that the brute wasn't needed to deal with such a weak coward.

Thrasyllus blurted out the simple proposition: Capture one man; kill anyone else with him. They would evenly split the bounty on the man's head, but anything else taken from the dead men was Seker's to keep.

That had been enough to catch the pimp's attention. It was enough to stave off a beating and find a quiet place to talk. Thrasyllus had heard Vorenus tell the librarian that he was traveling with only a single companion, so he explained that there was no need for many men. Thrasyllus thought that the massive brute alone could handle it, but Seker had laughed at that. The brute, he said, was an old and broken man who could hardly walk. He would be fine in a fight at close quarters—"He could break you in two if I gave him the word, if you're lying to me about this"—but he would be close to useless getting from shore to ship. So Seker had agreed to pay for three close-lipped men he knew who were good with bows. Their wages, he said, would be paid out of the scholar's share of the bounty on the man they were meant to capture.

Thrasyllus hadn't told him who the Roman was. He'd only told him the amount of the award Caesar had once offered for his head. That was enough, it seemed, for the greedy little man.

Things had happened fast at that point. Seker had sent for the scar-faced brute, who lumbered awkwardly into the carriage that was summoned. In short order they had picked up the three men with their wickedly curved bows—how the pimp knew such men, Thrasyllus didn't ask—and they were headed through the Sun Gate, riding toward the canal east of the city.

After that it was a simple matter of finding the spot for the ambush and waiting for the right barge to pass by.

There weren't many on the water. Traffic on the canal grew more sporadic the farther one journeyed from the great city, and the sun drifting toward the horizon had made it quieter still.

Between passing ships, Thrasyllus tried to think through what lay ahead. The men he was with were clearly practiced, efficient killers. They had the element of surprise. They would kill most of the men on the barge very quickly. And they would capture Vorenus. With luck, the Roman was as good a fighter as the high bounty on his head would indicate. He would kill a few of these men before he was taken. What happened after that would depend on how many were left behind. Too many, and he'd have no choice but to take Vorenus back to Alexandria to claim the bounty. That was what he'd told Seker they were going to do.

What he hoped to do, however, was something very different. If only a couple of men were left, Thrasyllus could try to convince them to follow his plan to take the prisoner to Elephantine Island and the promise of greater rewards. Gods willing, they would agree.

The astrologer's fingers ran across the little satchel at his side. Before he'd left to come find Seker, he'd taken a knife from one of the scriptoria of the Great Library. It wasn't a large weapon by any means, but he supposed it would do. Embedded in the right place in a man's back, even the smallest blade would surely kill. A man's life always hung by the thinnest of threads. Books had taught him that. They'd even given him some idea of where and how to strike.

Whether he would actually have the courage to do it was another question entirely.

He closed his eyes and prayed silently that it wouldn't come to that. When he opened them, he saw that Seker had turned to look back and was staring at him, his eyes glinting in the red light of the setting sun. "A devout man, are you?"

Thrasyllus nodded. "I am."

The rat-faced man sniffed. "You'll be screaming the names of many a god if you're wrong about this boat. And they won't help you." He looked over to the much larger man beside him. "The brute here will see to that, won't you?"

It had been painful for the big man to crouch down beside them on the sunken path. Whatever injuries he'd sustained during his life, they clearly ran far deeper than the scars visible across his face. But there was something else about him that Thrasyllus had noticed. More than once he had shown signs of a kind of inner pain, as if he was tormented by memories of the things he had done. When Seker spoke of his threats, the brute's broad shoulders hunched up almost as if he'd been struck. "I'll do what I need to do," he said.

"That you will," Seker said. Turning back to Thrasyllus, he said, "I recognized his talent right away. He's hard as a wall and strong as any three other men put together. Surprising since he's a Roman."

"Was," the big man growled.

Seker's smile was full of a kind of sneering delight. "That's right. He doesn't like his own kind anymore. So tonight should be fun, as long as he doesn't have to run." The rat-faced man chuckled quietly in the dim light, but the big man didn't react. He just stared out at the water.

Thrasyllus tried to smile, but he was anything but amused or even remotely calm. Men were going to die soon. Many men. He prayed that he'd get over the guilt. And he prayed, too, that he wouldn't be among the dead.

For many minutes they waited in silence. The darkness rising behind them brought the first stars into view. The light of the high moon was beginning to take over from the dying sun, and the last birds of the day were chittering toward their nests.

Ahead of him, the brute shifted uncomfortably. Without turning his head, he spoke quietly back to the astrologer. "You're certain the barge didn't already pass?"

Thrasyllus shook his head, even though the big man wasn't looking. By his calculations they should have been well ahead of the barge. "Impossible," he said, praying that it was true. He didn't want to even try to imagine what might await him if it had. He didn't doubt the big man's efficiency at causing pain. Not to mention the disappointed bowmen. If the barge didn't show, Thrasyllus was sure he'd be lucky to leave this bank alive.

The big man sighed. "I hope you're right," he said. "Best to get the killing done."

Thrasyllus nodded, as if he had any notion of what it took to kill a man. The satchel at his side seemed to grow heavier with each passing heartbeat. Could he really take a man's life? Could he really bury the blade and feel the blood? Could he stand to look even this vile pimp in the eyes as he did it?

No. He couldn't face even so loathsome a creature as Seker. He would have to do it in the back.

If he could do it at all.

Please, he thought, let them go with my plan.

"Is that it?" Seker said quietly.

Thrasyllus looked out. Backlit by the last light of the dying sun, a barge was coming up the canal. It was laden with textiles, piles of rugs and cloth. Two men on board had been speaking, the murmur of their voices sweeping across the still water, but it was too low to hear what they said, and they stopped before he could recognize whether one was Lucius Vorenus.

But it had to be, Thrasyllus thought. The timing was right, and with night falling any barge still on the canal must be hurrying from something.

"Well?" Seker whispered.

"It should be," Thrasyllus said. "But we need to know which one is the Roman. You can kill everyone else. But don't kill him."

"Easier to kill them all," the big man rasped.

"You can't kill him." If they killed Vorenus, what would he do? He hadn't even thought about that. "We agreed," he whispered urgently.

The brute seemed to shrug, and Thrasyllus saw that there was a gladius in his thick hand. He was tensing, as if the prospect of killing made him feel young again. As if it made him feel alive.

By the gods, Thrasyllus thought, he likes this. They all do.

Though he could make out no details against the sunset, he could see that the two men who had been talking were lounged amid the piles at the front of the vessel. They seemed relaxed, unaware of the bows being drawn in the tall reeds along shore.

"Home," one of the men said.

It was a single word, but it was enough. The man was a Roman. It was him.

The big brute gasped or grunted, Thrasyllus couldn't tell.

The barge was coming abreast of them. So close. Seker looked deadly in his expectation.

Thrasyllus nodded vigorously, and Seker immediately turned toward the bowmen below them and gave a soft whistle.

"He's in front. On the left," Thrasyllus said, his whisper rising in his urgency. "Leave Vorenus alive."

The big man lurched as if he'd been struck, and he actually half turned around to look at Thrasyllus. "Vorenus?"

Thrasyllus simply nodded dumbly, shocked at the thought of what he'd just done. He could see the man at the tiller now, too, a perfect target of black against the crimson sky.

The brute's eyes went wide, and he suddenly stood, rising up from the shadows. Seker tried to reach for him, but it was too late. The big man had already turned toward the barge that was sliding up before them. The next moment, when he shouted the word, it seemed to be ripped from his throat, from the very center of his soul. "Vorenus!"

Below, as if in response, the first arrows sang out.

9

CLAIMING THE REWARD

CANTABRIA, 26 BCE

The last place that Juba wanted to be was in the command tent. Something had happened to Selene while he was away at the meadow, and he was desperate to find out what it was. She insisted that she was fine, but the look in her eyes when she had come forward to embrace him was unmistakably fearful. She was scared, and he wanted to know why.

But rather than have the opportunity to discover the truth, he was here with the others in the tent. Octavian had called them back as the sun set, and he had told them that in the morning he planned to engage in a full assault on Vellica, the Cantabrian hillfort across the valley that stubbornly refused to surrender to their siege.

So now Juba was listening to another of the long-toothed Roman commanders give another long-winded excuse about why he didn't think the time was right for such an attack. The opinion was nearly unanimous. It seemed that every man in the tent but himself, Tiberius, and Carisius had voiced disapproval. The Cantabri were still too strong, they all insisted. More time would weaken their resolve, their strength, their walls.

It didn't matter. Juba knew his stepbrother's own stubbornness was a match for any fortification, much less the minds of the men in this room. And Caesar's mind was made up. He wanted a full assault, and a full assault he would get. All this discussion was merely for show.

And a show it was. Octavian sat upright in his seat, his face set with determined focus as he listened to the complaint. Though Juba could well imagine the disgust that was churning through his stepbrother's head, not a bit of it was shown on his face.

At last the commander stopped talking.

"Thank you," Octavian said. His voice was calm and collected, almost paternal despite the other man's greater age. He nodded thoughtfully, and then he turned to Carisius, the highest ranking field commander, who'd sat in a kind of brooding silence staring at the crude map of Vellica that had been placed before them at the center of the table. "And you, Carisius? What is your wisdom in this matter?"

The older man's eyes narrowed at the map. Tracing his gaze, Juba could see that he was staring at the outline of the gates of the Cantabrian fort. Vellica filled the top of the kidney bean–shaped hill completely, and it had but three gates— each of which presented a substantial problem for the Roman forces.

Vellica's main gate was actually the one farthest from the Roman encampment, at the northwestern end of the fort. The slope of the hill was far less steep there, and the existing main road would surely speed any Roman troops who approached from that direction. The Cantabri, aware of this, had dug significant trench works to narrow the field along which they could be engaged, and they'd built a high defensive tower beside the gate in order to repel any attack. From the reports of the Cantabri prisoners they'd taken—many of whom had been released earlier in the day to spread Caesar's offer of a reward for Corocotta's capture—it seemed that the second tower visible within the hillfort helped guard a second defensive wall that had been built in case the initial gates and tower were overcome.

The second gate, smaller than the first, stood midway along the eastern side of the fort. The terrain was very steep there, and approach could only be made by means of a narrow path that hugged the side of the hill, making a final switchback right at the foot of Vellica's walls. It was a natural choke point, and Juba was certain that the Roman dead would make the way impassable long before they could breach the stout entrance.

That left the third gate, which was essentially the rear entrance to Vellica. It was, by plan, the gate closest to the Roman encampment, on the southeast end of the fort. In some respects, it suffered from the same problem as the second, since it could only be engaged from a ramping sweep of earth that started to the west. Anyone attempting to breach the gate by such an approach would have to do so by marching uphill, under relentless assault from the walls of the fort above them. On the other hand, there was no final switchback, and a stretch of trees in the valley below would give the Romans at least some measure of cover as they readied for the final push.

In light of these facts, Octavian's plan was simple but sensible. The Roman forces would march west out of the encampment, crossing the valley on a direct path for the woods below Vellica. There the three legions would divide, with two continuing their march, paralleling the walls of the fort as if intending to come around to assault the main gates. This was a diversion, intended to draw defenders away from the rear gate. At a signal, the third legion left behind in the woods would then make a direct assault on that minimally protected gate, bringing up battering rams beneath the cover of their shields.

It was a good plan, Juba felt. He certainly couldn't think of anything better.

All eyes were on Carisius, who took a long, steady breath, his own eyes still riveted to the map. "The plan is a sound one, Caesar. No man here has ventured a better one."

There was a murmur from around the table, but it was true: they'd spoken against it, but no one had offered an alternative except delay. "Yet you hesitate," Octavian said.

Carisius finally looked up from the table and met Caesar's eye. Then he nodded once, slowly. "I do. For the same reason we all do, the reason that has gone unspoken."

Juba quickly scanned the room and saw that many of the men suddenly appeared frightened, as if fearful of what Carisius might say.

"I speak of the ghost," Carisius said. "That's what the men call him. The ghost who haunts—"

From the head of the table, Caesar cut him off. "You mean the rat. The slinking, hiding rat who feeds on the crumbs of a much larger force. Corocotta. You're scared of him."

Juba saw Carisius instinctively open his mouth to deny the accusation, but then he stopped, apparently recognizing that honesty would serve him best. Though the other men all seemed to be looking everywhere but at Octavian, Carisius continued to look him in the eye. Juba felt a great deal of respect for him. "Yes, Caesar."

Octavian nodded. "I understand your concern. A rat he may be, but a rat that has proven difficult to catch."

Carisius took a breath, then gestured to the map. "The legions will be exposed as we march on Vellica. We don't know how many men Corocotta has with him. He could easily attack our flank."

Young Tiberius, like Juba, had been silent the entire meeting, watching it unfold from his brooding darkness. But now, at last, he spoke up. "Corocotta is a brigand, Carisius. We don't know if he would expose himself to help the Cantabri."

Juba saw a touch of heat flush the commander's face, for Carisius to be addressed so informally by such a young and inexperienced man, but the commander was too politically astute to make any attack of his own. "It is true that we do not know if he would do so," he said. "But it would be prudent to be prepared if he were to do so."

"And I think he probably will," Octavian said. His gaze was leveled at his stepson, and his tone was both authoritative and instructive. "His actions have indeed shown him to be supportive of the Cantabri cause. Even if he isn't working from Vellica, he is clearly taking any opportunity to attack our weakness." He turned his gaze now to Carisius, and as he did so his tone shifted to respect. "So as you have wisely said, we should expect an attack on our flank during the assault."

"But how?" one of the other officers said. "We don't even know how many men he has."

"I think not many," Octavian said. His eyes flicked over to Juba for an instant before they took in the whole of the room. "Perhaps a dozen men at most. Maybe even less."

Several voices rose up at once, incredulous at the thought that so few men could cause such devastation and terror.

Caesar held up a hand, and the silence was almost immediate. "Corocotta will likely attack, but he should not be your concern. I will deal with him."

"One million Sesterces," someone whispered.

Octavian smiled. "It may be that this will be enough. But there are solutions even if it is not."

His stepbrother wasn't looking at him, but Juba could feel the press of his thoughts focusing in his direction. Juba was the solution, after all. The weapon to counter Corocotta. If the ghost indeed had the Shard of fire, what better defense than the Shard of water, the Trident of Poseidon, which he alone knew how to use?

A silence fell over the table for a few moments. Juba could hear the sounds of the encampment outside, and it made him yearn all the more to get up and run from the tent, run to the arms of the woman he loved.

Finally it was Carisius who spoke. "So we will assault Vellica in the morning," he said.

Octavian nodded. "Yes. You know your men. You know the plan of assault. Make ready the attack."

There was a murmur among the men, but at whispered commands several of the lower-ranking officers turned and hurried from the tent. Most of the men around the table began to rise.

Carisius had not moved. "I understand that Caesar intends for us to ignore it," he said, and for a moment all movement stopped and everyone turned to him. "But may I ask from what direction you think Corocotta will attack?"

"Perhaps you will ask him," said a small voice.

Heads turned once more, this time to the entrance of the tent, where one of the officers, who had been holding it open while he turned to listen to Carisius, stepped aside to allow a little girl to hobble into view. She appeared to be lame in her left leg, walking with the aid of a cloth-topped crutch of wood placed under her right arm. She had a dirty face and dirtier brown hair, and her clothing was hardly more than a tattered, soil-stained shift covered by a patched cloak. Behind her strode a bearded man with dark, shoulder-length hair and furred boots that matched his wolf-fur cloak. He carried what looked like a wooden spear in his right hand, the iron point held up as if he used it as a kind of walking staff. He had the bearing of a man of great importance. Both of them had the dusted complexion of the Cantabri.

Juba saw that three legionnaires and two praetorians walked in a half-circle behind him, their swords drawn and ready to plunge into his back. Another legionnaire, who'd been carrying a torch to mark their passage through the dark encampment, fell away behind them.

The officers stepped aside as the odd pair made their way into the steady lamplight of the command tent. More than a few men who had been on their way out returned to their positions to learn about this new development.

Caesar stood, and Juba and the other men at the table followed his lead. The men at the end of the table opposite Octavian—including Tiberius, who appeared to be of an even darker spirit than usual—moved away in order to clear a space for the visitors to stand. Carisius, Juba noted, had deftly flipped the map in the commotion.

The legionnaires who'd accompanied them departed as the man and girl took their position at the end of the table, but the two praetorians did not: they stood directly behind the visitors, swords at the ready. It turned Juba's stomach to see that one of the two blades was prepared to cut through the back of the little girl's neck.

"Caesar of Rome," the lame girl said, balancing off of her crutch to bow slightly, "Lord Corocotta has learned of the reward you have offered for his capture." She made a sweep of her hand toward the big man beside her. "He has come to collect it."

The bearded man gave only the slightest of nods.

Juba at last managed to pull his attention away from the Cantabri and look to his stepbrother. He found him smiling. "You are Corocotta?"

The big man's chin moved up and down once.

"And you have come to collect the reward?"

Corocotta stared for a moment, unblinking, then turned to look down at the little girl at his side. Still leaning heavily on her crutch, she spoke up to him in the guttural language of their people. Theirs was a strange tongue, Juba thought, before reminding himself that they no doubt felt the same about the Latin otherwise spoken in the tent.

Corocotta smiled at something she said, then turned to stare once more at Augustus Caesar. His smile in his dark beard was broad and white. "Yes," he said, the foreign word forming oddly on his lips, then he said something else they could not understand.

"One million Sesterces," the girl translated. "Lord Corocotta was told it was one million Sesterces."

Octavian looked past them to one of the praetorians. "How many did they come with?"

It was the one whose sword was aimed at the little girl's spine who answered. "It was only these two, Caesar. They announced themselves at the gate."

"I see," Octavian said.

Juba happened to be looking at his stepbrother, and so when Octavian's gaze quickly passed around the room, their eyes met. Rather than passing by quickly, however, Octavian's gaze locked on his own for several seconds, his eyes widening and imploring. Juba knew him long enough to know that his stepbrother was trying to tell him something. But what?

Caesar's attention once more turned to the Cantabri leader who'd killed so many of his men and destroyed so many of his supplies. "If I give the order," he said, addressing Corocotta directly even as the little girl translated, "those men will kill you."

Corocotta slowly turned his head to take in the praetorians at their backs. Then he smiled once more and his big shoulders shrugged as he looked back to Caesar to answer. At his side the girl translated again, "If you give the order, they will try."

"You have killed many Romans," Octavian said.

"And you have killed many Cantabri."

Juba was listening to the conversation, but he was also intently studying Corocotta. Octavian wanted him to see something. He was sure of it.

"You are either a very brave man or a very foolish one," Octavian said.

"And you the same," Corocotta replied through the girl.

A few of the Romans gasped, and Juba quickly glanced back at his stepbrother, expecting to find him angry. Instead, Octavian was smiling, and he seemed to be looking at the bigger man with a new respect. "We have a saying in Rome, that the victor is brave, the defeated a fool."

Corocotta nodded as he spoke and the girl continued to translate, "The same is spoken in Cantabria."

"As in all lands, I suspect," Octavian said. He paused, and the two leaders stared at one another for several seconds. "I will attack Vellica tomorrow."

"Sir," Carisius said, "I don't think—"

The Cantabri's barbaric tongue cut him off. "Corocotta had suspected you would do so," the little girl translated. "Your supply lines are weak and exposed. You cannot delay. And your offer for his capture shows your desperation." She blushed a little at what she had just said, and then gave a kind of apologetic bow, her hands still gripped firmly on the crutch for support. "Begging your pardon, my lord."

Octavian brushed her comment away with his hand. The little girl was some kind of prisoner or slave of the Cantabrian leader, and Juba knew that his stepbrother—like most Romans—would view her as little more than a necessary nuisance. Whoever she was, she was only useful for her ability to speak both Latin and the Cantabrian tongue. Her opinions mattered nothing at all.

It was the same attitude about the relative value of human life that Octavian had shown in ordering Juba to use the Trident of Poseidon to kill Quintus, the loyal slave who had helped to raise Juba.

The Trident. The Shard to control water.

With a start, Juba realized what it was that Octavian was trying to communicate. If Corocotta indeed had a Shard to control fire, he would have it with him. It would be here in this room. And wherever his stepbrother kept the Trident with which Juba could fight that power, it wasn't here. If Corocotta had the Shard and used it, he might be able to kill them all.

"You are right," Octavian said. "Your attacks have weakened us. You have done well."

Corocotta tilted his head in acknowledgment when the words were translated for him, but he didn't otherwise respond. Juba was studying him intently, head to toe. The Shard had to be here. He had to have it with him. That was why he was so confident. But where? What would it look like?

It would have a black stone somehow, wouldn't it? The Trident did. So did the Palladium. And so did the Aegis of Zeus. Surely the Shard to control fire would be the same.

The man had leather bands around his neck, and animal claws and crystals were tied upon them, but none of them were dark in color, much less the deep, light-swallowing blackness of the stones in the Shards.

"Vellica, too, runs low on supplies," Octavian said. "You have weakened our supply lines, but that has not weakened our siege."

"I agree that you are wise to attack Vellica now," Corocotta replied.

"It will fall tomorrow," Octavian said.

"Perhaps," Corocotta said. In addition to the spear in his hand, the man had a sword at his hip, and the ball of its pommel was just visible when his movememt shifted his fur cloak: it was a simple bronze, though, little different from the weapon that the praetorian held level at his back.

"When it does, we will be the victors," Octavian said. "And those who remain in the city, no matter how bravely they fight, will be the fools. Should I offer them the chance to surrender before the attack?"

Corocotta shrugged. "If you did, they would not take it. Among the Cantabri it is said that it is better to die in honor than to live in shame. They do not believe there is honor under Roman rule."

"And you? What do you believe?"

Corocotta thought for several long seconds after the little girl finished translating. "I believe in Roman gold," he said. "One million Sesterces."

Juba saw that Tiberius frowned, but several of the Roman officers chuckled at both the audacity and the forthrightness of the man.

Octavian also laughed for a moment. "The man looking out for his own head is perhaps the wisest of all," he said. He appraised the big man once more, and Juba wondered if he, too, was looking for the Shard. "Very well. I offered one million Sesterces for the capture of Corocotta, and it seems that Corocotta himself has claimed it." He turned to Carisius. "An odd position, is it not?"

Carisius nodded. "It is, Caesar."

Corocotta had turned a little to see the new man Caesar was addressing, and that's when Juba saw it. The Cantabrian's big-handed grip on the spear had shifted for a moment, and when it did Juba saw a sliver of black.

Octavian nodded, then looked down the table to Tiberius. "My son," he said, "in your studies, what do you know of honesty among leaders?"

Tiberius seemed surprised to be addressed, but he recovered himself quickly. "A good leader must be a man of his word," he said. "For his word must be obeyed."

"Exactly so," Octavian said. One by one, Octavian questioned the highest officers in the room. To a man, they agreed with Tiberius.

Juba stared at the big man's hand, trying to see it again. A part of him wanted to think the sliver was merely a shadow, but in his heart he knew that it had been more than that. The darkness, when he had seen it, had *swallowed* the light. Hadn't it? Surely it wasn't a trick of the light. Surely it wasn't his imagination.

No. It was the spear. It had to be the spear. And if he already held the Shard in his hand, then he could unleash its power at any moment. Dear gods, Juba thought, imagining the control he must have over it to hold it in check so easily. If he and Selene could achieve such skill—

"Juba?"

Octavian's voice snapped Juba from his thoughts, and when he blinked his vision away from the spear he saw that everyone in the room was looking at him, including Corocotta and even the little girl.

"Caesar?"

"We were noting what a strange position I find myself in. Either I must dishonor myself by denying the reward and killing him, or I must pay my own enemy," Octavian said.

Juba swallowed hard, unable to prevent his eyes from flicking once more to the spear before addressing his stepbrother. Had the man's grip tightened? And what was it about the spear? It reminded him of something, tickled at a fact long-forgotten in his mind. "A difficult position, to be sure," he said.

A few of the other officers murmured under their breath. Juba thought he heard a whisper about the useless "dark prince."

"So it is," Octavian said. "But do you have any advice, Lord Juba?" His stepbrother's eyes narrowed, boring into him with what Juba felt in his heart was almost a plea.

Juba nodded slowly as his mind raced. The spear. A spear. A Cantabrian spear. "There's another option," he said.

"Oh?"

Juba looked toward Corocotta, saw that he was staring as intently at him as Juba had been staring at his hand. Juba felt a cold sweat forming on his forehead despite the heat of the oil lamps on a warm night. "Do not make an enemy of him," he said.

A few of the officers murmured a little more openly, a kind of laughter in their tone. "He already is our enemy—" Tiberius began.

"But he needn't be," Juba said, cutting the young man off more quickly than he would have liked. He could see the heat rising in Tiberius' face, but Juba had more important concerns right now. If he was right, Corocotta might be able to kill them all with hardly more than a thought. He'd been able to do the same, had he not?

"Go on," Octavian said.

"What I mean," Juba said, "is you should pay him to keep your honor, but pay him as a friend to keep your strength."

Octavian's eyes narrowed, but he had a growing smile on his face. "As at Actium," he said, "you have found the wisest way forward."

Juba knew he meant it as the highest compliment, as a direct rebuke of the snickers and disrespect from the other men in the room. He knew it was meant in kindness. But he just wanted to be sick.

Octavian turned to address the Cantabrian leader, who had been silent through the Romans' exchange. "Let it be known that Caesar is a man of his word. One million Sesterces. It is yours, Corocotta. On the condition that you join Rome."

Corocotta looked slowly between Octavian and Juba as the little girl translated. Then he thought for a few seconds before answering. "One million Sesterces. I will stand beside Caesar tomorrow," he said.

Octavian smiled, clearly pleased, and in that moment the memory that had been niggling at the back of Juba's head suddenly rushed into the forefront of his mind. "Olyndicus," he blurted out.

Octavian had been ready to speak, but Juba's outburst had interrupted him. He looked over with a mixture of amusement, confusion, and a hint of annoyance on his face. "You have something to add, Lord Juba?"

Juba stuttered, feeling the stares of his fellow Romans and, most especially, the steady, intense scrutiny of Corocotta. He hadn't meant to speak aloud, but now that he had there was no turning back. "Olyndicus was a leader of the Celtiberians here in Hispania," he said, addressing the room. "He was defeated by Lucius Canuleyus almost one hundred fifty years ago. A hard man, it was said. A good leader, who fought long and hard against Rome." He focused in on the Cantabrian leader. "I wonder if he is considered a hero among your people?"

The little girl translated, but Corocotta's stare did not leave Juba. His eyes were filled with an intense heat.

"He is," he finally replied. "Olyndicus was a great man."

"This is no time for a history lesson," one of the older

Roman officers said, but Caesar's raised hand silenced any further comments.

"He had a great power," Juba continued. "I remembered it just now. It was in the history of Diodorus Siculus, I believe. They said that Olyndicus carried with him a lance—a spear—that had been given to him by the gods of the sky." Corocotta's fist tightened very clearly on his spear, and Juba turned back toward his stepbrother. If the fire was to come, he didn't want to see it. As he continued to speak, he tried to implore him with his eyes. "The Lance of Olyndicus could devour men where they stood, leave them in ashes. The spear could control fire."

Juba had always known that Octavian was a consummate politician. He'd seen it when he'd watched him take control of Rome after Julius Caesar's death. He'd seen it when he'd watched him pull the strings of the senators who'd declared him an emperor, who'd named him Augustus Caesar. But never, until this moment, did he see how powerful he truly was at the game of kings.

Realization of the reality, of the danger, showed itself only in the faintest tremble of emotion that flexed upon Octavian's cheek. His eyes didn't widen. His gaze never flickered to Corocotta and his spear. His expression didn't change. He simply nodded, then pursed his lips thoughtfully for a moment before turning toward the big Cantabrian. "He indeed sounds like a great man. Is this story as it is among your people?"

Corocotta's bushy beard nodded. Then, to Juba's shock, he held forth the spear in his fist. Though at first he spoke to Caesar, to the room, his fiery gaze finally settled upon Juba. "The Lance of Olyndicus was held safe for many years," he said, "until one was found who was worthy to wield it. I have brought it here to you, for with it I have killed many men of Rome. But for one million Sesterces Corocotta has agreed to stand beside Caesar when Rome marches tomorrow. I am a man of my word, and that should be enough. But I, Corocotta, give you the weapon in my hand as promise that I will keep my word. Will Rome do the same?"

"It will," Caesar said, and at a snap of his fingers the praetorians sheathed their swords.

The little girl, still clutching her cloth-covered crutch beside the big man, looked relieved that the long negotiation had not come to violence. As Corocotta remained standing with his spear held out before him, the whole room seemed to let out a long breath.

Caesar turned to Juba. "For your knowledge, my brother, I give you the honor of accepting the weapon."

Juba bowed slightly, then began to step around the table. Many of the officers, he noticed, were looking at him with jealousy or, in the case of Carisius, open confusion. The look on the face of Tiberius, he saw, was more akin to a brooding anger. Juba knew he'd need to deal with the young man at some point, somehow make amends for cutting him off in front of the other men, but now was hardly the time.

At last he came around the end of the table to stand before the big Cantabrian. The bearded man was even larger up close, and his eyes seemed to be ablaze, but he moved not a muscle while Juba quickly flipped his hands under the folds of the cloth sash that was wrapped over his shoulder. Covering his hands, Juba hoped, would prevent him from inadvertently using the Shard, yet it would appear to the other men in the room as a simple sign of respect. Then, moving slowly in reverence and in fear, he reached out with his covered hands and gripped the spear.

For the space of several heartbeats, Corocotta held fast, staring at him. Juba tried to return the determination, but in the end he had to blink. The Cantabrian gave a kind of satisfied grunt and then released the spear. He took one step backward before at last returning his gaze to Octavian. "A man of my word," he said.

"So am I," Caesar replied, and he immediately directed Tiberius to see to the reward, which was ordered to be ready by the dawn. Then he commanded a tent prepared for Corocotta and his slave, while Carisius and the remaining generals were once more sent to prepare the legions for battle.

Everyone snapped into motion, and in less than a minute Juba was alone in the tent, holding Corocotta's spear in his cloth-covered hands and wondering what on earth he should do next.

10

Blood on the Water

The grains that Petosiris had carried into the city had been replaced by piles of textiles, and Vorenus and Khenti relaxed among them at the leading edge of the barge, the waters of the canal once more slipping beneath them. This time the barge was headed east, away from Alexandria and toward Schedia and the Nile. And it was not the breaking day that lay ahead, but the growing darkness of night, which was quickly rising before them in a yawning wall of black, only just beginning to show the pricks of a few scattered stars.

They were hardly more than an hour from the city walls, but the buildings that had crowded against the waterway had long since begun to thin, and the air was beginning to taste clean again. The noise of crowds that had been a constant buzzing din within Alexandria's walls and its initial tumbledown suburbs had dissipated into the hush of the dark, broken only by the occasional barking of a dog or the steady, echoing clatter of a cart, homeward bound from the surrounding fields.

Getting out of the city had been much easier than getting in. Night had pushed most of the traffic from the waterway, and the guards had all gone to other posts. It had been at least half an hour since Vorenus had seen another soul on the canal.

Caesarion had been right about meeting with Didymus. The librarian had been more helpful than Vorenus had dared to hope, and it had simply been good to see him again—even if the joy of that reunion made the loss of Pullo that much harder to bear.

It seemed, too, that Vorenus' fears of discovery had been largely unfounded. There was no sign that anyone had recognized him coming or going from the Great Library, and within the office of his old friend he'd felt safe and relaxed for the first time in many years.

Vorenus sighed and leaned his head back, looking up into the dark. This, too, was relaxing, he thought.

Behind them, at the rear of the barge, Petosiris and his young assistant were at the tiller, guiding the craft on its steady advance.

"I am glad you learned what you needed," Khenti said from beside him.

For as long as Vorenus had known him, the only thing that ever seemed to matter to the Egyptian was the immediate mission. When they'd met to walk back to the harbor from the Great Library, he'd never even asked what was discussed. He only wanted to know if Vorenus had found what he was looking for and if they needed to go anywhere else before leaving Alexandria. There was something undoubtedly reassuring about his single-minded sense of purpose, but all the same he missed the company of Pullo, who could be stubborn and impetuous and a damnable fool, but was the only person Vorenus had ever truly loved.

"I am, too," Vorenus said. "Seems I was wrong to have been so worried that we would be seen."

"And it will be good to return home," Khenti said.

Vorenus nodded. "Yes, it will," he said. It took coming back to Alexandria to help him realize the truth of what home was to him. Long ago, campaigning with Julius Caesar in Gaul, he'd thought of home as nothing more than the seven hills and gleaming columns of Rome. Despite his many years in Alexandria he'd still been that Roman at heart: what fondness he'd had of the Egyptian city had been for its reminders of what he'd left behind. But the war had changed all that. He was a man without a country now, a man hunted by his countrymen, a man haunted by the place of his birth. If Alexandria had remained a foreign place even after so many years there, the little island of Elephantine they had fled to—perched as it was amid the wide waters of the Nile at the very edge of the old kingdoms of Egypt—was far stranger. But it really was his home now. It wasn't the ancient sandstone buildings clustered upon it that made it so, nor was it the strangely forgotten Jewish temple where they'd hidden the Ark. It was the people. It was Khenti. It was Caesarion and Hannah, the beautiful Jewish girl that the young man had come to love. And it was Pullo, too, since hardly a day passed that Vorenus didn't reflect on how his old friend would have laughed at something that was said or seen.

Vorenus let out a long breath in a sigh, turning to face his Egyptian companion. Khenti was sitting against a pile of packed cloths, but he still seemed more rigidly upright than Vorenus thought necessary since they'd escaped Alexandria. "Where are you from, Khenti?"

The Egyptian had been peering out into the night, but he turned to answer the Roman's direct address. "From? What does this mean?"

Khenti's native tongue was Egyptian, but he was thoroughly adept at the Greek that had been the standard tongue of Cleopatra's court. It was this that they used to converse with each other, since his knowledge of Latin was sparse at best. But even with his excellent Greek, every now and then a word or phrase would cause him to stumble.

"I'm wondering where were you born?" Vorenus clarified.

Khenti shrugged, but there was something like the hint of a smile on his night-shadowed face. "I am an Egyptian, Roman."

"No. I know that. I mean . . . Where did your parents live? In Alexandria?"

"Ah. Yes. I understand. I do not know the answer to that question, Lucius Vorenus, since I do not know the place of my birth."

Vorenus blinked at him in the dark. "You don't know?"

The Egyptian shook his head. "I do not."

"I'm sorry."

"I do not know why you would be so. My home is where I am."

Vorenus thought about that as the barge drifted forward. Ahead he could see the small, decrepit dock of an old farm, just visible in the growing dark. Khenti was right, he decided. It didn't really matter where you were from. It really only mattered where you were. And perhaps, he thought as he watched the water push against the wooden feet of the dock, where you were going.

"Home," Vorenus said, and he felt the full satisfaction of the word.

The sound of a bird whistled to their left. The reeds rustled as if something was about to take flight, but then, for a frozen instant, nothing stirred.

Khenti half-turned in that direction, and Vorenus was aware of the Egyptian's hand sliding toward the sword at his side.

Vorenus opened his mouth to say something, but in that moment a ghost arose from higher on the embankment, where the path leading to the dock had worn a kind of trench through the rising earth. The dark red of the last rays of the sun splashed directly upon the man's skin, making it appear to be bathed in fresh blood. It deepened the crossing scars that were scattered across the face Vorenus had known, and age or injury had stooped his once powerful neck, but the broad shoulders were the same. And the voice with which he shouted out was the same one that Vorenus heard in haunted dreams of the past.

"Vorenus!" cried the ghost of Titus Pullo.

There was time for a single heartbeat of shock and exhilaration. Then Vorenus heard the thrum of bowstrings loosed. And in the next instant, something hot and wet spat across his face as an arrow ripped across Khenti's side and embedded itself in the cloth between them.

Vorenus saw Khenti roll forward and down toward the top of the deck, making himself small, and then Vorenus' own instincts thrust him in the opposite direction, away from the darkness of the embankment on which he had seen the ghost of Pullo. His legs kicked until his feet found purchase and he flung himself back and to the side, putting the pile of rugs between himself and whoever or whatever was hunting them in the growing dark.

He hit the other side of the deck with a grunt, and all at once sound returned to the world. The young deckhand was screaming from the back end of the boat, and there was shouting from the shoreline, accompanied by the high clear ring of metal swung against metal. Closer, Vorenus heard the splash of a body moving through water.

And closer still, the black shape of Khenti rose up in his vision, the curved blade of his Egyptian sword flashing moonlight in his hand as he ran toward the rear of the barge.

Another bowstring loosed, just one this time, and Vorenus

both heard and felt its whistle as it sang through the night air above the deck, narrowly missing Khenti, who did not falter in his run.

Once more the familiar voice of his old friend bellowed from onshore, "Vorenus!"

Vorenus blinked as if he were waking from a dream. The shout rocked something loose inside of him, and when he looked down at his hands he saw that they had already answered the call: his fingers were now tightening around the familiar grip of his unsheathed sword. He arose from the cover of the piled rugs.

At a glance, he took it all in. The barge had turned. Something had happened with Petosiris back at the tiller. In seconds, the ship would run aground into the side of the canal, only feet from the old wooden dock that he'd seen. Beside the dock, the man who could not exist—the man who looked like Pullo—was knee-deep in the reed-filled marsh, swinging his sword before him like a scythe. Someone was before him, hidden in the reeds but still visible as he struggled to back away from the charging beast that Vorenus knew so well. A second man had slipped out of the marsh in Pullo's wake. He was dropping a recurved Egyptian bow from his left hand, while his right was drawing a long dagger. He was looking at Pullo's back.

"Pullo!" Vorenus shouted. With sudden urgency, no longer thinking but simply reacting, he jumped around the intervening piles of rugs, took four sprinting steps to get up to speed, and then leapt from the deck of the barge just as it hit the shoreline and shuddered from beneath him. He cleared several feet of water and landed left leg first on the old dock.

His foot slipped for an instant, and he felt his tendons groaning from the unfamiliar strain, but already his momentum was carrying him forward. His right leg came down on the wood ahead of him as if stretching across a great leap. It planted, and then the muscles of his thigh tightened and released, propelling him onward, out of control now, right at the man who had his blade out and ready to strike Pullo down.

Vorenus had his own gladius held before him, hoping that in this initial assault he could push it through the man, but the action of bringing it forward had taken too long. Vorenus was hardly the young man he'd once been. The time he'd taken had given the man he attacked a chance to turn and bring his long dagger around to defend himself. The edges of their weapons clashed loudly, each ringing off the other and away. Vorenus felt the sting of the other man's blade gashing across his forearm where his leather legionnaire armor once would have been.

Vorenus' sword point was turned away, but there was no stopping the weight of his body. An instant later, Vorenus had smashed into the man, shoulder-first, as if he were breaching a door. The mass of him lifted the would-be killer off his feet, and Vorenus tumbled over him and landed with a lung-clearing grunt against the grassy foot of the embankment.

The stars above him spun as Vorenus fought to get air in his lungs and ground beneath his feet. A part of him—the memory of a younger him—shouted in his mind, ordering him to move faster, to get up and engage first, to attack and kill before the enemy was prepared. But Vorenus was no longer that man. His shoulder and side pounded for attention in their present pain, and the muscles of his right thigh were screaming in distress.

And his sword! Where was his sword?

Vorenus had managed to gather himself up to his knees, but he got no further as his hands rifled through the grass in the darkness.

"Looking for this?"

Vorenus froze and then slowly looked up. The man he'd knocked to the ground was on his feet, standing above him with his long dagger in one hand and the Roman gladius in the other. He was smiling triumphantly. He started to raise the gladius back for a strike.

"I'll make it quick, old—"

His words were cut off by a throttled gasp as the tip of a second gladius crunched through his chest. The dagger in the Egyptian's hand dropped in front of Vorenus, who instinctively picked it up and then staggered to his feet and backed up a step as his friend who ought to be dead—big, beautiful Pullo—gave one half-turn to the embedded blade and then jerked it free from the man's back with a wet and slopping sound that made Vorenus thankful for the night. The lifeless body sagged to the ground like a stringless puppet.

"Vorenus!" The big man stepped over the corpse as if it were a log. In the moonlight Vorenus could see his friend's concern on a face that was still recognizable despite the jagging of new scars that lent it the look of a weather-beaten tent, more patches than cloth. Dampness shone on those torn cheeks, though Vorenus couldn't tell whether from blood, sweat, or tears. He saw, too, that his friend didn't step with the same thunderous gait that had shaken the decks of Mark Antony's flagship at Actium. He moved instead with an upright, almost straight-legged lumber, as if he walked on painful stilts.

"I'm okay," Vorenus managed. He wanted to reach out and touch him, to assure himself that this was real, that Pullo was really still alive. He wanted to shake his hand as they once did, he wanted to embrace him as they never really had, and—just in the back of his mind—he wanted to punch him square in the thick jaw for letting him think he was dead for so long. "Gods, Pullo, I thought you—"

Pullo, too, had seemed abruptly paralyzed once they faced each other in the night. But as Vorenus started to speak, he cut him off. "There were three," he said. "This is two."

Vorenus suddenly remembered the splash of water and the barge turning. He quickly reached down to roll over the dead Egyptian and retrieve his gladius. "The boat. Khenti is there."

Pullo was looking over toward where the path to the dock disappeared into the rising embankment. "Go on. I'm behind you," the big man said. "I've got to do something first."

Vorenus nodded as his old friend started lumbering away. Then he, too, began to move, running up along the dock. From the darkness behind him he heard Pullo's deep voice. "I'm always saving you," his old friend grumbled.

The chaos could only have lasted a minute or two, and by the time Vorenus reached the back of the barge there was nothing left but an eerie quiet over the canal, broken only by the soft sloshing of water and reed against the barge as it rocked back and forth against the shoreline. Khenti was standing there in the dark, his curved sword in his hand and the body of another Egyptian attacker at his feet. On the deck just ahead of him, below the free-hanging tiller, lay the deckhand, the side of his neck ripped out by a well-placed arrow. Petosiris was a few feet away, a short blade in his hand, collapsed against a stack of textiles. His eyes were open, but they saw no more.

Khenti wasn't looking at any of them. He was staring out into the night of the shoreline, unmoving but for the steady rise and fall of his chest. "I was too late," he said.

Vorenus nodded. From where they were positioned, Petosiris must have been letting the boy take a hand on the tiller when the first arrows struck. The young man had surely been killed instantly, but it looked like Petosiris had survived the arrow that had struck him in the chest. He must have tumbled backward, getting cover and drawing his blade. He'd tried to defend himself against the killer who'd quickly climbed aboard, but the wound had left him too weak and too shocked. By the time he'd arrived, Khenti could only avenge him. "Nothing you could do," Vorenus said. Little comfort, but it was true.

"That is Titus Pullo." Khenti's voice was so emotionless he could have been talking about a tree.

Vorenus looked back into the dark and saw his old friend making his way up the dock. Pullo had sheathed his sword now, and he was instead carrying a small leather bag in his big hand. At the end of the dock he waited until the barge bobbed close enough for him to reach out with his free hand, pull it close, and clamber aboard.

"Khenti." The big man was smiling when he drew near. "It's been too long."

The Egyptian gave him an approving nod, then looked back toward the night. "One man got away," he said.

Pullo sighed. "I'm not a runner. Never was before and I'm certainly not now."

"It sounded like a horse," Khenti said.

"It was," Pullo agreed. "And like I said, I'm not a runner."

"Pullo," Vorenus finally managed to say, his voice half exasperated with joy and his own roiling emotion. "Gods, we thought you were dead."

"I was."

"How? How did—?"

"I went to work for a man named Seker."

"Who?"

"The last man who's dead back there. Stabbed in the back."

"You killed him?" Khenti asked as he finally sheathed his blade.

"No," Pullo said, frowning. "Sadly, I did not. The other man did. The one who got away."

Vorenus peered out into the night, too. "Who is he? Do we need to worry about him?"

"I think he's a scholar, if you can believe that." Pullo chewed on his lip. "But a coward. And a frightened one at that. He hired all these men—and me—to ambush this ship, kill everyone, but take you for the reward. Please believe me, I didn't know it was you. I didn't know who he was after. When I realized . . . I tried to stop them, Vorenus. I tried."

Before Vorenus could reply, Khenti turned away from the night to look at him. His hand came up to hold his side, as if he were scratching an itch. "So you were recognized at the Library," he said.

"You went to the Library?" Pullo asked. "Did you see Didymus?"

"I did," Vorenus said, smiling. "We spoke of you. We thought you were dead, Pullo."

"I knew you'd gotten away," Pullo said. "And I didn't want to endanger anyone by going to Didymus. So I found work where I could." His voice trailed off for a moment, and then he shook his head and tossed the bag he was carrying to Vorenus. "Well, anyway, this belonged to the man I worked for. Meant to be payment for these bowmen." He looked down at Petosiris and the deckhand. "I'm so sorry, Vorenus. Were they . . . friends of yours?"

"Business associates," Vorenus said, his voice quiet. "But they were good men."

Pullo frowned, his eyes unreadable despite the moonlight. "Too much death," he said. "I'm sorry, Vorenus. I didn't know. I never thought I'd see you again."

"Nor I, you," Vorenus said, and he was suddenly moved to

reach out and embrace his old friend, clapping him on the back even as the bigger man squeezed him so firmly that he thought a rib might crack. "Gods, it's good to see you, Titus Pullo."

"And you've no idea how glad I am to see you, too, Lucius Vorenus. And you, as well, Khenti—" Pullo's voice broke off and his wide grin froze as he released Vorenus to look at the Egyptian warrior. "You're bleeding."

Vorenus spun around. Khenti had reached over to place one hand on the tiller, while the other gripped his side. His face looked pale in the moonlight. Even as Vorenus started to speak, the Egyptian teetered, and the two Romans rushed forward to catch him.

As quickly as they could, they pulled him over to another pile of textiles and laid him back. As they did so, the moonlight finally landed on his chest and flashed on the thick dampness there. Vorenus could see the ragged line across the side of his shirt where an arrow had carved across his torso, and he suddenly remembered that first arrow strike, when he'd felt something wet hit his face. It had been blood. Khenti's blood.

He'd already lost so much. Vorenus could see it now where it had pooled on the deck. How had he not seen it before?

The Egyptian's face contorted as Vorenus pulled his hand away from his side and placed his own upon the wound. He felt it pumping weakly against his palm. "Oh, gods, Khenti—"

"Leave the barge." Khenti's voice, always so strangely calm, was all the stranger for now being strained. "Canal is not safe anyway. Go north. Sea road."

Pullo loomed over them both. "Khenti, I'm sorry. Just . . . I'll go get some help. They put me together. Maybe you—"

Khenti smiled, and Vorenus was surprised that he had the kindest and warmest of smiles when he did so. "You're Pullo and Vorenus," he said. His voice grew quiet. "I do not think you can ever die."

The Egyptian's eyes had a distant focus to them, as if he was looking somewhere far beyond them. Vorenus pressed his hand harder against the wound. "Stay with us, Khenti," he said. "It's not far to the city. Then we'll get you home."

At the last word, Khenti blinked and turned his head slightly to look at Vorenus. He was still smiling. "This *is* my home, Roman. Remember?" Then he looked over at Pullo. "And you've just found yours."

"You're right," Vorenus said. "Just hold on. We'll go home. All of us."

Khenti had turned to look up at the stars, still smiling, but beneath the hand of Vorenus his heart beat no more.

PART II

The Spear of Destiny

11

The Power Within

CANTABRIA, 26 BCE

But for the dead, Juba was alone in the meadow.

Dawn was breaking over the hills to the east; its first bright rays fell on the sides of the burned-out husks of the wagons that had been ambushed there, starkly contrasting with the long shadows that stretched behind them. What was left of the bodies of the men had been buried, but he still felt their presence here in a kind of hushed and watchful quiet.

His horse tramped its feet uneasily beneath him. He reached down to pat its neck, steadying it—and himself, he supposed.

There were two long, canvas-wrapped bundles behind him on the rear of the horse, both carefully bound to his saddle with thick leather straps. It was, he thought, a remarkable sign of trust that Octavian had allowed him to bring Corocotta's spear here, alone, so that he could test it. It was more remarkable still that he had allowed him to bring the Trident as well. "If you lose control of the one, my brother," Caesar had told him when he was called to his tent in the early morning darkness, "you may find the other necessary."

And although Octavian's assault on Vellica was set to begin with the dawn—now, Juba supposed—his stepbrother had told him to go away from the death and din of the battle, to find a quiet place behind their lines in order to discover whether he could control the spear's power. After all, Octavian had mused, the Cantabrian might want it back.

It was that trust, more than the two artifacts behind him, that had Juba lost in thought for the moment. Octavian hadn't trusted him for years, not since that day at the villa in Rome when he'd confronted Juba about showing the Trident to a woodworker. The day that he'd first made Juba use the artifact's power to kill, to rip the life out of the slave Quintus.

Juba closed his eyes against the memory, and against all those that followed, all the men he'd killed with the power of a god.

In all that time, not once had Octavian let the Trident out of his possession. Not once had he let Juba handle it alone.

And now here, at the edge of the world, he'd given it to Juba—along with the spear of Corocotta. What did that mean?

Juba realized that he had begun to frown, so he opened his eyes and tried to smile. Whatever else it meant, he had two Shards of Heaven with him. Three, if he counted the Aegis of Zeus back in his tent. What it meant to have them was a question that certainly would need answering, but for now it was enough to have them.

And to see how they worked.

He dismounted and walked the horse to the burned-out remains of the wagon, where he'd stood with Octavian. Tying off the lead, he took a moment to stare once more at the crate and its unnatural flame scars that had surely come from the Lance of Olyndicus. It was, he thought, like a gashing wound. However the Shard was activated, it seemed that once it was in use it was like the spray of a fire-breathing chimera. That was different from the Trident and Palladium, which had always welled up energy in a concentrated effort—unless he and Selene had not yet tapped the fullness of their powers?

Juba turned away and, reassuringly patting his horse along

its neck and flank, returned to his saddle and the two long bundles tied behind it. His hands paused as he began to reach for the leather straps and brass buckles. Though he'd helped Selene learn to control the Palladium, he'd not used a Shard himself in many years. Being this close to the Trident made him yearn to grip it once more, to feel its power course through his veins.

Besides, if there was a new way to focus its power—like the scar upon this crate—he should practice doing so before he tried to handle the spear.

Taking a deep breath, he let his fingers open the straps. He lifted free the bundle holding the Trident of Poseidon.

The artifact was just as he remembered it. The long, polished wood shaft fit neatly into the socket of the triple-pointed spearhead—a perfect fit made by a craftsman in Rome who'd been repaid for his talents first with Juba's coins and then, later, with the knives of Octavian's men, who would suffer none to know of this secret weapon. The three points of the spearhead were unlike the head of any other trident he had seen: the center spear pointed directly forward, as expected, yet although the ones to either side were broken off, it was clear that they did not angle forward, but instead shot out directly to left and right—as if a double-ended spear had been shoved through the base of the first. Around and down the silver metal of the head were two intertwined snakes—one bronze and one copper in color—whose mouths opened forward like they were weapons on their own.

And in the middle of it all was the Shard of Heaven, the real weapon. Set in a metal housing, it was a blacker-than-black stone that seemed to draw in the very light of the air around it. A similar stone was set within the Aegis of Zeus, which had belonged to Alexander the Great before Juba had taken it, and a similar stone was embedded within the crystal-like rock that was the Palladium. And if he had succeeded in taking control of it back in Alexandria, Juba was certain he would have found another stone, probably the biggest of all, within the Ark of the Covenant. Each Shard seemed to control a single element: the Ark, earth; the Palladium, air; the Aegis, life; and this Trident, water. The Lance controlled fire. The Shards of Heaven, each a remainder—or so Didymus had said—of the throne that had been destroyed when the angels in heaven had tried to resurrect the one God, who died giving free will to creation.

As he lifted the Trident—being careful to grip it by the wood and not the metal snakes, which functioned as conduits of the power of the Shard—Juba observed how the stone within its housing was looser than he last recalled. He had first noticed it loosening after Octavian had made him use the Trident to sink a Roman bireme at sea. Octavian had let him handle the Trident only once after that: at Actium, where he called up a far greater wave to swamp Mark Antony's flagship and send it to the deep. The act had nearly taken the life from Juba, for through some means he did not understand the Shards could give power to their users—but they could also wrest power away if the users were not prepared, taking their very lives. This was the reason, Juba was certain, that Octavian would never use the Trident himself: if he failed to control its power, it would consume him.

What it meant that the stone had grown looser, Juba was not sure. Perhaps it meant that using the Shard diminished its power in some way—though he had noticed nothing similar happen to the Aegis and the Palladium—or perhaps the housing was simply ill-fitting for the black stone. Finding out if it was an issue of fitment seemed simple enough, but then Juba had never touched the stone directly. He feared very much what would happen if he did.

Juba walked ten paces or so from his horse. He planted

the Trident butt-down before him, still holding on to its wood shaft as he looked between the interwoven snakes at the broken, charred heap of another cart not far away.

Taking a deep breath, Juba moved his hands up to grip the bodies of the two snakes where the curves of their curling bodies made a pair of handholds on each side of the Shard itself. He closed his eyes, letting the metal grow warm beneath his skin, letting that contact become a kind of unity. Then, letting out his breath, he fell back down into himself, back into a darkness that was him and not him. He pulled it up into his hands, pushed it into the stone, and then pulled it out before him, to make it ready to strike out toward the cart.

He knew at once the power of the Shard. He knew it as he remembered it—a pool of molten metal bubbling and churning in its hot rage to be free—but for a moment nothing happened. No energy flowed forth. The ruined cart stood unfazed.

Of course. Every other time he'd used the Shard, it had been with a clear water source: the sea, a barrel of water, a jug of wine. But the meadow was dry, even parched. What could the Shard use?

And then he felt it: a tingling upon his skin, like the tiniest of raindrops dancing in feather-light song. A few at first, and then more and still more. The metal beneath his grip grew warm.

Juba opened his eyes and saw what was happening now. A fine mist was forming, swirling into a kind of wispy cloud before him. Like the wind that Selene had raised with her Palladium, what Juba had raised was the semblance of a storm. It strained with an urge to dissipate, but with concentration Juba bunched it as tight as he could and then pushed it forward with as much mental strength as he could muster.

The droplets splattered against the side of the cart.

Juba let go of the snakes and once more gripped the wooden shaft. He licked his lips, noticing how much drier the air around him had become.

That was where the water had come from, he decided. The Shard had drawn it out of the very air.

Juba smiled at the wonder of that, but then he frowned. The Trident was no match for the power that the Lance had shown. The concentrated force that Corocotta had managed to burn these carts and kill these men . . . it was so far beyond what Juba knew.

For that matter, where did that Shard's fires come from? There was no fire in the area for the Cantabrian outlaw to manipulate, and what fire was upon the wind that it could be gathered in such abundance?

Juba thought back to the previous night, when Corocotta had stood before them with the artifact in his possession. He was surely ready to use it then, so how? Would it have drawn substance from the torches? That seemed so little. Yet he had held it out nevertheless, his thick hand enwrapping the black stone itself as he stood ready . . .

Juba's eyes widened.

Corocotta had not held the staff or some other part of the Lance. He had held the Shard itself.

He'd held the Shard.

Juba swallowed hard. Then, biting his lip, he slowly raised his right hand and placed it, palm down, atop the Shard of Heaven.

If he had imagined the power of the Trident to be like a pool of molten metal, this was like pressing his hand down into its surface. The pain was white-hot, but not fire, not flame. It was something both liquid and solid, something that writhed around beneath his palm almost like a creature alive. In rippling flashes, pulsing with each beat of his stunned, lurching heart, it took more of him—though whether it climbed up his flesh or pulled it down, Juba could not tell. He fought to pull himself away, to pull back, but the searing shocks just pulled him on, deeper and deeper into a bright, screaming light.

He had closed his eyes at the lurching shock of the power, and as it rushed up his arms and began lapping like waves against his chest, shaking him into convulsions, he opened them as if he might witness his flesh consumed.

What he saw instead was that his hand was unharmed, but it was crackling with ripples of lightning that flashed in hot sparks across his skin.

His jaw was clenched by the agony of the power rushing through him. It was the only thing preventing him from screaming out whatever last gasps of breath he had.

His shaking legs gave way, and he began to fall backward, his hand still wrapped around the flashing stone as if it was rooted upon it.

The horizon fell away. The sky rose like a great hood over his eyes.

He saw the gathering storm.

Above him, wispy streaks coalesced and grew into a churning black pillar of cloud that spun up into the pale blue summer sky, looming over the parched landscape. Lightning flashed in its depths, like hungry beasts in a dark cage.

Juba's back struck the ground, and what air he had in his lungs coughed out in the same moment that a bolt of jagged lightning flashed down and exploded into the Trident with an explosion that shook the earth.

Juba somehow unclenched his jaw, and he screamed back against the pain and the power, willing it out of his body and into the Shard. Above him the lightning flashed again, menacing, but he pushed that away, too. It did not strike.

The shocking fear that had threatened to consume him

slowed and halted. He began to take deeper, steadying breaths. He could feel the presence of the power that was now coiled within the Shard, he could feel it poised like a beast ready to leap and rip his heart from his chest. But it did not jump. It sparked and crackled there, as if it was watching, as if it was waiting.

Juba—his hand still locked upon the terrible black stone—managed to rise to his knees and then stand, panting at the exhaustion of his willpower. He could smell rain in the air. He could feel more lightning roiling above him, ready to be commanded.

Bracing himself, gritting his teeth in the effort to keep the power controlled within the Shard, Juba focused on the remains of the cart and *willed* the gathered power into its destruction.

Released at last, the lightning struck out from the Trident, hot and bright, a jagged bolt of energy that ripped through the air and impacted the charred wood like the crack of a mighty whip.

The cart exploded outward from the impact in fragments of blackened wood and cascading sparks. And at last, as the energy dissipated and left him, Juba finally managed to let go of the Shard, dropping the Trident to the ground.

Juba fell to one knee, gasping air, his eyes riveted on the destroyed cart. Broken splinters kicked high by the discharge clattered down to the grass around him. The air smelled strangely sweet.

What he'd just seen, what he'd felt . . . the power was simply indescribable. It was unfathomable.

"My God," he panted. "My God."

At the sound of a quiet rumble, he at last turned to look upward at the sky. The clouds, so quickly summoned into being, were breaking apart. The coiled fury that had been there moments earlier was now idly drifting away on high, indifferent breezes. Juba watched it for a few moments, then he sat down roughly into the grass, staring at everything and nothing.

He'd had no idea the true power of the Trident. It wasn't just the movement of water. It was storms. Lightning. It was the power of Poseidon. The power of God.

And something in his heart told him that there was still more that it could do. That he could do.

Knowing what he might do with it made him want to laugh. Knowing what he'd already done with it made him want to be sick.

For several minutes, Juba didn't move.

Then, collecting himself at last, he picked up the Trident from where it had fallen—being careful not to touch the snakes or the Shard itself—and walked it back to the bundle behind his saddle. Only as he was placing it there did he notice that it had changed. The stone no longer shook within its housing. It was stable. Solid. It had, Juba was certain, grown.

But how? And what did it mean?

Juba frowned. He was too exhausted to think. He felt weary straight down through his bones.

And he still had another Shard to test.

Very carefully, as he settled the first artifact into place, he pulled out the second: the spear that Corocotta had carried into the tent and handed over with such ceremony. Then he walked back to the spot where he'd stood to use the Trident.

Hours earlier, in the darkness of the command tent, he'd seen a glimpse of the stone in the spear. It had been only a glimpse. But seeing it now in the light of the breaking day it seemed different than he had expected. It was a glossy black stone, but it didn't swallow the light the way the stones did upon the Trident of Poseidon and the Aegis of Zeus. It was instead dark in color yet flickering with strands of the growing light around it, like burned glass.

The stone in the Palladium could seem different from the others, too. Another question he would consider later.

There were no obvious ways to hold the weapon, so Juba simply gripped it as he would any other spear. Widening his stance, the spear firmly in his hands, he couched it against his hip, the spear point aimed at one of the wagons across the way. Then he closed his eyes and sank back into himself with a sigh, mentally bracing for the rush of the power he'd felt when he'd wielded the Trident or donned Alexander's armor.

Nothing happened.

Juba blinked. He shifted his grip—gently at first, but then with increasing fervor. The spear didn't react. It was as if it was nothing but an ordinary weapon, adorned with a black stone.

In desperation, he held it before him and wrapped his fist around the stone, just as Corocotta had.

Nothing.

But it *had* to be the Lance of Olyndicus. It was there last night. Corocotta would not have come without it. And whatever else the man was, he was no liar. Juba had seen his reaction when he mentioned Olyndicus, and he'd said he had it with him. But if this wasn't it, where was it? Where had the Cantabrian and his little crippled slave hidden—

Juba gasped, and he spun to look down the road back toward camp, toward the war.

The battle had begun. The legions would already be marching, strung out across the valley.

Juba ran toward his horse, hastily shoving the useless spear back into its bag and once more pulling free the Trident.

He spurred the horse into speed even as he pulled himself into the saddle. He'd been a fool. They all had. He knew where the Lance of Olyndicus was now.

He only hoped he wasn't too late.

12

The Battle of Vellica

CANTABRIA, 26 BCE

As the sun rose behind her tent, Selene looked out to the west. The two praetorians who were waiting for her looked expectant, but for several heartbeats she could do nothing but stare at the emptiness of the camp around her. The legionnaires were already on the move. Few had been left behind, it seemed, as the men formed up for the attack on Vellica. And though she could not see them, she had no doubt that atop the high hill across the valley, the men of Vellica were readying their weapons, too, preparing for the coming assault.

Many men would die today. Hundreds, she was certain. Perhaps far more if the Romans actually succeeded in breaching the gates.

So many lives would be lost.

But not the one she wanted.

Augustus had called Juba into a private meeting for some hours before the dawn. Afterward, her husband had sent her a message before he rode out of the camp alone, headed south along the road. The message was short, and it was unspecific— as all their communications had to be, in case they were intercepted by Caesar's men. But hidden in its brief lines was enough to know that he had both the Trident and the Lance in his possession, and that he would return soon. There was great hope that they might have vengeance on the man who'd taken her family from her.

Yet now two praetorian guards had come, requesting her presence at Caesar's side.

"The emperor was most insistent, Lady Selene," the one nearest to her said.

Though hearing Octavian's title made her stomach turn, Selene turned her eyes from the empty camp and smiled at the man. "Of course. I would certainly not dare to keep him waiting. If you'll just give me a moment."

Before they could object, Selene ducked her head back into the tent.

In the semi-darkness, she tried to calm her fearful heart. Why would Octavian summon her? Had Juba's mission been some kind of test through which Octavian had discovered their betrayal?

Her gaze darted around the room, not even sure what she was looking for as the yawning sense of panic swelled up within her.

And then she saw it: Juba's locked chest. The one with the false bottom under which he'd long hidden the Aegis of Zeus, beside which she had placed the Palladium.

Not two minutes later she was emerging from the tent with a slightly more formal dress—more appropriate, she explained to the praetorians, for meeting the son of the god they'd made Julius Caesar to be. What that dress held beneath its elaborate folds—clutched close like the treasure that it was, like the salvation it might be—she did not say.

. . .

The emperor of Rome was not far from the palisades of the Roman camp. The general staff—perhaps a dozen of the highest-ranking men in the army, along with the signalmen—were gathered on the ridge of the wooded hillside, from which they had a clear view of the open valley below and the hillfort of Vellica beyond. Augustus, Tiberius, and the three generals who commanded the individual legions of the army were on horseback. The other men stood around them in their battle finery, straight-backed and stone-faced.

Corocotta was nowhere to be seen, though a cart had been drawn up behind the general staff that was laden with boxes: the reward, Selene suspected, for Corocotta having turned himself in.

Juba was also nowhere to be seen.

The praetorians led her to the edge of the gathered staff, bowed, and then pulled away to stand apart, with four others of Caesar's guards, closer to the palisade behind them. Selene waited until Octavian noticed her, and then she gave a small bow, keeping her arms tight to her body so that the artifact she had hidden there wouldn't show.

"Lady Selene," Octavian said, "it is good of you to join us."

"You sent for me," she replied.

"So I did." Octavian smiled as if he were her father, rather than the man who'd led her father to fall on his own sword.

"I cannot think that I will be of much use to you here," Selene said. She motioned to Carisius and the other Roman field commanders. "I know little of the arts of war."

Tiberius shifted atop his mount beside Caesar. "Few women do," he said.

"It is only too true," Selene said, as graciously as she could manage. Tiberius, she saw, was staring fiercely at the valley below, as if he was determined not to look at her. Did he truly hate her so?

"So it is," Octavian agreed. "But only because they are not trained for it. Perhaps that is for the best. War is blood and death. I have learned this. The fewer who see it the better."

Blood and death, Selene thought, is all you have brought to the world. "As you say," she said.

"Columns moving, Caesar," Carisius said.

Selene turned toward the valley, following the intense stare of Carisius and the other generals. Where the hill rounded into the plain of the valley, the woods thinned and stopped. The three legions were appearing there, like glittering snakes forming out of the wooded dark. The men marched six abreast, in three columns that were hundreds and hundreds of rows in length, and she could hear now the steady thump of their feet upon the earth. At the heads of the columns the standards of each legion were held high in the air: banners crisp and bright, and the golden eagles atop them flashing in the first rays of dawn. In their discipline and in their display, she thought, the Roman army was truly a beautiful and powerful sight.

"I didn't call you here to speak of war," Octavian said. "I wanted to talk to you about your mother."

Selene's head whipped around. "My . . . mother?"

Octavian was calmly looking back and forth between her and the advancing army below. "Cleopatra," he said. "I've been thinking about Alexandria and what happened there."

Selene stared, feeling an instinctive heat rising in her chest. For a moment she had the urge to reach for the Palladium, but what then? What could she do with it? Blow down his own banners? Knock him from his horse? Now that she thought about it, she realized how foolish she had been to grab the Shard. It was desperation. It was panic. It was emotion. It was everything her mother had taught her not to be.

"My mother is dead," she said. Speaking the words made her rage flash and then fade. What good were the lessons of a woman who'd lost?

But what use was the Shard in her dress?

Octavian had been looking to the columns, and when he

turned his gaze back to her it was once more a look of pity. "She is," he said. "And it's important to me that you know that I did not want her to die. But she made that choice, Selene. I was not pleased when she took her own life. Why do you think she did so?"

"Because she loved my father," Selene said, voice flat.

"Caesar's your father, Selene," Tiberius said.

Octavian raised his hand. "By adoption," he corrected. "And I would be a fool if I did not recognize that there is a difference. You yourself know this well, my son."

The darkness grew upon the face of Tiberius, and still he stared straight ahead at the marching men.

"Your mother loved Antony," Octavian said.

"She did."

"She wanted to join him in death."

"She did."

Octavian smiled. "There is something beautiful in that, I think. They will write stories about it one day. There is something noble and admirable about it. And I am sorry that this same choice, beautiful though it was, meant that I could not know her better. I am sorry that she had to die. It wasn't right, what happened."

This was, Selene thought, perhaps the closest thing to an apology that she would ever receive from him for the loss of her family. But it wouldn't bring back the dead, she reminded herself. And if he expected her to forgive him, she would not give him that pleasure. "What would you have preferred?"

"I was a younger man then," Octavian said. He looked back to the legions for a moment. "I wanted a Triumph. I wanted glory."

Selene, too, looked out toward the advancing men. The trained discipline of the men meant that the three columns moved like living things. "Is that not what you want now? Isn't that what you want here?"

"Glory? If there is glory here, it belongs to Rome."

"Rome cares nothing for Vellica," Selene said. She saw that a few of the other officers surrounding them tensed up, but none interrupted or seemed to even acknowledge her.

"For Vellica? No. Not even for the whole of Cantabria," Octavian agreed. "But Rome cares for its honor. These lands belong to Rome, and we will not suffer the dishonor of losing them."

"The Cantabrians were here long before Rome claimed these lands."

"This is true. And the pharaohs of old were native Egyptians before your ancestor, Ptolemy, replaced them with Greeks. I don't favor a claim because of its antiquity. I favor a claim because it is true and just and right."

Justice? What justice had Rome ever brought for her? Or for Juba? Where was justice for her dead brothers? For Caesarion?

"It's peace, Selene." There was a fervor to Octavian's voice that brought her attention back to him. She saw that he was staring at her with a focused intensity. "That's what lies beyond this bloodshed," he said. "Perhaps not for these men here. Perhaps not for me or even you. But in generations to come there will be a Rome without war. Without bandits upon the roads. Without squabbles amid petty kings. There will be a peace the likes of which no one has seen before: the *Pax Romana*. That's the dream, Selene. That's the glory. I didn't always realize it before, but I know it now."

"The Peace of Rome." Selene spoke the words as if they were a foreign thing.

"When all the world is Rome," Tiberius said, "there will be no one left to fight."

Selene blinked, speechless as she looked between Augustus and Tiberius, one staring at her, the other staring away. For a moment she wondered if Alexander the Great had ever spoken such words. Had peace been his goal, too?

"Cleopatra understood this," Caesar said.

"My mother?"

"She knew it better than most. My father, Julius. Your father, Mark Antony. She may have loved them, but she was no fool. Egypt is pyramids and tombs in the sand. Its time has come and gone. Rome is the future. She and I wanted the same thing."

Selene didn't know if she wanted to scream or throw up. She shook her head, knowing that she shouldn't be doing so.

If Caesar was upset by her show of disagreement, though, he didn't show it. Instead he straightened up in his saddle, and he swept his arm over the marching legions toward the hillfort ahead. "You tell me Rome doesn't care for Vellica. But don't you see? This land, these people . . . all of it will be Rome. You've seen their contempt for human life. Coming here you saw with your own eyes the carnage they have wrought. They are lawless barbarians, and a restless brutality is all they've ever known. I can change that, Selene. We can all change that. We bring them peace. We bring them Rome."

"The Cantabrian, Caesar," one of the officers said.

Augustus turned in his saddle to look back where Corocotta was striding out of the palisades of the camp, flanked by two praetorians. The little crippled slave girl who served as his translator hurried as fast as she could in his wake, hobbling with a crutch under her arm. The Cantabrian slowed as he passed the wagon, seeming to gauge it with his eyes, and then he was standing beside Selene, towering over her in a way that for a moment made her imagine a bearded, wild-haired Pullo—except that where Pullo was a man who'd been quick to smile and laugh and tousle her hair, Corocotta's face seemed to be fixed in a fierce look of determination, and he acted as if he gave no thought to her presence at all.

"Corocotta," Augustus said. Though on horseback, he didn't need to look down far to address the standing man. "I am glad you have come."

The Cantabrian didn't look back to see if his translator had caught up. He simply began to speak, his rough voice a low rumble.

Panting, appearing pained, the little slave girl came up to stand at his side. "My lord Corocotta," she said between gulping breaths, "he says he is . . . a man of his word. Said he would stand . . . beside the Lord Caesar."

Augustus smiled and nodded toward the cart. "One million Sesterces. I, too, am a man of my word."

Corocotta looked back at the cart, grunted, and then stepped forward ahead of Selene so that he stood between her and the mounted Augustus. The other members of the general staff shifted themselves to give him plenty of space in which to position himself, and Corocotta turned to face the valley below, crossing his arms as he did so. Without looking at the man on horseback beside him, he spoke something in his strange language.

The crippled girl moved forward so that she stood behind Selene, to the right of her master, leaning tiredly on her crutch. "Lord Corocotta says that you started without him," she translated.

Augustus smiled and for the second time in as many minutes he gestured toward the columns that were now halfway across the open valley. "Just getting into position," he said. "You've come at the perfect time. Carisius?"

The field general snapped to attention. "Yes, Caesar?"

"Signal halt."

"Yes, Caesar." Carisius turned back toward the valley, and from the side Selene was certain she saw a smile on his face. "Praetors, signal your centurions. *Consiste.*"

Three other generals nodded and spoke the order to three more men, who in turn spoke to three men who lifted the horns that stood at their feet and hefted them onto their shoulders. In perfect coordination, the three men stepped forward two paces from the group. Moving from left to right, they each blew a single note that echoed over the troops, and Selene recognized that each of the horns—metal tubes that ran in a near-circle from a man's lips around his back and over his shoulder—gave a different sound. Her supposition that each tone was meant for a specific legion was confirmed when the three columns immediately halted their march.

Corocotta grunted, though Selene didn't know if the sound signified approval of the precision or annoyance at the break in the action.

"Very good," Augustus said, and at the same time Selene heard a kind of unintelligible shout from the walls of Vellica. They, too, were getting ready for the fight.

"I believe we have their attention, Caesar," Carisius said.

"Then let's give them something to look at," Augustus replied. "Form up the right and center. Leave the left in column for the flank."

Carisius nodded and signaled to the two praetors of those legions. *"Ad aciem."*

Seconds later, the right and center horns sounded again. And in their wake she heard the distant barking of the centurions ordering the legionnaires into battle lines.

The front rows of the two columns stood still, but behind them the rest of the legions, to Selene's amazement, rolled forward and out, unfolding as they morphed from a vertical line of men to a horizontal one. In a matter of minutes the battle line of the Roman legionnaires appeared to be at least a thousand men wide and perhaps three or four men deep. When the last row locked itself into position, the men in front gave a unified shout and readied their shields in time with a great stomp of feet.

Corocotta growled something, and a moment later Selene heard the little crippled girl behind her translate it: "Corocotta says the obedience of the army is very impressive."

"So it is," Augustus said. "This is the point where the enemy usually runs away."

A couple of the other officers suppressed chuckles as the slave girl translated, but Corocotta did not reply.

For a moment there was silence over the field. Then, to Selene's surprise, the rear gate of Vellica opened and a column of Cantabrian warriors began to issue out, jogging down the curving earthen ramp against the wall of the hillfort. A great cheer went up from the other side of the valley.

The officers around her shifted a little on their feet, and as Selene turned from the valley to look around at them she could see that they, too, were surprised. Several of them were exchanging whispers. Whatever plans the Romans had designed, she decided, a pitched battle on the valley floor was not among them.

From the corner of her eye, Selene caught movement from behind her, and when she turned to look she saw that Corocotta's crippled slave was staring at her. The little girl no longer had the crutch under her arm but had instead moved it forward, almost as if it were a walking stick. Out of instinct, Selene started to smile at her, but her smile froze when the girl silently mouthed a single word: *Go*. The girl's eyes were wide and imploring. She had a look on her face that Selene recognized but could not place. *Go*, she mouthed again.

"Caesar," Carisius said. "Orders?"

Confused, Selene instinctively turned toward the emperor of Rome.

For a moment Augustus appeared to be frowning, but he seemed to catch himself and he let out a lighthearted laugh. "Well, we don't need to open the gate now," he said. "Left legion, form a line. Archers, up a volley. Catapults, load and loose. For victory and Rome!"

As he spoke, Carisius relayed the orders down through the ranks and for a moment it seemed everyone around Selene was shouting at once. All three horns began to sound in complex notes. Below her on the hillside she heard shouts in the trees and an answering of trumpets signaling the readiness of the catapults, whose tops she could see now that she knew to look for them. A cry went up from the legionnaires as the Cantabrians streaming down out of the gate formed into their own lines at the base of the opposing hillside.

Her mother's servants, Selene suddenly remembered. That was what the crippled girl's look had reminded her of: the sorrow and fear and duty and despair that was etched on the faces of her mother's servants after she'd brought them the asp whose venom would take Cleopatra's life and their own.

Go.

High streaking whistles pierced the air: a volley of arrows streaming up from the Roman bows to rain down on the massing Cantabrians.

Heavy thrums and crashes as the taut catapults loosed their missiles up into the sky.

Corocotta roared something beside her, a sound like the doom of a god.

"*Impetus!*" Carisius shouted over the din, and across the valley the horns began resounding and resounding, sending the legions into the charge.

Go.

A trap. Somehow. Some way. To stay was to die.

In the same moment she realized it, over the chaos of the noise, Selene heard Juba shouting her name.

Selene's body tensed to run in response, and the world seemed to slow down as she started to turn back toward the palisades of the Roman encampment. Corocotta's arms, she saw, were no longer crossed. He was turning toward Augustus, reaching for him with hands like great mauling paws. The little slave girl was turning, too: she no longer leaned on her crutch but had pulled it up to brace it against her hip, point out. She was spinning to point it back the way they'd come, back toward the Roman encampment and the group of praetorian guards gathered there. The wrappings, Selene saw, had fallen from its top, revealing it to be a silver-tipped spear, seated in a wide socket. And at its base, gleaming like a liquid flame, was a black stone.

Still turning to run, Selene threw her momentum toward the ground, watching as the girl—crying, trembling—closed her small, fragile hand around the Shard.

The girl screamed, an inhuman, horrifying sound, and fire erupted from the point of the spear, ripping through the air in a white-hot line that lanced into the praetorians. For an instant she saw the clear face of one of the men who'd brought her to Caesar illuminated by the light of a second sun before him, but then that torrent of heat washed over him and melted him into a blinding glare.

Selene closed her eyes from the shocking light of the flame. She hit the ground, rolling flat onto her belly, and the world abruptly lurched into speed once more.

When it did, all she heard was screaming. And when she opened her eyes again, all she saw was fire.

Juba didn't have the Lance of Olyndicus. Neither did Corocotta. A small voice in her head wanted to laugh at what their arrogance had wrought: no one had given thought to the little girl who might kill them all.

In seconds, the hillside around her had been engulfed in chaos and flames. The girl's mouth was frozen open, as if she were still screaming, but no sound came from her throat now. Her body shook, quaking as the divine power of the Shard flowed through her and out through the spear point that she jerked from praetorian to praetorian, burning them alive with the fire of a hundred suns and at the same time running a barrier of flaming earth between the general staff and any help they might get from the encampment. Corocotta was behind her. He had wrestled the emperor of Rome from the saddle, and he had pulled Caesar's own dagger in order to hold it at his captive's throat to ward off any attacks. Most of the other officers were backing away in horror and fear. A few were running down the hillside, away from the fires, toward the line of catapults in the trees below.

Tiberius, Selene saw, was among them. Even from behind she recognized him running away.

As she stared after him, a part of her hoping that the little girl would turn the Lance to follow him, she heard again the sound of Juba's voice, calling her name upon the wind that suddenly swept across her face.

Juba!

A wind!

Selene's hands scrambled into the folds of her dress, searching.

She'd had it. The Palladium. She'd had it right here, standing right here—

As Selene rolled to her side to look back where she'd been—already reaching across the earth in desperation to find the Shard—a darkness passed over the hillside, as if a great canopy had been passed over the sun, sending all into shadow.

A deep, threatening rumble broke overhead.

Selene's arm was outstretched before her, and with wide eyes she saw the fine hairs upon it stiffening and rising, stretching toward the sky. In twin terror and fascination, she rolled to her back and stared up at a sky that had been, moments earlier, bright with the blue of dawn.

No longer. Dark gray clouds were forming up out of the air, as if by some magic they'd been pulled out of the ether itself. They streamed together as they were born, coalescing and spinning, squeezing each other into a spinning, roiling mass that flashed and rumbled from the power within.

It had been a long time since Selene had believed in the gods. She'd been nine years old when she'd learned that the One God, if he'd ever existed, was dead.

But still in this moment she prayed for mercy from whatever god had come with such vengeance to behold.

Closer, she heard Carisius shouting above the din of fire and wind and the sounds of war still raging in the valley below. "Riders! The flank! To arms!"

Selene blinked, the world slowing again as she looked away from the gathering combustion of the heavens to where Carisius, still somehow on horseback, was pointing off down the road leading away from the encampment. There were a dozen riders pounding up the road there. Cantabrian riders.

And another rider was in front of them: Juba. Beautiful Juba. In his hands he held the Trident of Poseidon. In his face he held agony and determination.

He twisted in the saddle, looking back at the pursuing riders even as the hooves of his steed kicked clods of earth into a kind of thick rain. He held the Trident out, facing them.

Selene felt the sonic pulse of the thunderous crash in nearly the same instant that she saw the bolt of lightning tear down from the clouds above. It impacted the Trident or Juba—or both—and then it ripped out and into the riders behind him. There was a flash and a crack of sound like the shattering of a stone, and the middle of the line of Cantabrian riders exploded.

The other riders fell back. Juba rode on, bearing down upon her, the look on his face a near match for the wild, mindless terror in the eyes of the horse beneath him.

Corocotta shouted out, and a blast of colder air rushed across Selene's skin as the blazing fire of the Lance suddenly fell silent. The little slave was turning around now, following Corocotta's instructions. The Shard in her hands was coming around, too, as she hobbled tiredly to face the other way. Toward Juba.

At last, Selene saw the Palladium. It was on the ground, fallen into the grass where she'd stood. She lunged for it, gripping it hard, leaping into the darkness within, pulling the power up as quickly as she could.

Faster! her mind screamed. Faster!

In her haste she couldn't control it. Every time she tried to pull the power up, it slid out of her grip, like a fish fumbling back into the waters from which it had come.

She opened her eyes in the horrible realization that she wasn't ready, that she wouldn't be able to help. She saw the little slave girl unleash the power of the Lance once more, in a line of pure flame that shot out at her husband.

In an instant there was an explosion that knocked the Palladium from Selene's grip and flung her backward into the grass.

Selene blinked up into the darkness of a stormy sky and saw that a torrent of rain was coming down like a stream, like a waterfall of slashing mist that descended down and down to the Trident in the hands of her beloved.

Juba had dismounted, and he was trudging forward, driving the rain before him through the Trident, where it impacted

against the slave girl's fire and sent both heavenward in a gey-
ser of angry steam.

The slave girl made a sound like a long groan, and she staggered backward a step.

Juba strode forward, foot by agonizing foot.

And then he was there, almost beside Selene, nothing but
the hot, wet smoke of fire and water in the air. He fell to his
knees, face anguished. With one hand he reached out, straining to hold the Trident against the torrents of energy that were
pounding into him, straining to reach her hand.

Their fingertips touched, skin to skin, and began to curl
around the other. A lifeline. A way out.

A darkness beyond the storm rose up from behind her, and
before she could cry out, Corocotta's fist fell heavy against
Juba's cheek. The Trident fell from her husband's suddenly limp
hand. There was a mighty roar of air and water, fire and storm,
all swallowed up into the heavens—and then the powers that
had beaten down upon the hillside were gone.

The other Cantabrian riders were there, dismounting and
running. Selene saw one take the slave girl up into his arms
as she collapsed. Two grabbed Octavian and began binding
his hands.

From somewhere came the sounds of shouts and blades
striking one another, and a small part of her mind wondered if
Carisius and the other generals were fighting to reach Caesar.

But she didn't really care. What mattered was Juba.

She lifted herself to crawl forward, to cover him with her
body, to somehow protect him in all this madness, but when
she looked up she saw Corocotta looking down upon her,
grinning. He barked something and two more of his men hurried up and began dragging Juba away. A third had a bundle
of cloth and went for the Trident.

"No!" Selene screamed, scrambling to get up, to go to her love.

Something heavy struck her on the back of the skull. The world reeled, and she pitched forward.

She was vaguely aware of her body falling on something hard and round. Some strangely detached part of her mind wondered if it was a rock of some kind, but then all the voices of her mind fell silent and she drifted away into the dark.

13

The Island in the Nile

As he stood at the railing of the boat ferrying them up the Nile, Vorenus was glad for many things. There was the sun rising on another day. There was the old friend at his side whom he'd long thought dead. There was the prospect of ending his long journey to Alexandria and back. There was the fact that the ferry would reach the island long before the heat of the day sent the cooler breeze that was moving over the waters into retreat.

But most of all, he was glad that his feet had finally stopped hurting. After surviving the ambush, he and Pullo had followed Khenti's dying advice and left the canal, heading with all possible speed north to the road along the Mediterranean shore.

All possible speed wasn't as fast as it used to be.

If they'd not stolen two horses from a farm on the second day, Vorenus feared that they would be out there still, trudging along in the dirt. He was fifty-two now, and while that didn't seem to him to be a particularly lengthy age, Vorenus had to admit that he'd not been entirely kind to his body over those decades. And now he could hardly remember having felt so many pains in his feet and in his aching joints—except that he seemed to be thinking that very same thought more and more these days.

That's what getting old was, he guessed. Each day more tired than the last.

Each day, perhaps, less useful than the last.

Yet whatever toll those years had taken on him, Vorenus knew that they'd done far worse to his friend.

Pullo had tried hard to be strong, to keep up with Vorenus, just as he had for so many decades of their serving together in the Roman legions—just as he had in their last posting in Alexandria, when they'd served the royal family of Cleopatra— but his body was simply too broken to do so.

Of course, it was a kind of miracle that he had lived at all.

Pullo had refused to tell the tale of his survival and his sub-sequent years—"I'll only speak it once," he'd said when they lay down to sleep that first night—but if he didn't know bet-ter about the nonexistence of divinity, Vorenus would think it truly the work of a god that the man still breathed. He had seen with his own eyes the amount of rock that Pullo had brought down upon himself in order to secure their escape from Alexandria with the Ark. It was impossible to think any man could have lived through it.

Except here he was. Bent and battered. Scarred and sore. But breathing. And despite it all, still the man he'd always known: quick to laugh, loyal to the end.

Ahead of them, the wide, slow surface of the Nile split apart. Between the two arms of the river was the sandstone head of an island ringed by a shoreline of round rocks and thick water grasses. Palms and other green trees rose beyond them, adding their lighter scents to the heavier smells of the mud-laden river.

"Is that it?" Pullo asked.

Vorenus nodded, forcing himself to swallow down the instinctive smile he felt forming on his face whenever Pullo spoke. "It is. Elephantine Island."

"It's so close to Alexandria."

"I suppose so." Vorenus glanced over his shoulder. There were a dozen other passengers on the ferry, all of them native Egyptian laborers. Not one of them showed the slightest interest in the conversation between the two Romans in traveling clothes standing at the bow of the vessel. And even if they had been interested, from the looks of them, Vorenus was quite sure none would understand the Latin in which he conversed with Pullo. "The Ark had been housed here before, though. There was a temple for it already here. That was important to Hannah. And there were allies here. It was safe."

"Was," Pullo said.

Vorenus sighed in agreement. Pullo had known little about the young man who'd hired Seker to ambush them on the canal, but he'd known that he was probably a scholar of some kind. One of the prostitutes that Pullo had helped protect during his years as Seker's personal thug had called the man her "little astrologer." That and the fact that he'd known where to find Vorenus could point to only one conclusion: the visit to the Great Library had been compromised. And that meant that anything discussed there, including the location of the Ark, had also been compromised.

Vorenus had been brooding on the matter during the days of their journey across the plains to the sea and thence to the Nile. He'd been thinking about it every day since, as they made their way up the mighty river, passing ancient pyramids and temples.

No matter how much he turned the matter over in his mind, though, his conclusion was always the same.

The Ark had to be moved.

Hannah would fight it, he knew. She believed it was some-how the bonds of fate that the Ark had returned to the temple where it had lain in secrecy from the time it had been stolen away from Jerusalem, until it had been moved to the land of Kush, farther up the Nile to the south. Her family had kept the Ark safe through those centuries, had kept it safe through the centuries beyond after it had fallen into the hands of Alexander and been placed in the hidden chamber built be-neath his greatest city to protect it. And now Hannah had managed to bring it safely back here, a new home in old ruins. Her brother had died to see it happen. The other keepers had died. She wouldn't want to leave.

And that meant Caesarion wouldn't want to leave. He was twenty-one years old and in love.

"A nice place to live," Pullo said.

It was true. Elephantine was like a bright green teardrop in the rolling waters of the Nile. It was beautiful, and it was peaceful in ways that Vorenus had learned more and more to appreciate. "It's not Alexandria," he said.

"Some parts of Alexandria are nicer than others."

"True," Vorenus said, once more wondering what Pullo had done and seen in their time apart.

The boat tacked and slid through the water to the east. Soon Elephantine began to pass by on their right as they made their way under sail against the current. Looking ahead, Vore-nus could just see the first blocks of old buildings and weath-ered columns rising out from the verdant vegetation that covered the quiet island.

Pullo saw the architecture, too. "It's beautiful. But an odd place for a Jewish temple."

"Well, this all started as a trading center," Vorenus ex-plained. "A real mix of people. The first cataract has long marked—"

"Cataract?"

"Rapids in the river. There are five or six of them, I've heard. You'll see the first just upstream of the island. For a long time, the first cataract marked the border of Egypt. Farther south was the kingdom of Kush."

"Where the Ark was before Alexandria?"

"Good memory," Vorenus said, beaming over at his friend. As Alexandria was falling to Rome, their old friend Didymus had brought them to the Temple of Serapis, where they'd met Hannah and the other keepers of the Ark. There they'd learned much about the history of the Shards and how that particular artifact had passed from Egypt to Jerusalem and back. "I'm impressed you can remember that," he teased.

Pullo grinned, and for a moment it felt as if they were back in the legion. "Don't be too impressed, though. It's about all I remember. The king kept it, right? And then he made an agreement with Alexander the Great: the conqueror would leave Kush alone, but in return the Ark would be kept safe in Alexandria. Is that close?"

"Essentially. They secretly used the Ark to help build the city, including the construction of the Third Temple to house it."

"A third one?"

"That's what Hannah calls it, though as many places as the Ark has been I don't know what makes something a temple or not in her eyes. I think maybe it has something to do with the design of it. Or maybe how long the Ark was there. The first two were in Jerusalem. The third was in Alexandria, and she sometimes calls this one the fourth. But since it was here before it ever went to Alexandria, and somewhere in Kush between . . . well, I don't know. I guess I haven't actually thought to ask, but I'm sure Hannah has her reasons."

"She's a remarkable girl," Pullo said. "I remember that."

"A woman now," Vorenus corrected. "We're getting old, remember?"

"Can't forget that even if I'd like to."

"Also, you'd figure it out soon enough, but I might as well tell you: she and Caesarion—"

"I knew it!" Pullo cut him off with a hearty laugh that also reminded Vorenus of younger times. Then the big man clapped his back—a sudden blow of camaraderie that, while painful, was something else he had missed all these years. "I knew it that night. The way he looked at her. I knew it." Pullo beamed—proud, Vorenus suspected, of both his own keen observation and Caesarion's choice.

Either way, Vorenus couldn't help but smile, too. "I think everyone saw it. And the important thing is that he's happy. Truly so. She's been good to him. And good for him. It was hard, you know. He lost his mother and his home that night."

"A kingdom, too. Egypt would have been his, Vorenus. Rome, too. *All* of it should be his."

"You know he never wanted any of that," Vorenus replied. Caesarion's status as the son of both Julius Caesar and Cleopatra had meant he was destined to rule the world, and they both knew that he would have been an extraordinary ruler—most especially because he didn't want the power for its own sake. It was that same status that had made him Octavian's foremost enemy during the civil war, the reason that his continued existence couldn't be known to anyone.

They were silent for a minute as the ferry swept into another tack on its way up the river. The colonnade that marked the location of the small harbor on the southeast corner of the island was just coming into view. Farther upstream, on the mainland shore of the river, a group of fishing boats was moving into the little town of Syene, which housed the local Roman garrison.

"I heard the boys died," Pullo said, his voice tightening up. "I assume he knows?"

Vorenus nodded, remembering Caesarion's younger half-siblings, the children Cleopatra had born to Mark Antony. "He does. Ptolemy Philadelphus died not long after they reached Rome. Just an illness, we heard. Bad luck. Alexander Helios died only a little later."

"He was always so sickly."

"His sister is well, though," Vorenus said, forcing himself to focus on happier thoughts. "I was actually there when our little Cleopatra Selene stood up to Octavian. It was extraordinary."

Pullo raised an eyebrow. "Oh? I would have liked to see that. Always hated that devious prick."

"She was made to marry Juba the Numidian as a result. The one who used the Trident against us at Actium."

"He's the one who cut my legs," Pullo interrupted. "The one Caesarion fought off."

Vorenus looked over at him, surprised at the sudden sharp hostility in his friend's voice, and the unexpected disclosure of what had happened while they were apart. He wondered if he should press him about it, despite Pullo's insistence on only telling the tale once.

Pullo said nothing more, though, and Vorenus decided to leave it alone. The ferry was turning into Elephantine's little harbor. They could see workers moving about the docks as they brought in the catches of the early morning and directed cargo from one place to another. "Well, I have a hard time believing it myself, after Actium and all," Vorenus finally said, "but every report we've had seems to be that they're happy."

Pullo grunted.

"Anyway, they're bound to be king and queen of Mauretania, from what I hear. And I'm just glad she's well. She's a good person in her soul. They all were."

Pullo nodded, and then his eyes widened as he looked out over the water at Elephantine. "Well, speaking of the prick, there he is."

There was a small square at the head of the docks, and standing there, more than twice as tall as a man, was a bronze statue of Augustus Caesar, shining in the early morning light, his eyes of glass and stone turned to look down upon the water with a look of calm, penetrating authority.

"Our emperor is rather fond of himself." Vorenus sighed. "The idea, I think, is that anyone who even passes by the island knows they've entered the territory of Rome."

Pullo chewed the inside of his lip. "Caesarion has to see this every day?"

"He doesn't come down here much, I suppose. Our rooms are on the other side of the island, and he and Hannah don't much leave the temple where the Ark is, anyway."

Behind the massive statue of Augustus there was a low wall that had been put up for defense in a long-ago era, ringing what was clearly a motley assemblage of stone buildings. Among the many gray threads of morning fires weaving their way through the sky were a few thicker columns of smoke rising from the town: the fires, Vorenus knew, that were burning in the courtyards of the several temples on the island. One to Khnum, the ram-headed god of the river's dangerous cataracts. Another was to Satis, the gazelle-horned goddess of the river's life-giving floods. And amid still others, there was a dilapidated temple built to honor the one true God of the Jews—once real, but now as equally gone as his counterparts on the island. It was there that the Ark had found its temporary home.

"Someone ought to tear it down," Pullo said.

"What?"

"The statue." Pullo was staring at the bronze statue of Caesar as if he might strike it down himself. "These are Caesarion's lands. It isn't right."

Vorenus patted the big man on the back. "I know. But Caesarion doesn't care. Not really. He cares for the safety of the Ark, Pullo. And his love of Hannah. Nothing else matters, bless him."

Pullo sighed, but he nodded. "You said allies."

"What?"

"You said before that Hannah wanted the Ark here because it had allies. Are there more keepers here? More Jews?"

Vorenus smiled. "More keepers? No. More Jews? Well, that's a trickier question."

"You're hiding something. You've always been a bit of a scholar like that, you know."

"Being smarter than you hardly makes a man a scholar," Vorenus said.

Pullo laughed again. "True enough. By that measure there'd be a dog or two in Didymus' care."

The ferry slid up against the dock, and the river water that rolled off its wake sloshed against the wooden pilings. Two crewmen jumped over to the dock boards, carrying lines that they pulled tight and hastily tied off to cleats. One or two of their fellow passengers stood to disembark at midship. Together, Pullo and Vorenus began to move in that direction.

"Don't be too hard on yourself, my friend," Vorenus said as they walked. "I've never met a dog who could out-think you. Though one or two of these holy cats that the Egyptians like might give you a run for your money. But anyway, I don't mean to be tricky. Not really. It's just that our allies here call themselves Jews, but I don't think most Jews would agree that they are."

The other passengers who were leaving had already reached the dock, and Pullo motioned for Vorenus to go first. "I don't understand."

"Neither did I," Vorenus admitted. "They're called the Therapeutae."

Pullo just stared. "Thera—"

"Don't worry. You'll learn soon enough." Vorenus stepped out onto the dock with his left foot, keeping his right on board the ferry as he offered his crippled friend a hand to help limp up and out of the boat. "Suffice it to say, my dear Titus Pullo, that you're about to find out that the world is a far bigger and stranger place than you or I ever knew."

14

THE OUTLAW KING

CANTABRIA, 26 BCE

Juba awoke with a headache that throbbed like a hammer inside his skull. Eyes still shut, he groaned.

"Thank the gods," said a familiar voice.

Juba squeezed his eyes shut even harder against the pulsing behind them, but he couldn't squeeze out the pain. He took a deep breath and found the air thick with humidity and the scents of human waste. He shook back a stomach-curdle of revulsion and released the breath in a long exhale that came out as an anguished sigh. Then he willed his eyes open.

Octavian was kneeling beside him, his features lit by a dim candle. There was a look of honest relief upon his face. "I thought you were dead."

Juba closed his eyes again and raised a hand to his forehead. His fingers were rougher than he remembered, and his arm ached with a bone-deep exhaustion he'd never experienced before, but it still felt good to rub his forehead. "I'm alive," he rasped. His throat was drier than it ought to have been, too.

His jaw had hurt when he flexed it, and when he brought his fingers down against it they found his face swollen and bruised, hot and painful to the touch. Trying to think back through the throbbing in his forehead, he remembered Coro-cotta punching him. Right when he was reaching for Selene—

"Selene!" He gasped, flinching from the pain of it.

He started to rise up, the need to see her overwhelming the pain of his body, but Octavian's hands caught him at the shoulders and kept him from moving too far. "Go easy, brother. She's not here. They didn't take her."

Juba panted for a few seconds in a horrible mix of pain and fear as his panic subsided. Then he nodded and allowed himself to fall back down again. He lay for a while, eyes closed, swallowing the angry pains, hoping the throbbing would abate. When it showed no signs of doing so, he tried to focus on questions. Why was he so tired? And what had happened? Octavian said Selene wasn't taken. Which meant they had been?

He found himself instinctively starting to grit his teeth, so he forced himself to relax.

Start simple, he told himself. Where am I?

He opened his eyes again, and he looked around.

They were in a room. A very small one.

A windowless room, he saw as he slowly stretched his neck to peer into the half-light. Two simple cots, a clay pot for the voiding of bowels, a single tallow candle burning beside it, and a heavy wooden door.

Not a room, Juba realized. A cell.

"I need to get up," he said.

It took his stepbrother a few moments to respond, and Juba could see him frowning in thought. But when he did reply, it was in a kind and agreeable tone. "Okay," he said. "Just go slow."

This time Octavian's hands helped to lift him as Juba rolled into a sitting position. He grunted, groaned, and then swung his feet off the cot on which he'd been stretched out. The leather soles beneath his feet scuffled on a floor that might have been hardened clay. He flexed his legs against the resistance of the earth, and he was rewarded with fresh pains in his muscles to compete with the throbbing in his head.

Octavian let him go and shuffled backward to sit down on his own cot. The eyes of the emperor of Rome, the man who had been proclaimed Augustus Caesar, were dark with exhaustion, and he moved with the weariness of one who had been broken.

"How long?" Juba asked.

"I think it is only a day after the battle. Perhaps two. It's hard to tell the night from the day here."

Juba coughed, wincing at the strain of his rib cage. His head still throbbed.

"You don't look well," Octavian said.

Juba looked up and grinned weakly. "Nor do you. Are you hurt?"

Octavian shook his head. "I thought for a while that . . . well, I didn't think you would recover."

"I'm fine. Just weak. Where are we?"

"In Vellica." Octavian's voice was flat as he told Juba how the battle had begun, how they had been surprised by the opening of the gates of Vellica, and how Corocotta's slave had then surprised them further by attacking the Roman leaders with the Lance while a hidden Cantabrian cavalry force had swept in to carry them away.

Juba nodded. It was, he thought, a beautiful plan on the part of the Cantabrians. Then he frowned. "Why did they need to open the gates, though? Why risk that engagement if their plan was to capture you?"

"I think they wanted to be prepared to charge and wipe out all of us if the legions went into disarray."

"They didn't?"

Octavian actually managed a slight smile despite his tiredness. "They brought you and I around the battlefield and through those gates. Already the legions were advancing and the Cantabrians were preparing to fall in and close the gates."

"That's good," Juba said, then wondered why he should care for the fate of the Roman legions. He stared down at the hard earthen floor between them, lost in thought.

Footsteps marked the approach of men beyond the door, and Juba looked up to see Octavian stand and straighten himself. For a man who had lost a battle and been living in a cell for a day or more, shitting in a pot, he managed to look remarkably regal.

There was a sound of a bar being moved, a lock turning free, and then the door swung inward in a wash of the light of a torch.

Juba, squinting through both the pain of his aching head and the shocking brightness of the flame, saw that two Cantabrian men had entered the room. He first looked at Octavian, who stood with his back straight and chin high. One of the men smirked, then looked over at Juba. "Awake," he said in rough Latin. "Good. The king requests your presence now."

The man turned to his companion and said something to him in their barbarian tongue. An order, Juba guessed, as the man approached to help him stand and walk.

Juba thought for a moment about refusing to go. He thought about demanding to know where it was that they were being taken. But then he realized that it didn't really matter. He was too tired to object. Too broken to fight. So instead he simply nodded when the man stepped over to him, and together they began the painful labor of lifting him to his feet and getting him to walk again.

. . .

Their prison had been underground, housed beneath a small building that had been built for this purpose. And while every movement brought fresh hurt to his aching body, Juba decided that for now stairs were his greatest enemy: to reach the top he had to be held upright between Octavian and one of the Cantabrians as they struggled to make their way up and out of the stench-laden hole.

When they finally got him outside the building, Juba asked them to stop while he tried to straighten his back and stand on his own. There was still a trace of the sun's fading glow in the sky, he could see, but stars were already beginning to light the firmament. The air was cool and crisp on his skin, and it tasted of the wood-burning cook fires that were so familiar from the Roman camp across the valley.

His stomach rumbled.

Now that the flatter ground of the fort lay before him, Juba insisted that they let him walk on his own. It was painful, but it was, he thought, a good pain. Blood was moving back into his limbs, and whatever it was that the Trident had taken from him, he felt like moving would begin to get it back.

The two guards shrugged, seemingly happy not to help him further, and then they led Juba and Octavian through the winding labyrinth of buildings that were crowded inside the hillfort. There was movement and noise seemingly everywhere. Juba saw hundreds of men and women, their faces lit by torch-light, but none jeered or spoke to them as they passed. Only a little boy reacted—making a gesture like his stomach was bursting out. What it meant among these people, Juba did not know.

Around another building, they found themselves facing a wooden stairway that climbed up the wall of the fort. Juba's mind wailed, but he resolutely began climbing the steps one by one, leaning against the wall for support. In the end,

Octavian once more had to get his shoulder under Juba's to help him make the climb.

The stair ended at the walkway that ran along the inside of the top of the wall. Torches set at intervals along this battlement hungrily licked the night air, and beyond them, in the distance across the valley, Juba saw the lights of the Roman encampment. His heart ached in his chest, and he longed to shout Selene's name—but of course no voice could carry so far. For all that he could reach her, his wife might as well be in distant Rome.

The hulking figure of Corocotta stood with a small gathering of other Cantabrians not far away upon the battlement, above what Juba recognized as the gate that Octavian had hoped to breach during the battle. When they got closer, Juba saw that the little slave girl stood beside Corocotta, leaning tiredly upon a simple wooden walking stick. Like everyone else, she had her back to them as she stared out into the night.

When the guards stopped short and announced themselves, Corocotta and a few of the others turned and looked at them appraisingly. "Hail, Caesar," Corocotta said, smirking.

Juba blinked in surprise, but Octavian appeared unfazed. "No interpreters this time?"

Of course he speaks Latin, Juba realized, kicking himself for underestimating the man. He had only pretended not to do so in order to have his slave with him as an interpreter.

"I am not as uncivilized as you think," the big man said. He nodded to the guards and then turned back to what lay beyond the wall.

The two guards pushed Juba and Octavian forward toward the wooden parapet, and at last they saw what held the attention of the Cantabrians. Seven thick stakes had been set into the ground there in a row. Two were empty, but Roman legionnaires were tied upon the remaining five. Or what was left of the legionnaires, at least. Only the man on the last of the stakes was still alive, and he was weeping in a panicked horror. The man on the opposite end of the row, Juba saw, was charred and blackened, his face frozen in the same kind of contorted scream that Juba recognized from the ambush of the Roman supply train. The three dead between them weren't burned, but they were covered in sheets of blood that had streamed from their eyes, their noses, their gaping mouths. Their red-stained corpses were recognizably Roman only by the garments that still clung whole to what was left of their blood-drained bodies.

Juba had seen this sight, too. He had done this to a man once, moving his blood, tearing him apart from the inside, pushing the life from him in torrents as he writhed and choked. He had held the Trident in his own two hands and *willed* it to happen, murdering his slave, Quintus, upon Octavian's order.

For his silence. And so that Octavian could see if it could be done.

Juba's stomach lurched and he hunched over, dry-heaving the emptiness of his belly.

Corocotta made a rumbling sound that might have been a laugh. "You would prefer your Roman crucifixion, I am sure," he said. "But we do not have the skill for that art here. And I am not uncivilized. I give them a choice. More than you would do for my people, I am sure." He nodded toward the empty stakes. "Two have chosen life."

Juba got control of his heaving. Octavian, he saw, had not seemed to react to the terrible scene. "Your people," he said, his voice as calm as if they were speaking of the pleasantly cool night air. "You're no outlaw. You're king of the Cantabrians."

Corocotta smiled behind his thick beard. "And king of you, Caesar. Does that make me king of Rome?"

"Rome is greater than one man. The legions pressed on without me."

"This is true," Corocotta said. His arm swept out into the darkness of the valley. Juba tried not to imagine the corpses that probably still rotted there, the feasting of the wolves and carrion fowl. "I had expected them to run. I brought out my army so that they could charge into the rout. I expected to destroy three legions yesterday, I expected three golden eagles in my hands. It is a credit to your men, but it disappoints me that we failed in this."

"Rome is greater than one man," Octavian repeated.

"So you say. And we shall see. But whatever my disappointment, it is nothing against what else I did not expect." He looked over to Juba, who tried to stand straight despite his show of weakness. "When you spoke of the Lance of Olyndicus, I was surprised that you knew so much. I now see why."

The king barked out a command, and two of his men came forward with a bundle of cloth. They bowed as they held it out before the little slave girl, who pulled the wrappings away and then handed off her walking stick before she lifted up the Trident of Poseidon and set it before her. The wooden staff had been sawn down, Juba could see, so that the head of the Trident, and the black stone of the Shard that gave it power, was no longer at his eye level but hers. She leaned on it, her hands gripping the wood and not the winding metal snakes around the Shard. Juba could not see her face, but her shoulders were sunken in a look of pure exhaustion and despair, and they trembled as if she wept.

"I am fascinated by this," Corocotta said. "It is like the Lance, yet it is very different. Though we have not yet managed what you did, we have been learning how it works."

"You are killing these men in cold blood," Octavian said.

"You are invaders here. I do not think you have the right to object. And we need to learn how it works." He gestured back toward Juba. "Did you not make your slave do the same?"

"He's not my slave."

The king scoffed, "He looks like one."

Octavian faltered—the first time that any emotion had troubled his demeanor since they'd heard the footsteps approaching the cell. "He is my brother."

Corocotta laughed, a long and mocking sound that rumbled over the battlements and into the darkness. "And you think me cruel," he finally said.

Juba's body felt shattered, but as much as he'd gone through he felt like he would recover. But this girl—this crippled slave girl—was she a sign that there was a point where he wouldn't be able to do so? Was that what had happened to her? "It's killing her," he said.

Corocotta turned. "It is killing you, is it not? Little by little, it takes what you are. Some comes back, Caesar's brother. But not all." His voice was like a sneer for a moment, but then he returned to his casual tone and went back to addressing Octavian. "Many cannot use the Lance at all. It is hard to find someone who can survive the powers, and I think the same must be true of this object, too. That is the reason you will not use it yourself, Caesar. You are no fool. This one of mine does not have long before she is used up, I think. And then I will find another. They say that Olyndicus used it himself, but he would have been a fool to do so. Like us, he surely used a slave."

A slave. Juba stared at the back of the little girl, at her trembling shoulders. For all that she had tried to harm him, he wanted to take her in his arms and hold her while they wept.

Octavian had not replied, and the king of the Cantabrians turned back to the whimpering legionnaire below. "And that brings us to your choice, my friend," he bellowed. "Give your allegiance to me, as two of your brothers have, or we see if she is more efficient at killing a man this time around. That last one did not suffer long."

Juba felt Octavian's body tense up beside him, and then his stepbrother sprang forward, leaping into the side of the little girl and sending her sprawling as he wrested the Trident from her hands, spun it around to Corocotta, and placed his hands upon the twin snakes that coiled around the head of the weapon and the blacker-than-black stone at its center.

He shouted at Juba to run, and then his voice choked off as his eyes rolled back into his head and his body began to shake as if an unseen giant had gripped him in an angry fist.

"Octavian!" Juba shouted. He tried to lunge forward, but the guards easily caught him and held him. He watched, powerless, as Augustus Caesar fell to the ground, spasming, his knuckles turning white as they gripped the Trident harder and harder.

Corocotta laughed again, and after a few seconds he loomed up over the fallen man and harmlessly kicked the Trident out of his grip with his boot. Octavian's body jerked once, twice, and then was still but for its ragged, gasping breaths as his lungs fought to keep him alive.

"Take them back," he said to the guards. "See that Caesar lives." Then he motioned to the little slave girl to retrieve the fallen Shard before turning back to the legionnaire in the darkness below. "As for you," he boomed. "It seems Caesar has spoken."

15

The Peace of Rome

Standing at the main gate of the Roman encampment, staring out over the night-shadowed valley to the distant glimmer of torchlights that marked the battlements of Vellica, Selene thought of many things. There was the hopelessness of knowing that Juba had been taken behind those distant walls and there was nothing she could do for him. There was the despair of knowing that although she had managed to protect the Palladium when her body had fallen upon it, it was useless in the face of what she had seen of the powers of the Lance and the Trident. There was the horrible awareness of the unburied dead that littered the darkness below.

But above all in this moment, she thought of a growing discomfort in her mind, the possibility that Octavian was right: that he and Cleopatra had wanted the same thing.

Just the thought of it made Selene feel ill.

But was it true?

And if it was true, what did it mean?

She had been ten years old when Octavian had taken Alexandria. Ten years old when she had seen her father's bloody body cradled in her mother's arms. Ten years old when she'd run from that horror, intending to somehow find Octavian and kill him. Ten years old when she'd sworn to him that she would marry Juba the Numidian to preserve the life of Lucius Vorenus. Ten years old when she'd smuggled the asp to her imprisoned mother, pushing the basket forward with its offering of death.

She had sworn to her mother that she would avenge her. It was the last time she'd seen her alive. They were her final words to her. And not a day had gone by in the years since that she hadn't dreamed of that vengeance, plotted it. She'd fallen in love with Juba, and that, too, had become part of the plan.

All to destroy Octavian. All to destroy Rome.

And yet . . . was Octavian right?

The Peace of Rome. That's what he'd called it. And Rome *was* safe, after all. No bandits in the woods. No fighting upon the streets. She'd enjoyed that security every time she'd snuck out with Tiberius to wander the streets at night. She'd known it even on the night she'd used him to steal the Palladium.

What was it that Tiberius had said on the morning of the battle? Make the world Rome, and there'd be no one left to fight.

Impossible, of course. No one could conquer the world. Even Alexander had failed.

But it was true that within Rome's borders there could be peace. Had that been what her mother had sought from first Caesar and then Mark Antony? Forge an alliance with Rome, become one with that eternal city, and there could be peace from one side of the sea to the other. Security and prosperity.

The Peace of Rome.

Selene shook her head. Even beyond her love for him, she felt she needed Juba at times like this. A few years older, a few years more experienced in knowing the ways of the world, he often saw to the heart of a problem. It had been Juba who had persuaded her that killing Octavian alone would solve nothing. It was what Octavian stood for that needed to be destroyed. It was Rome itself.

But at what price? Was the Peace of Rome a truly horrible dream? Or was it perhaps something real, something tangible that was worth setting aside their need to avenge the fallen members of their families?

Selene stared out into the darkness, out at the hillfort that was so close and yet a world away.

Carisius and the other members of the general staff had been locked away with Tiberius in the days since Octavian and Juba had been taken. They were working hard to keep up the facade that Caesar was with them, too; from the moment Selene awoke after the attack, she had been aware of the Roman leaders' efforts to hide what had happened that morning.

Part of this secrecy, she knew, was a matter of simple political expedience. The generals understood that it was best for morale—especially in the face of the army's defeat in the battle, after the attack on the general staff resulted in a loss of strategic control upon the field—if the men thought Caesar remained in authority within the camp. The other reason for the secrecy, however, was that the leaders simply didn't understand what had happened. She had heard as much as she lay still upon the field, for the leaders had huddled there, arguing about what had been done and what needed now to be done. There had been a storm, they agreed. There had been fire and lightning. But nothing of it made sense. She'd heard them whispering what they had seen to one another, each man disbelieving the other's account, each man unwilling to believe even his own eyes. Tricks of nature, some said. Cantabrian magic, others argued. And still others thought it was the vengeance of the gods for some Roman offense. Whatever the reason chosen, though, all were agreed that the fewer who knew what was happening, the better.

None of them had asked Selene what she thought of it all. And none had seemed to give the slightest heed to her as she tucked away the little statue upon which she had fallen and hurried back to her tent to hide it once more.

Selene had later tried to meet with them, to learn what she could of what was happening, but the praetorian guards had turned her away from the tent. Whatever plans they had for getting back Caesar and her husband, they clearly did not require the presence of a fifteen-year-old girl, no matter how much she had experienced and how mature she was.

Selene sighed into the night, and she tightened the shawl that she had pulled around her neck. She didn't want to return to her tent, didn't want to face the emptiness there, but Juba was beyond her reach now.

Perhaps, Selene thought to herself as she turned and began the walk back toward her tent, the morning might bring news. For all she knew, the morning might even bring Juba back into her arms. She could kiss and hold him, and she could tell him how maybe, just maybe, they could learn to live in the Peace of Rome, the peace of Augustus Caesar. She didn't know what it would be to live in a world without vengeance, and she didn't know whether her mother would be disappointed or proud that she would even think of it.

She had just decided that the answer was a little of both, when she came around a corner, saw her tent, and then froze.

Someone was inside it. Pale light spilled from the thin crack of the flap, flashing to the shadow of movement within.

For a second, her heart leapt in her chest, but then she noticed how quiet the camp had grown around this place, how no one walked the paths nearby. And she saw the shapes of the praetorians in the darkness to either side of the tent. She did not need to turn in order to know that Caesar's guards had melted out of the gloom behind her, too.

Not that she intended to run. There was no sense in doing so, for she had nowhere to go.

Instead, Cleopatra Selene once more pulled tight the shawl about her neck, letting its closeness be a comfort. And then, holding her head high as a queen of Egypt should, she walked to the tent and Tiberius.

.   .   .

Augustus Caesar's adopted son was alone in the lamp-lit tent, sitting at the small table that had been set at the foot of the bed Selene shared with her husband. That bed was exactly as she had left it: the feather-stuffed mattress atop its raised metal frame covered over with a fine white linen sheet, crowned with pillows set against the iron lattice of the headboard.

Little else about the space was so pristine. The wooden drawers of her traveling dresser had been pulled and over-turned, scattering clothing upon the slatted floor. The desk had been torn through. And in the corner, someone had opened Juba's locked chest by taking an ax to the wood. It was splintered like an open wound, broken nearly in half in the intensity of the search. Whether or not the lower compart-ment had been breached—where the Aegis and the Palladium were hidden—Selene could not tell.

Tiberius did not look up when she entered. Before him on the small table were a clay pitcher of wine and two gilded cups—hers and Juba's—a strangely peaceful scene amid the chaos surrounding him. The cup facing him was empty, but his hand was wrapped around the other, and he stared into the thick red of the wine within.

"How dare you enter this space," Selene said. "My husband—"

"Is not here," Tiberius interrupted. His eyes were dark and

unreadable when they slowly rose to meet hers. "And we don't know if he ever will be again."

Selene swallowed. Was that a threat? A portent of some news that they had received? "Until we know one way or another, I—"

"Knowing," he said, looking back into his drink as he interrupted her once more. "That's so much of it, isn't it? What we know and what we don't know." His fingers turned the cup before him.

Selene instinctively wanted to run for the chest, to see what he knew, but of course that was foolish. The worst thing she could do would be to draw attention to it. So what would her mother do?

She was just starting to open her mouth when Tiberius abruptly looked up. He had an apologetic smile on his face. "But where are my manners? Please, Lady Selene, sit down. Let me pour you a drink."

Selene didn't move. "I'm not thirsty, Tiberius."

"Oh, I insist." Tiberius stood, and in a step he was beside her, his arm clamped to her shoulder, steering and settling her into the opposite chair. Still staring at her, he picked up the pitcher and poured a stream into her cup before refilling his own and sitting down.

Selene lifted the cup with two hands to ensure that it would not shake. While he took a long draft, she took only the smallest of sips before she closed her mouth and let the wine simply wet her lips. When he started to lift his own drink away from his mouth, she did the same, setting the cup down and smiling across the table at him, trying to project the air of serenity that her mother had always possessed. "It's good wine," she said.

Tiberius nodded as he held his cup—Juba's cup—in the air and examined it. "The vineyard is not far from here. They tell me it is one of the best in this region. Not a wine of Rome, but a wine of Romans."

"The vintner should be commended."

Tiberius half-frowned. "Difficult," he said, sloshing the thick red liquid in the cup into circles. "When these Cantabrians rebelled, the vineyards and villas were targets in the first strike. From what I heard, the winemaker and his family were hung from the rafters of their villa. They were still alive when it burned."

"Oh." Selene blinked down at the wine, then removed her hands from her cup and folded them in her lap where their shaking could not be seen.

Tiberius took another long drink before setting down his cup. "They are not civilized, Selene. You have to understand that. They are barbarians. Heathens. They know nothing of law and of order."

"Whose law?"

Tiberius stared at her. "Caesar's."

"And what if he doesn't come back?"

"Some say the next Caesar would be Agrippa or Marcellus. But we both know it will be me. I am the adopted son of Augustus, just as he was the adopted son of Julius. I will be Caesar after our father's death. I may be Caesar now."

"You don't know if he's alive?"

"If I were Corocotta I would have killed him already. I would have killed them both."

Selene opened her mouth to say something more, but the words choked off in her throat. She had to swallow hard to keep her fear in check. Juba is alive, she told herself. Juba *has* to be alive. She would see him again. She just had to survive.

Survive. How many times had her mother thought the same? Had she thought it before she'd taken Julius Caesar into her bed?

"They've made no contact," Tiberius continued. One of his fingers idly traced the rim of his cup. "And they took the wagon of gold with them. I'm not sure what more they could expect to get out of Father, and of course Juba is worth nothing on his own."

Selene's arm twitched, and her hand curled up in a fist, but she pushed her anger back down. "But he's your father," she managed to say.

"Yours, too," Tiberius corrected, and his lip ticked upward in the faintest of smiles, laced with cruelty. "And he said it himself yesterday morning, didn't he? By adoption. For us both, my sister."

Something about the way he said that last word, like the sound of a slithering snake, sent a tremor up her spine. Like the asp that she'd brought for her mother, hissing in the corner before Octavian ran it through with a spear.

"But the difference between us, Selene, is that even before I was his son, I was a Roman." One of his fingers continued to trace the rim of his cup. "You were an Egyptian. Without him, you're not even a citizen. Not even by that beast you call a husband, who is no better than a Numidian."

Selene tightened up, and his eyes narrowed even as his smile grew.

"Ah, yes. The last time I was here you slapped me for speaking ill of him. But now you begin to see the place you're in. Until Augustus returns—*if* he returns—I am Caesar now. It's my law, Selene. My Rome. And you're the daughter of the woman who brought war upon it. You're the daughter who still dreams of continuing that war."

"Tiberius, I don't—"

His hand balled into a fist and slammed down upon the table, cutting her off. "Enough!"

Selene gasped, but said nothing.

"Enough of your lies. Your games. The last time I was here, girl, I told you that I'd find out what you took from the Temple of the Vestals that night. I promised you. It's time."

"I—I don't understand."

"You do understand," he said. He stood abruptly, staggering for a moment before making three heavy-footed steps toward the corner of the tent. For the moment his back was turned, and the thought of running once more flashed through her mind, but she knew the guards would catch her. And his anger would not be lessened for it.

Then she saw that he had stopped in front of Juba's chest, that he was leaning down to reach through its broken lid.

Oh gods, she thought.

When his hand came up he held the small bag, made of her own royal Egyptian cloth, which held the Palladium of Troy. "I recognize this," he said, turning to her. "You carried it that night. I remember. The very same one. You had it with you."

He walked back over to the table, but he didn't sit down. He only stood there, looking down upon her. With one hand he held the object inside while with the other he unwove the strings that were binding the bag shut. Then he pulled down on the cloth, exposing the Shard. "Tiberius," she said, trying to keep her voice from cracking.

He looked at it and laughed. "Not a statue of Horus after all. You lied to me. Because of this. Because you're a part of it. Just like yesterday. The fire. The lightning. The storm. It was the same as I saw that night. The same as that wind that left my cousin half blind."

Selene swallowed hard, thankful that his eyes were fixed on the little statue and not her. "I'm sorry about what happened to Urbinia," she said, her voice small. "But what you think you saw—"

"I know what I saw," he snapped. "And I saw it yesterday, too."

"I had nothing to do with yesterday," she said, the truth of the words giving her strength.

"But you know what it was." He stared down at her, and she could see the fierce anger in his eyes. And with it a rising, terrible passion.

"Tiberius," she said, trying to sound gentle, trying to sound calm. "I think you should go now. The day has been long. We've had too much wine." Her eyes fell to the statue still half-hidden in its bag. Thankfully, he hadn't yet touched it directly, hadn't yet had a chance to feel its power. "It's just a trinket. I took it, though. You're right. And the wind . . . the gods must have been angry. Like yesterday."

"I saw it," he protested.

Selene's gaze returned to meet his, and she smiled, reaching up with one hand to rest it on his. "Please, Tiberius. Put it down. No more of this."

For a second he simply stared down at her fingers upon him, and then he recoiled, eyes widening. "You filthy witch," he spat.

"No," Selene gasped. "Tiberius, I—"

His free hand shot forward, slapping her out of her chair. Her legs kicked the table as she fell, and her full cup of wine was flung onto the white linens of the bed. "You slapped me," he growled. "How does it feel?"

Still stunned, Selene tried to crawl away from him, her fingers gripping and pulling across the slats in the floorboards, though she had nowhere to go. She felt but didn't see his footsteps rocking the wood beneath her, and then he kicked her in the stomach.

Selene coughed, doubled up. She heard him let out a noise

of anger and frustration, and then she heard something crash above her, the sound of something hard being broken.

She tried to say his name, tried to beg for him to stop, but there was no air in her lungs. His rough hands picked her up by the hair, and she gasped as he lifted her and shoved her forward onto the wine-stained bed. Unable to hold it back any longer, she began to cry in voiceless sobs.

"You think you're grown up," she heard him saying from behind her. For a moment she looked back and saw him. He'd shed some of his clothes, and his skin was pale in the lamplight, sickly and weak. "But look at you," he said. "Just a scared little girl, aren't you?"

His hands ripped at the wraps of her clothing, and she kicked and screamed out. He paused and punched her in the back of the skull.

"Don't fight it," he said. "Your mother would have taken it. She always spread her legs for Rome."

The world was spinning, jerking as he manipulated her clothes and her body. Her face was wet with spilled wine and shed tears. She gasped as he exposed her at last and began to press into her, pronouncing that he'd make her a woman.

But she did not scream again. As she opened her eyes to look across the stained bed to where Juba would have rested his head, she saw that Tiberius had thrown the Palladium against the iron headboard. It lay there, nestled as if it were sleeping. And when he thrust into her at last, when she swallowed her horror and revulsion, she watched with hatred and hope in her eyes as the little statue rolled over.

It was broken. And through the crack in the rock she could see a blacker-than-black stone, gleaming in the lamplight.

16

The Way of the Teacher

As the sun rose to send its first rays of light upon the life-giving Nile, Vorenus sat upon one of the rocks along the northeastern shoreline of the island and watched Caesarion strip off the last of his clothing and walk naked to the edge of the great river.

At twenty-one years old, the young man was clearly in the prime of his life. The son of the beautiful Cleopatra and the powerful Julius Caesar, Caesarion had unquestionably handsome features, with a lean-muscled strength that spoke of both the training at arms that he'd continued to refine with Vorenus and the physical labor of a life that for the past four years had been led on the frontier of Egypt. Four years far away from the glorious palaces in which he'd been raised. Four years away from the kingdoms of Egypt and Rome that had been ripped from his grasp, unrightfully stolen from him by Augustus Caesar.

And yet as he took his first steps into the Nile, walking with his face toward the dawn and the outstretched, saffron-robed arms of the abbot waiting in the water, the young man who should have ruled the world was happier than Vorenus could ever remember him.

All because of Hannah, the mysterious Jewish girl who had taken them to the Ark, who had watched over Caesarion as he recovered from his struggle against Juba the Numidian in trying to control it. She was indeed a lovely girl, and there was no doubt they were attracted to each other from the beginning, but it was also clear that something far deeper than surface appearances drew the two of them together. Vorenus had never seen two people fall more madly in love. If he had any reason to believe in such a thing anymore, he would have called it fate.

It was, he thought as he watched his old friend Titus Pullo limping up the path among the rocks, almost exactly the opposite of the surface passion that most men counted for love.

"Did I miss anything?" Pullo asked when he got close.

"Just started. But I've never seen it, so for all I know he's almost done." Vorenus scooted over a little to make room on the rock for Pullo to sit.

The bigger man eased himself back onto the stone with a tired sigh. "Well, I'm glad I made it."

As his friend sat down, Vorenus saw that Madhukar, one of the monks, was walking behind him. So small was the brown-skinned man—and so large was Pullo—that even in his gold-orange robes he'd been fully hidden behind the Roman. Vorenus stood at once and, turning to face the man, placed his palms together, brought the tips of his forefingers up to the bridge of his nose, then bowed.

Pullo, just having seated himself, sighed and nodded at Madhukar. "Can we pretend I did that earlier?"

The monk's smile creased through the laugh lines upon his tanned face as he returned the greeting of Vorenus. "We can indeed, my new Roman friend. And a pleasant welcome to you, Lucius Vorenus. Your safe return yesterday pleased us." He let go his hands and nodded toward Caesarion, who had stopped in the knee-deep water and seemed to be reciting something. "As you know it greatly pleased Joachim, too."

Vorenus rose and gestured toward the place on the rocks that he had vacated.

Madhukar's smile was, as ever, quick and genuine. "No, dear boy," he said, waving his hands gently before clasping them behind his back. "You have traveled far more than I these past days. Rest, please."

Despite the four years that he had been living among these strange monks, it still amused Vorenus that even the ones like Madhukar, who was at least two decades younger than he was, treated him like a young man. It was, another monk had once told him, because he had a younger soul—though for the life of him Vorenus couldn't think what that meant.

"Joachim?" Pullo asked.

The monk was looking out at the river, so Vorenus casually elbowed his friend in the ribs and with wide eyes nodded hard in the direction of Caesarion.

Pullo looked confused for a moment, but to Vorenus' great relief he caught on quickly. "He . . . ah, was waiting?"

Madhukar nodded, his back still to them. "Oh, yes," he said. "We wanted him to cleanse himself as soon as he was ready, but he insisted that you be here to see it, Lucius Vorenus."

Out in the Nile, Caesarion had walked the rest of the way to stand in front of the abbot, Rishi, who was waist-deep in the flowing waters. Once there, the young man made the same gesture to him that Vorenus had to Madhukar. Rishi's face was shadowed by the rising sun, but he appeared to be smiling. He raised his arms, and he spoke something to the sky. As he did so, Caesarion cupped his hands into the water in front of him and brought it up over his face four times, saying something each time.

"Why four?" Pullo asked. He waved away something that buzzed around them on the morning air.

"One for each of the four truths," Madhukar said without looking back. "The truth of suffering. The truth of the origin of suffering. The truth of the end of suffering. The truth of freedom from suffering."

Pullo made an agreeable sound, as if he understood, but Vorenus didn't need to look at his old friend to be sure that the same confusion was on his face that was so often on his own whenever the Therapeutae spoke of their strange ways.

Rishi lowered his arms and, pressing his palms together, once more made the customary gesture of bowing to the young man while touching his forefingers to the space between his nose and brow. Caesarion returned it, and then he took two steps into the deeper water and ducked beneath the surface.

"They call it cleansing," Vorenus said to Pullo. He kept his voice quiet, for this was, he knew, a solemn moment.

"A cleansing of what?"

"I would say his soul, but Madhukar here would probably correct me on that. He'd say it is only cleansing his body."

"So I would," Madhukar agreed.

Caesarion appeared, repeated words after Rishi, then immersed himself once again.

"Why the river? This town has baths doesn't it?"

"A still bath would not do," Madhukar said. "Proper cleaning requires living water, which washes away the impurities."

Vorenus saw Pullo staring out at the silty water of the Nile. He smiled. "Not cleansing from dirt, Pullo. I asked."

Again Caesarion appeared, and again he spoke something before disappearing under the water.

"Does he do this four times, too?"

"A good guess." Madhukar's voice was quieter now. "But it

is three times. The first for the wisdom of right view and right intention. The second for the promise of ethical conduct through right speech, right action, and right living. The third for the assurance of focus to achieve right effort, right mindfulness, and right concentration. Together these are the Teacher's Eightfold Path to release from suffering."

Vorenus had often heard the Therapeutae talk of the Teacher, though they said little of who he was beyond cryptic comments that he had lived in another country far to the east. They were reluctant to say more, Caesarion once explained to him, because they wanted to emphasize the Teacher's humanity. To exalt him, they feared, would lead people to honor him beyond what he was, perhaps even to worship him. Having seen firsthand how the people were taught to honor Cleopatra as a living goddess—and how they tried to do the same to Caesarion even when he disdained the notion himself—Vorenus thought their concern was indeed valid, even if it did leave him wanting to know more about the mysterious Teacher.

Out in the Nile, for a third time Caesarion spoke, went under, and at last reappeared. He once more exchanged bows with Rishi and then the two men started making their way toward the shore, both beaming.

"It is done." Madhukar's voice sounded proud, though Vorenus suspected it was more pleasure at another's joy than happiness for himself. If there was one thing he'd learned about the Therapeutae, it was that they were selfless almost to a fault.

"He's converted, then?" Pullo asked. "He's one of you?"

Madhukar at last turned back around to face them. "Yes and no. Ours is not like other faiths. One does not need to convert to anything to act properly. When the Teacher was asked how to become like him, he answered that a man needed only to act as he did. He taught that it is not our rituals or our beliefs that make us right or wrong. It is the truth of our deeds. Your friend is set upon that path now."

On the shoreline, Caesarion was exiting the water with Rishi. Other monks approached, bearing saffron robes. Everyone was smiling.

"But wasn't that a ritual?" Pullo asked.

Madhukar nodded. "When our forefathers came here from the east, they brought one truth, but they found another. From the Jews they learned of a powerful belief in the one God, a supreme being Who had created heaven and earth. We came to spread the wisdom of the Teacher, but we are not so arrogant to think that there are no other truths in the world. So we learned from the Jews about their faith that was built around God, a faith built of and for the earth. For the Jew, you see, faith is about how to live properly in this world, how to make each and every act more sacred, more befitting the divine spark that gave us life. This moved our fathers, for ours, too, is a faith about living properly. Not for a deity, and not for this world. For what god would create such suffering in this world? But here, on this island, at this temple, our forefathers met Hannah's people, and we learned of their secret belief in the death of that one God, and the ways in which this brought about both freedom and suffering. We saw the ways in which this was like our own thoughts, and we saw fit to bring our peoples together into a fuller understanding of who we are. As Therapeutae, as the Greeks began to call us, we view the teachings of the Jews and that of the Teacher as two sides of the one very real truth: there was one God, our creator, Who set in motion the wheel of life and Whose death brought us into the cycle of suffering that we may learn in time to lift ourselves out of life and into the wholeness of being with what remains of His universal presence. So we bring together many of the ways of both peoples. Joachim, your young friend, has set himself upon the path of the Teacher in right wisdom, conduct, and focus. But he has also undertaken the ritual of baptism in order to become one of the Jewish people."

"He's a Jew?" Pullo asked.

"And one who follows the Teacher. He is both, you see." Madhukar turned to Vorenus, who had been watching their exchange with interest. "It is indeed good that you were here for this," he said, though the look of happiness on his face turned to one of sorrow. "It is a misfortune, however, that you suffered such losses on the way."

"Thank you," Vorenus said, bowing his head slightly. "Khenti was a good man."

Madhukar nodded slowly, closing his eyes for a moment. "He carried much with him, I fear."

Vorenus nodded, trying to digest what this meant among the monks. Though he had tried hard to learn it alongside the young man they knew as Joachim, the Therapeutan way of thinking remained as immeasurably strange to him as it surely was for the confused Pullo. Caesarion, however, had latched on to it quickly, declaring that it was, among all the philosophies in the world, the closest to his own beliefs.

It was also, Vorenus suspected, a kind of bridge for Caesarion between his own beliefs and that of Hannah's Judaism.

As if bidden by the thought, Hannah came out onto the shoreline and embraced Caesarion in a powerful hug. She had been waiting, Vorenus knew, in a small room that kept her from seeing the young man's nakedness. It was a strict rule among the Therapeutae—as it apparently had been among both the Jews and the disciples of their Teacher—that men and women were to remain modest among one another outside of marriage. They were also segregated during their times of communal gathering in the temple. Having seen how unfocused

Pullo could be around women, Vorenus understood the principle, even if he did think that they went a little far in having a short dividing wall cutting their sanctuary in half.

Still, the segregation wasn't as bad as it could be, Vorenus supposed. Caesarion had told him that the Teacher had apparently advised men to practice complete celibacy in order to better concentrate upon their meditations. Their Therapeutan descendants, however, had adapted to the Jewish acceptance of worldly passion and pleasure—albeit confined to marriage. "In the end life is suffering," Caesarion had once told Vorenus, "but that doesn't mean that there aren't very real joys to be shared."

And so it was in moments like this. Vorenus watched as the monks smiled and laughed while the two young people shared their embrace.

Caesarion was going to marry her. Vorenus was certain of it, and he couldn't be happier.

"What is it that you worry Khenti took with him?" Pullo suddenly asked.

Vorenus blinked back to the two men beside him. "Ah, my curious Roman friend," Madhukar said, "he took what he has been. What he has done. These things will carry with him in his next life."

Pullo's brow furrowed. "The Elysian Fields?"

"There are those who speak of such things. Of a life beyond in a heaven. I have not died in this life, so perhaps it is so."

"But you don't believe in it," Vorenus said.

"Just so. As I have told you before, our Teacher showed us another path, another way. To continue in life is not our goal."

"You want to die?" Pullo asked.

"In a manner of speaking. In truth we want to live to be released from life."

"That's death."

"This is not so." The monk's voice was gentle and soft as the breeze. "It is release."

Pullo looked confused, and Vorenus let out a little chuckle. "I've heard these same things, Pullo. They didn't make any sense to me, either."

"But I do want to understand," Pullo said.

Vorenus saw a genuine pleading in his friend's eyes. Pullo had never cared for the gods. When they were younger, when they'd known far less about such things, Pullo had mocked Vorenus for believing. And yet here the big man was, wanting to know the belief of the Therapeutae. What had happened to him while they were apart?

"It is difficult to understand," Madhukar admitted. "It took the Teacher many years to learn the truth: life is suffering. You know this. You need only look around to see that all the joys of life are matched with an infinity of sorrows. Joy, one might say, is only possible because of that sorrow, for if all life was joy you would know it not for the joy that it is. We need sorrow and pain in this life, if only to know the importance of those blessed moments without them. But still, in the end, from the child trembling in the cold night to the worm drying upon the earth, the one truth of life is suffering. So we want to break the cycle of our being. Going to the Elysian Fields—to a heaven, as some call it—would only be to continue to exist, no matter what form you imagine for it."

Pullo chewed on his lip for a moment, thinking. "So you want to be released from existence?"

"Released from suffering, yes."

"So that's what happened to Khenti? He was released from existence? He's just gone?"

"I cannot know. I can only say what we have been taught. But I would say that he has not gone into nothingness, if this is your concern."

"Tell him about the flower," Vorenus said. "It's about the only way this ever made sense to me."

If Madhukar was offended by the negativity of the statement, it did not show. The monk instead gave an acknowledging nod. "I'm glad at least something in these years is getting through your Roman skull."

Vorenus wanted to tell the monk that it wasn't his fault—that what he had seen, what he knew now of the death of the one God and the futility of a life of pious belief, had left him unable to believe in anything anymore—but instead he just smiled. "I'm an old dog and this is all a new trick," he said.

Madhukar chuckled a little. Pullo still had a kind of frown on his face. "Flower?"

"Ah, yes." Madhukar waved his hand to a patch of leafy green growing a little ways down the path among the rocks. "Imagine for a moment a seed. Placed in fertile earth it will take root. Care for it, and it will grow. Tend to it, and it will bloom. But only so long. In time the caterpillar will gnaw upon its leaves. The wind will sweep away its soft petals. The frost will kill its roots. The flower will die, and it will fade back into the earth from whence it came. Perhaps a new flower will grow in its place, rising from the very dust of the old one, rising in birth in the moment of death. It, too, will take root and grow. It, too, will live and die. So it is for most of us. We live. We die. We live again. And each time the value of our being sows the ground of our new life for good or ill. What we are matters very much for what we will be."

"In other words," Vorenus said, "after death, Madhukar thinks Khenti probably took on a new life."

Madhukar shrugged. "It is what the Teacher taught."

Pullo's face had softened. "So you live a good life in order to live a better one again? And that's the release you seek?"

"It is a noble and proper thing to live well," Madhukar agreed. "But rebirth is not release. The flower that returns must suffer again. The caterpillar. The wind. The frost. No, release is to no longer be the flower. To be a new thing now: the butter-fly, the air, the chill itself. To become one with the very fabric of creation."

"To know the mind of God," Caesarion said.

Everyone turned to where the young man was walking up the path, holding hands with Hannah. Rishi and the other monks were nowhere to be seen.

"Welcome," Madhukar said, exchanging acknowledgments with them both. Then he looked around at them all and opened his arms in a gesture of completion. "I am glad you are all come together at last. I do not doubt that you have much of which to speak, and I have work to tend to elsewhere. The bees won't keep themselves. May you all find solace and peace in this place."

The little monk bowed once more to them all, quickly em-braced Caesarion in a joyous hug, and then retreated back down the path.

"I'm really glad you were here for this," Caesarion said. "And especially you, Titus Pullo. Thinking you dead and now seeing you alive . . . well, it's amazing."

Pullo smiled, and without leaving his seat on the rocks he reached out and grabbed the younger man with one big paw and pulled him in for a hug that was at once playful and fatherly. "I did miss you, little pharaoh," he grumbled.

And I missed this, Vorenus thought, recalling the shared memories of a time before war and the Shards of Heaven en-tered into their lives.

Pullo let Caesarion go, tousling his damp hair with one hand while with his other he quickly wiped at his own eyes.

Seeing them smiling suddenly brought back the memory of another day in Alexandria, when they'd first learned that Juba the Numidian was trying to attain the fabled Scrolls of Thoth, thought to hold all the secrets of the gods.

"Is everything all right, Vorenus?"

Vorenus opened his eyes when Caesarion spoke, not having realized that he'd closed them. "All is well." He blinked back dampness as he looked at his old friend, so beaten by the world, and the boy they'd come to view like a son, so ready to enter the next stage of life with the young woman he loved. "I was simply thinking how it is that things can stay the same even as they change."

"Time passes," Hannah said. "All things change."

Vorenus nodded respectfully. "So it does."

Hannah's eyes twinkled as they so often did when she saw to the clear truth of things. "But you were thinking of something specific, Lucius Vorenus."

Vorenus couldn't help but smile at how he was exposed before her. Even from the first time they'd met her, the young Jewish girl had read them all like a book. It was one of the first things, he suspected, that drew young Caesarion to her. Wise and wise again, he thought to himself. "I was thinking of the house of Asclepius," he admitted. "After the assassin's attack in Alexandria. Do you remember it?"

"I do," Caesarion said. "You saved many lives that day, Vorenus."

Vorenus nodded, though he didn't feel the least bit heroic for what he'd had to do. "I remember we talked about the Scrolls of Thoth, how they were said to hold all the knowledge of the gods. You told us that if we actually found them you would destroy them. You said you had no desire to know the mind of God."

"I remember it well." Caesarion smiled. "And that's still

true to a point. But remember that back then I guess I thought God was alive. But He's dead, remember?"

Vorenus shivered despite the warm morning air. It still bothered him to hear it said so plainly. No matter how much it made sense of the world, he didn't want to believe that God was dead.

"Dead," Pullo said. "But you still do believe there *was* a God?"

"How could I not?" Caesarion exchanged a smile with Hannah and squeezed her hand. "I know that the monks here say that their Teacher didn't speak of a god, but I do think there was one. Nothing else explains the Shards. At the same time, it's like I told Didymus back in Alexandria: no just God could allow such injustice in the world. So it makes sense, as Hannah and her people believe, that for God to give His creation the free will to live on its own, He had to unmake Himself. His death was His greatest gift."

"But the monks say life is suffering," Pullo said.

"The gift indeed comes with a price," Hannah replied. "But remember that we prefer to dwell on what lies within ourselves, not that which dwells without. As the monks here say, through right wisdom, right conduct, and right focus, we can achieve release."

"To be unmade ourselves," Vorenus whispered. The stark truth of it struck him so suddenly, so abruptly, that he couldn't help but speak the words out loud. It was as if they had been spoken into his very soul.

The smile with which Caesarion met him was kindly, almost paternal. "And so to know the mind of God."

"A hard thing to understand," Vorenus said, looking at the ground.

Caesarion stepped forward and put his hand on Vorenus' shoulder. "An even harder thing for many to accept."

For a moment there was silence amid the gathering on the rocks. And for all that Vorenus might have thought he would hear next, it was not the voice of his old friend.

"I accept it," Pullo said. "But I know it's not everything."

Vorenus looked up, but it was Hannah who spoke first. "How do you know?"

"Well," Pullo said, a smile creasing the ragged lines of his scarred face, "I know there's more, because I died."

17

The Moon Takes Flight

CANTABRIA, 26 BCE

In the dark before the dawn, Selene left Tiberius sleeping. Pulling her shawl close about her as she left, she pretended to be unhurried. Not one of the praetorians outlined by the watch fires around the tent stopped her as she turned toward the baths on the far side of the encampment and began to walk. Not one of them even looked at her.

She tried not to limp, though she ached from the bruising and the strains of muscles and joints that had been twisted in the rape. She tried to walk tall and proud, like the queen that she should have been.

She didn't need to try not to cry, though. She had had enough of tears. This night had seen the end of them. Only vengeance was left. Vengeance and her love for her husband, stronger than ever.

Juba. Beautiful, kind Juba. She wasn't sure whether she would tell him what had happened. She wasn't sure if she could.

It wasn't her fault. She had tried to fight. Tiberius had simply been too strong. It was true, and she knew it in her soul, yet she felt a horrible guilt. Another man had been inside her, and it left her feeling dirty, soiled in ways that she feared would never become clean.

But that wasn't why she walked toward the baths.

She walked toward the baths because they were away from the main gate, away from any hint that she was escaping. And escaping was exactly what she intended to do.

Around her, the camp was heavy with the smells of the fires along the paths between rows of tents. A few legionnaires stood guard or walked from one place to another on the various ceaseless duties of maintaining order within the encampment. The air was crisp, and Selene kept her heavy shawl held close as she walked. From time to time she looked behind her, but she saw no one following. The praetorians, it seemed, had judged her no threat to leave.

The baths were situated toward the rear of the encampment, but when she arrived there she paused and then, as if making a sudden decision, walked onward, toward the latrines along the rear wall of the camp.

These latrines, she knew, were among the least used. And here the legionnaires had built a few enclosed areas, one in particular being designated for the few women in the camp: most of them camp followers, but a few were wives like Selene who had come for one reason or another. It was a simple plank-built structure, only large enough for three or four women at a time to squat over the rock-lined channel, but it was enough to shield private business from public eyes. And privacy was precisely what Selene needed now.

Entering the latrine, wrinkling her nose at the bitter, thick smells, she was grateful to find the little space unoccupied. The early hour had more than one use for her this day.

With the wood door pulled shut behind her—taking one last glance back out to see that no one was watching—she lowered the shawl off her body and exposed the satchel and the Aegis of Zeus hidden beneath.

She'd had to be careful removing the breastplate from its

hiding place, and she couldn't bother to tighten its straps for fear that they would make too much noise and wake Tiberius from his wine-drunk stupor, but she had felt certain that she couldn't leave either of the Shards where they were. Tiberius knew too much. He'd come too close to engaging the Palladium last night. She had to get it and the Aegis of Zeus away from him.

Carefully, Selene tightened the Aegis as best she could. It was too large for her by any measure, but by cinching every strap to its limits, she found that she could keep the armor of Alexander the Great from moving too much around her smaller body. It was good enough, she supposed. And she didn't have much choice.

As she took a deep breath and tried to relax she realized that the armor felt warm against her breast: a deep warmth that nuzzled up against her, settled into the center of her being. It was comforting, she decided, though it trembled with a power she could not define.

Whatever it was, she was certain she would need it.

She resettled the shawl upon her shoulders, covering the armor as effectively as she could and tying it tightly about her neck.

Next, she took from her small satchel the Palladium.

The rock statue had been broken when Tiberius had thrown it against the iron headboard. She'd seen the crack as she'd lain upon the bed and taken his weight. She'd stared at it. She'd remembered all that she had seen in the battle between Juba with the Trident of water and the little girl with the Lance of fire. Both of them had been holding the stones, the blacker-than-black Shards of Heaven themselves.

Carefully, Selene knelt. Ignoring the proximity of the open channel of refuse, she gripped the statue in both hands and swung it hard against the corner of the stone wall of the latrine trough. The rock sparked and chipped. She swung again, and this time her aim was true: she struck the jagged crack perfectly and the top half of the statue fell away with a clatter into the dirt.

Selene stared. The stone, like all the others they'd seen, was of a glossy darkness, a pit with no color. It was about the size of a throwing stone. It was smooth and round, like a slightly flattened egg, and if it wasn't still nestled within the lower half of the Palladium like a jewel within its setting, the Shard would have fit perfectly in the soft flesh of her palm, wrapped in her fist.

Selene stood, and she took one more look outside. No one had approached the latrine. Nothing stirred in the darkness.

It was now or never, she decided, and after one last deep breath, like a diver getting ready for the plunge, she held the base of the little statue in her right hand and placed her left upon the top of it, her palm cupping over the smooth black surface of the Shard.

The power surged up or pulled her down—she could not tell which—and she clenched her jaw to keep from screaming. For several seconds it threatened to overwhelm her, but she knew something of the surge and how to control it from her practice with Juba.

But this power was far greater than anything she had tapped into before. It was, a part of her thought, as if she'd had a mere basin of water before and now was given the sea.

She became aware that each time the tumultuous power of the Shard in her hands bucked up, hungry and wanting to devour her, another force pushed it back—another wave of power that was both her and not her. The Aegis of Zeus.

Selene at last unclenched her jaw and forced herself to breathe again, first in labored gasps and then, as the forces steadied, in longer, calmer breaths. She felt giddy, standing in the latrine with a dragon writhing in her hands, begging to be released.

And so, looking up, she released it.

The sides of the latrine buckled and broke inward as torrents of air were suddenly sucked into the space. They shoved upward, like a massive battering ram, and the thin planks that made up the roof splintered away, hurtling up high into the night.

The wind died down. Selene panted, grinning. Somewhere in the distance she heard the shouts of the men at the gate watchtower.

Let them stir, she thought. I'm going to go rescue my husband, and I'm not going that way.

And with that, staring up into the starry void, Selene called down the power of the four winds, and she took flight.

•   •   •

From far up above, invisible against the blackness, Selene soared in silent circles above Vellica.

She cried as she flew, not in tears of rage or anger or pain, but in tears of sorrow and hope. Her mother, Cleopatra, had ruled on Earth as the physical embodiment of Isis, and upon her death she had intended to take her place within the heavens, ruling unto eternity among the stars with her husband, Osiris. It had been a beautiful story once, but Selene had learned too much to think it true. Her parents were simply dead. Dead like the one God who was the only true God there had ever been.

Only now Selene was among those stars herself, like Isis upon her kite wings, trying to bring her husband back home. And she felt her mother with her. And her father, too. They weren't gone. They were here. They were in the wind. She felt as if with only a little more power she could reach out and touch them, bring them back, and enfold herself in their loving arms once more.

Just a little more power, she thought. I could conquer death itself.

Against the far horizon to the east, the sky began to glow with the fire of dawn. Reluctantly, as if pulling away from a dream, Selene shook herself into the present and circled lower toward the lingering shadows, closer to the still-slumbering hillfort.

The guards on the walls brushed hair from their eyes as the wind passed over them, but no one gazed upward and saw the girl in flight.

Selene held herself amid the air above the center of it all, slowly turning and watching the few people moving as they came and went in the pre-dawn. What she was looking for, she didn't know. Certainly she didn't expect Juba to be held out in the open. But she hoped to spy some clue as to where he was, some sign of what she might do.

She knew she ought to be more tired. She ought to be exhausted, given the amount of power that was coursing through her. But the steady warmth of the Aegis against her breast made her feel as if she'd never been more alive.

At last, just as the sky was growing light enough that she feared she would need to fly away, Selene saw something that could help her: Corocotta's little slave girl, hobbling between buildings on her way toward what Selene could only imagine was their own latrine: a small building against the outer wall not unlike the one she'd just left behind in the encampment.

Not far away was a secluded pocket of shadows, created by piled crates and barrels. Selene floated there, then she dropped down to the ground and landed in a soft crouch, quiet as a cat on its paws—the only sound the clatter of debris that swirled about her as she descended.

The wind cut off abruptly, but she held the power close as the noise subsided, listening. Hearing no shouts of alarm, she took her hand off the Palladium, already missing its power, and then slipped it into the satchel at her side.

The dust that had been kicked up settled around her quickly as she lifted the shawl over her head, made herself small, and slipped between the shadows to where the little slave girl was just leaving the latrine. She had a different crutch now, Selene saw. It wasn't the Lance of Olyndicus. That, she imagined, Corocotta kept close to himself, as Caesar did the Trident.

Panicked, realizing that she had no real plan, Selene looked around, trying to decide what to do. She thought about calling out to the girl, luring her into the shadows, but of course she could not speak the girl's language. To speak would only give herself away.

But, seeing there was no one else in sight, she made a decision. Stepping out from the darkness, keeping her head low, she walked straight for the latrine herself, walking so close to the little slave that her shawl brushed against her. And then, pivoting quickly, she swung around behind the girl and clamped her hand over the girl's mouth.

She lifted as she pulled her back toward the shadows, surprised at her own sudden strength—was that the Aegis, too? she wondered. The little girl kicked and tried to scream, but Selene's grip was too tight for anything but the most mumbled sound, and her legs did nothing but flail in the air. The girl dropped her crutch as she struggled, and Selene kicked it ahead of her into the darkness from whence she'd come.

Selene carried the struggling girl in that same direction, keeping the crutch ahead of her, all the way back to the quiet spot where she had landed. There she leaned forward to whisper in the girl's ear, "I'm going to set you down. I'm going to let go. Please don't call out. You didn't hurt me, and I don't want to hurt you. Do you understand?"

The little girl had stopped kicking as she talked, hanging limply, and when Selene was done she simply nodded her head once up and down.

"Thank you," Selene said, and she leaned forward to set the girl's feet upon the ground, releasing her mouth as she did so.

The slave took a deep breath, but to Selene's relief she did not scream. She steadied herself by leaning on a barrel to her right, and then she carefully turned to face her. "Who are you?" the girl whispered.

Selene leaned down and picked up the girl's crutch, holding it forward as a kind of peace offering. "My name is Selene," she said, keeping her voice quiet. "I need your help."

The little girl studied her for a moment, then took back the crutch. "You're the one I saw with Caesar. How did you get here?"

"I have my powers, as do you."

"I could call the guards. You would be no match for them. Corocotta will destroy you."

Selene opened her arms, allowing the shawl to part and bring the Aegis of Zeus into view. "Corocotta is nothing before the power of the gods. He's just a man." She released her arms and leaned forward. "He is nothing without you."

The crippled girl had been staring at the breastplate, staring at the Shard. "I am a slave."

"Only because you are not yet free," Selene said. "What's your name?"

The girl swallowed hard. "Isidora."

Selene blinked. It was a beautiful name. A Latin name. "You're a Roman?"

Isidora nodded quietly. "They killed my family, took me when I was young."

"Your name means 'gift of Isis.' Did you know that?"

The girl looked up. "Who is Isis?"

My mother, Selene wanted to say. Me. Fate. She smiled, warmly and genuinely. "Someone who wouldn't want you to live in chains."

Isidora's eyes flashed with dampness in the growing light. "What can I do? I am only a girl."

"And you are more powerful than Corocotta can ever be. You are stronger than he is. That's the reason he makes you use the Lance, isn't it? It will destroy him. He knows that."

"It's destroying me," Isidora whispered. "That stone will destroy you, too."

"I've come only to take my husband back. That's all." That was all, wasn't it? She could leave the power behind after that, couldn't she? Or perhaps she could use it just awhile longer.

Tiberius. In her mind she saw his pleading, his begging as her powers ripped him apart. *Yes. Tiberius.*

"Selene?"

Selene shook herself. "Yes?"

The girl had a look of confusion on her face. "I asked who your husband was."

"I'm sorry," Selene said, trying to get her bearings again. What had she been thinking? Those thoughts of destruction didn't feel like her own. "My husband . . . He was the one who fought you."

"The water." Isidora nodded in remembrance. "He is a slave, too."

Selene started to object, then nodded. "In a way. But in our land a slave can be a prince. He is that, too."

"And you are a princess? You answer to this Caesar?"

"No man rules me. I am a queen, and I have come to take back my king. No matter who or what stands in my way."

Isidora nodded again, then her eyes got wide. "I can't—"

"You tried to warn me," Selene interrupted. "Back on that hillside. You didn't want to hurt me any more than I want to hurt you. So I know you won't call out for help. But please, just tell me where my husband is. Where are they holding him?"

Isidora's mouth opened and closed. "I cannot tell you," she finally said. She looked Selene in the eyes. "But I can show you."

"You will take me there?"

Isidora nodded, and a smile crept across her face. "Yes, Queen Selene. And then you will take me with your king to this place where I will not be a slave."

"I will, Isidora," Selene said, thankfully. "I swear it."

The little girl nodded curtly and adjusted her weight on the crutch. "But first you will help me get my things. You're going to need my help in more ways than one."

18

Unquenchable Fires

Octavian—Augustus Caesar, son of the god Caesar and emperor of Rome—was dying. Juba laid another wet rag upon his stepbrother's fevered brow.

"Such a fool," Juba said, though Caesar could not hear him and there was no one else in the cramped little cell. "Such a fool."

Octavian had indeed been a fool, thinking that he could grab the Trident and use it so easily. He'd seen with his own eyes what it had done to Quintus back in Rome. And yet to have done it anyway . . . "Such a fool."

And why? What could he have been thinking? It had all happened so fast. Juba replayed it in his mind: Octavian lunging out, wrestling the Trident from the little girl, and shouting. What was it that he had shouted?

Juba removed the rag and squeezed it out into the little basin of tepid water they'd granted him. He resoaked it, vainly hoping it would be cooler than the air in this closed space, and resettled it on Octavian's brow.

His stepbrother moaned but did not otherwise respond.

Run, Juba abruptly remembered.

That was what he'd shouted. Right before the power of the

Shard had taken him and sent him to wherever he was now—
Caesar had told him to run.

"You were saving me," Juba whispered, staring down at the
man he had hated for so long. "You were giving me a chance
to get away."

It didn't make any sense. When Juba had awoken in this
cell after the battle, Octavian had been relieved. Easy enough
to understand, since he was the one who could use the Trident for him. A slave. That's what Corocotta had thought him.
No different than that little girl whom he'd he been using to
wield the Lance. Of course Octavian didn't want him to die.

And yet this—so foolishly seizing the Trident, trying to
give him a chance to get away—this was something else.

Was it caring?

After all that Octavian had made him do—Quintus, those
first men at sea, the hundreds at Actium—after all the death,
was it possible that all along Octavian had truly viewed him
as a brother? As family?

Sudden sounds stirred him from his thoughts. There was
shouting, distant and muted. A noise like a roar.

Juba stood, trying to listen, the sodden rag in his hand
dripping into the little basin. There was a bang that sounded
as if it came from the building above them, and on the other
side of the cell door heavy steps pounded down the hall as a
guard shouted something he could not understand.

Screaming. A heat in the air.

Then a sudden eerie silence between the door and the distant commotion.

"Juba?" a voice suddenly shouted. "Juba? Are you down
here?"

Juba blinked in the dim light. "Selene?" It couldn't be her.
But it sounded—

"Juba? Are you down here?"

"Selene!" Juba dropped the rag in the water and jumped to the door of the cell. He banged on it and shouted into the wood, "Selene!"

There was a thump against the wood beneath his hands, and then her voice was close. "Juba! Get back from the door!"

"Selene! What are you doing here? How did you—"

The air in the room seemed to groan, and Juba felt himself being pulled against the damp wood. The flame of the tallow candle flickered as it stretched in his direction.

"Get back!" he heard her shout.

Juba shoved himself away from the door, and—feeling as if he were fighting a horrible tide—he managed to throw himself on top of Caesar just moments before the wooden entry to the cell exploded inward with a splintering crash.

Wind erupted into the room, and clattering, broken boards. Juba shielded his eyes with one hand as he steadied himself with the other, the wood scattering across his back as he covered the emperor of Rome.

In a second, the wind was gone.

The little light had guttered out, and when Juba shook the debris off his neck and looked up at the open doorway, he saw Selene, his love, backlit against the light in the hallway. The shawl about her shoulders was drifting in what looked like a leftover breeze, and she was cradling something in her hands.

"Selene?"

"You're all right," she said, and she dropped what she had been holding into a satchel at her side.

"Selene, how did—"

She rushed forward as he stood, and she threw her arms around his neck, cutting off his words with kisses as if she'd never thought she'd see him again.

Juba embraced her in return, and as he did so he felt the hard plate between them. The Aegis of Zeus. The Shard.

Selene pulled away from his lips. Her eyes and cheeks were wet, but she was smiling. "We need to hurry," she said. She kissed him one last time, and then she let go of him and ran back to the hall. She was out of sight for only a heartbeat, and when she returned she had the Trident. She threw it to him, and he caught it.

"I don't understand how—"

Above the tumult they both heard a girl shouting Selene's name.

Selene's eyes were wide. She grabbed Juba's arm and started pulling him forward. She was far stronger than he ever remembered. "We need to go."

Juba took two steps, feeling like this was some kind of dream, and then he snapped out of it and stopped. He looked back at Octavian upon the bed. "I can't just leave him."

Selene's grip bruised his arm. "There's no time!"

Juba met her eyes. Her big, beautiful, bold eyes. "I can't, Selene."

The love of his life looked back and forth between them. Then she nodded. "Hurry," she said, already reaching down for the fevered Caesar. "Come on."

. . .

Outside, the world was on fire.

Selene had helped to carry the unconscious Octavian up the steps out of the little prison, and when they reached the top all Juba could see at first was smoke and flame. The walls of several buildings nearby were ablaze, and at least three men were blackened, smoking corpses in the open area around them. Corocotta's slave girl stood at the top of the steps as they came up. Her back was to them, but Juba could see the Lance of Olyndicus was once more in her little hands, a tongue of fire flashing out against a group of men who'd tried to come around one of the buildings to their left.

Selene pushed Caesar's weight onto Juba, then spun away from him and knelt, facing to the right.

Juba turned in that direction—speechless, paralyzed with shock—and he saw that four archers had taken position behind an overturned and smoldering wagon. They were drawing back on their bows.

Selene once more had something in her hands. Juba opened his mouth to cry out, knowing that it was already too late as the men loosed their strings. For an instant he could see the heads of the missiles flying straight and true, the wood shafts behind them vibrating from the acceleration of their flight, the rising curtain of gray smoke curling and twisting behind them as they sliced through it.

In the same moment a wind struck him against his back, pushing him forward a step toward the killing shafts. But a step beyond Selene the wind *bent*, turning upward toward heaven in a glorious sweep of natural power that he could see in the dust that it scraped from the ground and carried up with it in what seemed a wall of cloud. The four arrows hit it and were pushed upward, sailing high.

Then Selene's cupped hands jerked forward, and the wall hurtled forward as well, as if commanded—bowing down upon itself and rushing forward like a wave. It crashed into the charred wagon, slamming it back into the archers, who fell screaming.

The booming voice of Corocotta split the crackling noise, echoing off the walls of the fort and the buildings around them, shouting commands that Juba could not understand.

"This way," the slave girl urged.

Juba turned back toward her, saw that she was pointing toward a break in the fires. Through it he could see a gate of the hillfort. A way out.

Caesar was a dead weight, so Juba crouched down and let

his stepbrother fall over his back and shoulders. With a grunt, still feeling barely recovered from his own weakness but knowing there was no other choice, he stood up and hefted him onto his shoulders, just barely managing not to drop the Trident in his right hand. "Selene!" he shouted. "Let's go!"

There was no need. Selene was already passing him, calling the crippled girl by name—Isidora, Juba noted—and half-picking her up to help them move faster.

Corocotta continued to shout, and when they were nearly to the break in the fire, Juba finally saw why: Cantabrians were storming up the stairways to take positions above the gate. Dozens of bows were already being drawn against them.

No wind, no fire could stop them all.

"Down!" he shouted, and in the same moment he flung Caesar from his shoulder into the backs of the two girls—bruises are better than holes, he thought—and held out the Trident of Poseidon. He wrapped his hand around the Shard.

In an instant the power was there. In an instant he was a god.

The lightning crackled into being around him like sharp fractures of a hidden light.

For the space of that single heartbeat Juba had shut his eyes. When he opened them, men began to die.

The bolts pulsed out of him, through him, ripping across the air, searing it with a speed beyond the eye. The hungry tongues cracked out like whips of the purest white fire and men were struck down where they stood: shaking with the energy, unable to move or scream. The thunderous boom of the torn air threatened to send Juba backward, but he held on.

Hungry. He was hungry. The Shard was hungry.

More and more power rushed down and out of him. He

felt like laughing and crying all at once. This is life, this is power, he thought. And a voice answered, No, this is death, this is destruction.

Only when the wind of God struck him across the face did he let go.

Juba staggered, and he buckled over, his hand falling off the Shard and onto the wooden shaft of the Trident as he leaned on it for support. He gasped for air, and for a moment he could hear nothing else.

Blinking, he looked around and saw the broken fog of smoke twisting angrily through the violated air. Bits of paper and cloth fluttered in the quiet. And all those who'd stood before them were dead. They had been scattered upon the walkway above, some crushed back against the battlement, others fallen with their black-streaked limbs dangling obscenely over its edge. Still others had fallen to the ground and lay in broken piles before them.

He'd killed them.

In a second, he'd killed them all.

No bird called out. Nothing and no one made a sound, as if the world itself could not accept what he had done.

"Juba," a voice said. "My love, Juba."

He blinked, looked over, and saw Selene. She was crouched, her hands held up in front of her open satchel, palms out as if she meant no threat to him. Her face was dirty and streaked with tears. Behind her Isidora was pushing herself to her feet, her eyes wide in fright. She appeared to be backing away.

"Selene," Juba said. "I don't know how—"

She nodded. She smiled. And she bent down to put her head under one of Caesar's motionless arms. "Help me. We have to hurry."

Juba hesitated for a moment, then he nodded, too. He

stepped forward, feeling dizzy, and he set the Trident down upon the earth in order to help Selene carry Octavian between them. "Take it," he said to the girl. "I can't."

Isidora looked to Selene, who nodded. Then she came forward and picked up the Trident, leaning into it and the Lance as if they were walking sticks.

Selene started forward, and Juba simply followed. They stepped over bodies, and he saw the twisted expressions upon their smoking faces. His stomach heaved, and he vomited upon the ground, upon his feet. Still he trudged on in mute horror, climbing steps as she climbed them, bearing the weight as she bore it.

Shouts began again. A few arrows struck the wood around them as they climbed. One shot through the air so close that it tore across his arm. He felt the pain. He looked down and saw the blood. But he was numb to it now.

Just keep walking. Step by step. Body by body. Rising.

At the top of the stairs Selene walked them to the edge of the battlement. She leaned Caesar against it, standing him up beside Juba amid the men he had destroyed. Isidora was shouting, and he felt sudden heat as walls of flame shot up from the wooden walkways to their left and right. He was aware that there was fire raging below him, too.

Whether Isidora had set the stairway aflame behind them or whether the Cantabrians had done it, he didn't know.

Didn't matter. There was nowhere to go either way. This was the end. In flames amid the dead.

"Juba," Selene was saying. "Stay with me. Hold on to Octavian."

Juba nodded. Tears were streaming from his eyes, but when he looked out over the edge, he could see the stakes still mounted there, with the bodies of the legionnaires Corocotta had tortured. Beyond them was the valley, stretching out toward the Roman encampment. And flashing gold across it, in the light of the early morning, he saw eagles.

He heard horns.

Juba turned to tell Selene, and he saw that she was pulling Isidora up beside him. The little girl hugged close to his body even as he held Caesar's. The fires were very close.

"Hold on tight," Selene said over the flames. She put her left arm around Octavian's back. Her right hand fell into her satchel and enclosed something there. She leaned close. Juba felt once more the hard plate of the Aegis. But he felt, too, the love of the heart behind it.

A wind rose around them, and Juba felt his weight lifting.

"Now jump," Selene said. "I'll catch you."

19

WHAT LIES BEYOND

ELEPHANTINE, 26 BCE

Caesarion, his hand still on the shoulder of Vorenus, turned to look back at the man they'd all thought dead. Truly dead. "You *died*, Pullo?"

"I believe I did."

There was a depth in Pullo's eyes now. Caesarion had noticed it from the moment they had joyously greeted each other the day before. It was a depth that had shocked him even more than the horrible scars that crossed Pullo's face like the cracks in the clay of a dry riverbed, even more than the painful way in which the broken man walked now. There had been no such depth in his eyes when last they'd met. Back then, Pullo was mirth and unbridled passion. Now, though the same hints of his old happiness were there, they were like flashes of light at the edge of a great pool. Caesarion had thought it was sorrow, but Hannah had said that it was wisdom. Perhaps she was right, as she so often was, but he wondered, too, if there was truly a difference.

"You died," Hannah repeated.

Pullo nodded. "Though I've never spoken of it."

"In Alexandria," Vorenus whispered. "Beneath all that rock."

Pullo nodded again.

"It was a brave act, Titus Pullo." Hannah's tone was almost reverent. "You saved our lives. You saved the Ark, and in so doing saved many lives more. You were like Samson among the Philistines."

"Samson?" Vorenus asked.

"An ancient hero among the Jews," Hannah said. "He was the strongest of men, and when he was captured and blinded by his enemies, placed in their temple, he pulled it down upon himself, killing them all. It was the sacrifice of a great hero, and his story has been long told among the Jews."

"Just as yours has been among us," Caesarion said. Then, fearful of too much emotional solemnity, he playfully punched the big man on the shoulder as he walked back over to Hannah's side. "Not that you're for sure the strongest of men, mind you."

Pullo laughed at that, a rumble that felt like a sigh of relief.

"Though you are the strongest I've ever known," Vorenus said, his heartfelt love and respect for Pullo abundantly clear. "But even so, my friend, how did you make it out? That much rock . . ."

Pullo's rumble subsided, and he took a deep breath. "I don't remember everything. But I remember enough. We'd thought he was dead. Juba, I mean. So when we took the Ark down to the platform under the bridge I didn't even think to look behind us. My fault, I guess." He looked up at Hannah, his brow knitted with sorrow. "I am sorry for your brother. I failed him. I failed you all."

"You did not." Hannah's voice was both stern and forgiving. "It was not your fault. As the keeper of the Ark, his life and those of the other men who died that day were in my keeping. I have had to make my peace with Jacob's soul. Don't let it be your burden, too."

"It's true," Caesarion added. "Don't carry more than you need to carry."

Pullo nodded, though he didn't look convinced. Still, he took another deep breath and began to tell his tale.

"Well, he cut me across the backs of my legs. Hamstrings. You know how it's done, Vorenus. I'm lucky he wasn't as efficient as you or I would have been useless even if I did survive. He didn't cut all the way across, I guess. I can still make my way around. Just not much good in a hurry, as they say.

"I remember screaming and falling, but then I don't remember a whole lot for a little bit. Just flashes of what was happening around me. The unnatural wind. The surging power from the Ark. And Didymus talking to me. He was a good man, you know. After everything. He wanted to help.

"And then I saw how Juba was coming back. He was like a man possessed, you know. The look in his eyes, the ceaseless focus despite all the wounds he'd received."

"Ah, yes," Hannah said. "It was the armor he had on, Pullo. It's one of the Shards of Heaven: the Aegis of Zeus. It has the power to preserve life, to heal and protect the body."

"Healing." Pullo chewed on the word for a moment. "Sounds right. I don't know how many arrows he'd been pinned with, but he was still coming. Like a mindless thing."

"There are stories of Alexander the Great being the same when he wore it," Caesarion added. "They say he had a singular focus of determination, perhaps of rage. The Aegis must do that to men somehow." He looked at Hannah hopefully. "Do any of your stories say that? About the Shards driving men mad?"

"Not that I know of," Hannah said. "But we aren't meant to use them. Few who have ever done so have survived."

When she answered him there was a look in her eyes that she gave him occasionally. It was not unlike the one he remembered on the faces of servants in the palaces of Alexandria who had thought him to be the living embodiment of the god Horus. It was a look that made him uncomfortable, and so he looked back to Pullo. "So you knew he was coming back for the Ark?"

"I did. He was going to get it. I knew I couldn't stop him. And you'd only barely managed to do it once, if you'll forgive me for saying so."

Caesarion held up his hands. "I don't disagree at all, Pullo. I was unconscious at that point."

"Anyway, I don't know why, but it was right then that I remembered those explosives that were there to bring down the bridge. I didn't know if they would kill us all, but I didn't think I had much choice. So I blew them up."

"I saw it from across the harbor," Vorenus said. "It was horrific."

"I remember the flash of fire. Red and orange. Hot and angry. And then everything became a white light. There was wind. Water. Earth. Waves upon a shoreline. It was like all my memories, all my life, all at once. Things I've done and said. Things that made me laugh. Things that wake me in the night."

Pullo's voice had become a whisper, and Caesarion became aware of how he had leaned in to hear him. Everyone else had, too.

"And then I sensed a darkness rising, like a great wave that would carry me away." The big man paused for a moment, his head down and his eyes closed. After several long and steady breaths his head came up and he looked his old friend in the eye. "It was frightening, Vorenus. I don't care about admitting it now. But it was also . . . well, it was comforting, too." He looked around at them all. "It was the end, I guess. And it felt like that darkness was where I was supposed to go. So it felt right. My fear melted away, drifted away. I was ready. And it was then that I heard it."

"Heard what?" Hannah asked.

"A voice. Out of the dark. Only, not words. More like a breath of air, but when it hit me I understood what it was saying. It told me I needed to come back. I wasn't done. And the darkness fell back away, and I saw beyond it in just that moment. Just for a flash before I woke up."

"What did you see, Pullo?" Vorenus had leaned in even farther.

"Heaven," the big man said. He looked at Hannah. "That's what you call it, isn't it? We would've said the Elysian Fields, but I guess it's the same thing, really. It was white shores. The sun coming up over a wide country of soft, green hills."

Pullo's eyes turned to look out toward the Nile, but Caesarion could tell he wasn't looking at the river. Not now. He was looking beyond them all, at a far green country.

No one spoke. Everyone seemed wrapped in their own thoughts and questions, but no one dared disturb Pullo from his dream.

After a time Pullo blinked away the memory, and he smiled, looking back at them all. His expression reminded Caesarion of the look on Rishi's face when he talked of the Teacher. "I only saw it in a glimpse," Pullo continued. "But whatever it was, I can tell you that what the monk said a little while ago isn't true: not everything after this life is suffering. The place I saw was beautiful. But it was so much more. It seemed like a place I could run forever."

"Was it only what you wanted to see?" Vorenus asked.

Caesarion blinked for a moment, uncertain of the older man's tone. Was he attacking the truth of Pullo's vision?

If he felt any hostility, Pullo didn't show it. He simply shrugged. "You know, I've thought about that. Maybe. Maybe not. But it felt real to me." He sighed. "Anyway, as soon as I saw it the whole thing was snatched away, almost like a cord that had been tying me to that place had been cut. I awoke in the rubble."

For a little while they were all silent. Bees buzzed in the air, dancing between flowers.

"How'd you get out?" Hannah asked. "I saw how much rock there was."

"You'd know better than me about how much rock there was, though it certainly felt like a lot when I was under it in the dark. The way it had fallen there was space around my head and part of my chest. Like a pocket, where there was enough air to breathe, and at times I could smell the sea beyond the smells of the shattered stones. A few times I heard birds and even distant voices. I couldn't tell time, but I'm guessing I was under there a day or two. But the bridge needed to be rebuilt. So eventually people came down to clear the rubble. They found me.

"They were pretty amazed I was alive, but I think the weight of the stones actually stopped a lot of my bleeding. Lots of bones were broken. And my back was really badly burned." The big man laughed lightly and gestured to his face. "If you think this is bad, then you don't want to see what I look like back there.

"Anyway, they took me to that same House of Asclepius you were in, Vorenus. And wouldn't you know it, but that same old priest helped bring me back to the land of the living."

"Did he recognize you?"

"He did, amazingly enough. For all that I'd been torn up and smashed and burned, he knew who I was. There were a lot of fevers the first couple of weeks, and he gave me a lot of medicines for the pain. But when I really finally came out of it, he told me how he'd destroyed my legionnaire uniform and that he'd told people I was just an unfortunate fisherman who was in the wrong place at the wrong time." Pullo chuckled. "He had no way of knowing how bad I am at catching fish."

"Patience was never your strong suit," Vorenus agreed, smiling.

"Well, anyway, he got me back to what you see here. I offered to do what I could to repay him, but he said that the Lord Pharaoh had always been a loyal supporter of his house, and that he owed you, Caesarion."

"He was truly a good man," Caesarion said. "The finest healer I ever met."

"He certainly proved it again with me."

"And thanks be to Asclepius," Vorenus said. "Why didn't you contact Didymus, tell him you were alive?"

"I thought about it. But by then I'd heard that you had been executed out on Antirhodos, my friend, that you had been killed, my lad, and that the Lady Selene had been captured and would be forced to wed Juba the Numidian. I'd heard nothing of the Ark, though, so I thought maybe it had gotten away. Meeting with Didymus—well, I just thought it wouldn't do any good, and if I was recognized it could lead to Juba and Octavian maybe finding the Ark through him. Besides, what good was I now anyway? Better to just let it go and move on."

Vorenus sighed. "You were certainly right about the troubles of being recognized at the Great Library."

"The blame for that is mine," Caesarion said. "You had been against meeting with Didymus. Khenti's death is mine to bear."

Vorenus nodded. Then he reached over and patted the knee of his big friend. "But if not for that tragedy, I suppose we would not have met again. Good can come from evil things."

"All is not suffering," Hannah said, smiling.

"That's one way of looking at it," Pullo said. "Seker found me in the slums a year or two ago, where I was doing anything I could do for the coin to buy bread. He hired me and paid me well enough. I didn't like hurting people, but he told me I wouldn't really need to."

Caesarion smiled. "One look at our giant here and people got in line? I know the feeling. As a kid I was scared to death of the great Pullo. Still am, I think."

Color blushed the big man's cheeks, turning his scars into rivers of dark blood. "Well, he was right, anyway. Mostly I just stood around and grunted now and then. I really can't tell you much beyond that. This scholar came to us about kidnapping someone he said was worth a pretty coin. I didn't know until the moment of it that it was Vorenus here. Was like seeing a ghost."

"For me, too," Vorenus said.

"Well," Pullo said, his voice taking on a mock-defensive tone, "I *did* die. So maybe I *am* part ghost."

"The finest ghost I could ask for," Caesarion replied. "Any special powers come back with you?"

Pullo frowned and bit on his lip in concentration as he turned his hands over and back in front of himself. "Doesn't seem so. Just the strength of Hercules, but that's nothing new."

"Just the same old Pullo, then," Vorenus said.

"Older old Pullo," the big man replied, cracking his neck for emphasis.

"I don't think so," Hannah said, interrupting their companionship. When Ceasarion looked over, he saw that she had that look upon her face again, only this time she was giving it to Pullo. "Not the same man at all. He was sent back. That makes you quite special indeed, Titus Pullo."

Pullo blushed. "We don't know what for. And maybe it was all in my head. I don't know."

"I don't think so," Hannah said. "I think you saw beyond."

Pullo seemed suddenly nervous to be the center of everyone's attention. "Well, anyway, that's my story. And I don't think it's the important thing right now."

The big man looked over at Vorenus, who started to open his mouth, then closed it again.

"What is it?" Hannah asked.

Vorenus stared at the ground and shook his head for a moment before looking up to address them. "He means the Ark. We need to move it."

"Why?"

When Vorenus didn't answer her right away, Caesarion started putting the pieces together. "Because of this scholar, Thrasyllus. You think if he heard enough to know to attack you on the canal, he might have heard enough to know that we are here."

"He might have."

Caesarion frowned. It was possible, he supposed.

"He never said anything about this place," Pullo said. "Or about the Ark. Or about you, Caesarion."

"Doesn't mean he doesn't know," Vorenus said. "He killed Seker, right?"

Pullo nodded in agreement. "He did. Stabbed him in the back."

"So he's capable of deceit," Vorenus said. "He wants to hide something."

"He also probably didn't have the money to pay what he promised," Pullo pointed out. "When he saw that everything had gone wrong he might have just killed the man for his money."

It was a valid point, Caesarion thought. "If he knew about

me, though, why go after you? I mean no offense, Vorenus, but I can only imagine that my head is worth rather more than yours these days."

Vorenus smiled. "No offense at all, Pharaoh. Honestly? I think he might have been greedy. Maybe he wanted to use me to get to all this. So he could have the Ark all to himself."

Caesarion found himself frowning again. "Maybe."

"He never struck me as a schemer," Pullo said, "though I'm admittedly not the best judge of character. I have been friends with Vorenus for quite a long time, which says a lot."

Everyone smiled, but the mirth didn't last long amid such serious matters. "I think it's something we need to consider," Vorenus said. "It would be prudent to move the Ark."

Caesarion nodded. Prudence was indeed wisdom, though the danger seemed slight. He turned to Hannah. She was the keeper of the Ark, after all. Any decision would have to be up to her. "What do you think?"

Even frowning she was more beautiful than anyone he'd ever laid eyes on. Love did that to your point of view. Caesarion had read enough stories of love to know the truth of that old wisdom. But he also knew that it didn't really matter when you were the one in love.

"Hard to say," she said. "You're right that this is a danger, Lucius Vorenus. And it is true that we should be mindful to protect the Ark above all else."

Pullo's brow raised. "But?"

Hannah chewed on the inside of her cheek as she thought, an odd habit that Caesarion had long found endearing. "But we cannot jump at shadows," she finally said. "We cannot move the Ark at every whisper of something that may be wrong. It is hidden here for now, safe with the help of people we know and trust. It will need to be moved at some point, but to do so we would have to get it into the open. That might only compound our dangers. This is why the Ark was placed in Alexandria so long ago: we could not continue to move it. The Shard needed a home where it could be safe. And it *was* safe there. For three centuries it was safe."

"And you think this can be its home now?" Pullo asked.

"I don't know," Hannah admitted. "Perhaps not. But it served as a temple for the Ark once before. Perhaps it can again."

"Though it had to be moved from here because it was unsafe," Vorenus pointed out.

Hannah nodded. "This is true. But it was a different time. We don't know what is to come."

"The truth is," Caesarion said quietly, "that we know precious little at all."

Pullo made a scoffing noise. "I think Vorenus is right, but then I usually do. At the same time, this Thrasyllus is just one man. What harm could he do?"

Vorenus looked at the ground. "Khenti is dead because of that one man."

For a few moments everyone was silent. Then, at last, Hannah let out a heavy breath. "He can do little enough alone. The only danger now would be if he got help, right?"

Vorenus thought for a long time, then he finally agreed.

Hannah nodded. "Then it is settled. The Ark stays here for now."

20

Growing in Darkness

Almost two months after she rescued Juba and Caesar, Selene sat with her husband on a bench outside the room where Caesar continued his recovery. Praetorians stood to either side of the door before them, faces impassive, eyes straight ahead. Selene's hand slid across the stone, touched his, and their fingers intertwined. They so rarely touched these days, and the connection made her want both to smile and weep.

Neither of them had spoken of the traumas they had suffered while they were apart. Between their exhaustion and the uncertainty of what would happen to Caesar—and what his health might mean for them—it had been as if a distance had settled between them since Vellica had burned, since the legionnaires who'd swept forward at the first signs of smoke had found them all, stumbling from the hillfort's walls, carrying the fevered Octavian. Tiberius, Juba later learned, had objected to the assault, but Carisius had nevertheless called out the legions. He had come down onto the field personally when word came up through the ranks that Caesar was in danger, so Selene and Juba had been standing by Carisius when the burning gate of Vellica gave way and the legionnaires entered the hillfort and began sweeping out what was left of the Cantabrians, sending them fleeing into the rocky hills.

After they had returned to the encampment, Juba had asked no questions as to why his wife had hurried ahead to the tent, insisting that he check to be sure that Octavian was still alive. His exhaustion, Selene suspected, had overwhelmed any suspicion.

Still later, when he'd come at last to the tent, when they were alone, Juba had asked only the briefest of questions about how she had done what she did. He'd nodded. He'd told her how brave she had been. How proud he was of her. He'd helped her out of the Aegis, and a profound weariness had overtaken her. The Shards hidden as best he could manage among their things, he'd helped settle her into the bed. He never even asked why unfamiliar sheets were upon it.

She'd burned the old ones.

The door to Caesar's room opened, and one of the assistants appeared. "He is calling for you now," the man said.

Juba nodded, stood, and with his hand still in hers helped Selene do the same. She smiled in a gratitude that ran to the core of her heart.

As they passed the door, the assistant leaned close to whisper, "Be brief. He is still weak." Then he quietly closed the door behind them, leaving them alone with the emperor of Rome.

He lay in a bed of great cushions and silks, propped up on pillows. The doors to the balcony behind the bed were open, and Selene could see the ever-breathing waves of the sea over the roofs of the city beyond them. In the room she shared with Juba they could taste the salt of those waves, but here the air was thick instead with medicinal oils and burning incense that drifted on the trembling little breeze.

Octavian had never been an imposing man. Unlike his adopted father, Julius, or his great rival and Selene's father, Mark Antony, he could little intimidate with his stature. His

success, his power, lay in his determination, his will to domi-
nate, and his shrewd cunning to forego small battles in favor
of final victory in a larger war. That, and his singular focus on
his goal.

The Peace of Rome.

If he was an unimpressive physical figure in his best days,
he was startlingly weak now. His face was gaunt, his skin pale
and stretched over his cheekbones. His eyes were dark-rimmed
and sunken, and when he smiled and beckoned them forward
it was with frail arms.

"Lord Caesar," Juba said, bowing low before advancing to
the bedside.

Selene followed suit, and the two of them sat in chairs that
had clearly been set there for just such audiences.

"I've seen better days," Octavian said, his voice a tired rasp.

Juba smiled. "Could be worse, Caesar."

"Indeed so. I'll be bedridden all winter, I fear, but I could
be dead, my brother. I should be." He closed his eyes to take
a deep breath. "You saved me," he said when he opened them
again. "Both of you."

Selene nodded her head in a kind of bow, hoping it would
hide her moment of panicked fear. What did Octavian remember of the escape? Had he seen them using the Shards?

Juba's hand was once more in hers, and he squeezed it in
reassurance, steadying her. "We could not leave you behind,"
he said.

"Yes, you could have. And perhaps you should have."

"Lord Caesar," Selene started to object, "we would never—"

His frail arm raised again, cutting her off. "You have more
cause to hate me than most, Selene. I will not have us pretend
otherwise. But that morning of the attack . . . I tried to explain why."

Selene nodded. "The Peace of Rome. It is a worthy dream."

"I am glad you think so," he said. Once more he took a deep breath, though his voice was seeming stronger than it had been. "I want you to be a part of it. Both of you."

"How can we serve, Lord Caesar?" Juba asked.

"By becoming what you were meant to be."

"I don't understand," Selene said.

"A queen, my lady."

Selene blinked. A queen? For a moment Selene's heart soared, as visions of a return to Egypt danced in her head. But she pushed them away. Whatever paths were set before her, no road could lead her back to Alexandria. Caesar would never allow it. To think otherwise was a childish, foolish hope.

"And you a king, my brother. Naturally." Octavian laughed lightly for a moment before a cough cut him off. Juba reached out to hold his shoulder as he shook, and then lowered him back into the pillows when the fit had passed.

"Shall I get someone?" Selene asked.

Another raspy deep breath from Caesar, and he shook his head. "Please don't. They've no idea what ails me." He turned to Juba. "But you do."

Juba nodded. "You should not have done that. You shouldn't have grabbed it. You knew the danger."

"Only too well. But I had to do it. You're no slave, my brother. I was wrong to use you as I have." There were tears in Octavian's tired eyes. "I only hope you can forgive me."

Juba's jaw tightened, and Selene wondered at the emotions that must be surging through him. He squeezed her hand once again. "I have. You did what you thought right. Sometimes the hard decision must be made for the greater good. A great man once told me that, in the tomb of Alexander the Great."

Caesar nodded in remembrance. Selene remembered it, too. She was there that day, though Octavian did not know it. She listened from behind a door as her future husband negotiated for the lives of her and her brothers with the man who would become the emperor.

"Peace is a greater good," she whispered. It was true, after all, though she still wasn't sure if she could live it. She abruptly realized that her free hand was resting against her belly, and she consciously moved it away.

Octavian shifted on his pillows. "I do believe in that dream," he said. "I always will. But I know now there are things that should not be done. There are powers that cannot be used again."

"I agree," Juba said.

"And so tonight will be your last night in charge of the watch." Octavian's voice, though still weak, nevertheless managed the tone of command. No matter his physical appearance, he was, Selene thought, every ounce a leader of men. "You will prepare at once to go to Mauretania."

"Mauretania?" It was a frontier province, south of Hispania on the other side of the sea. It was almost as far from Egypt as it was possible to be.

"I cannot have you in Egypt," Octavian said. "But you will be a queen, Selene."

"Thank you, Lord Caesar," she said.

"I realize, too, that I never formally gave you both a wedding gift."

"Already you have done so much," Juba said.

Octavian simply smiled. "There was a wagon in Vellica. A wagon Corocotta had taken from me."

Selene nodded, but it was Juba who spoke. "One million Sesterces."

Octavian shrugged his thin shoulders. "Corocotta managed to take a few bags with him before he fled, but yes, most of it was still there when the legions arrived. It's yours now.

It will go with you to Mauretania, though I may keep the wagon."

Selene just stared, as did Juba. Octavian let out another weak laugh.

"I . . . I don't know what to say," Selene said.

"You need say nothing. You saved my life. You saved Juba's. You gave me victory in Vellica, a victory that will be proclaimed across the empire as a most glorious and honorable win—omitting, as it must, my capture, my illness, and whatever it was that you did to bring us out of there. History will never know the truth of what happened, Selene. I do not think I want to know it. But I do know that whatever happened, however it happened, you alone succeeded where my legions could not. And whatever else you might think of me, please know I am a man who pays my debts. I reward those who are loyal to me. I only hope this will be true for the king and queen of Mauretania."

Juba's fingers were tight against Selene's. "For the Peace of Rome," she said.

Juba let out his breath, and his fingers relaxed in hers. "Peace," he agreed.

Octavian's eyes shut for a moment in a look of pure relief. Even his breathing seemed easier, as if a great weight had been lifted from him.

Had he been worried, Selene wondered, that they would turn against him? Had he so well guessed the truth of those dreams of vengeance?

"One thing more," Octavian said. His eyes opened, and he stared at Juba.

"Yes?"

"When you leave me, when you go to Mauretania, you will take the Trident and the Lance with you."

"Take them?"

"I wish never to see them again."

Juba opened his mouth, but then simply nodded.

"They are yours now," Octavian said. "Do with them what you will."

"Yes, Caesar."

Octavian seemed to relax even further. "I should rest now. And you must prepare."

Selene and Juba thanked him, bowed, and stood. But just as they were leaving his bedside, Caesar spoke once more. "I would be rid of them, Juba. Destroy them. Throw them into the sea. I felt the darkness. They aren't meant for us."

. . .

The sun was setting as Selene lay nestled in her husband's arms. Her head resting on his shoulder, her hand making circles across his chest, she watched his breathing beginning to slow and felt the last tremors of his pleasure pass through his body.

"Thank you," he said, and the muscles of the arm beneath her rolled as his hand came up and ran through her hair. It was the first time they'd made love since Vellica. The distance that had been between them was gone. He was her Juba again. And she his Selene.

Selene's eyes fluttered as a breeze rolled gently through the open doors to the balcony, tasting of the clean sea, so different from Caesar's room. Out in the distance, she could hear the calls of the seabirds following fishermen as they brought in the last of their day's work to the harbor. She felt more at peace than she had for many weeks, for a moment even forgetting the darkness growing within her.

"So how are you?" Juba asked.

Selene smiled, and she raised her head to kiss him in answer before settling back down again.

Against her cheek she felt his smile. "You'll be a great queen, my wife."

"Mauretania," she whispered.

"I'm sorry. I thought you'd be happy."

Selene hadn't realized that she'd been frowning. She turned it into a smile and kissed him again. "I am happy. Sorry, I was just thinking about home."

"I understand. It isn't my home either. But you know he can't have me in Numidia, just as you can't be in Egypt."

"I know."

"But we can make it *our* home, Selene. Far from Rome. Far from all this. We can just be you and me there. Alone together."

"Alone together." Selene playfully poked at her husband's ribs. "I like the sound of that."

Juba grinned. "Until we have children anyway."

Selene gave the quickest of smiles before she turned away from him to hide what she could not keep from her face. She tried to steady her racing heartbeat as she made a show of gathering up the blankets that had been kicked down to the foot of the bed during their lovemaking. "A new start," she finally managed to say.

His fingertips ran along her naked back. "A chance to put everything behind us."

Not everything, she thought to herself. She took a deep breath, pulling up the gathered covers as she crawled back up to him and nestled against him once more. "A king. I know no one who could be a better one."

"I hope so," he said. "With you at my side I feel I can take on anything."

"Well, I'm not going anywhere."

His arms enfolded her in a hug.

For a moment Selene said nothing as she thought about what it all meant. "Can we truly do it?" she finally asked. "Be loyal to Rome?"

"I don't know anymore." Juba's voice was unsteady, uncertain. "I have so much cause to hate him. But what he wants to build, what he wants to achieve—"

"The Peace of Rome," Selene whispered.

"He really did talk to you about it?"

Selene nodded. "Just before the battle started. He told me that Rome is civilization and justice. He told me how peace reigns in Rome, and that wars like that at Vellica might be necessary right now, but that peace is on the other side of them."

"Do you think he's right?"

Selene bit her lip, thinking. "I think my mother would have thought the same thing. I think there's a reason that she worked so hard to ally herself with Rome. So, yes. I think he's right. And a part of me hates him even more for it."

Juba squeezed her again. "I think so, too. And I think he cares for me. Truly, like a brother. I think I'm one of the only friends he thinks he has in this world. And if he ever treated me badly it was only because he loves his dream even more." He took a deep breath. "I may not have known that before, but he's sick because he tried to save me. That's what he was talking about. When he grabbed the Trident, he couldn't control it and it almost killed him. He did it to try to save me."

Selene nodded, thinking back to that moment in the Cantabrian prison. "That's why you couldn't leave him."

"It's why I'm loyal, I guess."

Selene looked up at him and saw the mix of emotions there: the feeling that he was betraying his father, betraying his home, betraying *her*. Her fingers brushed his cheek. "I know. I understand."

He smiled at her, dampness at the corners of his eyes, and she felt the relief coming through him. She was glad he didn't know what Tiberius had done. It would ruin him.

Outside, the world moved closer to darkness. She laid her head back down and held him close, not wanting to let him go.

"And now he's given us the Shards," he finally said.

Selene stared out into the coming night. "What will you do with them all?"

She felt him shudder. Memories, she knew, of their escape. Memories of what he'd done, how many men he'd killed in the impulse of a moment. He had nightmares about it, nearly every time he slept, though she pretended not to know.

She pressed herself closer to him, wishing she could shield him from the pain. "You saved our lives. All of our lives. You did what you had to do. You had no choice."

"That still doesn't make it right," he whispered.

Selene didn't know what to say. How could she? In these last years not a day had gone by that she did not hate herself for bringing the asp to her mother, though she knew it was what she had to do. And now, these last weeks not a day had gone by that she did not hate herself for what Tiberius had done to her, though she knew she'd had no choice.

Her hand, without her thought, rested on her belly.

"I never dreamed of this." He shivered beneath her. "I don't want them. I don't want the power anymore."

Selene at last raised up to look at him. She saw that he was staring off into the shadows of the room. "I think that's why you must have it," she said. She tried to smile. "And that's why you'll make a good king."

She saw the corners of his mouth lift slightly, but still the darkness fell heavy upon him. She was wrong when she imagined that her old Juba had at last come back to her this afternoon, she decided. A part of him was still in Vellica, and might always be.

"Four Shards of Heaven," he said.

Selene saw them all in her mind: the Trident, the Lance,

the Palladium, the Aegis of Zeus. Even Alexander never had so many.

He shook his head. "I would like to destroy them, like he said, but I don't think that's even possible." He took a deep breath. "They must be kept safe. And they must never be used."

Selene nodded, though in her mind she felt again the closeness of her mother's memory as she'd soared with the Palladium. What had that meant? She yearned to feel it once again.

"Selene," Juba said.

Selene blinked her focus back to her husband, her king.

"They must never be used. We must not let what happened in Vellica happen again."

Selene nodded, consciously forced her hand to move away from her belly. "I understand," she said. "We aren't meant for such things. We can't take it."

His smile, she thought, was genuine and beautiful. "We will keep them secret and safe. We must hardly even speak of them."

Selene swallowed the memories of Tiberius that flashed against her mind, and she agreed, enfolding herself into the warmth of Juba's embrace for the last minutes before the dark.

He lingered as long as he could, but his duty called him away. He dressed, kissed her, and was gone.

Selene rose, too, wrapping herself in a thick robe to ward off the deepening chill. Winter was coming, she thought.

And then the spring, she reminded herself. A new start. A fresh start.

It had to be.

. . .

It took Isidora less than an hour to procure what she required. The crippled girl had followed Selene and Juba to Tarraco, and she had been given a small room close beside theirs. She had become a kind of maidservant to Selene, content to serve her as best she could on the new crutch that they'd had made for her.

She sat now upon the seat on the balcony, holding up the little glass vial, her face half shadowed by the flickering light of the oil lamps that had been lit inside the room.

Selene took the vial, then set it upon the stone rail of the balcony, as if it were hot. Her hand lingered beside it for a moment before it quickly withdrew. She pulled her robe closer.

The contents of the vial were a dirty green, flecked with spots of brown and yellow. She tried to appear disinterested, but in truth her heart was revolting in her chest. "What is in it?"

"I don't think you want to know, my lady."

Selene nodded. She had heard tales of such potions. "And it will . . . expunge it?"

"She said it never fails, though it will be painful."

Isidora let out her breath, long and unsteady, and Selene realized that she, too, was nervous. "Surely less painful than other solutions."

"Yes, my lady. But you will be ill before your body begins passing it."

Selene looked out to where the lights of the city were flickering. Somewhere out there, her husband was receiving reports, keeping the watch. "Did she say how long?"

"Before it begins? An hour. Perhaps two."

"And it will leave me unharmed for the future? It won't prevent me from another—with Juba?"

"She said it would not. I was very clear on the need for that. She said she understood."

"Good." Juba said he wanted a fresh start. A family.

"Are you sure there is no other choice? You could go away,

we could hide it. And then afterward claim it is mine. Give it away. Expose it. The potion . . . When I was asking around, some said that it can kill."

Selene swallowed hard. "I've nowhere to go. I'll stay with my husband. This must be done."

"Then drink it all," Isidora said. "The woman said you must drink it all."

"I will." She looked back at the girl. "I had no one else to trust in this. Thank you."

"I owe my life to you, my lady. You know you don't need to thank me."

"And you don't need to serve me. I didn't take you from one slavery to put you in another. You are a Roman citizen. You can return home. Juba and I, we can give you enough coin—"

"There's nothing left for me there. You did save me from slavery, Lady Selene. For that I thank you, and for that I choose to serve you. Not as a slave, but as a citizen. If you'll have me."

Selene smiled, despite her fears. She reached out and took the girl's hand. She squeezed it. "And I will indeed. Thank you, Isidora."

Isidora bowed her head to kiss her hand. Then, when she let it go, she looked up with a question on her face. "Lady Selene, may I ask you something?"

"Of course."

"What you said before, back in Cantabria, about my name— you said it means 'gift of Isis.'"

"I did. Yes."

"And you said Isis wouldn't want me to live in chains. You said it like you knew her."

"I suppose I do, in a way." Selene once again recalled that feeling she'd had when she was flying, that sense of her mother's presence. "In Egypt, where I come from, Isis is one of the greatest of the gods. She is a goddess of nature and magic. They say that a long time ago her husband, Osiris, was killed by the god of the desert, named Set. The murderer dismembered Osiris and cast the parts of his body across the world. But Isis was loyal to him. She traveled across land, river, and sea until she had brought them all together. And then, with the secret spells of the god Thoth, she raised him from the dead, and together they conceived a child, Horus, who destroyed Set and reestablished peace and prosperity in Egypt. Because of this Isis is the perfect mother and wife." She smiled at the girl. "She is also a great friend to slaves."

"I like this goddess. Do you worship her?"

Selene wondered what to say. Should she tell her that there had only ever been one God, and that He was dead? That the Lance Isidora had used to kill so many men was one of the Shards, one of the pieces of the throne of God's unmaking? No, she decided. Not yet. Perhaps not ever; they must never speak of it.

"In Egypt many people believe that the queen of Egypt is the embodiment of Isis. And that after her death she becomes one with the goddess."

"You believe this?"

There was something like hope in the crippled girl's voice, and Selene recognized the longing in her eyes. Isidora wanted something to hold on to. Something permanent beyond the world of pain and suffering that she had known. She wanted the gods and goddesses. Selene recognized it, because she wanted it, too. "My mother was the queen of Egypt," she said.

Isidora blinked. "Cleopatra? Your mother was Cleopatra?"

"She was. You have heard of her?"

The girl's eyes were wide. "I heard she was very beautiful."

"She was. My mother was the most beautiful woman I've ever seen."

"And she fought against Caesar. With Mark Antony."

Selene nodded. "He was my father."

"They say they died together. She killed herself with an asp so that Caesar wouldn't—" Isidora's eyes got wide and her face flushed. She lowered her head. "Oh, I'm sorry, Lady Selene. I didn't mean to talk . . . I'm sorry."

"It's all right." Selene reached out to raise the girl's face gently so that she could look her in the eye. "It was years ago. And it is true. My father fell on his sword when our city was defeated. And my mother chose the snake's poison over a Roman Triumph." That she herself had brought Cleopatra the asp, she didn't say.

"Anyway, my mother was supposed to be Isis, but she was really only a woman. I know why people believe in the gods, Isidora. I understand the fear. And it doesn't matter to me what you choose to believe about this world, so long as you learn to believe in yourself."

"I *do* want the gods to be real," Isidora whispered. "I want to think I will see my parents again."

Once more Selene recalled that feeling of closeness with the memory of her mother in the skies above Vellica. It couldn't have been real, but it had felt so very much like it was, like she could just reach out and touch her, as if her face was just behind the thinnest of veils. Selene felt like she would give anything to see her mother's face again. "I wish that, too."

Isidora blinked in the half-light. "You must hate him."

"I have great reason to do so."

"But you saved his life."

Selene nodded, thinking about what Juba had said. The Peace of Rome. A dream that perhaps existed beyond vengeance. "I did."

"I do not understand, my lady. But I will trust you. I will follow you, whatever your choice."

Selene opened her mouth to tell her what a fool's errand it was to follow her, how so little good had come of her choices, but she knew it wasn't what the girl needed to hear. "We will leave these shores," she said. "You need to know that. I understand if you don't want to go."

"Is it far?"

"Not far. Caesar has given us the kingdom of Mauretania, south across the sea. He has given me a great dowry as a late wedding gift, and we will rule there as king and queen."

"I will go with you. I told you, there's nothing for me here."

"I'm glad."

Isidora smiled, as if she'd never heard such a kindness. Then her eyes widened a little. "So you are a queen."

I always was, Selene thought. She smiled and nodded.

"Then may I ask one more question, my queen?"

"If you promise not to address me like that in private."

Isidora's smile melded into a blush. Then for a moment she seemed to be searching for the right words. "Is it . . . was it for this gift that you did not kill him?"

"It was not," Selene said, glad that her motives were far beyond wealth. But if not that, then what were they? How could she explain what she herself still didn't understand? The Peace of Rome. The words had haunted her dreams for weeks. "Nor was it for the kingdom. I didn't kill him because I think that he's right."

"So you have made your peace with Rome?"

Selene felt her eyes begin to drift toward the little glass vial for a moment, and she had to force herself to look at Isidora. "Almost."

Isidora nodded. "I am glad. I've had enough of war." She leveraged herself up and took her crutch. "Will there be anything else?"

"No, thank you." Only now did Selene let her gaze fall upon the vial. She had to do it. And it had to be tonight.

"I can stay if you need." Isidora's voice was a whisper.

Selene swallowed hard, tried to smile as she looked away from the glass to the girl who would be, she was certain, her friend. "I'll be fine." A part of her had hoped that saying it would help her believe it, but it only spiked her fear. "But please stay close, my gift of Isis. I may call upon you if I need help."

Isidora's smile was broken with worry, but she nodded and bowed before retreating to the door. Once there, her hand upon it, she paused. "I remember when I was younger I did believe in the gods," she said. "I still want to. But I don't believe in them. I can't. Not anymore." At last she turned back to look over her shoulder as she leaned on her crutch. "But I do believe in you, Lady Selene."

Selene knew nothing to say, but Isidora only nodded once more and then opened the door, limping out into the growing night.

When the door was shut, when she was alone, Selene turned and looked out again over the town. Juba was out there somewhere. Her husband. Her king. Her lover.

He didn't know what she carried, what Tiberius had given her, what was growing in the dark. It would destroy him if he did. It was vengeance, and it would destroy them both. He couldn't know. It couldn't survive.

She took a deep, long breath of the cool night air. Then, before she could change her mind, she reached for the vial and swiftly uncorked it.

"Some things we must never speak of," she said.

She raised the glass to her lips, and she drank.

PART IIII

THE GATES OF HELL

21

THE ASTROLOGER'S ALLY

CAESAREA, 25 BCE

Even from out on the waters of the bay, Thrasyllus was stunned by the level of the construction under way in Caesarea. For months the Mediterranean had been buzzing with tales of how the new king and queen of Mauretania had renamed the seat of their kingdom in honor of Augustus Caesar and were engaged in a massive program of public works that seemed destined to make it the jewel of the western end of the sea. All along the shoreline he could see that workers were busy: from the bustling port to the scaffolding that clambered over buildings old and new, which were fast rising, built in a style that Thrasyllus quickly recognized as half Greek and half Roman. It had the feel of a new beginning, and a new beginning was everything Thrasyllus intended to have in his life.

After his failed attempt at capturing Lucius Vorenus, Thrasyllus had been wracked with guilt and despair. The gods had given him such clear direction in leading him to the Roman outlaw, but then all had been lost. And what was worse, he now had blood on his hands. He'd killed Seker and taken his coins that night beside the canal—slashed at the man with a blind rage that made him feel sick every time the memory came back. Even now he didn't like to look at his hands, for fear that he would once more see the thick blood upon them, clinging to his skin, dried to grit beneath his nails.

On the journey back to Alexandria that night, he'd thought about going to the Roman authorities for a reward, to tell them what he knew about Vorenus being at Elephantine—and even the conspiracy of Didymus working with him—but doing so he would have to admit to his own act of murder and his complicity in several more. In the new order of Augustus Caesar's Rome, such violence would not go unpunished. And even if he somehow went unpunished by the Romans, Thrasyllus was certain they'd never let a murderer lead the greatest library the world had ever seen. All was lost.

With no other prospects, he'd once more rented his old room in the city, feeling guilty to be using the slain man's coins but grateful not to be forced to once more beg of Apion and Didymus at the Great Library. To assuage the guilt and pass the time, he'd bought cheap wine by small casks.

Whatever else he expected of his life, he never would have imagined that a week later there would come a knock at the door, and that he would open it to see Lapis standing in the same hallway where he'd first met Seker and the giant, scarred Roman who had doomed the ambush.

One half of her face was bruised near to black, her cheek swollen to the point that all he could see of one eye was a pupil surrounded by red. A line of blood had run its way down the side of her head, smeared into hair that clung to her scalp. Her clothes were disheveled and torn. More blood was smeared upon her body. Her one good eye sparkled for a moment when she saw him, the slightest smile turning up like a wince at the corner of her mouth. "Stargazer," she whispered, and then she'd fallen forward into his arms.

Thrasyllus looked over to her now, where she stood not far away along the railing of the ship, smiling and talking with another of the passengers, an older woman who appeared to be somewhat wealthy.

The gods had taken his dreams away, only to give him one that was greater.

He had given up drinking that night. The money that he'd once spent on wine he now spent on salves and bandages and medicinal aids to help bring her back to health. When her health still teetered, when she fell into a fever that refused to break, he paid for someone to sit with her while he set aside his pride and went to the Great Library, begged for forgiveness from Apion, offering to submit himself to the lowliest work in the inkroom if only he would also be allowed to access the books on medicine. When he'd come home that day, he'd brought with him a copy of the inscriptions on the Asclepeion at Epidaurus, two texts by Erasistratus of Chios, and a bouquet of fresh flowers from the harbor market that he set in a vase by her bedside.

Day after day he'd fallen asleep upon the latest medical texts he'd brought home from the Library, and day by day he succeeded where the physicians had not: he stopped Lapis's internal bleeding, he broke her fever, and he was able to greet her with a smile and the latest bunch of fresh flowers when she at last opened her eyes and smiled at him once more.

Down along the railing, Lapis laughed: a sweet sound, like the song of a morning bird. She took leave of the woman she'd been speaking with, and she began walking in his direction, a smile that could stop the sun upon her face.

She still had a slight limp from what the men who'd taken her had done to her legs, but she'd somehow melded it into a sway of her elegant hips that never failed to thrill his heart. Beyond that, there was nothing to show that she had been beaten so close to death upon the streets.

"My stargazer," she said, coming up to lean against his side.

Her head fell against his shoulder as she joined him in looking out over the waves. The salty breeze off the water raised strands of her black hair, tickling at his cheek.

"You seem to make friends wherever you go," he said, smiling into the sunshine.

She pinched his side playfully. "And you should try talking to people. You can't learn everything from books, you know."

"I know. I just don't have the knack like you do."

"It just takes practice. I wasn't that good when I first had to talk to strangers. I just got better at it over the years."

Thrasyllus nodded, decided to take the conversation in another direction. "So what did you learn from that stranger?" he said, nodding back to the older woman she'd been talking with.

"Not much. Only how to meet the king and queen."

Thrasyllus stiffened and looked down at her. She was still staring out to sea, but he could see enough of the curve of her cheek to see that she was smiling. "You're serious, aren't you?"

Lapis nodded. "Very much so."

"But how—?"

"Trade secrets."

"But really, how did you—"

"She's married to a wine trader," Lapis said. "As it happens, he's friends with the man who supplies the palace. She said she shouldn't have any problem getting you an audience."

Thrasyllus just stared for a moment. "What did you tell her about me?"

Lapis pulled away and turned to look him up and down. "Only the truth: that you were one of the finest scholars in the world. Well, that and the fact that you have a message from the Great Library of Alexandria, which is a little true."

Meeting with Juba and Selene had indeed been his plan, and he'd made no secret of that with Lapis. Caesarea could be a fresh start for them both, he'd told her. It was a chance for a new life, far away from what they had been in Alexandria, far away from what they had done and seen. And he had information that he'd learned at the Library that could help him find favor with the new king and queen. They could use the last of the precious few coins they had to get there, to find a room, to find work. Then he'd find a way to meet with the young royalty. So this was indeed the plan. He just hadn't expected it to happen so quickly. "How long?"

"A few days at most. I was very charming."

Thrasyllus felt like laughing at the perfection of it, at the perfection of her. It would work. He'd lie and tell them he had a message for them from Didymus. Not really a lie, he supposed. What he'd learned about the Shards *did* come from the old man in the end. So of course they would want to see him. Then he could tell them what he'd overheard about the strength of these items being greater in sacred places. And they'd reward him, give him a chance to start a new life. Maybe even let him start his own library here.

"I . . . I hope that was all right," Lapis said, her voice suddenly uncertain.

Thrasyllus shook himself from his thoughts and smiled at her. "Of course it is. I'm just . . . amazed at you, that's all."

Lapis smiled back, and he continued to be astonished that her warmth felt so genuine. "Do you remember what I told you, my stargazer? After I woke up. After I'd come to your room because I didn't know where else to go and you were one of the only ones who'd ever been nice to me. After you saved me. Do you remember what I said?"

Thrasyllus had to look away from the intensity of her azure

eyes. He blinked out across the water at the growing city of Caesarea. "You said I could have you. All of you. That you owed me your life."

"And that I would repay you with whatever was left of the life you gave me. So I am. My old life is done. Seker left me, and I don't know what became of him. There's only you. And if you want to see the king and queen of Mauretania, then by all the gods of heaven and earth I will see it done."

Not for the first time, Thrasyllus thought about telling her that he'd killed Seker, that he'd bought her this freedom—but then he knew he'd have to tell her that in so doing he'd taken away her protection, that he'd left her alone in the streets to be taken and beaten.

Without meaning to do so, he found that he had pulled his father's coin out and that he was rubbing it between his fingers as he thought.

"What are you thinking, stargazer?"

Thrasyllus caught up the coin in his hand and squeezed it hard. "I'm thinking that I adore you, Lapis. Opening the door that night was the best thing I've ever done. And I'm thinking that I need to get better clothes. I can't meet the king and queen of this place dressed as a simple traveler."

"Truly so."

"But we hardly have anything left. We still need to find a room. Food. Work. Not to mention—"

One of her thin fingers came up and rested gently upon his lips, stilling his speech. She smiled in a look that was at once proud and mischievous. "I thought about that." She pulled her finger away and her hand slipped into the fold of her robe for a moment. When it came out, she was holding a small coin purse that he did not recognize.

He started to ask where she'd gotten it, but then he realized he already knew. The wine trader's wife. Lapis hadn't just been talking to her.

Thrasyllus reached out and enfolded her in a hug.

The gods indeed worked in mysterious ways, he reminded himself. And no way was more mysterious than love.

22

The Temple of the Ark

The night was heavy with a thick fog, and the twisting earthen path between buildings of mud-brick and stone could be confusing enough in clear daylight, but Vorenus wasn't the slightest bit worried he would get lost. Even if he hadn't walked the meandering route a thousand times before, Vorenus would have known he was getting closer to the temples by the unmistakable whisper of frankincense that floated ever stronger in the cool, pre-dawn air. Over the smell of the sporadic torches and oil lamps hanging beside doorways that gave a feeble push against the cloudy shadows upon the island, that sweet lemony-pine aroma drew him onward into the night.

Pullo, limping at his side, yawned in the dark. "Do you think they got any sleep at all?"

Vorenus didn't need to ask who he was referring to. Caesarion had been staying up for far too many nights this past year, working with the information that Vorenus had brought to him, trying to better understand the functioning of the Ark of the Covenant. As ever, Hannah had been by his side through it all. "I doubt it."

"Seems like she should be getting more sleep, even if he doesn't."

Vorenus shrugged. Caesarion and Hannah had been married for only two months when she had announced the happy news that she was pregnant. But rather than slow down their work, it seemed to have only intensified it, as if they were in a race with the coming of the child. When Vorenus had asked about it, Caesarion would only say that the child made it all the more urgent that they understand how to use the Ark and how to keep it safe. "I suspect they know best."

"I hope so." Pullo looked around, as if he'd just noticed the shadowy cloud pressing about them. "Heavy fog tonight."

"The time of year for that."

"Can't hardly see but ten feet." Pullo sniffed. "But I can smell it now," he said, smiling.

Vorenus smiled, too, glad that he wasn't the only one who recognized the scent.

Truth be told, despite all that he had learned, the aroma of incense still thrilled him. Vorenus had visited more temples than he could count in his life, and for many years he'd believed that they brought him closer to the gods. A temple might not be the home of a god, but it was nevertheless a kind of access point to the divine. It was a sacred space, and being there had always made him feel less insignificant for the connection with powers greater than himself, as if a little slice of the divinity of the place could be carried with him.

It didn't feel quite like that anymore, of course. None of those gods had been real. And the one God, the one real God, had died giving life to creation. The prayers being chanted, the songs being sung, they were just whispers to old stones. No one was listening. The stone gods did not make a sound.

But he still liked the fragrance. It warmed his heart, in the same way that the smell of certain meats on a cook fire could remind him of his mother and home. It was a memory. It meant something. Even after all this time.

"You know, I never thought much about that smell," Pullo said. "What made it, I mean."

"It's frankincense."

"I know." Pullo yawned again. "I mean to say that I never thought about it being something people bought and traded. It was just something that was always there in all the temples."

"I hadn't thought about it either," Vorenus admitted. "When I was younger I think some part of me just assumed it was the aroma of the gods themselves. That's probably the point of it for the priests, anyway. The sweetness of the air is meant to mimic the sweetness of the gods themselves."

"Funny. I've never heard of the gods being sweet at all." Pullo spit into the fog. "Mostly in the stories they're every bit as rotten as the rest of us."

Years ago, Vorenus would have chided him for his words, would have told him it was dangerous to wrong the sacred powers, but to his chagrin the sacrilegious old bastard had been right to doubt and disbelieve. The gods were made of men's fears, men's desires.

"Anyway," Vorenus said, returning to the earlier subject, "I hadn't thought about where it comes from, either. Until all this mess with Petra it seems like none of us ever did. Except Caesar, I suppose."

There was no denying it: the man whose oversized bronze statue stood watching the harbor not far away was proving to be a stunningly capable leader. Augustus had a grand vision for himself and for the empire, but he also had a practical sense of what needed to be done to make that vision a reality. Everyone knew that the Nabataeans, hidden away in Petra, their secret city carved deep into the mountains, were growing rich from the spice trade, but they were doing so largely by geographic good fortune. As middlemen, they received the incense and other spices from the growers in Arabia Felix and then sold them at great profit to the traders of Rome. Vorenus could easily imagine how this practice would anger someone like Augustus, who wanted not only all the roads of the earth to lead to Rome, but all its coins to flow there, too. Worse still, the Nabataeans, with an effective monopoly on the trade, were holding Rome hostage to higher and higher prices. The incense was a necessity, after all. The temples needed it, and the last thing any shrewd leader desired was to anger the priests. Other leaders would have perhaps negotiated with the people of Petra, but Augustus had instead decided to circumvent them: he ordered Aelius Gallus, the prefect of Egypt, to find a direct trade route to the lands of Arabia Felix, the source of the frankincense. If Gallus could establish a Roman route, Petra could be cut out altogether.

"Truth be told," Pullo said, "Caesar really is doing some good."

"Some." Augustus Caesar had also ordered Vorenus killed, after all. And he'd torn Egypt apart. "Though hiring the Nabataeans themselves to guide Gallus through Arabia was foolish."

Pullo let out a chuckle and shook his head as if in disbelief at the notion. "I can't imagine it ending well."

"Nor I. And maybe it's already ended. Gallus left . . . what? Six months ago? And not a message since. If I were a betting man, I'd wager the Nabataean guide didn't exactly show him the straightest route. Probably just took him out into the desert to die."

"Well, it certainly makes things easier around here for now." Pullo waved his arm vaguely in the direction of the east, toward the Roman garrison town of Syene, just across the Nile.

Though several Roman cohorts remained there, it was nothing like the military presence before Gallus had drawn men away for his expedition. "I don't like being so close to the legions, so the fewer the better."

"Agreed."

Coming around the last turn of the path, they emptied out onto the King's Street, one of the main roads through the town. The pair followed it south in silence for less than a minute before they found it narrowing as it was hemmed in by the large Temple of Khnum looming up on their left and what remained of the ancient temple of the Jews on their right.

The Temple of Khnum, ram-headed god of the Nile's cataracts, was a sprawling and magnificent place: columned and open, with colored tiles and statuary. It was, like most temples Vorenus had known, meant to invite the eye and impress with its grandeur. The incense burned alongside the fires there night and day, and the priests were ever-busy tending to their prayers and to the constant watch they kept upon the level of the Nile, as did the priests of the nearby Temple of Satis, goddess of the flood. Measuring the water level on the stone walls of what they called a Nilometer, a flight of steps that ran like a corridor down into the water, the priests at Elephantine would be the first to detect the yearly flood upon which so much of the kingdom's crops depended.

From Vorenus' point of view, the ancient temple of the Jews was everything that the Khnum temple was not. Sitting across the narrow King's Street from that ornate complex, the Jewish temple seemed more like a warehouse than a place to honor God. The walls of the building were not much taller than two men—far shorter than the grand pillars dedicated to Khnum that in daylight would shadow the walls—and they were squat and thick, built of featureless mud-brick that was unbroken by windows or adornments of any kind. Neither a sign nor any other marker indicated the presence of the temple beyond its simple, heavy wood doors.

Stopping in the cramped street, Vorenus pulled open one of the old temple's doors for his friend and then followed him through, carefully shutting it behind him.

Within the outer walls was a rectangular courtyard that had once been holy ground. Centuries earlier, though, the Jews had been forced to leave the temple, and the Khnum priests had taken it over for use as stables—an act, Hannah was sure, of deliberate desecration. The animal pens were thankfully unused now—they lay in wooden ruins to either side of a cleared, rough path through the courtyard—and the lingering stench of the animal inhabitants was largely overpowered by the incense that floated over the wall the courtyard shared with the larger temple. Yet, the memory of the desecration of the place still persisted—a fact that the Jews had used to their advantage in hiding the Ark here.

Stepping around a pile of rubble in the middle of the courtyard that Hannah said had once been a sacrificial altar, Pullo and Vorenus came to the door of the inner building, the sacred shrine itself. Like the rest of the temple, it was unimpressive from the outside: the same functional brick, with no ornamentation or great artistry upon it. The roof was made of simple cedar beams.

It was what was inside, Vorenus knew, that was so important.

Pullo knocked at the door of the shrine, and they had to wait nearly a minute before latches were unhooked and the door swung open on its bronze hinges.

Hannah was there, smiling with a bright-eyed kindness that contrasted with the dark circles under her eyes. One arm was casually draped across her round belly as if she was resting it there. With her other arm she gestured inward. "Please, do come inside."

Vorenus gave a slight bow of acknowledgment, and then he and Pullo stepped inside, and the door shut behind them.

The building had once been split into two parts: the initial room that they had just entered, and then an inner sanctum farther on. The dividing wall between the two spaces had been broken away over the centuries, however, so that in the middle of the room it remained only as a kind of low bench between the two spaces. The side in which they all stood had been taken up by Hannah and Caesarion's shared bed and the rudimentary makings of a home, including a long table stacked with scrolls and books, among which Caesarion sat, on the bench, with his face hidden in a leather-bound codex. On the other side of the low dividing wall stood the Ark.

It didn't matter how many times he'd seen it, Vorenus still felt a sense of awe and wonder to be near the ancient artifact. Though he'd never seen it used—he'd only heard stories of what it had done in the past—he was nevertheless certain he could sense the raw power of it, like a low thrum filling the room that he could sense in his bones even when his ears could not hear it.

It also never ceased to amaze him how new it looked. It was, quite obviously, a kind of box, wrought of rich acacia wood that was so highly polished that it shimmered in the reflected light of the four lamps in the first room. The bottom was slightly larger than the top, so the sides angled inward, drawing the eye up the thin lines of metal that formed intricate designs of vines and leaves over the wood. On the broad side of the Ark that faced them, those metallic lines twisted into a symbol like an inverted pyramid set within a circle, a horizontal line cutting across its bottom third. Hannah had

worn just such a symbol on a pendant on the night Vorenus
had first met her. Caesarion wore one now.

The top was trimmed with gold, and two small statues
crowned it, one gold, one silver. They were, Hannah had once
explained, meant to be angels, kneeling toward each other,
heads bowed, their wings swept forward as if they were reaching for one another. And between them, flat against the surface
of the Ark's top, was a pitch-black disk, perhaps the breadth of
Vorenus' forearm.

"Thank you for coming, despite the foggy night," Hannah
said. Her voice was quiet, almost a whisper.

The Ark seemed to have that effect on them all: though for
years Vorenus had been coming to this place, he'd found that
their mutual sense of reverence never wavered. "Of course,"
he replied.

Hannah smiled, her face beaming with the unmistakable
vibrant beauty of pregnancy, and then she turned toward her
husband at the table. The young man still didn't seem to have
noticed their arrival. "He gets like this."

"I've not been that focused in a long time," Pullo replied.

"Perhaps never," Vorenus whispered.

Hannah grinned and quietly walked over to stand behind
Caesarion. She bent over and kissed the top of his head. "My
love, they're here."

Caesarion startled, and at last blinked away from his book
to look up at her and then Pullo and Vorenus. His face softened with genuine relief, though his eyes gleamed with excite-
ment. "My friends, please, come and sit."

There was another bench on the opposite side of the table,
and the two legionnaires found places that were clear enough
to sit down upon it. Hannah carefully lowered herself beside
her husband, who smiled at her and reached over to place his
hand upon her stomach.

Hannah's smile was deeply warm. "She's been active today. I think she's excited."

"It could be a boy," Vorenus said.

"I still think it's a girl," Pullo said.

Caesarion looked adoringly at his wife. "The mother always knows best."

"And my mother said that girls are carried low," Pullo said. "And look, she's carrying the baby low."

"Actually, the saying is that girls are carried high," Vorenus pointed out.

"So it is." Hannah rested her hand over Caesarion's, and they both smiled as the child within her moved once more. "But I don't think that's true, anyway. I just have a feeling it's a girl."

"Boy or girl," Caesarion said, "he or she will be more beautiful than we can possibly imagine."

"With two such parents," Vorenus agreed, "it will be so. I can't wait to meet him."

"Or her," said Pullo.

"Beautiful," Caesarion whispered, patting his wife's belly once more.

Hannah squeezed his hand against her, but then nodded toward the piles of writings before her. "That's not why we're here, my love."

Casearion let out a long breath and finally pulled his hand away. He turned to Pullo and Vorenus. "We think we figured it out."

"Figured what out?" Pullo asked.

Caesarion nodded his head in the direction of the artifact over his shoulder. "The Ark. Why it's weaker here, like it has lost some of its strength. When I used it I could sense that."

Vorenus knew that Caesarion and Hannah felt that it had lost some of its powers, but he'd never really asked how they had known it—though he'd always suspected it must be because they'd tried to use it. "I thought you didn't want it used," he said to Hannah.

"It's true. I didn't. I still don't. But you've said it yourself, Vorenus: the Ark isn't safe here in Elephantine."

Vorenus started to open his mouth to ask why they hadn't followed his advice to move it, but Caesarion held up his hand. "It's still safer here than out in the open. All the choices before us have ill outcomes. It has been that way from the moment we left Alexandria. We all know this."

"It's only a matter of choosing the least evil," Pullo said.

Hannah nodded. "Here we have a place of relative security. The Roman garrison is over the water in Syene and only rarely do they come here. Whatever disputes between the priests of Khnum and the Jews who built this place—the ones who were here when my family once kept the Ark in this very place—they are forgotten. And the Therapeutae have welcomed us as the long-lost cousins that we very much are. No one would think to search here for us, for the Ark."

"But if they do," Caesarion said, acquiescing to the arguments of the elder man, "then this place is little capable of protecting the Ark. You are good men, my friends, but all of us together could not stop even a cohort."

"Though a century, perhaps," Pullo said, seeming to puff up at the thought of taking on a hundred men.

Vorenus patted the bigger man on the back. "Not even in our younger days. And we are anything but young now."

"Speak for yourself," the big man muttered. He pointed at his hideously scarred face. "This alone will turn back half of them."

"I think it's charming in its way," Hannah said, causing the furrows on Pullo's face to flush dark.

"Point is," Caesarion said with a smile, "staying here has

been the best of our bad options. But we felt we needed the power of the Ark to help even the odds if it came to it."

Vorenus nodded. "So you tried it."

"I did. Just a little at a time, learning to control it, learning how to control myself. The power . . . it's beyond description. But it's less than what I felt in Alexandria, like it was disconnected from something."

"Didymus said that the Ark drew power from sacred spaces," Vorenus said, remembering what the librarian had told him in Alexandria during the mission that had cost Khenti his life—but which had brought Pullo back to them. "Alexandria was one of them."

"Right. But this is a sacred place, too, is it not?" Caesarion swept his arm across the space inside the shrine. "A temple, built by Jews to honor their God, constructed according to the instructions given in their scriptures by the prophet Moses, the same man who had built the Ark itself. A place where centuries ago the very Ark had been kept, surely just there, where it sits now. What could be more sacred than this? And yet its power was lessened. Still extraordinary, but still less."

"So this place is not as sacred as Alexandria," Pullo said. "Maybe it isn't the making of a building that makes it sacred."

"It seems not," Caesarion agreed.

Vorenus thought back to their walk in the fog. "It's like the incense," he said.

"Incense?"

"Something Pullo and I were talking about on the way here: what they burn in the Temple of Khnum, the frankincense that Gallus and his army are wandering Arabia trying to find. I grew up thinking of it being holy. But it isn't. Not at all. It's just an aroma. It has nothing to do with the gods. But I still like it, it still makes me happy to smell it, to be in those places. All because of what they are in my memory.

Maybe that's what makes a place sacred. Not where it is or what it looks like or what spices they have. It's the people who have been there, the memories of that place. Maybe we leave a part of ourselves where we have believed. Maybe this place . . . well, maybe not enough people believed here."

Caesarion indeed looked like a proud teacher. He turned to Hannah and smiled at her. "You've just explained it far more beautifully than we ever could, Vorenus," she said.

"Your father never taught you any of this?" Pullo asked.

Hannah sighed. "He taught me much, as did my mother. But so many generations have passed since the Ark was used. We were only tasked with protecting it, remember, we were never meant to use it. No one is."

"And no one will," Caesarion said to her, "unless the safety of the Ark is at stake and there simply is no other way."

Vorenus looked over to the Ark. At Actium he'd seen something of what one of the Shards could do, and this was said to be the greatest of them. He truly hoped he would never need to see it used. "So what now?"

Caesarion at last turned back to the two old friends. "Well, that's why we brought you here. We want to move it. We want to take it to Petra."

Vorenus was tempted to shake his head, so strange a suggestion it seemed to be. "Why Petra?"

"Well," Caesarion said, gesturing toward the books around them, "unless I'm wrong, that's where it is from."

23

The Rising of the Moon

CAESAREA, 25 BCE

It seemed like the sun had hardly risen in the sky, and already Selene wanted to go back to sleep. She didn't understand it.

Not that the daily rule of a kingdom was generally exciting. She'd seen enough of her mother's duties to know what to expect, but it didn't make living the truth of it any easier: ruling a country could be an awful bore.

But the tasks were never unimportant. Her mother had taught her that, too, and it had served her well. This morning, for instance, it had been meetings about repairs to the city's main aqueduct. The growing city needed more water, and the old structure was showing signs of being inadequate. If the aqueduct failed, great swaths of the city would be without fresh water. People would die. Chaos would ensue.

Nothing could be more important, she knew that. Yet she still found herself needing to concentrate not to yawn or get distracted as the engineers and artisans explained in detail what was wrong and how best to fix it.

Many rulers, she knew, didn't sit through such interminably detailed accounts of the works they conducted, but that wasn't Juba's way. He wanted to understand the matter—not just in vague waves of the hand, but at the level of chisel and stone. More than once he had surprised those delivering reports by asking for the opinions of the actual laborers themselves. It was unheard of for a king to ask a commoner for his advice, but to Juba it was a simple matter of who had the best information.

It was exactly how her half-brother Caesarion would have ruled if he had lived to take his rightful place upon the thrones of both Egypt and Rome. She could think of no higher praise than that.

And it made her love him all the more.

So she stilled her yawns and generally tried to match her husband's hard focus as he received final clarification on the additional work to be done on the vital structure.

"I see," he said, leaning forward from his seat beside her on the dais. The light from the open balcony behind them stretched their shadows forward onto the polished tile floor of the chamber, and for a moment her attention was caught by the way those darker forms of their enthroned selves looked like statues of the kings and queens of old. Her own shadow needed only a headdress to be her mother's.

We become our parents, she thought. Whether we welcome it or not.

Juba's shadowed form turned to face hers, and she could see the hazy outline of his thickening beard. It gave him a look of wisdom, he thought, and an authority that came with the age he still thought he lacked—as if he had forgotten that all kings were once young. A few weeks earlier she'd pointed out to him that at twenty-three he was a year older than Alexander the Great had been when he'd invaded Asia and begun the destruction of the Persian Empire. He'd laughed at that and told her that Mauretania would be good enough for him.

"What do you think, Selene?"

It took Selene a moment to realize that the shadow was speaking to her, and she looked up from the floor and smiled

at her husband, noting that the beard also made him hand-
somer than ever. "I think your words on this matter are wise,"
she said.

It was rare for her to lose focus like this, and it didn't surprise her that her observant husband had sensed it. His eyes
were twinkling at her with both a kind of amusement for having caught her and a shared pity for their duties. For all that
he seemed born to rule, she knew he'd rather be in bed, too.
Though perhaps not sleeping.

"It appears we are agreed, then." He turned back to the
man who had been placed in charge of the project. "I'll trust
you to see to the matter efficiently. Regular reports will be
thorough and unflinching. Remember that problems in exe-
cuting the plan will not be treated as harshly as attempts to
cover up those problems will be."

The man bowed and retreated along with several other in-
dividuals involved in the project. Selene saw that as he turned,
he was smiling. He had been thorough in his preparations, he
had answered truthfully, and he had been rewarded with over-
sight of the project, which was a key promotion. And like so
many of the men they hired, he seemed relieved that the king
and queen had no tolerance for half-measures or empty ges-
tures. They were going to build Caesarea—and the kingdom
of Mauretania around it—based on a foundation that was as
devoid of rotting corruption as possible. They expected the
best work out of the best people, and they would pay what it
took to get that, because it was the only way to sustain the
dream that they were building.

As the chamber emptied of one group and the herald waited
at the door for the command to bring in the next, Juba leaned
over toward Selene, whispering quietly so that neither the
guards nearby nor the servants in the corners of the room

might hear. "You can go back to bed, my love. I'll delay any-thing of great importance."

Though many queens were mere child-bearers for their kings, present as figureheads at the most formal functions but otherwise uninvolved in the daily workings of the realm, Juba and Selene had agreed—without ever needing to discuss it—that Mauretania would have a true king and queen, who ruled side by side and hand in hand. "I should be well," Selene re-plied, shifting in her seat to move tiring muscles. "I don't know why I'm so tired this morning."

"Well, I know I didn't keep you up late. For once." Juba grinned, and it was clear that there was still a young man behind his beard.

Selene narrowed her eyes. "Maybe that's the problem."

His eyebrows raised. "In that case, my queen, you'll be full of energy tomorrow." He nodded in the direction of the door. "Still, we can take a break. The aqueduct was the most pressing thing. I'm sure everything else can wait."

She shook her head and yawned in the middle of it, which almost made her laugh in the most un-royal of ways. Why *was* she so tired? "I'll be well. I will. Call in the next."

Juba nodded his head, turned to face forward again, and then waved to the herald.

The herald bowed, disappeared through the doorway, and then returned again a few moments later with a young man in tow.

He was a handsome-enough man, well dressed, with deeply tanned skin that immediately reminded Selene of her home-land. She sat up a little straighter and focused on him as he approached. He was clearly nervous about the audience. Most people were, but there was something even more skittish about him, as if he half-expected to be struck by someone. It made her want to pity him. But then as she watched him get closer she realized, too, that he was someone that she felt she'd seen before. She couldn't place where, but she was certain she'd met him.

The herald brought him up to a spot some five paces in front of the thrones, then stopped and bowed low. The young man with him stopped at his side, hesitated for a moment, and then awkwardly did the same.

"Thrasyllus of Mendes," the herald announced. "Come from the Great Library of Alexandria."

As the herald backed away once more, Selene found that she had leaned forward in her seat. To her right she sensed that Juba had done the same.

"Welcome, Thrasyllus of Mendes," Juba said.

Thrasyllus opened his mouth to say something, then closed it and bowed again. "My Lord King," he said. "Thank you for agreeing to see me. And you, too, Lady Queen."

Juba waved at the titles as if he might brush them away, but Thrasyllus appeared too wide-eyed to have noticed. "So, you've come from Alexandria," Juba said, clearly trying to coax him out of his shock.

Thrasyllus nodded but still said nothing.

"It's been a long time since I've seen Didymus," Selene said. "Is he well?"

"He is, Your Majesty. Very well indeed."

"We're pleased to hear it," Juba said. "What business do you have?"

Selene saw the young scholar's eyes flash away from them, toward the guards nearby. *That* was what was making him nervous, she realized. Was it because he was a threat? "I think I remember you from somewhere," she said. "Did I meet you in Alexandria?"

Thrasyllus let out his breath as if he was relieved to be talking of something other than what was on his mind. "You did, my lady . . . my queen. You both did, in fact. During the, ah, fall of the city, when you both came to the Library. I was the one who brought you to Didymus."

"Of course," Juba said. "I remember."

Thrasyllus nodded and smiled gratefully, but once more Selene saw his eyes move toward a servant who was walking quietly from one shadow to another, tending to some of the plants that stood among the pillars and statues lining the walls. Not a threat, she decided. He was nervous because he had expected to talk with them alone.

Selene made a show of making a welcoming gesture with her arms, allowing the movement to subtly give her control over the room. "We are glad you have come, Thrasyllus, and I know we both want to hear more about how things fare in Alexandria, and what news you have from the Library." She abruptly stood, and she heard Juba immediately do the same. "But let us not sit in chairs to hear of it. I think a walk out of doors would do me well on this beautiful morning."

Juba started to say something, but she looked over and a message unspoken passed between them. He smiled grandly and stepped down to stand before her, offering up his hand. "A walk outside would do the three of us much good, I'm certain."

As she took her husband's hand and began to descend, Selene caught the look of pure relief on the scholar's face as he realized that Juba had just said they would be alone.

Whatever the young man had to say, she decided, it was going to be interesting.

.   .   .

The sun was shining even higher in the sky as Thrasyllus took leave of them and moved away.

When he was gone, Selene turned and placed both hands

upon the railing of the long palace balcony they'd been walking along. Stretching out below her, the city of Caesarea was a hive of activity: hammering and crashing, yelling and laughing. They had come so far. For a time she had thought she'd actually left everything behind in Cantabria. But it wasn't true. It had never been true. And now more than ever, the old thoughts were coming back. Vengeance. Death.

And hope, too.

Juba came up behind her and placed his hands gently upon her shoulders. "What are you thinking, my love?"

So many things were swirling in her head that she could not find the words for them. How could she tell him that despite all that they'd tried to leave their old ways behind them she needed this last chance to put her mother's spirit to rest, to put herself at rest? She'd sworn vengeance for her mother, and she'd left it unfulfilled. And she'd felt her mother, closer than ever as she'd flown above Vellica, using the Shards. If even more power could be pulled from the artifacts, what could they accomplish? Could they ally with a greater power? Could they send Tiberius to his grave? That alone could bring her peace, could it not? And maybe they could do more. Maybe they could break the very walls of death, see those whom they'd lost. Juba's father. Her parents. Her brothers. And how to convince Juba to help? He'd sworn never to use the Shards again, and she'd tried to do the same—tried, God knew it, and failed.

At last she let out a long sigh. "It's a lot to think about."

"It is. I can understand why Didymus sent the news of what he'd discovered in person rather than in writing."

Selene nodded. "We saw the power of the Shards in Cantabria. Just the beginnings of it."

"And it was terrible."

Juba's voice was shaking with emotion, and Selene turned

to see that there were tears at the corners of his eyes. His nightmares, she knew, had never gone away. The sight of his face
brought fresh ache to her heart. She nodded at him, knowing
she couldn't deny the truth. "Used in anger. Used to destroy.
Yes." She reached up and gently brushed away the tears. "But
you had no choice, my love. We would have died."

Her husband cupped her hand against his cheek, and he
closed his eyes. "It was wrong."

"But don't you see? You had no choice." She swallowed
hard, nodding at her own argument as it unfolded in her mind.
"But what if you *did* have a choice, my love? What if you could
use that power not to destroy, but to create something new?"

After a moment his eyes opened. They were hurt and angry,
but they were longing, too.

Selene half-turned to take in Caesarea with a sweep of
her arm. "We just heard about the troubles with the aqueduct, how desperate parts of this city—*our* city, Juba—are
for something as small as clean water. And you can give it to
them. You. The Trident. You can use it to give your people
what they need."

Her words seemed to chase away in the air, and there was
silence between them for a moment. "That's not what you
really want."

"It is."

He swallowed hard. "Then it's not *all* you really want. I
know you, Selene."

It was true, and it was pointless to deny it. He knew her as
well as she knew him. *Almost.* "He says that according to
Didymus, the power of the Shards is greater in some places
than others. We saw part of what they were capable of in
Cantabria. But what more can we unlock?"

Juba looked down at the stones beneath their feet, and he
spoke in the faintest whisper. "I'm scared to find out."

"And I'm scared not to try and find out. When I had on the Aegis, when I flew with the Palladium, I felt something. My mother." Selene reached up and put her hands on his shoulders. "I felt her as if she was so close that I could reach and touch her as easily as I'm touching you. I think it was because I was using two of the Shards at once. They amplified each other somehow. Do you remember how Didymus explained what they were?"

He finally looked up and met her eye. "Fragments of the Throne of God, broken when the angels tried to use it to bring God back."

"Don't you see? Bringing the pieces together, we can recover the power of the Throne. If it could be used to find God, couldn't some smaller part of that power enable us to reach things that are still closer?"

He sighed, long and low. "Your mother is dead, Selene. There's no bringing her back."

"And your father, too. But what if we could speak to them, even for a moment? A chance to tell them how much we missed them, how much we loved them. And even if we cannot achieve that, my love, imagine what else we might do with what we have in our hands. We've been given an extraordinary gift, a chance even Alexander did not have. Four Shards are within our control. Brought together in the right place, in the right moment, what limits could there be?"

"I've told you before, Selene: I'm no conqueror. This land is all that I need. I've made my peace with Rome. I thought we both had."

Since Thrasyllus had been speaking with them she'd felt a crack had been forming in the wall that she had built up inside of her. Now, at last, she let it break and give way. She saw again the face of Tiberius, felt once more his hands upon her. The memories, held so long at bay, began to surge forward one after another, and she had to turn away to look at the city, to not let Juba see the despair on her face. "I have," she managed to croak out. "With Augustus Caesar." Her breath caught in her lungs, and once again she placed her hands on the railing—this time to keep from falling.

Juba's arms came around her, starting to pull her into an embrace. "Selene, what are you not telling me?"

"He raped me."

His arms froze. "What?"

"Tiberius," she whispered. Now that the words were unbottled, they started to flow. "While you and Caesar were prisoners. Tiberius came to our tent. He took me." Her tears broke free completely and she spun around, sobbing out of control. "Oh please, my love. Forgive me for not telling you. I wanted to tell you so many times, but I wanted to try to leave it behind, just like you said. You wanted to come here and make a fresh start. Please, Juba, I—"

He held her close. "You should have told me. But I understand. You need no pardon from me. But Tiberius . . . Tiberius . . ."

She stopped sobbing long enough to catch her breath. "There is more."

He looked incredulous. "What more could there possibly be?"

It took her a moment to find the words. "He left me with child."

"He what?"

"It was his. I am almost certain of—"

She felt a tremor of rage go through him. They'd tried for so long to have a child themselves. "*Almost* certain?"

She looked up into his eyes. "Could we have borne it if it were otherwise? Could I have carried it in my womb, nurtured it, given it life, only to look down and see the eyes of the man who'd taken me, who'd ripped me apart upon our bed? Oh gods, Juba. And now we've not been able to have our own. All because of him. What I've done—"

There was silence for a moment. She could feel the struggle within him: his rage at Tiberius, his love of her, his need for his own vengeance, his awareness that her decision to abort the child might be the reason that they'd had none themselves. She buried her face into his chest, gripping him hard.

For a long minute they stood. His arms tensed, released, and tensed again. "It's not your doing," he finally said. His voice was calm, but it was the calm of the eye of a storm. "It's his."

She nodded against him.

"What would you have us do?"

Selene swallowed hard. Vengeance. Power. Maybe even a chance to see her mother again. "Carthage isn't far. We go there." She took a deep breath. "We bring the Shards together. We see what power we have."

"Tiberius isn't in Carthage."

"No, but there are many sacred spaces in Rome. We can use those when the time comes."

"Take the Shards to Carthage. See what we have." She felt him nodding above her, working it out in his mind. "What of our parents? Your mother? My father? Do you think they can really be reached? Can the Shards break through death itself? Can we reach the other side?"

"I don't know. Maybe. My mother felt so close in Vellica. With just a little more power . . ." She squeezed him again. "But we can find out together. In Carthage. And if not, we'll find what we need to put their souls at peace. To put *our* souls at peace. We have to make him pay."

"And he will pay," Juba said. "We can make him pay."

"I just want to be at peace."

"We will be. There's a peace on the other side of war."

Selene looked up at him, saw that he was gazing out to the bay. He looked back down at her and smiled, his love undiminished, but with something steely and hard in his eyes. They kissed, and she wanted it to last forever.

When he finally pulled away, it was to turn back down the walk. "Isidora!"

Selene's handmaiden was never far away, and she appeared within moments, hobbling out into the light from one of the doorways. "Yes, Your Majesty?"

"The young man who just left the palace. Send the order to have him brought back. We would speak with him more."

Isidora bowed as best she could on her crutch and began to turn.

"Wait," Juba called out. He squeezed Selene in his arms. "Then tell the steward I want preparations made for our most able ship to head to sea with us aboard."

"Shall I tell him where?"

Juba looked back to his wife. "To Carthage. We sail for Carthage."

24

FIRE ON THE WATER

The plans to move the Ark to Petra finally done, Pullo and Vorenus stepped outside to stand watch in the courtyard while Caesarion helped Hannah lie down in their bed. She'd put up a good show during the planning, but he could tell how very exhausted she was. Neither of them had slept much while they considered what to do to keep the Ark safe, but of course she was needing to sleep for two now. Thinking of the unborn child, Caesarion ran his hand across the fabric over her belly. Resting it there, he felt the baby kick. Boy or girl, he thought with a proud smile, it was going to be a fighter.

Hannah lifted her hand to touch his face, and he looked up to meet her eyes. "Must you really go now?"

He nodded. "You know I don't want to, but the sun will be up in an hour. I would like to be in Syene as soon as the port is waking up. The sooner I can start making the arrangements, the better."

She nodded and yawned as she settled back into the cushions. "I know. But surely Vorenus could do it."

"Vorenus can't speak Coptic, and it may well be that the captain least likely to ask questions will be a native." He didn't point out that Vorenus might be recognized as the man who had hired the last captain they'd needed—who had died in their service on the canal east of Alexandria.

"Just be careful," she whispered, but already her eyes were closing.

Caesarion pulled the covers tight around her. He kissed her forehead, eliciting a happy sigh from her, and then he stood and put a few coins into his pouch for the day. Just enough to get to Syene and back, plus a little extra advance for whichever captain he hired to come to Elephantine, load up the crate that would hold the Ark, and then ferry it and its four companions down the Nile to Gebtu, where they could join one of the many caravans that trekked across the Nile to the Red Sea port of Myos Hormos. From there, they would need only to arrange passage across the waters that Moses had once used to drown a pharaoh, sailing up the gulf to Aila, where further caravan travel up the King's Highway would take them to the fabled city of Petra.

Simple enough, Caesarion thought, shaking his head and smiling to himself. If not for Hannah's sleeping he might even have laughed at the absurdity of the plan—though he was nevertheless certain it was the best chance they had. Elephantine had been a sanctuary, and a welcome one. What he had learned from the Therapeutae had given him a peace he could not have imagined. But it couldn't last forever. In Petra, that secluded mountain stronghold of the Nabataeans, there was a chance they could quietly hide the Ark in a place where it might never be found. And, if it ever was, it was the sort of sacred space where the fullness of its power could be used.

Caesarion took one last look at the artifact in the other room, wondering at the strange workings of history. Yes, he thought, it would find a home there. After all, unless he was wrong, Petra was where it was born.

. . .

Outside, Pullo and Vorenus were standing beside the altar in the courtyard, talking. Caesarion never tired of seeing the two of them together once more. Were it not for the ruins in which they stood, the Egyptian robes that covered their familiar Roman swords, and the scars of mind and body they all carried now, he might have thought he was back in Alexandria again.

Aside from the fog, that is. He couldn't ever remember seeing a fog so thick upon the city.

"So," Vorenus said, looking up at his approach, "we will expect you by nightfall?"

"If not sooner. Hannah's asleep."

Vorenus smiled, but it was Pullo who answered. "We'll see that she gets her rest."

"Thanks."

Caesarion grasped each of their forearms in turn, then was starting to walk away when Pullo called out to him. "I still think it's a girl," the big man said. "We're placing bets."

"And I'm down for a boy," Vorenus said.

Caesarion frowned in mock concentration. "Put me down for a boy, then," he said. "Keeps the sides even."

The two old legionnaires nodded, smiling, and Caesarion bowed to them in Therapeutan fashion before he turned and made his way out into the fog.

Leaving the temple by the side door, Caesarion entered into the narrower stretch of the King's Road as it ran between the temple of the Jews and that dedicated to Khnum. After a moment of thought about which way to go, he decided to make his way through the larger temple: the path was better lighted that way.

The walls of the Khnum temple were higher than those of the Jewish temple, its broad doors perpetually open. Caesarion stepped through and began walking along a long, stone-crowned colonnade that stretched across the side of the complex. Oil lamps set upon the square-shaped columns marked the path, drawing pools of clouded light against the darkness, and he followed them with quiet steps. A handful of souls moved in the shadows, but the world was at peace for the moment, and he was glad for it. Around him the smooth walls of the inner shrines moved in and out of view, the figures and hieroglyphs painted upon them seeming at times alive in the shifting mix of lamplight and clouded air.

A new infusion of Roman coin had spurred building projects across the empire, and Elephantine was no exception. There was the mighty bronze statue of Augustus at the harbor, of course, but even temples like this one were gaining new markers of success as Caesar tried to quell resentment of the removal of the pharaohs by supporting local priests where they were useful to the administration of the conquered territories. The priests of Khnum and of Satis—the goddess celebrated in an adjacent, smaller temple—were very much among those. At the far end of the complex, Caesarion had to step around the tower of scaffolding that surrounded a pair of new obelisks that were being raised where they could be seen from the river below, dominating the skyline of the island as viewed by anyone who passed on the Nile. When it was finished, the sight would be impressive, he was sure.

Exiting the Khnum temple, he turned northward, following the wide, paved walkway that extended above the shoreline toward the harbor, separated from the rocky drop by a low defensive wall. The temple of Satis immediately arose to his left, and he passed the entrance to the all-important Nilometer on his right, which was little more than a wall around the stepped gash that had been driven down like a channel into the waters below.

The sky was less dark now, the fog slowly starting to thin

as dawn approached. Men would be beginning to stir at the harbor. His timing could hardly be more perfect.

A few minutes later Caesarion came down the last set of steps to the inner market area of the harbor. The oversized statue of Augustus was there, looming over the docks that extended out before him and disappeared into the fog that still hung heavy upon the Nile. The docks were otherwise abandoned, and Caesarion was surprised that he didn't even see any movement from the harbor's little lighthouse: the light at its top was lit, as it always was, but there was no sign of movement inside or around it. The night harbormaster ought to have been there, keeping watch over the docks when he wasn't walking them, but Caesarion could see even in the dim light that the lighthouse's door was open to the night and not even a candle was burning inside. Perhaps, he thought, the harbormaster had gone off to the far end of one of the docks, invisible for now in the fog. Rather than call out, Caesarion just stood for a time staring up at the big bronze man with his piercing eyes.

For all that they had been at war with each other, Caesarion had never actually met the man who'd conquered Egypt. This wasn't really surprising, he supposed. When it came to warring states, it was their men, not the men who led them, who met face-to-face, shed blood to shed blood. History would surely be written differently if it were otherwise.

Still, a part of Caesarion would have liked to have met Octavian. He had to be an impressive man to command armies as he had. He'd drawn great men to his side, and he'd achieved great things. That one of those things was the conquest of Egypt and the stripping away of everything Caesarion had known was a point of personal issue, but in truth he couldn't fault the Roman emperor for many of his decisions. Meeting him, he thought, would indeed be interesting.

Looking around the docks again, Caesarion suddenly saw a man sitting upon some crates a little ways down one of the closer docks. Chiding himself for not seeing him before—whether from the shadows or the fog—he began walking in his direction.

The man didn't move, though Caesarion's footsteps were certainly loud enough on the wooden dock. Nor did he move when he was hailed in greeting.

Noise came over the water then. Muted by fog and distance, the sounds were indistinct, moving in and out like waves. But they sounded, he thought, like screams. Like battle.

Still walking, he turned his eyes in their direction, looking south and east across the great river in the direction of Syene, the little town on the eastern bank of the Nile. There was light there in the darkness, and it wasn't the light of the dawn.

It was the light of fires.

A chill ran up the back of Caesarion's neck as he crossed the last stretch of wood to where the harbormaster sat upon the crates.

In the darkness he could see no blood, but the shafts of the two arrows sticking out from his body—one in his gut and one centered upon his chest—were evidence enough of his fate.

Caesarion instinctively dropped low, squeezing himself behind the man and the crates, away from the dark water from which the killing shafts had sailed.

Almost in the instant that he did so, thin whistles of wind pierced the fog, and two more arrows impacted where he'd been standing. One thudded into wood, while another plunged into the harbormaster's corpse with a wet, meaty sound. Out in the dark, someone cursed.

Caesarion panted for a moment, trying to decide what to do. Staying was hardly an option: sooner or later whatever ship was on the water would get an angle to reach him. And if Elephantine was under attack, he had to raise the alarm. He had to try to warn Hannah and the others. They had to protect the Ark.

Crying out would do little good. What he needed, he decided, was to ring the harbor bell. And that meant getting to the lighthouse.

He crouched. He took one deep breath, then another. And then he flung himself away from the crates, keeping as low as he could while he launched himself into a sprint.

Arrows shot out from his left, and he heard them nipping through the air, somehow missing him. He heard muffled commands in a language he did not know, and the voices were fearfully close. Without breaking stride, he chanced a single look in that direction. There were black boats gliding through the water, boats full of men, and they were going to come ashore between him and the Ark.

Control what you can, he told himself. The bell. Raise the alarm. Go!

The attackers, whoever they were, apparently only had a few bowmen who could make the ranged shot against him, because by the time the next salvo came he was reaching the end of the dock, where he had space to dart and dodge in a jerking, serpentine rush. The arrows flew past him—four, he thought— and he saw them strike the walls of the lighthouse ahead with splintering cracks. All of them were high, he realized, probably because the bowmen were still in the boats.

He crouched lower, making himself small as he continued his quick movements, and when he heard the first snap of the next salvo, he kicked his legs forward, sliding feet-first into the open doorway of the lighthouse as the arrows sang over his head.

He crashed into the darkness of the first floor, overturning chairs and smashing into a table with such force that he sent papers and ceramic pots scattering.

Even before he came to rest his mind was screaming at him to get up, to move, to sound the alarm.

There were footsteps pounding on the dock as Caesarion struggled to get his feet under him, shuffling and slipping on papyrus sheets until he managed to get upright and begin fumbling in the dark for the stairs.

He tripped over the first step, but then he was scrambling upward, taking the steep steps two at a time, determined to get to the top, to warn his friends before he was caught. Men burst into the room in his wake, just strides away, and Caesarion pitched over cases of scrolls and boxes that had been placed against the walls of the stairwell. He heard the men cursing as they stumbled behind him.

The stairs ended in a small circular room with a ladder rising to a trapdoor. Caesarion hardly broke pace, leaping up onto the ladder and then jumping upward off of its rungs, his arm extending out and throwing open the wooden panel at the ceiling.

After the dimness below, coming into the sudden presence of the lit beacon at the top of the lighthouse felt as if he'd come face-to-face with the sun. Caesarion had to shut his eyes against the harsh glare even as he pulled the rest of himself up the ladder. He clapped the trapdoor shut just as the men chasing him reached the top of the stairs, and then he stood over it, letting his weight hold it down as he blinked and squinted at his surroundings. There was a pile of wood within arm's reach, meant for feeding the burning harbor beacon, and he pulled it to him, unceremoniously dumping it down upon the trapdoor as he hopped back off of it. For a moment the men pushing from below got the edges of it to lift, but then the wood crashed down and pushed it shut again.

It wouldn't hold them away for long—already their pounding was shifting the logs and rolling some away—but it would be enough. He only needed a few seconds. It might be all that stood between life and death for his friends. For his love.

It was all he could do. It would have to be enough.

Caesarion, once pharaoh of Egypt, took two steps around the fire, grabbed the rope of the bell, and raised the alarm over Elephantine.

25

The Wheel Turns

ELEPHANTINE, 25 BCE

Vorenus was sitting with Pullo upon the ruined altar in the middle of the Jewish temple when the harbor bell began to ring. He bolted up to his feet, and he turned in the direction of the sound as if he might discern something through the thick walls that surrounded them. He saw nothing but the fog, seeming to show the faintest light of a coming dawn.

Pullo had lumbered up, too. "An attack?"

Vorenus nodded. The ringing was no steady chime. It was panicked, frightened.

"What do we do?"

It couldn't be Romans. They were all gone into Arabia, weren't they? But if not Romans, who?

"Vorenus, what do we do?"

"See that the doors are secure," Vorenus replied. "Keep them fast. I'll awaken Hannah."

Pullo, as if he were still within the legion, snapped to attention at the order, and he shuffled as quickly as he could toward the door that Caesarion had taken.

Caesarion! He'd gone toward the docks. He ought to have reached them by now, and if he was—

The bell clanged once more, and then it stopped.

There was an eerie silence in the air, a hush as if some violence had silenced the ringing alarm.

Vorenus felt a yawning pit open in his belly, even as he hoped against hope that the bell had only been a false alarm.

But then he heard, echoing through the buildings of the city, the sounds of battle. The island was under attack.

"Hurry, Pullo!" he shouted, swallowing his dread as he ran for the inner shrine.

The door opened just as he reached it. Hannah was there. "Where's Caesarion? What's happening?"

"I don't know," Vorenus admitted. He skittered to a halt in front of the doorway, looking beyond her to where the Ark was standing, serene and still, where it had been for years. "But gather your things. If he comes back we may need to be ready to move."

Hannah nodded and spun back toward the chamber. Vorenus stood at the doorway for a moment longer, measuring the Ark with his eyes.

"Vorenus!" Pullo called out, pointing from one door of the courtyard across to one he hadn't yet reached. It was opening.

Though Vorenus had long since lost his uniform as a Roman legionnaire—it was far safer to appear to be a common man these days—he hadn't lost his gear. Beneath his loose-fitting robes he still had a chain shirt, and at his side he still had his bone-handled gladius. As he spun through the dirt and began sprinting for the doorway, the blade was in his hand with hardly a thought. Old habits died hard.

The door creaked, opening slowly as Vorenus closed the distance to it. A hand appeared, fingers tentatively curling around the wood, and then—just as Vorenus was preparing to barrel himself into the wood and shove it backward—Madhukar's brown face appeared in the gap.

Vorenus pulled up, catching himself. "Madhukar!"

The Therapeutan man looked relieved as he stepped inside and helped Vorenus push the door closed. "We are under attack," the monk gasped. "It's Nubians, from Kush."

Vorenus sheathed his gladius. That answered one question, at least. Kush was the kingdom south of Egypt, the land just beyond the cataracts. With so many of the Roman legions away in Arabia, this would be the perfect time for them to come down the Nile and make an assault on Egypt's riches. He reached down to lift the heavy wooden beam that would bar the door.

Madhukar's hand fell upon his shoulder. "No, my friend. We must leave. They will burn the town."

Vorenus froze. "Burn it?"

The Therapeutan nodded vigorously. "It is their way. We have boats on the other side of the island. We'll sail for the western shore."

Pullo had come up, having barred the other doors. "Boats?"

"Yes. Enough for you all."

Vorenus looked back toward the shrine, toward Hannah and the Ark. Where was Caesarion? "We can't leave."

"To stay is to burn," Madhukar implored.

"But we can't leave it," Vorenus said, but even as he spoke he found himself looking between them. It was a foolish thought he was having. They were three older men. She was one very young and very pregnant girl. But Pullo, even crippled as he was, might well be stronger than any other two men on the island. And his own bones . . . maybe he had enough in him for one last push.

"Can't leave what?" Madhukar asked, but already Vorenus was running back to the shrine. Pullo was running after him, and when Vorenus glanced back he saw that the big man seemed to have guessed his plan. He was beaming through the scars on his tattered face when he caught the eye of Vorenus. "We've done crazier things." He laughed.

The plans to leave Elephantine had been set in motion earlier in the night, so it hadn't taken Hannah long to put the last of her things into a sack that was already filled with books and clothes. She turned when Vorenus burst in, and she didn't need to speak the question that was so clearly written on her face.

Vorenus shook his head. "He's not back yet."

Her face fell with despair. "How are we going to—"

"My God," Madhukar whispered as he came up behind them.

Vorenus didn't look back. "Pretty much."

"Is that—?"

"The Ark of the Covenant," Pullo said, pushing his way past them all and hulking into the shrine. The space seemed at once smaller for his presence.

"I didn't know," the monk said. "I'd heard the stories in your books, but I didn't—"

"Now you do," Vorenus said, and he hurried forward to join Pullo in retrieving the Ark's smooth carrying poles from their places at the side of the room. They began to thread them carefully through the metal rings affixed to its sides.

Madhukar just stared. "What are you doing with it?"

"They're going to try to move it," Hannah said, the disbelief clear in her voice.

Vorenus got his pole situated, stared at the beauty of the Ark for a heartbeat, and then fetched a heavy canvas sheet that he threw over the top of it. "That's right," he said. "And we need you to help."

"Us?" Madhukar sounded incredulous.

From the other side of the Ark, Pullo spread his big arms, taking a wide grip on the pole there. Vorenus took a position at the back of his own side. "Just you, Madhukar," he said. "My side. Let's start with a few steps."

"You're mad," Hannah whispered.

Maybe, Vorenus thought with a shrug. "Hurry, my friend. To stay is to burn, remember?"

The Therapeutan hurried forward, looked between the two former legionnaires, and then took position where Vorenus pointed. "Only a few steps at first. We don't have to get it far. Just outside. Then onto a cart. Then the boats. Then safety."

Hannah was right. It was, as he heard himself say it, utter madness. But he simply didn't know what else to do. They couldn't leave the Ark, and he was certain that the old monk was right. If they stayed, they died. As good as he and Pullo were, they surely couldn't hold off a Nubian army forever.

"On the count of three," Pullo said. "One. Two. Three."

The men strained, and the Ark lifted high enough that they were able to shuffle it forward a few feet before Madhukar had to set his end down. "I just need to change my grip," he said.

Vorenus adjusted his own, smiling over at Pullo, a man who never ceased to amaze him. Then, when Madhukar was ready, they lifted it and went a little farther, getting it just past the low, broken wall between the two chambers of the shrine.

"Good," Vorenus said when they paused for breath. He glanced up to say something to Hannah, but she was nowhere to be seen.

"On three again," Pullo said. The scars on his face were hot with blood.

Again they lifted together, and this time they made it to the door. Just as they set it down there, Hannah appeared in the frame. She was panting, her face flushed, and she was holding her belly protectively, but she was smiling. "A cart," she said. "I found a cart."

She had indeed. They could see it in the courtyard, a four-wheeled wagon littered with hay, sitting perhaps halfway between the doorway and the altar. It was a battered, rough-looking thing, but it appeared big enough to hold the Ark. "There we go," Vorenus said. "We're going to make it."

That he could smell smoke in the air, that he could hear distant screams, he didn't say.

Foot by foot, grunt by grunt, they stepped the Ark out of the doorway and into the open air. Minutes passed, but they brought it up behind the cart, lining it up as best they could before they set it down. Madhukar was panting, and he'd begun to say little prayers beneath his breath, though Vorenus did not understand them.

The sounds of battle were pressing close.

Up to now they had only lifted the Ark a few inches from the ground while shuffling alongside it. Standing beside the cart, Vorenus could see that the bottom of it was easily as high as his aching hip.

A horrific scream echoed up from the Khnum temple, and they all instinctively looked in that direction. It was, as they listened, just one scream of many in the town. And when Vorenus saw how the sky was growing brighter he didn't know if it was the rising sun or the burning of homes, of goods, of people. He swallowed hard, tasting the acrid smoke, and forced himself to look away, back to the Ark. There was no other choice, was there?

Pullo, he saw, was smiling at him as they once had in battle. "Just one more lift," he said.

Vorenus nodded. Madhukar took his position, and with a heave they raised it a foot, then nearly to Vorenus' knees, before Pullo groaned and they began to lower it. The Ark came to the ground and the big man let out his breath in a sob. "I can't." When their eyes met, Vorenus could see his eyes were red, and he was freely weeping. "Maybe once . . . I'm not what I was. I'm sorry, Vorenus. Gods, I'm sorry. I can't do it alone."

"Then not alone," Hannah said. She pushed herself up beside him, gripping the pole tight.

"Hannah," Vorenus said, "You shouldn't—"

In reply she took one hand and pulled free the necklace she had around her neck. The emblem upon it was the same that was upon the side of the Ark. All the keepers had one. "My family won't fail. Not while I live," she said.

The door of the temple that faced the Khnum temple shook as someone tried to open it. There were angry shouts coming over the wall in a language that Vorenus did not know. It was now or never. "On three," he said.

Pullo repositioned himself, and Madhukar, even gasping for air as he was, counted them down.

They lifted as one, and they were just inches away from getting the bottom edge of the Ark up and over the lip of the cart, when Hannah screamed in pain.

"Back down!" Vorenus urged, and they were able to get the Ark back to the ground before Hannah had to let go of it. She gasped, then doubled over, gripping her stomach in agony.

Pullo caught her, lowering her to the ground beside the Ark. "Hannah," he was saying, "oh, gods, Hannah . . ."

Vorenus started to ask what it was, but the moment he had rushed around to her side of the Ark and saw the way she was holding her belly and the horrified look on her face he knew that there was no need. "No," he gasped. "Oh, please no."

Hannah's body tensed, and when she opened her mouth the scream that tore from her was as if her very soul were being torn apart.

Vorenus wanted to weep. He wanted to cry out at the injustice of it all.

But none of that would help.

A second of the barred doors to the temple was shaking now. The shouting was very loud, and the smoke was thicker than the fog. Vorenus let out his breath, and once more his gladius was in his hand. The battle calm fell over him, that eerie sense of peace he'd known at Actium, at Gaul, at those moments when all hope of survival had left him and he had resigned himself to his fate, freed himself from fear, freed himself to simply do what needed to be done.

"Madhukar," he said. "You need to go. Now." He nodded toward the last door, the one they'd intended to take the Ark through. "I'll bar it behind you."

The monk had crouched down beside Hannah, and he was holding her hand. When he looked up, his eyes were wide and wet, but there was a peace behind them as he shook his head. Then, with a kind of regretful smile, he stood and hurried across the courtyard to the door, which he began to bar.

Pullo was feeling Hannah's belly as she gasped in uneven breaths. "She is bleeding badly, Vorenus. I think the child may be coming, but it is not good."

"So is the enemy." Vorenus said. "Let the monk do what he can. I need you, Pullo. I can't do this alone."

The monk came back and once more knelt beside the agonized young woman. He and Pullo whispered urgently. Around them the doors were crashing against the bars as they were rammed from the outside. Vorenus turned toward the nearest of them, and he absently gauged the familiar weight and balance of the blade in his hand. For all the twists his life's story had taken, he never would have expected that his end might be in blood upon the sands of Egypt.

So be it, he thought.

Pullo walked up to stand beside him. He used the shining tip of his own sword to point toward the second door that was likely to fall. "I'll take this side."

Vorenus looked at his old friend, so battered and broken. He couldn't imagine they would last long, but he knew there was nothing else to be done. And while Caesarion lived there was still hope. Time was all they could offer him, all they could offer Hannah and Madhukar and the child to come. It was all they had left to give to the Ark.

Titus Pullo swept his blade back and forth in the air, stretching his tired muscles. "It's been too long."

Vorenus smiled. Then the first door finally gave way, and it began.

26

The Citadel of Carthage

Walking up the hill in the darkness of Carthage, carrying the cloth-wrapped Trident before him like a sacred offering, Juba thought of many things. He thought, first and foremost, of his beloved Selene, who strode behind him, her hands wrapped protectively around the satchel in which she held the Palladium, the Shard that could control wind. He'd long known that he loved her, but the clarity of his resolve since he'd learned of her rape had made clear to him the desperate nature of his passion for her.

And his fear of what Tiberius had taken from her.

Looking back, it still shocked him how quickly he had abandoned his desire to live in peace and to come here instead, to unlock even greater power from the four Shards of Heaven in their possession—shocked him, though never for a moment had he regretted the decision. It was, he was still certain, the right thing to do. It was the only way he knew to end the suffering that she had borne for so long in silence. It was the only way he could destroy the haunting memories of Cantabria: her rape, his destruction of all those men.

Truth be told, Juba knew that he had never fully abandoned his desire for vengeance upon Rome for what had been done to his family. Like Selene, he might have made his peace with

Caesar, peace with Rome itself, but he had in so doing found a new face to hate, a new enemy that needed to be destroyed.

They had to kill Tiberius. How else could Selene find comfort in the night, knowing that he had raped her and yet lived? And how else could Juba find comfort, knowing of her pain?

The streets of Carthage were quiet as they passed between homes and buildings: Thrasyllus and Isidora walked ahead, Juba and Selene following, and the shadows only furthered the oppressive silence between them. Each of them, Juba supposed, was wrapped in private thoughts.

He'd ordered the guards to stay behind with the ship, along with Lapis, the wife that Thrasyllus had insisted be brought with them. The captain in particular had been deeply concerned about the king and queen journeying through the city on foot in the night, but orders were orders, and he obeyed, leaving the four of them to make the trek up to the summit at the center of the city alone.

Juba had been a little surprised when Thrasyllus had told them how Carthage was among those sacred places where the full powers of the Shards might be better accessed. At first, Juba had thought of sacred places as being only the ancient temples in Rome and Greece, or the distant holy city of Jerusalem. Yet the more he'd thought of it, the more he'd come to recognize that this was only a reflection of his own experience, the bias of his Roman upbringing and what he'd learned about the truth of the one God. If sacredness wasn't about the gods themselves—and how could it be, if none of them was real?—then it was about the belief of the people in their gods. And for that, Carthage was a sacred place indeed.

Juba knew his history, after all. He knew how Carthage had fought Rome over the centuries, vying for supremacy of the Mediterranean Sea. He knew the brilliance of Hannibal, who'd driven a Carthaginian army from the Iberian peninsula across the Pyrenees, across the Alps, to bring them down upon Rome. He knew how even today the cry of "Hannibal at the gates" meant a message of disaster to a Roman.

He knew, too, how because of all this Cato the Elder had stood up before the Roman Senate and declared that ultimate victory over their enemy across the sea had to be achieved at all costs, that Carthage had to be utterly destroyed. "*Carthago delenda est*," he'd said. *Carthage must be erased.*

And so they tried.

It never was, though. Sacked, yes. Left in waves of devastation and disrepair when the Romans finally seized the city and sold its inhabitants into slavery 120 years earlier, but hardly erased.

It was simply too grand a place. Built on a natural peninsula, it was easily defended from land, and formidable seawalls held back incursion from the water. It commanded fertile lands. And its seaport was one of the most magnificent structures Juba had ever laid eyes upon: there was a long and deep rectangular harbor that extended away from the sea, the daily docking point for hundreds of ships from lands far and wide, and at its head a short canal led to a second harbor, round this time, and filled with the naval might of the city.

He'd first seen that harbor as a child, after the death of his father, when he was being transported to Rome in chains, to stand in his father's stead through the triumph of Julius Caesar. He was too young to remember it in anything but hazy flashes, impressions of its bewildering size. When he'd come back as a young man, this time leaving for Rome as an adopted member of Caesar's family, secretly carrying with him the Trident of Poseidon, he had half-expected Carthage and its seaport to be less impressive, that its immensity would be so much the lesser because he was no longer a small child seeing it through a child's shocked, naive eyes.

Instead, he was impressed all the more. Year by year the seaport drew more wealth to the ancient city. It grew grander with each passing season. And around it, in the century and more since they had razed parts of the city, the Romans had built a new and prosperous city from its ruins. The old city had been laid out in concentric rings that emanated from the heights of Byrsa Hill at its center: there stood the fortified walls of the royal citadel and the great temples dedicated to Ba'al Hammon and Tanit, the supreme couple in a pantheon of elder gods. The new city, in Roman fashion, was laid out on a grid, and the once sacred places atop the hill were shunned now, tainted by the memories of what had been done there.

Everyone knew that the Carthaginians had practiced child sacrifice. Ba'al Hammon had been an especially hungry god, and no one knew how many children had been fed screaming to his flames. The sacrifices had assured fertile lands and abundant crops, calm seas and full nets. They had assured good water and fine weather. They had assured success at war, the blessings of Ba'al, something greater than the innocent lives that fed him and kept him strong.

At least for a time.

Such was the way of faith, Juba had long since decided. No god was forever kind to his people, for no god was greater than chance and the inevitability of change in the world. All there was, in the end, were the men and the gods they made to favor or curse themselves, depending on the winds of fate.

That, and the belief that the people left behind.

And in that case, what place could be more sanctified, more full of belief, than the temple of Ba'al Hammon, where so many faithful had taken their children, their beloved offspring, and had given them over in sacrifice to the hungry gods?

"Is that it?" Isidora whispered.

The young girl and Thrasyllus had stopped walking where the buildings on either side of them, arched in a line across the slope, came to an end. As he and Selene caught up with them, Juba saw that ahead there was a darkness of ruinous stones and shattered pillars strewn among trees and brush: the despairing summit of Byrsa Hill, the center of the old city destroyed by Rome, the once-beating heart of a faith whose victims were still said to haunt it day and night.

For a moment Juba felt new fears infect his resolve. But when he looked at Selene he saw that there was hope written on her face, a hope of peace beyond the pain. A hope for vengeance for all that she had suffered. Seeing it, he remembered why he had come here. For her. He would do anything for her.

"It is," he said. Then he strode forward. And as he pushed his way onto a path occluded by overgrown brambles, he felt the darkness open around him and welcome him inside.

. . .

The temple of Ba'al Hammon was, like so much of what they had passed on the summit of Byrsa Hill, a broken place. Its gates had long since been ripped away. The walls encompassing the open-air temple had been torn down. The pillars that once stood in rows leading to the altar had been toppled and smashed. Weeds made lines of green along the cracks in the dirt-strewn floor, and ropes of vines and brush made black webs between the pitted stone of statues beaten by chisel and storm into twisted lumps unrecognizable as men or gods.

There had once been a great bronze statue of Ba'al Hammon at the head of the sanctuary, seated on his throne, flanked by sphinxes, the curling ram's horns atop his head just visible beneath his tall crown. The god's arms had stretched out before him, palms up as if ready to receive a gift, and his bearded face had stared out over the assembled believers, impassive and unrelenting to the pleas of the mothers and the fathers—and the wailing infants who were placed upon those hands to sate his hunger and appease his need for tribute. The arms and hands were raised slightly upward, sloped so that as the child struggled it slid, inexorably, down the hot metal and into the yawning pit of fire at the god's feet.

The statue had long since been torn down, melted in the forges of Romans who brought to Carthage a new set of gods to feed.

But the pit below was still there, black and dark. As he and the others had lit torches around the desolate place of worship, Juba had not dared to bring a light toward that gaping maw of death. He had no desire to see what might remain in its depths. No one else had looked either.

Juba stood now at the center of the circle of flickering light in the sanctuary. The four Shards in their possession had been carefully laid on the ground before his feet. Thrasyllus had read many books on their voyage from Caesarea, and he seemed to know much of the knowledge of the Shards that Didymus had entrusted to him, but in the end he could tell them very little about what to expect beyond the assumption that the objects should be more powerful in this place.

The young scholar stood with Selene and Isidora near the edge of the lit torches. By common assent, they had all agreed that Juba would be the one to test his Trident first. He had experienced more of the power of the Shards than anyone.

First, however, he reached down and picked up the Aegis of Zeus. He and Selene had both experienced the ways in which it had extended their endurance and strength, and Juba was certain that if the Trident was truly so much more powerful here, he would need the help of the Aegis to control and survive it.

It worried him to put it on, because he remembered so little of the last time he had worn it, in Alexandria when he had tried to seize the Ark from Selene's brother, Caesarion. He'd been wounded badly in the struggle with those trying to keep it from him, and the Aegis, he was certain, had been what had saved his life—just as it had saved the life of Alexander the Great from his own hideous wounds. The Aegis had kept him strong.

But it had done more, too. The Aegis had kept him angry. It had kept him enraged. It had blinded him to suffering; it had fed an all-consuming intent to fulfill his desire to take control of the Ark, no matter who or what stood in his way.

And yet Selene had worn it without such effects. He had talked with her about it many times since they had made the decision to bring the Shards to Carthage, though he had never admitted to her that he was sure he had killed Caesarion in his Aegis-fueled rage. She said that she had felt no anger forcing itself upon her when she wore the armor. Instead, she felt a powerful capability of strength and insights about how to use the Palladium to achieve her needs.

The Aegis enhanced life, they decided, and at the same time it amplified the emotions of the wearer. Juba's anger had turned to white-hot rage. Selene's fear had turned to a piercing recognition about how to save his life. The Shard gave them each what they needed.

I need it to keep me strong, Juba thought as he pulled the armor over his head and onto his body. He began to pull its straps tight around his torso. For Selene, he needed it to help him find a way to kill.

He felt it at once. The Shard that settled against his chest was warm, and it calmed his nerves. He'd felt the same thing in Alexandria, but there was something more this time: a whisper at the edge of his mind, like a voice in the distant dark that only he could hear.

He turned to Selene to say something of it, and he was shocked at his sudden awareness of her heartbeat, her breathing. He was aware, too, of the looming shadows behind her, a wall of darkness like a wave that was poised to topple over them.

"Are you well, my love?" Fear and worry were written across Selene's face, and Juba could feel the pulse of her anxiety.

Juba nodded and tried to smile. "I am. But there is more power here. I can feel it."

He turned back to the Shards before him, and he took a long, deep breath, clearing his mind. Then he lifted the Trident and focused his thoughts. His hand reached out and wrapped around the Shard itself, just as he'd done in Cantabria.

The power surged, far beyond anything he'd felt before. It sparked through the tightening fingers of his grip. It danced along his skin, reaching up to consume him, to flow over him and pull him down into that black emptiness of the Shard. Clouds were forming overhead. He did not need to look to see. He could *feel* them there, gathering, pulsing like a heartbeat in the heavens. A wind was swirling into the sanctuary, and Juba felt even the ground beneath his feet tremble in witness of what he held in his grasp.

He staggered a step, felt his arm rattle as he strained against the tide, but then he felt the power of the Aegis pushing back, bracing him against the onrushing tide until he had finally controlled it, calmed it, and held it still.

But gods, it was strong. So very strong. It was as if what he'd felt in Vellica, the stroke of power with which he'd killed all those people, had been only a pool, and now he saw that beyond it lay the boundless sea.

This, he thought. This was truly the power of God. The power to do His will, to build up, to destroy, to do His will to the uttermost end. The power around Juba swirled now in ready currents, like a lacing through the fabric of creation, and he could reach out and grip it.

"Juba?"

He heard Selene calling to him, but there was another voice now, too. It spoke from the darkness that surrounded them. It spoke in the wind, and its words were a language he did not know, whispered into his very bones.

But he understood them all. He knew what the shadow wanted. And without thinking about it, he knew it was what he wanted, too.

Because it was for Selene. It was all for her.

In the gathering storm Juba reached out into that tower of midnight, that place where light was just a memory.

He reached out into the shadow. Then he reached for another Shard.

27

Life for Life

Caesarion had known he couldn't swim the full width of the river. It was too far, the current too strong, even if by luck he wasn't taken by a crocodile in mid-swim. Besides, there was nothing for him on the other side. Syene was in flames, and Hannah was here. Pullo and Vorenus were here. The Ark was here. While he still lived, he had to try to help them.

It was a near miracle that he lived. He'd rung the bell until the attackers were coming through the trapdoor, and then he'd jumped from the tower, tumbling painfully onto the tiled ridge of the building below. As the men shouted behind him, he'd then run and leapt for the Nile.

To his great relief, they'd not followed—whether because they couldn't swim, because they thought him unlikely to last against the beasts of the river, or because they just had better things to do, Caesarion didn't know.

It only mattered that he was alive. There was still hope.

He'd thought about letting the current push him north, down the river, but the crocodiles were thicker there. And it would carry him away from the fighting, away from his friends. So instead he'd turned and begun to drive his body hard against the current, staying as close to shore as he could once he made a wide berth around the harbor, which was swarming with attackers.

The screaming from the town was loud, the fires that sprang up glowed like eerie bubbles against the foggy night, and with each stroke of his legs and arms he was certain that toothy jaws would snap them away in the black water, but there was no choice.

He swam on.

His lungs burned from the struggle, his heart quaked. But then, just as fear and exhaustion threatened to take the courage from him, Caesarion saw it: a black doorway in the rock of the shoreline. A chance. Hope.

Caesarion swam for it, moving faster now as he angled across the current toward the shore, as he made one last thrust of energy, frightened that it would be in this last moment that he'd be taken to the black depths by the reptilian monsters that haunted the fishermen of the Nile.

Nothing came for him. He reached the doorway and splashed out of the water onto stone steps in a rock-hewn corridor so midnight black he couldn't see his hand before his face.

It was the Nilometer. Grasping for the wall to lean against it and catch his breath Caesarion felt the chiseled signs upon it, the glyphs and letters marking the depths of the water against the stone.

And that meant he was just across the walkway from the Temple of Satis. He'd only need to run a short way across those same paved stones he'd walked minutes earlier. Then through the Temple of Khnum, straight to the Ark and his friends—if they were still there, if they were still alive.

Caesarion shook the despair away.

Vorenus would fight. Pullo would fight. By the gods, his beloved Hannah would fight.

They were alive. They'd make it. He just had to get to them.

He pulled himself up, his breath slowing down enough for him to begin to carefully climb the stairs in the pitch dark-ness.

To his relief and terror, it did not stay dark for long. He wasn't five steps from the water when he heard shouts from above, and the gated end of the Nilometer was outlined in torchlight as attackers began to run past it.

Caesarion threw himself against the wall, trying to make himself small on the chance that anyone turned to look in his direction, but none did.

They passed by, but there remained glow enough to see the stairs now: temple buildings nearby were alight, and the screaming told the story of priests or servants still inside.

He hurried up the remainder of the stairs and carefully unlatched the gate from the inside. He looked in both direc-tions, saw no one. His luck, he decided, was changing.

Not about to wait for more attackers to show up, Caesarion took a single deep breath and then burst from the gate, sprint-ing for the Temple of Khnum.

He did not get far before the flash of fire, the ring of battle, and the cries of the dying made clear that the attack-ers had beat him there. He ran on, and on the paved walk and the stone walls before him he saw now the shadows of men traced by the flickering firelight like terrible, shape-shifting demons.

He ran on, not knowing what else to do, but certain that he'd never make it through the temple alive.

Ahead, melting out of the fog, he saw the scaffolding around the obelisks being built in front of the Khnum temple. And he saw a figure, a sword in his hand, pulling out of the clouded shadows beside them and moving in his direction.

The man had dark skin, darker even than a native Egyptian's. A Nubian, one of the men of Kush, Caesarion realized. From farther up the Nile to the south.

Caesarion's run hitched for a step, but there was nowhere to go, nowhere to hide. And if he could somehow get the man's weapon, maybe . . .

A fool's hope. Even with a Nubian sword, even if he could kill with it—which he wasn't sure he could do—he'd never fight his way across the floor of the temple. It was too far to cross. He'd need to be able to fly if he wanted to reach the Ark.

Caesarion's eyes suddenly widened at the thought, and he lowered his shoulder as if he meant to bull the man over.

The Kushite shouted something, and he seemed to laugh as he steadied the blade in his hand.

Three steps away, Caesarion raised himself up, almost as if he intended to embrace the sword that even now the Kushite was swinging toward his chest. Then, in the same movement, Caesarion fell away, kicking his legs out in front of him and letting his momentum propel him forward into a slide.

The Nubian blade arced through the air just inches above Caesarion's face as he passed beneath the blow—for a frozen instant he saw himself reflected in its metal surface, his face red in the firelight—and then he was reaching out with his right arm, grabbing the Kushite's leg and pulling it out from underneath him.

Already imbalanced from his swing, the man fell awkwardly, flailing out and dropping his sword as he hurtled down toward the stone. There was a hollow cracking sound as his head hit the ground.

Caesarion let go of his leg, scrambling up to his feet. He started to go back for the Nubian sword, but he heard more shouts of alarm in Meroitic, the language of the Kushites. Footsteps were pounding, too close.

Caesarion leapt up onto the scaffolding, clambering board to board, grasping at ropes, pushing himself in a mad rush.

Below him no one followed, but he heard voices and recognized a few words, now that he knew the language being spoken. He'd never spoken Meroitic, but he'd once heard it in the palace, when his mother was holding a diplomatic meeting to resolve a dispute with their southern neighbors. A farmer from Kush had been killed by Egyptian soldiers. Caesarion remembered how, because it was the same way these men intended to kill him: *archer*, he heard them say. And *arrows*.

The scaffolding around the obelisk reached the height of the Khnum temple, and so Caesarion jumped across to its roof. He'd planned to make his way over the roof, but flames were licking it in spots. So instead he began to make his way along the flat stones that had been set across the tops of the pillars that traced the perimeter of the temple.

He couldn't fly over it all, he thought with a smile, but a walkway above it would do just as well.

Fires began to rise in ferocity to either side of him, and he had to raise his wet sleeve before him like a shield as he ran through the smoke and heat, but he hurried on as fast as he could, eyes to the stone as he balanced one foot before the other. He took one turn, and he was heading now directly toward the temple of the Jews.

The Kushites hadn't expected him to gain that path, and he could hear their shouts of confusion and rage from behind and below him. Then, to his displeasure, he heard it from in front of him, and the arrows began to fly.

He crouched down, making himself as small as he could while he kept moving, kept his eyes to the stone. If it was destiny for him to take an arrow and fall, so be it. But he wasn't going to have his last thought be cursing himself for a missed step.

He carried on, arrows clattering against the rock below his feet or whistling as they carved the air around his body. One caught on his sleeve that he held before him, tearing through the cloth before it sailed off into the fog, but none struck him.

Ahead, his stone path turned, and he turned, too, looking down off the edge now at the King's Road below, which was bustling with attackers and the men, women, and children that they were dragging from their homes. Everything was screams.

None of it mattered.

Hurrying on, Caesarion saw the corner of the Jewish temple form in the darkness as the road below constricted. The doors had been broken and Kushites were streaming inside. He heard the clash of swords and the shouts of men.

And he heard, unmistakable, the screaming of his love.

Caesarion took two more strides to bring himself above the broken doorway, then he pushed hard against the high stones and launched himself off into the fog, over the King's Road, over the wall, and down into the courtyard of the Jewish temple.

It was no leap into the forgiving waters of the Nile this time, and Caesarion hoped that his fall might be broken by the Nubians who were entering the sacred space.

He was not disappointed.

Screaming, he crashed into the backs of the dark-skinned men, tumbling them and himself into a heap.

Even as he hit the ground, the lessons learned so long ago in hours of training with Pullo and Vorenus in the courtyards of the Alexandrian palaces kicked in as an instinct, a single, overriding thought: *Keep moving. Don't stop. To stop is to die.*

He heaved his weight and rolled, ignoring the pain of sudden bruising. Bodies pushed and fought beneath him, but his feet finally gripped and he scrambled up and over them.

Somehow the Shard had been moved into the open out of the shrine. There was a cart, and his friends had clearly been trying to load the canvas-covered Ark up onto the back of it when they had, apparently, simply run out of time. Pullo and Vorenus were valiantly holding back the oncoming Kushites. Pullo had been defending the door that Caesarion had jumped over, and Caesarion's slamming into the mass of men there had bought him time, but there were too many of them. Vorenus was on the far side of the courtyard, and he was staggering back, step by step, being driven ever closer to the Ark. His face and body were smeared with blood.

They needed help.

Hannah screamed again, and Caesarion at last saw where she had crumpled down beside the Ark that her family had sworn to protect. The canvas covering the artifact was partially pulled away behind her, so that her back was against its gleaming side, and the symbol of the Shard that was inlaid upon the acacia wood made a kind of circle about her head. Her face, framed by that thin curve of metal, was pale and contorted with agony. Her legs were drawn up, and she was holding her hands against her belly. Madhukar was on his feet beside her, the wiry little monk grappling with a Kushite who'd somehow made it past the former legionnaires. The Nubian had a dagger in his hand, and Madhukar was holding on to his wrist, trying desperately to keep the blade away.

Time, he thought. I need to give them time.

For a second Caesarion stood, hesitating, choosing among his love, his friends, and the Ark.

Then he felt the icy touch of a blade sinking into his back, just below the ribs.

Time.

He took in the smoky air with a short lurch of his lungs, which sent a jolting shock of pain down through his body.

The blade pulled free with a sudden, sharp jerk. What had been a cold finger became hot and terribly wet.

Time.

Caesarion gasped. Somewhere he heard screams. His. His friends'. Hannah's.

Time.

He crumpled down to his knees. His eyes fluttered for a moment. The world seemed to slow.

The end, he thought. No time.

A blade bright with blood—his blood—passed in front of his eyes, lowering to draw across his neck and speed the death that his wound had made inevitable. When it passed, he saw beyond it, across the courtyard, that Madhukar had been thrown backward against the Ark, and he was falling to the other side of it from Hannah. The canvas—now stained with sprays of crimson—was falling away with him, exposing the rest of the artifact. The two angels standing upon its top shone brightly in the firelight.

No, his mind whispered. No. No. *No.*

And then the whisper was a shout, and the voice that cried it belonged to Titus Pullo, whose gladius jabbed into the shoulder of the man holding the blade across Caesarion's neck. The man screamed, the blade jerked for a moment, and then it fell from his hand.

"Move!" the big man shouted. He filled Caesarion's field of vision, and the fist of the Roman's free hand swung over-head.

Caesarion blinked. *Move. Move.*

Another Nubian tried to take Pullo in the side, just as the legionnaire's gladius pulled free from the flesh he'd stuck it into. With no time to turn the weapon, Pullo just swung his arm backward, slamming the heavy pommel of his sword into the attacker's face. "Get up!"

Caesarion began to rise, and he realized that Pullo's fist must have gripped the back of his robes. The big man was lifting him up, trying to pull him out of harm's way.

Move. Time.

He gasped, and as the air filled his lungs Caesarion was aware that behind the pain there was still life to be had. Not long. Seconds, perhaps.

But it could be long enough.

His muscles twitched as Pullo pulled him, jerked him back into motion. Then his feet were underneath him, and he was stumbling forward toward the Ark.

Pullo was shouting behind him to run, to get away, but Caesarion knew there wasn't time enough for that.

And where would he go?

The Nubian who'd killed Madhukar was standing in front of the Ark, and the knife with which he'd killed the monk was still in his hand. Caesarion pitched into him, his lowered shoulder pushing the man off-balance even as his right hand reached around him, wrapped around the man's knife hand, and jerked it up and into his chest.

The man shuddered and gasped. He would take time to bleed out—as he himself would, an absent part of Caesarion's mind noted—but once the Nubian's hand fell away from the dagger, Caesarion let his body fall away, too.

He fell to his knees beside his only love. Her eyes were wide with horror and shock, and they seemed not to focus on him. Her breathing was in shallow, sharp, halting gasps. And the bottom of her dress looked as if it had been dipped in blood.

Like him, she was dying.

"Hannah," he managed to say. "Hannah, love . . ."

"Caesarion?" Her eyes blinked, winced as she tried to focus on his through the haze of pain. "Oh, God, love," she whispered. "So . . . sorry. Should've moved it . . . before."

"I'm here. It's okay. It's all fine."

A tear rolled down her cheek, then another, but something like a smile lit her face. "Up to you now. Ark . . . Save it, my love."

He nodded. "I will."

She smiled at that, as if she couldn't hear the sounds of battle around her, as if she couldn't see through his lies. "I think Pullo is right. About heaven."

Caesarion touched her cheek. "I know he is."

"He is," Hannah repeated.

She sighed out her breath.

He took in another.

Her chest did not rise again.

Caesarion bowed his head for a moment, then he leaned forward and kissed her cheek one final time. The tears on his cheek mixed with hers. "I'll see you there soon," he whispered.

He used the Ark to pull himself up, and he looked around at the temple for the last time. Pullo and Vorenus still lived. Helped by Caesarion's surprise tackle of so many of them, Pullo had beaten most of his attackers, but Vorenus was nearing the end of his strength. He was outnumbered, and he was staggering backward from the door he'd been trying to defend. His fight was only to prevent being outflanked now, and it was a fight he'd lose.

Hannah was dead. Caesarion wanted to weep, to curl up against her as he gasped out his last. Madhukar had died trying to protect her even as he must have known she was bleeding out her last moments on this Earth. Even as Caesarion watched, Vorenus parried one blow, twisted away from another, and then fell awkwardly onto his back.

God help us, Caesarion thought.

And in the same moment he remembered that there was no god anymore.

There's only us. Our choices. Our actions.

And she'd told him to save the Ark.

In his last act on this Earth, with the last resolve of his failing body, the child of Julius Caesar and Cleopatra, the once-pharaoh of Egypt who by every right should have ruled the world, fell forward across the Ark.

And this time, Caesarion's hands did not grasp it by the bronze and silver angels that adorned its surface. Instead, his hands fell palms-down upon the black disk set within the wooden surface.

This time he touched the Shard.

28

The Gate Opened

CARTHAGE, 25 BCE

On either side of him, Selene and Isidora were screaming, but all Thrasyllus could do was stare. He had, as a small part of his mind noted, never seen anything like it before.

He had known little of what the Shards were—they were artifacts infused with divine powers; he'd gleaned that much from what he'd overheard—but the full exposure of their reality left him petrified with fright, astonishment, and a yearning deep within to have the power for himself. Didymus and Apion could have the Great Library. With power such as this, he was certain he could have the world.

Before them, barely visible through a swirl of storm sparked with shocks of lightning that ripped through the vortex of air like probing, angry snakes, Juba was holding both the Trident and the Palladium. The Aegis on his chest glowed metallic blue with every flash of the energy surrounding him. In one moment he seemed to be laughing. In another he seemed to be crying out.

And through it all the power grew.

Thrasyllus looked up and saw that the spinning energy thickened and tightened as it rose, a column of pulsing black against the night sky. One by one, the stars seemed to be going out above them, and the analytical part of the scholar's mind

decided that the column must be opening up far above, unfolding itself and curling back down around them, like the
curvature of a great dark dome.

To his right, Selene's screams took on a new pitch of horror,
and he turned to see that Juba had hugged the Trident and
the Palladium to the Aegis, and that he was reaching down for
what they'd told him was the Lance of Olyndicus.

Isidora was trying to step forward to Thrasyllus' left, but
the strength of the storm was too great. She staggered and fell,
her walking staff tumbling away from her.

The lightning grew in its intensity, and for a moment Thrasyllus could see clearly that fire danced in horrible waves up
the flesh of Juba's arms, and the skin there was peeling back
and forth—one moment flayed off by the heat, the next
moment restored. It was as if his body fought against itself,
whether to be unmade or kept whole. Through it all, Juba
appeared to be smiling and crying and screaming an inhuman wail of horror.

At last the Lance came together with the other Shards at his
chest. The world erupted in a flash of fiery light, and there was
a great sucking sound riding the blinding glare. For the span
of a heartbeat Thrasyllus was being pulled forward, feet sliding
on the soiled rock floor, and then a wave of yawning sound
burst against Thrasyllus' chest, propelling him backward
against the stone and into fresh darkness.

· · ·

Quiet. A silence as still as the grave.

No, Thrasyllus realized. Not silent. There was a sound of
straining. Teeth grinding. Breath coming in short bursts. And
voiceless weeping.

The scholar opened his eyes.

The storm, the lightning, wind . . . all of it was gone.
All but two of the torches had been snuffed out by the tumult,

but those that remained licked hungrily at the suddenly stilled air in the ruined temple. By their light, Thrasyllus could see that Juba was kneeling where he had stood. He was trembling, and his arms were close about him, presumably still holding the other three Shards against the Aegis. He was the one who was crying, the scholar realized. Soundlessly crying.

"Juba?"

Thrasyllus turned at the sound of Selene's voice, and he saw that the beautiful young queen was on her hands and knees in the dim light, not ten feet away to his right. There was blood trickling down her forehead.

Juba was looking away from her. He did not turn. "You need to go." His voice was hushed, strained through clenched teeth. "Don't think I can stop it."

"Stop what?" She crawled forward a few feet. Thrasyllus could see the fear and despair on her face. Something was wrong. Everything was wrong. She knew it. She didn't want to believe it.

Thrasyllus had been lying on his back, and he rolled himself upright. Selene had crawled a few feet farther.

"What I've done, Selene. God . . . I don't even know why, Selene . . . it . . . it made me do it. The voice. The darkness."

She trembled now, too. Thrasyllus saw her swallow hard, building her courage. "Juba, my love, put them down. Please. Come—"

"I can't. You don't know. Just go." His voice trembled into a groan. "Please. I . . . can't hold it back."

She started to reply, but there was no time. Something broke in Juba. He gasped—a sound of both pain and relief—and power flowed out through him into the earth. Like tendrils of red-white fire it radiated outward, tracing along cracks in the stones, forming into glowing patterns that Thrasyllus dimly recognized as runes and glyphs, though he did not know the language.

Selene gasped as the lines shot across the ground and under her, but they left her unharmed. A moment later they were passing under Thrasyllus, too, an eerie line of ghost fire that whispered in an ancient tongue but touched him not.

It wasn't looking to harm them, Thrasyllus realized. It was searching for something. "Selene," he finally managed to say, overcoming his cowardice and fear. "I think—"

Out of the corner of his eye, he saw the dancing, darting lines find the edge of the black pit of Ba'al Hammon and then plunge into it like little rivers of phantom flame. Beneath them the glyphs and patterns dissolved, as if the power was flowing away, draining into that shadowed place of sacrifice that was soon glowing with a fierce light the molten color of fresh blood.

Juba groaned again, a long and agonized sound.

There was a snuffling from the pit, like that of a trapped beast scenting at the open door of its cage. And then a hand appeared at the lip of the stone. Long fingers with nails sharp as claws. The skin was crimson as it arose in the glow of the red light from the pit's depths, then pale and bloodless as it came over the edge and stretched out upon the surface of the rock. It seemed almost to caress that hard surface, and then the knuckles strained as it pressed down, beginning to leverage up the body that lay beneath it. Another hand arose and gripped the stone.

And another. And another.

The arms began to appear, with the lean but sculpted muscles he'd seen on the statues of gods, the forms of bodies made from the most perfect molds, untouched by time and worry. The skin over those muscles, now that he saw more of it, was the color of the Egyptian sands. Every movement the bodies made was smoothly elegant, a graceful dance that strangely reminded Thrasyllus of the movement of deadly cobras being charmed from baskets. Then, one by one, three hauntingly beautiful faces of what looked like two men and one woman were rising from the pit. Their eyes were black on black, gleaming like polished gems of obsidian. They were entirely hairless, and as they began to climb out onto the floor of the ruined temple he could see that they were naked but for the smears of the black-ash char of the pit. They were so perfect, so extraordinarily beautiful, that he could not look away. Yet at the same time his heart quaked at the sight of such unnatural perfection. And something inside of him—something so deep that he might have called it his soul—screamed with paralyzed terror.

For a fleeting moment, the thought came to the scholar's mind that he wished he still had the knife he had plunged into Seker's back outside Alexandria, and it nearly made him laugh despite his terror.

He was a coward. He'd known it back in Alexandria. He'd known it when he'd taken Seker's life, crying and shaking as he drove the blade home. He'd known it nearly every day since. And no weapon in his hand would change his cowardice in this moment, when all he could do was stand, still as the broken statues around them, and do nothing but bear mute witness to the rise of these beings.

Not that a blade could be of great use against such creatures as these. They were beings of the underworld, he was certain. Spawn of the utmost dark of creation.

Demons, Thrasyllus thought, the word coming to him out of the recesses of his mind. That's what they were.

In a sudden kick of bravery he managed to shout the word

to Selene as a warning, but his eyes never left the mesmerizing creatures.

Juba had summoned demons. And the three of them, in their horrifying beauty, had turned and were beginning to reach back down into the fiery depths of the pit.

They were reaching down for others.

29

The Bitter End

ELEPHANTINE, 25 BCE

Lucius Vorenus was out of time. He'd fought hard and bravely, but he had little left to give. And for every Kushite who fell it seemed two more took his place. There was nothing he could do now but stagger backward, fending off strikes, parrying and dodging as best he could while the Nubians pressed their attack.

He heard Pullo yelling, but in the tumult he could not hear what his old friend was saying. Not that Vorenus could do anything to help, no matter what the cry. He couldn't spare the chance to even turn and look. The attackers were becoming more coordinated as they pressed their numerical advantage.

Just let me go first, he prayed. I can't bear to lose him once more.

The Nubian to his left came at him high and hard, and Vorenus got his gladius up just in time to block the blow. The shock of it rattled through his bones, grinding his teeth.

The attacker to his right was jabbing at him, too, aiming for his exposed lower back.

His sword was still up for the first blow, so all he could do was twist away, buckling his knees as he tried to pivot away from the worst of the strike.

It worked. The blade missed him entirely.

In his younger years Vorenus knew he might have been able to catch himself from this position, tensing his muscles and then reversing his body's direction. He might have exploded out of his twisted crouch and run the long, wet curve of his sword's edge across the front of his attackers, carving a red line in space as he pressed into the attack.

But now, instead, his hip and knee gave way and he fell awkwardly onto his back. The thump of the ground coughed out of his lungs the little air he had left, and all he could do was just stare up into the sky above. It was brightening, he thought. The sun would rise soon. And there was a hole in the thick bank of fog, a ragged tear that had been ripped through the veil that had covered the island this night. Through it Vorenus could see a single star. It was a light of hope, he felt. Not for him, but for the fact that there was something far beyond the suffering of this world.

With or without them, the sun would rise again. And it would little note the horrors its rays shone upon.

He blinked, and at last he gasped the air back into his chest and could breathe again.

Too late.

One of the Kushites was looming up above him. His sword was poised like a spike.

Their eyes met, and Vorenus saw that he would find no pity in them.

Then, he saw in those same eyes a reflection of an unnatural green light, like a streaking sheet of ethereal flame. The man froze as he looked up. His eyes widened. What he saw struck him with terror.

Vorenus felt the world lift beneath his back, and he knew then the fear in the man's eyes: it was the fear of the power of God.

Once, when he was a young man, Vorenus had floated in

the waves of the sea. Still at night sometimes he could close his eyes and remember the motion of the water beneath and around him, the waves moving like a living thing. The memory of it had etched into his bones, soaked into his blood. Unmoving in his bed, his body could still feel that rolling rise beneath his back, pushing him toward the heavens before passing and letting him back down with a sigh.

This time, it was the earth itself rolling beneath him, and the instant after he saw the light in the Nubian's eyes and felt the rising of the earthen swell, Vorenus heard the ground break. Stones, tensed by the wave that kept lifting and lifting, shattered in a crack that sounded as if the very bones of the earth were being broken. Splinters of rock and clodded dirt hurtled through the air like a storm come from the underworld.

Vorenus spread his arms and legs as the force pushed up beneath him, as if fearful that the power below might finally break free of the confines of the shattering rock and fling him upward. The Nubian above him screamed and pitched over backward as the ground trembled higher and higher into the air.

It was unnatural. It was terrifying.

And Vorenus knew he had to get away from it. Whatever was happening, whatever was about to happen, he simply needed to get away.

Instinctively he began to kick away from the Nubians who'd been attacking him and who were all upon the ground now, screaming in terror. He flipped over onto his stomach as he did so, the better to crawl and scramble away.

But when he turned, he simply froze.

"My God," he whispered.

Not five feet from him, the floor of the temple ended in a jagged torn ledge, like the frayed edge of a ripped scroll. The walls of the temple to his left and right ended in similar tatters of stone. It was as if a great, unseen knife had cut the temple in half and was lifting this end of it into the sky, offering it to the heavens.

It was impossible, Vorenus thought. Impossible.

In the same instant, as if it recognized the same truth of its impossibility, the power that was thrusting it all upward let go. Everything hung, floating in the lightening fog—Vorenus, the floor of the broken temple beneath him, the snapped halves of the walls to either side of him—and then, with a roaring exhalation, it all fell back toward the shattered earth.

Vorenus didn't have time to imagine what destruction awaited them upon impact. But he knew enough to know that to stay was to die. So he shoved himself toward the edge as it fell. And when he saw the earth-bound half of the temple seeming to rise up to meet him as the sinking mass continued its ever-speeding descent, he leapt from the edge, screaming as he reached out, his limbs flailing in the air.

In his mind, he'd imagined that he'd make it to the other floor. Perhaps he'd land awkwardly and twist an ankle, but he'd make it.

Instead, the ragged edge of the temple's broken but otherwise unmoved paving stones hit him in the chest as he fell into them.

His hands scrambled for purchase, but already his impact against the edge of the rocks had him bouncing away. The last of the rock slipped away from his grip. From below and behind him he heard a crushing, sliding destruction, and he began to fall down into it.

Just as he was about to curse the gods he didn't believe in one last time, just as the floor slipped out of his sight and he started the fall into the chaos of crashing earth below him, a hand reached out and grabbed his forearm.

His shoulder pulled, stretched. The hand slipped along the scars that Vorenus still carried from the battle of Actium, but it stopped at his wrist at the same moment his own fingers wrapped around his savior. That arm was scarred, too, and when he looked up, dangling by one arm off what had become a cliff, he wasn't shocked by the face he saw. No matter the scars, no matter the years, it was the face of the only person he could say he'd truly loved.

"Got you," Pullo said, smiling down at him through the strain, squinting as a cloud of dust rolled up and over them from below.

Vorenus had dropped his gladius—he couldn't remember when—and so he swung his free hand up to grab hold of his old friend's wrist. "Not a good day to die," he panted.

"Not yet," Pullo said, beginning to pull with what Vorenus imagined must be the last of his herculean strength.

Vorenus held tight to his friend's grip, helping as best he could by kicking his way up off the shattered earth, until he joined Pullo on the floor of the temple. Clouds of dust continued to billow up behind them.

He was only beginning to gulp air into his lungs when he looked up and saw, illumined in the growing light, the Ark of the Covenant. The canvas he'd thrown over it had been pulled away, and there was the shine of blood upon the glorious angels atop it.

Pullo and Vorenus got to their feet, helping each other balance in their exhaustion. The world had grown strangely silent but for the still-resounding crash of falling rocks somewhere down below them. The battle seemed to be over. Most of the Nubians had fallen away, and the sounds of war with them.

The two old friends staggered forward, shoulder to shoulder. They saw Madhukar, a dead Kushite atop him. And then, stepping around the Ark, they saw Caesarion.

A long mark of smeared blood showed how the young man they'd known since he was a child had slid down the side of the Ark. He was seated now beside Hannah, his hand in hers, his head resting upon her shoulder.

"Caesarion!" Vorenus gasped. He fell down before the would-be pharaoh, to examine his wound.

The young man didn't move. His eyes were open, but they focused on nothing. What they saw beyond this world, Vorenus did not know.

"He's holding something." Pullo's voice was barely a whisper.

Vorenus looked down and saw that Caesarion had in his hand a bloody Nubian dagger. His fingers were loose upon the grip, and when Vorenus reached for it he was able to slip it out with ease.

"Oh, gods," Pullo said.

Still holding the dagger, Vorenus turned toward his old friend, then followed his wide-eyed gaze back to Hannah, to her belly, to the movement beneath her bloodstained clothes. He swallowed hard. He took a deep breath, took one last look at their perfect faces, and then readied the blade in his hand.

. . .

When it was done, Vorenus staggered backward from the scene. His eyes welled with the tears he'd kept at bay; he looked up at the heavens, begging for forgiveness, praying he'd done the right thing.

The babe in his arms cried. And though his heart was breaking and his own agonized weeping would not cease, Vorenus thought that its cries of life were the most extraordinary sound he had ever heard. For a long time it seemed there was nothing else in the world but this precious, perfect thing.

Then dimly, like a whisper at the edge of his mind, he

became aware of another sound. Steady, like waves on a far shore growing closer.

He cuddled the still-bloody infant girl against his chest. He blinked up.

The light of dawn had come upon Elephantine, dissipating shadows. The fog was lifting. No one still fought in the broken courtyard, which ended in a gash across the landscape. He could see that the entire upper tip of the island had dropped away into rubble and ruin, and in the distance he could see now the waters of the Nile, flowing steady and unconcerned for the lives and the deaths of man.

Some of the Nubians had survived, but they had dropped their weapons. They had fallen to their knees. Their voices were low, murmuring. Vorenus looked up in wonder. Though he did not know the language that they spoke, he knew their intent, clear enough.

They had fallen to their knees in reverence.

They were worshipping the bloodied Ark.

30

The Gate Closed

CARTHAGE, 25 BCE

Isidora lurched into view. Selene had not seen her, but some-how she, too, had been crawling forward to her left. The young girl was close enough now that she scrambled forward, pulling her weak leg behind her, and dove into Juba.

For the space of heartbeats they wrestled, screaming. En-ergy erupted around them in flares of chaos. Then, with a final burst of light, Isidora was rolling past him, rolling away from him, and she had both the Lance and the Trident in her hands.

The traces of power that had been feeding the pit dis-appeared as quickly as a candle snuffed by a cup. The glowing red from its depths flashed hot once, and then went dark.

The three demons—Thrasyllus had shouted the word, and she was sure that's what they were—who had come up from the pit began to scream in a pure fury that Selene knew she would never forget. Whatever they were, they struggled to reach down into the terrible void of the pit. A noise of horrific, unearthly agony welled up from below them. Selene looked over and saw that Thrasyllus had collapsed, fighting to cover his ears from the piercing wails.

But far, far worse was the too-human shrieking of Isidora, who writhed as storms of angry flames began to erupt from her body, breaking her apart as the uncontrolled power of the two Shards in her hands burned her alive.

Just as Thrasyllus had been, Selene was paralyzed at first. It was too much to comprehend, and in the vacuum of that understanding she simply froze up and stared at her dying friend. But when Isidora stopped screaming, when she ceased her torturous spasms, the wall of fear in Selene's heart finally broke.

Selene rushed forward, sliding in beside her husband on the dusty stone floor. Juba was shaking, as if he were having a seizure. His eyes were wide and bloodshot. In his hands he still held the Palladium close to the Aegis. Energy continued to cascade off him, forming a thrashing cloud that once more spun around the temple, whipping leaves and branches from the trees, and sparking with spirals of lightning. It was weaker now, though whether it was losing power or storing it up she did not know.

But she knew its potential. She knew its danger. When she had used the Shard in Cantabria she had felt the yawning darkness threaten to overwhelm her. She had contested it. She had controlled it.

And if she was going to save Juba's life, she would need to do it again.

Pulling what deep breath she could from the tortured air, ready for the worst, Selene grabbed hold of the Palladium.

What rose up against her was not the wave of power that she had felt before. It was a deep emptiness, an aching hollow of the power that had been, a feeble echo of what had surged about them less than a minute earlier. Whatever Juba had done, wherever these creatures had come from—and she was certain she knew—the gate he had opened had sapped the Palladium's power.

It was spent, but as she held it, joined to her husband

through it, she felt its power slowly rising once more. And she realized—in each beat of his Aegis-sustained heart, in each pulse of her own—the trickling rejuvenation that was giving the Shard new life was them. It was using them. The Shard *was* them. All the Shards were. They were born of God's powers, the same powers that He'd forsaken in giving true freedom, true life, to His creation. The Shards needed the spark of life to be used. They fed on it. They consumed it.

If it wasn't for the life-sustaining power of the Aegis keeping him alive, Juba would almost certainly be dead.

With a grunt, Selene wrested the Palladium from her husband's tensed hands. She enfolded it within her dress. What was left of the storm swirling around the temple of Ba'al Hammon dissipated and hushed away with a sigh. Juba groaned and slid back toward the earth as if falling into dreams.

Selene rolled around to crouch behind her husband, trying to pull him upright. He was so much bigger than her, so much heavier. And he was unconscious. Only the ragged rise and fall of his chest showed that her love still had life. She managed to get him into a sitting position, but she could do little more. Looking up, she saw that the three demons had stopped reaching back down into the pit. They were still kneeling beside it, but they were all looking back toward her. The horrible wailing had ceased. Their black eyes were dead, like black beads of glass.

"Thrasyllus!" she yelled toward the stricken scholar. "Help me!"

The scholar was still curled up on the ground. He had uncovered his ears when the noise stopped, but he was staring at the demons with wide, paralyzed eyes.

Selene tugged at Juba, moving him inches away from the danger. "Come on," she urged him. "Wake up, my love. Please."

One of the demons, the first one who had risen from the

pit, stood. She felt its stare piercing her flesh and bones, gauging her, studying her.

Selene tugged again, and this time Juba's weight shifted and he collapsed over onto his side again. "Oh, God. Move. Please."

The demon opened its mouth. Its teeth were perfectly formed, white, but the color of dried bones. Like so much else about the creatures, they were still wrong, still not quite human. The demon spoke, and the words moved in a wave like music, like an elegant song. Its voice swelled through the air, riding its own wind, touching and caressing the stones and the trees and the earth. It was, Selene thought, perhaps the most beautiful sound she had ever heard, the most beautiful sound she ever could hear. She did not know the demon's words, but she knew its meaning. As if it spoke to her very soul, she knew what it was saying.

The Shards. It was telling the others to get the Shards.

The other two demons stood. They opened their mouths in their perfect but unnatural smiles. Then all three turned and walked toward the charred corpse of Isidora, sliding with the grace of slow-moving dancers across the old stones of the temple.

"Come on," Selene whispered, gripping the straps of the Aegis and dragging Juba with them. When she could only move him a few feet farther away, she began to cry. "I'm sorry," she sobbed. "I'm so sorry. It's my fault. All my fault."

God had died to give them all the freedom to choose. Right or wrong, good or evil, she'd always had a choice. No one had forced her to sneak away from the palace so many years ago, to make her way to the Great Library, where she'd first learned about the Shards of Heaven. No one had forced her to confront Caesar. No one had forced her to bring the asp to her mother. No one had forced her to swear to avenge the death of her parents, or even the rape she had suffered at the hands of the vile Tiberius. No one had forced her to convince Juba to come here, to reach for greater power than she'd already been blessed to receive.

She'd had a choice. She'd always had a choice. That was what God's sacrifice had given her. That was His gift.

Yet she'd chosen vengeance. God had given her true life, and at every turn she'd chosen death.

No more. Weeping, she looked up at the great expanse of the heavens above her. The clouds and storm were gone. The stars shone down. God wasn't there. Even the heaven where He'd once existed wasn't there. Not truly. But it still felt right to pray upward, to direct her plea for forgiveness into that silent canopy of night.

And then she swore, to whatever memory was left of God, that she was done with vengeance. If somehow they survived, she was through with dreams of death. She would live in peace, no matter the cost.

Just let us live, she prayed. And if not me, then my husband. A good man. Let him live.

The demon who had spoken—the leader, Selene decided—had reached Isidora's body. It looked at it with disinterest for a moment, as if studying a foreign thing. Then the other two came, and they reached down with their perfect hands, each of them grabbing a Shard. Isidora's blackened fingers cracked and crumbled as they effortlessly lifted the artifacts away. Little was left of the Lance of Olyndicus, and even the metal housing of the Trident had been twisted and deformed by the energies that had consumed the young girl, but the two Shards were still there. They were untouched. They still gleamed, blacker-than-black stones, as hauntingly beautiful as the demons who held them. The leader kicked at the corpse, sliding parts of it across the weathered stones toward the black pit of death.

As if obeying some unheard call, the two beings wrapped their hands around the stones. Selene held her breath.

But there was no arc of fire. There was no rush of storm. Nothing happened.

The two demons looked up at one another. Then at the leader. As one, all three turned to stare at Selene.

No, she realized. Not her. They were looking at Juba. They were looking at the Aegis. They needed life. They needed the spark of God.

"Thrasyllus!" she screamed, plunged into sudden panic and pulling desperately at her husband. "Help me! Please!"

The demons were moving in perfect steps. They were smiling. "Thrass-lus," the leader said, smiling as it mimicked her words. "Please."

Then Thrasyllus was there, his hands by hers, and he was tugging and dragging Juba away. Her husband groaned, beginning to awaken, but he hadn't the strength to move.

The demons were very close now. They did not hurry. They moved with a steady and unrelenting pace, as if they had all the time in the world.

With the astrologer's help Selene had dragged Juba past the line of torches, close to the shattered gate of the temple. But it wasn't far enough. It would never be far enough.

They would get the Aegis. They would get the Palladium. With the four Shards together they could surely open the gate once more. Selene had wanted vengeance. In her selfish desire for it, she had unleashed unimaginable horror upon the world. They would make a hell on Earth. Her attempt to escape, like the desires that had brought her here, had all been for nothing. And the demons knew it, too. They made lyrical and beautiful sounds to one another as they approached. They were, she knew, laughing.

She stopped pulling. Thrasyllus stopped, too. Juba was leaned up against her, and Thrasyllus was close beside her on her left. He was crying and talking of his love for Lapis, then begging for his own forgiveness. He had lied, he said. They huddled in their despair, the three of them, awaiting the end. Selene leaned over her husband and saw that he was awake enough to look up into her eyes as she looked down into his. And when she reached down to kiss him one last time upon the forehead, to apologize, he had strength enough to whisper three words to her. "Go, my love," he rasped.

"Fly," Thrasyllus suddenly said.

Selene looked up. The astrologer was gazing at the stars, tears in his eyes. "What?"

"Mercury. Libra." His head jerked as his eyes moved across the heavens. He seemed ready to laugh at the foolishness of what he read there. "Signs say to take flight."

Selene's eyes widened. She rifled through the folds of her dress, searching desperately. The demons were just steps away, tall and mighty, terrible and menacing in their perfection. But in the last moments her hand found it, wrapped around it. She pulled it free, and then she moved one arm around Thrasyllus while with the other she placed the Palladium upon the Aegis.

Juba's hand had somehow fallen atop hers, and together they dropped down into the fast-filling dark, only to rise up again in flight.

Riding a shaft of wind, arcing against the moon and the stars, they flew for the shore, for the sea, for the ship that would speed them away. Behind and below them, the frustrated cries of the demons sang a wordless song of horror. And around them, upon them, the city was awakened to screams that soon filled the night.

EPILOGUE

The Light of the Sun

MEROË, 22 BCE

Vorenus stood on the northern balcony of the royal palace of Meroë, seat of the kingdom of Kush. He was, for the moment, alone with his thoughts. Most of the city was gathering below, all of them cheering the new temple that was about to be dedicated in honor of the Kushite victory over Rome—a victory that he knew was not true.

He had seen such a celebration before, years ago in Alexandria, when Antony and Cleopatra had returned from the battle of Actium. That, too, had been a lie. Rulers, he'd found, had a way of doing that.

Not that he could blame the Kandake. With Rome's conquest of Egypt complete, the Kushite queen knew that the next kingdom up the Nile—Kush, with its rich iron mines—would surely be the next target for their insatiable domination. So the Kandake had done what she'd had to do: she'd made a deal with the Nabataeans of Petra, who were already worried about what would happen if the Romans managed to open a direct route to the spices of Arabia. It was a masterful plan, one that Vorenus admired for its seeming simplicity. The Nabataeans would agree to guide the Roman legions from Egypt through Arabia, but they would take the most time-consuming and dangerous path possible. The Romans could be expected to react with trade sanctions against the Naba-taeans, but the Kandake agreed to help minimize their impact by opening up Kushite markets—including increased access to her precious metals—on favorable terms to the people of Petra. And in the meantime, while the Roman legions were wandering the desert of Arabia, the Kushites would have de-scended the Nile in a massive raid on a relatively unprotected Egypt, establishing their strength while burning towns like the one at Elephantine and destroying fortifications like the garrison at Syene. The power of Rome would be checked on two fronts.

It was a brilliant plan.

The only thing she had underestimated was Roman resolve.

Augustus had relieved the prefect of Egypt when he'd at last returned from Arabia with the limping remnants of the legions he'd marched into the desert. He'd appointed Petro-nius in his place, who had immediately set himself upon the task of restocking the garrisons, rebuilding the fortifications, and making plans for a counterstrike on Kush.

Pullo and Vorenus, who'd spent the years since Elephan-tine as guests in the Kandake's court, had told her it was com-ing, even as she'd set her workmen to constructing this temple dedicated to the very victory that had brought them into her presence—and cost Hannah and Caesarion their lives.

Below him, the people cheered as trumpets blared in song. But the thoughts of death had turned the eyes of Vorenus to the east, to the dozens upon dozens of sandstone tombs and pyramids lining the horizon. The necropolis of Meroë was sa-cred ground, and he'd found himself walking there more than once, in the silence, communing with the memory of Caesarion. He'd been a good man, the best of men, and it was wrong that he should die so young. He'd only just started his life.

It should have been me, he thought to himself. What he could have done differently, he didn't know, but that didn't change the guilt. He'd lived, though he was undeserving of more time on this earth. And Caesarion, a young man who deserved everything in the world, had died.

It simply wasn't right.

"Am I disturbing you?" said a voice from the palace behind him.

Vorenus turned and saw Syllaeus, the Nabataean who had played such a key role in the negotiations between Petra and Meroë. The dark-haired man had a mixed complexion, not un-like that of the Greeks in Egypt, and the way he held himself was mixed, too: his rough hands and his taut muscles spoke of a man accustomed to labor, yet the way he wrapped his robes about him and held his head high, he could just as eas-ily have been a man of the court. Vorenus had found him friendly and interested in what was happening around him in a way that seemed casual but was in truth constantly scheming for an advantage. For all these reasons and more, Vorenus fig-ured Syllaeus was a consummate politician: as likely to push a drowning man under as he was to save him. It was little wonder that he'd been the man who'd guided the Roman legions into the desert, able to walk the men to their deaths in the sands, smiling all the while, and somehow returned a free man, living to tell about it. He was impressive, to be sure, but Vorenus trusted the Nabataean no farther than he could throw him. And his back wasn't what it once was.

"Not a disturbance at all," Vorenus lied through his smile.

"I am glad for it," the Nabataean said. He walked up to join Vorenus at the balcony, looking out at the crowds. "A nice temple," he said.

Vorenus nodded. "People like a celebration."

Syllaeus yawned. It was midday, but Vorenus didn't doubt

the Nabataean had enjoyed a late night. He'd only been in Meroë two weeks, but his drinking and whoring was the talk of the city. Something else he had in common with many politicians. "The Romans will attack Napata in the coming days."

Napata was home to the more ancient royal palace of the Nubians, partway between Meroë and Elephantine. It was the last stronghold between the advancing Roman legions and this capital. And Syllaeus was noting the impending attack as casually as he would comment on the weather. Everyone knew the Romans were coming, but their speed was unexpected, even for Vorenus, who nevertheless tried not to act surprised. "I see. And the Kandake is aware?"

The Nabataean nodded. "I tell her what she needs to know."

Vorenus smiled at that. "Which means you think I need to know."

"So it does. We will be leaving for Petra earlier than planned. That is, if you and your friend are still planning to join me?"

Before it had passed into the hands of Alexander the Great, before it had been moved to Alexandria, the Ark, through Hannah's family, had been kept under the protection of the Nubians for many years. Centuries had passed, but the people of Kush had not forgotten their long-ago charge. When they had seen it on Elephantine, when they had witnessed its power, they had worshipped the Ark and once more taken it into their protection. But the Kandake knew that it could not forever remain in Meroë. Rome was coming, sooner or later. It was only a matter of time and circumstance before it would need to be moved to Petra, to the place where Hannah and Caesarion had wanted to see it go before they died. "We will go with you," Vorenus said. "All of us."

Syllaeus smiled as if this was the finest news he'd heard in days. "Excellent. I'll make the final arrangements. We will leave in the morning. With Rome on the way, we will need to take a longer route east from here to reach the seaports, but I'll see to it that things are comfortable for your, ah, cargo."

The Nabataean paused for the briefest of moments, and Vorenus kept his face impassive, the way he suspected Caesarion would have, the way Cleopatra would have expected.

"And of course for the two of you and the little one," Syllaeus continued. Then his eyes perked up. "Ah! Speaking of them now . . ."

The two of them turned toward the palace, and Pullo came lumbering out onto the balcony with his familiar half-limp. On his broad shoulders sat little Miriam, her brown hair bouncing lightly as she held up her hand to shield her eyes from the light of the sun. She laughed, a sound so innocent and pure that Vorenus knew it would never fail to lift the spirits of his heart. Pullo, too, was beaming.

Vorenus couldn't help but smile. Though he himself was more and more prone to thoughts of the darkness, his old friend had somehow regained some of his old, familiar mirth since Elephantine. Vorenus was thankful for it each and every day.

"I'll take leave of you all," Syllaeus said. He bowed, then swept back into the palace depths, whistling.

"Uncle Vor-nus," Miriam said, smiling as Pullo put an extra bounce in his step. "They're starting."

Vorenus grinned and reached up to jiggle a finger playfully at her rib. She giggled and pushed his hand away. "So they are, little one. Are you wanting to go down to watch?"

The three-year-old clapped. "Down!"

Vorenus nodded sagely, then tilted his head toward the balcony edge. "All right, Pullo. Over she goes."

Pullo stepped forward and Miriam squealed in mirth,

seemingly ready to take flight. The girl, near as they could tell, feared nothing in the world. Vorenus prayed that this would always be so.

When the big man didn't throw her, she grabbed his gray hair in her little fists and tugged. "Pul-lo. Fly!"

Pullo winced and grinned. "Just for that, Miri, I think we will be taking the stairs."

"Probably for the best," Vorenus said. "You need wings to fly."

Miriam spread her arms as if she were a bird. "I don't think so," the girl said. "I'll show you one day."

"I don't doubt it." Vorenus looked at his old friend. "Syllaeus says Rome will hit Napata soon. So we will leave tomorrow. Can you be ready?"

Pullo nodded, bouncing the little girl in distraction, then looked down to the temple and almost laughed. "Is that what I think it is?"

Vorenus peered down where he was staring, and he saw the procession moving toward the temple steps. Four men were carrying a small platform on their shoulders, and a head of bronze was upon it. It gleamed and flashed in the sun, so bright that even Pullo's bad eyes had been able to make it out: the head of the tall statue of Augustus that had stood over the harbor at Elephantine. "It is indeed. I think they're going to bury it under the steps of the temple. That way anyone who comes there will step on it."

Pullo let out a hearty, booming laugh. "I like these people."

"I do, too," Vorenus agreed. He smiled, though he worried over what the future would hold.

"Let's *go*," Miriam said plaintively.

Pullo nodded. "As our lady says."

The big man started to turn away when something else caught Vorenus' eye in the light. Vorenus stopped them, and he reached up to push the necklace that had been Miriam's mother's back into her tunic. He patted it there, against her skin. "Remember to keep it safe," he said.

"So she can keep me safe," the little girl said.

Vorenus smiled. He'd have time to cry after they were gone. "That's right. Now run along, you two. I'll catch up."

Pullo headed back into the palace. From his shoulders, Miriam was asking whether she'd be able to see through the crowds. Watching him bend to keep from hitting her head on the high palace archway, Vorenus just smiled as he let the tears come.

. . .

The story of the Shards of Heaven continues in
BOOK 3: THE REALMS OF GOD

GLOSSARY OF CHARACTERS

Aelius Gallus. Roman prefect of Egypt, he led an expedition to Arabia Felix that can only be described as disastrous. His Nabataean guide, Syllaeus, seems to have purposely led the Roman legions to their destination by the longest route possible, and most of the men died from the desert heat or unexpected disease over the six months they spent wandering. Worse, his long absence from Egypt left it open to a crippling attack from its Nubian neighbors in Kush.

Alexander Helios. Son of Mark Antony and Cleopatra VII, twin brother of Cleopatra Selene, he was likely born in the year 40 BCE. He disappears from reliable historical records after the fall of Alexandria in 30 BCE.

Alexander the Great. Alexander III, born in Macedon in 356 BCE, succeeded his father as king in 336. In his youth he led a number of Greek city-states to revolt against what had been a Macedonian-led alliance, and Alexander quickly set in motion a series of campaigns that led him as far north as the Danube and solidified his position as ruler of a united Greek state. Alexander subsequently moved his armies east against the Persian Empire, then the largest and most powerful state in the known world. He led his men to conquer Asia Minor and Syria, routing the Persian armies and defeating city after city. In 332 he entered Egypt, where he was declared to be the son of Ammon, an Egyptian deity.

For reasons unknown, he faced off with the armies of the Kush but refused to fight them. Instead of continuing his campaign south into Africa, he moved north and founded the famed city of Alexandria, which subsequently became the capital of Egypt. Returning east, he captured Babylon and put an end to the Persian Empire before entering central Asia and defeating several states. Alexander then journeyed toward India, where his armies, though successful, finally balked at fighting farther from their Greek homes. Throughout his long career, he is said never to have lost a battle, and though severely wounded on several occasions, he was still reportedly vigorously strong. Nevertheless, he died under uncertain circumstances shortly after returning to Babylon in 323 BCE. After his death, he was placed in a golden sarcophagus, which made its way to Alexandria, and his world-spanning empire soon broke into rival states. His golden sarcophagus was melted down around 81 BCE by Pharaoh Ptolemy IX Lathyros when he was short of money (an act for which the angry citizens of Alexandria soon killed him). Alexander's miraculously preserved body was at that time transferred to a crystal sarcophagus, which remained on display in the city until its disappearance around AD 400.

Apion. An Alexandrian scholar who wrote a commentary on Homer, he would later become famous for writing an anti-Jewish tract that was replied to by Josephus in his *Against Apion.*

Caesarion. Caesarion, whose full name was Ptolemy XV Philopator Philometor Caesar, was born to Cleopatra VII in 47 BCE. According to Plutarch, he was rumored to have been executed by Octavian after the fall of Alexandria in 30 BCE, though his exact fate is strikingly unknown. While later Roman writers questioned his paternity, there is little reason to refute the claim made by Cleopatra that he was the son of Julius Caesar.

Carisius. Roman coinage identifies Publius Carisius (Cassius Dio calls him Titus Carisius) as the general most responsible for putting down first the Cantabri and later the Astures tribes of Hispania.

Cleomedes. Very little is known of Cleomedes, a Stoic Greek astronomer active at some point between the middle of the first century BCE and the fourth century AD. His elementary astronomy textbook *On the Circular Motions of the Celestial Bodies* is widely regarded as poorly written and full of errors, yet it is also important for preserving the otherwise lost works of the earlier astronomers Posidonius of Rhodes and Eratosthenes.

Cleopatra Selene. Daughter of Mark Antony and Cleopatra VII, twin sister of Alexander Helios, she was likely born in the year 40 BCE. After the fall of Alexandria in 30 BCE she was placed under the guardianship of Octavia, the sister of Octavian, before being married to Juba II sometime between 25 and 20 BCE.

Cleopatra VII. The last pharaoh of the Ptolemaic dynasty, Cleopatra VII ruled Egypt from 51 BCE until her suicide at the age of thirty-nine after the fall of Alexandria in 30 BCE. As pharaoh she had an affair with Julius Caesar, to whom she bore his only known son, Caesarion. After Caesar's assassination in 44 BCE, Cleopatra took the side of Mark Antony in the civil war against Octavian and eventually bore him three children: Ptolemy Philadelphus and the twins Cleopatra Selene and Alexander Helios.

Corocotta. According to Cassius Dio, Corocotta was the leader of a guerrilla campaign against the Romans in Cantabria

who personally accepted from Caesar the award that had
been established for his capture. Little more is known
about him.

Delius. One of Mark Antony's leading generals, he defected
to the side of Octavian just prior to the Battle of Actium in
31 BCE, reportedly bringing with him Antony's plans for
the fight.

Didymus Chalcenterus. Born around 63 BCE, he wrote an as-
tounding number of books in his lifetime on a wide vari-
ety of subjects, though he is now primarily known as an
editor and grammarian of Homer. One of the chief librarians of the Great Library in Alexandria, his name Chalcenterus means "bronze guts," supposedly a statement about
his indefatigability as a scholar.

Galbus. Unknown to history.

Isidora. Unknown to history.

Juba I. King of Numidia, he allied himself against Julius Caesar in the Great Roman Civil War. After being defeated by
Caesar's forces at the battle of Thapsus in 46 BCE, he fled
the field with the Roman general Marcus Petreius. Trapped,
they took their own lives by duel, with the survivor being
aided in his suicide by a waiting slave.

Juba II. Probably born in 48 BCE, he was left an orphan by
the suicide of his father in 46. Adopted by Julius Caesar,
the man who'd caused his father's death, Juba was raised
as a Roman citizen and ultimately joined his adopted stepbrother Octavian in the war against Mark Antony and
Cleopatra. He was restored to the throne of Numidia after
the fall of Alexandria in 30 BCE, and around the year 25
BCE he was married to Cleopatra Selene. Some time later
he was given the throne of Mauretania. Juba was a lifelong
scholar who wrote several books before he died in AD 23.

Julius Caesar. Born in 100 BCE to a noble Roman family of

comparatively little significance, Julius Caesar achieved a position of unparalleled power within the Roman state and thereby laid the stage for the end of the Republic under his adopted son Octavian. A well-regarded orator and savvy politician, Caesar rose to prominence first as a military leader in the field, whose reputation won him election, in 63 BCE, as the religious leader of the Roman Republic. Returning to the military sphere in subsequent years, his extraordinary abilities were proved in successful campaigns in Hispania, Gaul, and Britain. His power and popular appeal eventually led to the Great Roman Civil War when he crossed the Rubicon with an armed legion in 49 BCE. Victorious in the civil war, Caesar voyaged to Alexandria, where a civil war had broken out between Cleopatra VII and her brother-husband Ptolemy XIII. Caesar supported Cleopatra, defeating Ptolemy and making her sole pharaoh of Egypt, and she, in turn, became Caesar's lover, bearing him his only known biological son: Caesarion. Returning to Rome, Caesar took solitary control of the state as a popularly supported dictator, effectively ending the Roman Republic. From this position of authority he instituted significant reforms to the Roman calendar, the workings of its government, and the architecture of its capital. Caesar was assassinated in 44 BCE by a group of at least sixty Roman senators, who reportedly stabbed him twenty-three times before he died. His popularity among the common people at the time of his death was so great that two years after the assassination he was officially deified. Though his murder had been intended to restore the Roman Republic to order, it served only to set off another series of civil wars. These conflicts culminated in the struggle between his adopted son Octavian, to whom Caesar had bequeathed the whole of his state and his powerful name, and his popular former general Mark Antony, who had taken residence in Alexandria with Caesar's former lover, Cleopatra VII.

Kemse. Unknown to history.

Khenti. Unknown to history.

Laenas. Unknown to history.

Lucius Vorenus. Along with Titus Pullo, Vorenus is mentioned only once in the existing record: in Julius Caesar's *Commentary on the Gallic Wars*, where their inspiring actions in battle are reported. His birth and death dates are unknown.

Madhukar. Unknown to history.

Manu. Unknown to history.

Marcus Petreius. A Roman general, he allied himself against Julius Caesar in the Great Roman Civil War. After being defeated by Caesar's forces at the battle of Thapsus in 46 BCE, he fled the field with Juba I, king of Numidia. Trapped, they took their own lives by duel, with the survivor being aided in his suicide by a waiting slave.

Mark Antony. A Roman politician, he was Julius Caesar's good friend and perhaps his finest general. In the years following Caesar's assassination, Antony struggled with Octavian for control of the Roman Republic, though an uneasy peace was reached in 41 BCE when Antony married Octavian's sister. The following year he had an affair with Cleopatra VII, resulting in the births of the twins Cleopatra Selene and Alexander Helios, and soon he was making his home with her in Alexandria, where she gave birth to another son, Ptolemy Philadelphus, in 36 BCE. Open war broke out between Antony and Octavian in 32 BCE, with their two great armies facing off at the battle of Actium one year later. Defeated, Antony returned with Cleopatra to Alexandria, where he committed suicide after the fall of the city.

Octavian. Born in 63 BCE, he was adopted by his great-uncle Julius Caesar just prior to his assassination in 44. Though he originally joined forces with Mark Antony to rule the Republic, their ambitions would not allow the peace to last, and the war between them tore the Roman world in two. His eventual defeat of Antony made him sole ruler of Rome, giving him the power to remake the Republic into the Roman Empire. Known most popularly as Augustus Caesar, the name he adopted in 27 BCE, he is rightly regarded along with his adopted father as one of the most influential men in history.

Petosiris. Unknown to history.

Ptolemy Philadelphus. Born in 36 BCE, he was the youngest son of Mark Antony and Cleopatra VII. He disappears from the record after the fall of Alexandria in 30, his fate unknown.

Quintus. Unknown to history.

Seker. Unknown to history.

Syllaeus. One of the chief ministers to King Obodas II of Nabataea, Syllaeus volunteered to guide Egyptian prefect Aelius Gallus and his Roman legions to the spice-rich lands of Arabia Felix. He instead led them to death and despair in the desert, returning to Petra a hero. In 9 BCE Obodas died, and Syllaeus was soon accused of his murder. King Aretas IV put him in chains and sent him to Rome, where he was declared guilty and flung headfirst to his death from the Tarpeian Rock.

Syphax. Unknown to history, though it is reasonably certain in the records that an unnamed slave aided in the suicides of Juba I and Marcus Petreius.

Thrasyllus. An Egyptian scholar, Thrasyllus of Mendes became famous as the personal astrologer of Tiberius Caesar. A

trusted servant and friend to the emperor, it is said that
he saved the lives of many in Rome by promising Tiberius
a longer life than he ultimately led.

Tiberius. Born in 42 BCE, Tiberius Claudius Nero became the
stepson to Octavian, the future Augustus Caesar, when his
mother was forced to divorce his father and marry the
powerful adopted son of Julius Caesar. In time he became
a strong field general, and he rose quickly through the ranks
to the position of heir apparent to Augustus Caesar. He was
unhappy, however, and for unknown reasons he retired to
Rhodes in 6 BCE, only returning to Rome in AD 2—after
much begging from Caesar. When Augustus died in 14,
Tiberius was declared his sole heir and would rule—a
reportedly depressed and dark figure—as Caesar until his
own death in 37.

Titus Pullo. Along with Lucius Vorenus, Pullo is mentioned
only once in the existing record: in Julius Caesar's *Commentary on the Gallic Wars*, where their inspiring actions in
battle are reported. His birth and death dates are unknown.

Varro. Marcus Terentius Varro (116–27 BCE) was a Roman
scholar of great renown.